"A natura
—Mi

PRAISE F

Patricia Briggs

DRAGON BONES book 1 of 2 story

"A heartwarming tale . . . delivers a thrilling coming-of-age story." —*Romantic Times*

"A lot of fun." —*Locus*

"An excellent read for everyone." —*KLIATT*

cont in this book

THE HOB'S BARGAIN

"[A] fun fantasy romance. . . . There's plenty of action, with battles against raiders and magical creatures, a bard who isn't what he appears, and an evil mage—but there's also plenty of humor, and some sweet moments of mischief and romance." —*Locus*

"I ran across Patricia Briggs—literally—at our local bookstore, while sorting through the shelves looking for another book. The cover art intrigued me, then I read the first page and went straight to the counter. This is a "Beauty and the Beast" story but unlike any I've ever read. Ms. Briggs blends adventure, romance, and innovative fantasy with a deft hand. Highly recommend this one to all my readers." —S. L. Viehl, author of the *Stardoc* series

"It is easy to like Patricia Briggs's novels. Her books are perfect for a Friday evening or a late Sunday afternoon when you don't want to have to *work* to enjoy your reading. Her books are clever, engaging, fast-moving, and with plots that manage to be thought-provoking without being heavy-handed. A warning, however—make sure you don't start the dinner cooking or the lawn watering before you curl up with one of her books, because you'll end up with a burnt dinner and a soggy lawn and an enjoyable few hours lost in another world." —*Romantic Science Fiction & Fantasy*

Ace Books by Patricia Briggs

DRAGON BLOOD

Patricia Briggs

2003
50TH
ANNIVERSARY

ACE BOOKS, NEW YORK

DRAGON BLOOD

An Ace Book / published by arrangement with the author

PRINTING HISTORY
Ace mass-market edition / January 2003

Copyright © 2003 by Patricia Briggs.
Cover art by Jean Pierre Targete.
Cover design by Rita Frangie.
Map illustration by Michael Enzweiler.
Text design by Kristin del Rosario.

ISBN: 0-441-01008-3

ACE®
Ace Books are published by The Berkley Publishing Group, a division of Penguin Putnam Inc., 375 Hudson Street, New York, New York 10014. ACE and the "A" design are trademarks belonging to Penguin Putnam Inc.

PRINTED IN THE UNITED STATES OF AMERICA

10 9 8 7

For
Michael Enzweiler,
Mary and Bob Kerns,
Ann Peters (aka Sparky),
and
Kaye Roberson;
my reading, writing, and riding buddies.

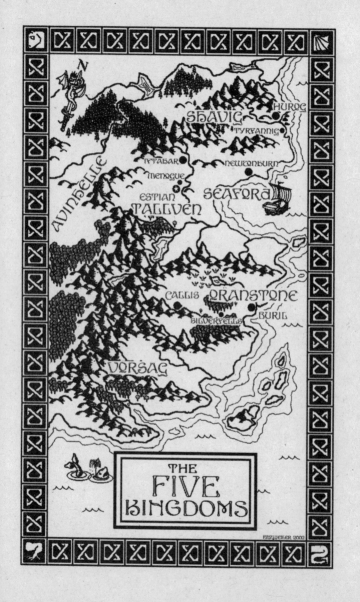

THE
FIVE
KINGDOMS

1
TISALA IN ESTIAN

It takes many years of hard work and dedication to produce a competent torturer. Young men just don't want to take the time to learn the craft.

—Lloth of Edelbreck, Royal Torturer

"IT'S JUST LIKE SKINNING A RABBIT," THE OLD MAN said to his grandson. There was strength in his grip that belied the age on his face as his sharp knife removed another sliver of flesh from Tisala's finger.

"I've never skinned a rabbit alive." The boy looked ill, like a newly blooded recruit, thought Tisala.

The old man lost all patience with him. "Don't be an idiot. Now watch."

The next move of the knife forced Tisala's attention back to her body. Eventually she would tell the old man what he wanted to know, but if she could wait long enough, they could trust none of what she said. But she'd only been there something under two days and already her body ached and her mind flinched away from what had been done to her.

"What do you know about Alizon's rabble, little girl? Tell me and I can quit hurting you," he crooned as his knife worked its magic. "I don't like hurting little girls, but you are hiding something our king needs to know. A brother shouldn't try to hurt his own kin. What Alizon is doing is wrong and you know it. All you need to do is tell me who's helping him and I can stop."

She didn't fear death, not even death by torture. Death was a constant companion in the battlefield, as often a friend as an enemy. Betrayal, though, betrayal was truly frightening. Best she die fast, before she could hurt someone she cared about. She'd bide her time and see if she could use her tongue as a goad to make the torturer slip. Someone had once told her that her tongue was her most formidable weapon, and it was one they hadn't taken from her.

"How can you *do* this all day?" asked the boy passionately. "Grandfather, cannot the mages make a person talk?"

The old man snorted. "The mages can make a person say anything the mages want him to, but they can't get real information from magic. Good information comes only from men like me. We save lives on the battlefield, give our king his victories."

"Why are you doing this one here, instead of in the castle?" Bravado, not curiosity, sparked his question. Tisala could tell that he knew the answer already.

"For secrecy." The old man's voice trembled, betrayed by age.

The boy sneered. "Because if his precious nobles knew what we did here to a noble woman, they'd join Alizon's rebellion. Torturing a weak woman is filthy work, unworthy of the king's torturer. He'll get rid of you, too, Grandfather, when you're done here."

Quite likely, thought Tisala.

"I do what I am told, boy. I am the king's man." The old man was so agitated, he slipped with the knife and blood cascaded down her arm and over his hand.

The boy looked at the mess, swallowed hard, then turned and ran, shutting the heavy wooden door behind him, leaving the old man distracted from his work, cursing the mother that raised her boy to be weak and foolish.

Tisala almost couldn't believe the old master was so stupid, but he continued to look at the door with the knife in his blood-slick grip—so near to her hand, held only by his inattentive clasp. Tisala never waited for second chances.

She twisted her wrist, breaking his grip, and then drove her shoulder forward. She caught the hand that held the knife and used it to slice the old man's throat.

Tied to the bench she lay on, she couldn't slow the old man's body down as it fell, nor move out of the way of the blood gushing from his ruined throat. But she held on to his hand with her own, damaged and bleeding though it was. Once the body hung limply, she slowly shifted her grip from his hand to the knife.

For a terrible moment, she thought the knife was going to slip from her weak grasp, and she'd be stuck tied to the table. But when the old man's arm slid away, the knife was still clutched desperately in her hand.

The knife, small but sharp, cut through the ropes as easily as it had sliced through her skin. Her body moved sluggishly, stiff from being tied too long, and weak from shock and the indignities visited upon it. She ignored her aches as best she could, and she found a bit of rag to wrap around her hand.

No one ran in to investigate the sound the body had made. Hope rose a notch higher as Tisala weighed her chances.

The boy had said they were not in the castle, but she knew better than to trust anything she heard in a place like this. Still, if it were not true, then she might as well slit her own throat now. She was hardly in any shape to walk unnoticed through the royal halls. Maybe the boy had been right.

The hope of escape made her fumble with the crude bandaging on her hand.

Where could she go? She had to make the right decisions but her thoughts flowed like mud.

She had friends here in Estian who would hide her.

If someone followed her tracks through the city—very possible in the condition she was in—she would be sentencing her friends to death.

She couldn't afford to run home to Callis in Oranstone on her own. If she went home now, she'd be signing her father's death warrant. Their public estrangement, ostensibly because she was tired of her father abiding by his oaths of loyalty to the king, was the only thing that kept her father out of Jakoven's cells. If he saw what Jakoven's man had done to her, he'd start a war on his own—and the time was not right yet.

She pulled herself back to the immediate situation. *Think, Tisala, think. Five Kingdoms under Jakoven's rule, surely there is someplace to hide.*

Outside of the city, Tallven was firmly in the hands of the High King Jakoven, whose family name it bore. Tallven was all grasslands, no mountains to hide in. To the south was Oranstone, where she couldn't go because of her father.

East was Avinhelle, and she had acquaintances there, but four years ago Avinhellish lords had conspired to betray the Kingdoms. Caught and humbled by fines and hangings, the remaining lords would hand her over as soon as they realized who she was in hopes of demonstrating their loyalty to the king.

West was Seaford, but she didn't know many people there. Seaforders were sailors and they explored the oceans, leaving politics to land-bound folk.

North . . . Shavigmen were coldhearted savages. She remembered seeing a troop of Shavigmen when she was a very young child, their pale hair strung out behind them as they charged down upon a hapless village on their monstrous horses. Remembered the cries of terror of her countrymen. "Shavig," they called. "Shavig."

Shavig. She shivered.

"Barbarian?" laughed Ward, pushing his exotically pale hair out of his eyes. *"Tisala, we're stubborn, obnoxious, and coarse. But we're hardly barbarians. We even* cook *our food . . . if it's convenient."*

Ward of Hurog. She had a sudden vivid image of him the last time she'd seen him, his sword red with Vorsag blood. He was strong, strong enough to stand up to King Jakoven if need be. Moreover he was *not* involved in the king's half brother Alizon's rebellion. He lived in a keep on the coast, not too far from the Tallvenish border. Surely she could find it.

Better yet, she had information for him—a payment of sorts for helping her.

She slipped on the old man's shoes to protect her feet and

took his cloak off the wall. She would have taken his clothing as well, but death had released more than just blood. Wrapping the cloak around her nakedness, she decided she could steal clothing before she left the city.

She opened the door and climbed up a long flight of stairs to another door. She opened it, too, expecting to find a hall or another room, but there was fresh night air and a set of stone steps that led up into a tidy alley.

The guard who stood in front of the door didn't even turn around, his eyes scanning the rooftops and the shadows.

"He'll learn, Master Edelbreck. Boys grow up," he said in the flat, nasal tones of an Estian native.

He didn't live long enough to understand that it hadn't been the torturer who'd opened the door behind him. The knife was very sharp, and Tisala took the guard's belt and sheath to carry it. His knife was crude, an eating utensil rather than a weapon and she left it on the ground beside the body. Leaving the sword was a more difficult decision. She longed for the reassurance of its weight, but in Tallven, only armsmen and nobles carried swords.

Swordless, Tisala disappeared into the maze of Estian, leaving no trail for the king's men to follow. *Cont. R-18*

2

WARDWICK AT HUROG

I've found that after the harvest is finished, I have time for renewing old acquaintances and discussing politics.

"YOU'RE CHEATING," OREG SAID, AND PAIN SEARED down my vision, weakening me until the flame I'd lit on the bowl of water flickered a sad, faded yellow and died. "I told you not to draw on Hurog—you might find yourself somewhere else when you need magic, and then where would you be?"

I wiped sweat off my forehead and glared at him. He looked more like a young man with dark hair and pale violet eyes than an old dragon, but appearances often lie—something I've found to be useful myself. Oreg looked young and vulnerable, and I looked big and dumb. Neither happened to be true.

Oreg ignored my wrath and nodded at the bowl. "Try it again, Ward."

He maintained the shield that separated me from Hurog's magic, and the pain made it difficult to work what power I had left. Losing touch with Hurog *hurt*.

"*Concentrate,* Ward."

Over the past few years I'd grown to hate those words.

But working magic with Oreg had become my refuge when the pressures of running Hurog grew too great. It's not easy to rebuild a keep.

Technically, Hurog, lands and keep, belonged to my uncle, Duraugh. But four years ago, my uncle proclaimed me Hurogmeten in my dead father's place. Ironically it was Hurog, not my uncle's richer estate, Iftahar, that gave him power to do so—for Hurog, which had lain in ruins by my own actions, was the heart of Shavig, northernmost of the Five Kingdoms of Tallvenish Rule. If my uncle, Duraugh of Hurog, called me Hurogmeten, then all of Shavig was prepared to go to war in defense of that proclamation.

King Jakoven, unwilling to begin a civil war when his seat was so uncertain on the throne, ignored Hurog. I stayed on Hurog land, where ignoring me was easier.

But even if my uncle had not returned Hurog to me, it would still have been mine, by bond of blood and bone.

I looked at the bowl of water and envisioned a flame roaring from the surface. My world narrowed to the water in the bowl. Something shifted in my head, and the stone bowl cracked as flame rained to the floor borne by a sheet of water. Power roared from the soles of my feet through the hair on the top of my head, and I shook with the effort of redirecting it back to where it had come.

When at last I stood empty, I realized the sound I heard was Oreg laughing.

He waved at the fire and it dissipated, leaving only a damp spot on the flagstone floor of the guard tower.

"If you can break through my shielding," he said, still fair hiccuping with laughter, "I suppose there's a fair chance you can pull magic from Hurog wherever you happen to be."

I felt a surge of triumph replace the emptiness, and I grinned at him. "I broke your magic?"

"*Hurog* broke through my spell when you called it," he corrected, and his humor gave way to bemusement.

I picked up the pieces of the bowl and set them on a small table. "Hurog's magic feels different to me than it did before I killed you," I said. I knew it sounded odd, but I never forgot

that I had killed him. He just hadn't died the way we both
had expected him to.

"Different how?" He perched on the edge of the only stool
in the tower. We'd furnished it sparsely so that there would
be less to burn when my magic went awry. The tower was
one of six on the wall surrounding the keep proper, so there
was only stone nearby. The scorched bits of rock on the
tower wall proved the wisdom of Oreg's choice of classroom.
Almost four years of work and I still had occasional, and
spectacular, miscalculations.

"Do you remember Menogue?" I asked. The hill with
Aethervon's temple stood deserted outside of Estian—deserted by people, that is. We'd had a vivid demonstration
that Aethervon had *not* left the holy temple when his priests
had died a few centuries ago.

"Yes."

"The magic here at Hurog isn't as focused as that was, but
I sometimes feel as if there's some intelligence behind it." I
looked at him. "Something that might break your shielding
when I called for it. It's gotten stronger the past few months,
ever since you taught me how to separate my magic from
Hurog's."

Oreg's eyebrows pulled together. "Interesting. Has the
connection between you and the land altered?"

I shook my head. "Not that I've noticed."

I LEFT OREG IN THE TOWER AND CROSSED THE BAILEY TO
the keep. I had a while before arms practice, and whenever
I had a spare minute, I worked on the keep.

Once Hurog had been made entirely of blackstone, but
many of the stones had shattered when Oreg's death had
destroyed the keep and its walls. Blackstone was expensive,
and when we started rebuilding, there had been little gold to
buy it with. Whatever quarry had supplied the original
builder with stone was lost to time, always supposing that
he'd gotten the rock from somewhere nearby, as was customary—Oreg didn't remember one way or the other.

But Hurog had an old granite quarry, so we'd used granite

instead and the result was . . . odd. Black pockmarked with gray made the keep much less imposing, and part of me regretted the loss of the old keep bitterly.

We'd rebuilt the inner curtain walls, except for a properly secure gatehouse. Instead we had only a primitive set of wooden gates while our blacksmith and our armorer labored mightily to supply the ironwork we needed. Most of the outside of the keep had been finished as well. Our progress had been unusually quick because of the aid of the dwarves, but I suspected that it wouldn't be completely rebuilt until my body was dust in the grave. The keep wasn't overly large by the standards of the Five Kingdoms, but neither was the workforce we had to rebuild with. The outer curtain wall was no more than a pile of rubble enclosing nearly thirty acres of land. I hadn't even had the heart to begin on it.

The harvest this year had been the best in memory, aided in no little part by the disappearance of the salt creep, which had been growing in the best of the fields since before my great-grandfather's time. *Magic,* whispered the people, and looked at me in awe. *Dragon bones,* I thought, and hoped the wheat we harvested wouldn't poison the person who ate it. It hadn't last year, or the year before. Nor, to my relief, did it seem to have any other unusual properties.

With harvest over, while others hunted for meat or sport, I worked on rebuilding the keep with whoever wanted to help. The dwarves came and went at their own whim—and there were none here now. Two days a week, I paid for a work party, but even with good harvests Hurog wasn't rich. We'd finished the roof and the inner supporting walls of the keep last winter, but it was still mostly just a shell of half-finished rooms.

From the inside, the great hall looked much as it had in my father's day, since I'd been firm on keeping the granite where it didn't show inside. The wall with the family curse written on it had taken the most time. Finding the correct stones and setting them in proper order was somewhat more taxing than the court ladies' puzzles, since each of the pieces weighed over a hundred pounds, and several stones had been smashed when Hurog fell.

My uncle thought I was foolish to work so hard on it, since the curse, which predicted Hurog's fall to the Stygian Beast of mythology, had already been broken. My brother, Tosten, said I did it because I'd been instrumental in breaking the curse. But I hadn't realized, until I saw Oreg's face, that I'd done it to protect him from the too-rapid changes of the past few years. When you're over a millennia old, change, even for the better, is a hard thing. And it was he, as much as I, who had broken the curse.

I touched the wall lightly with one hand and bent to pick up a grout bucket. For the past few weeks, we'd been working on the floors. One of the Blue Guard, an Avinhellish man, was the son of a mason. He'd taken one look at the cracked mess left on the floor of the great hall after the keep fell and declared it unfixable. If I'd known then the amount of work the stupid floor was going to be, I'd have timbered it, or even just left it dirt. It took us months to get the floor level enough for our mason. I think he took covert enjoyment in giving me orders.

The main doors of the keep were awaiting hinges capable of supporting their great weight, so there was nothing to slow the boy who barreled into the great hall. He stopped in front of me and opened his mouth, but he couldn't get a word out for lack of breath.

"Take it slow, boy," I said. We waited for a long moment and several false starts before he could speak. Meanwhile, I examined him for clues to his identity.

He was clothed rather well, even for a freeholder's son. The woolen trousers were newly dyed, and the shirt was linen—a cloth that had to be purchased, as flax didn't grow in our climate. The boy looked like Atwater's get, tall with dark eyes that swallowed the light.

"Sir, there's bandits, sir. Down by Da's farm. He sent me here to get you."

He was covered in sweat, and once he'd gotten his message out, he had to give his all to breathing again.

"Atwater is your father?" I asked, and he nodded.

I always knew when there was trouble brewing on Hurog land. Oreg said it was because I was tied to it by blood right, and told me that several of my distant ancestors had the same tie to the land. Hurog spoke to me—when I listened.

A swift touch of magic showed me that there was no fighting near Atwater's farm now, which meant that the bandits had been driven off. If Atwater or one of his family had been killed, I'd have known about it. They belonged to Hurog in a way that had nothing to do with law and everything to do with blood.

"Don't fret, boy," I said. "Atwater's been fighting bandits longer than I've been alive. Let's get my horse, shall we?"

IN THE END THERE WERE THREE OF US FOLLOWING THE boy. He plainly thought we needed more; I thought we could do with less. Rides with Oreg and my brother were always more interesting than pleasant.

My brother, Tosten, rode his new roan war stallion, a gift from our uncle, and came with the excuse that the animal needed exercise when he found me saddling my own horse in the stables.

Tosten was never going to be as tall as I was, but the past four years had given him a man's face and a fighter's body. He looked cool, competent, and clever (as some court woman said in my hearing). Competent and clever, I agreed with. Coolness might come with age—maybe in fifty years or so.

While I waited for Tosten to saddle his horse, Oreg showed up and, without a word, took out his own gelding. Except for his dark hair and half a head in height (Tosten was taller), he and Tosten looked enough alike to be twins.

"Bandits," I said in answer to Oreg's look as I mounted and lead the way out of the bailey.

"My brother spied them near our farm and Da sent me here for help." There was a hint of accusation in the boy's tone. Three people, it implied, would not be much help.

The air was chill with the coming winter. We'd taken the last of the harvest in this week. Oreg said he thought it might snow soon, but today the leaves still clung to the branches of the rowan and aspen in bright clumps that stood out against the dark greens of the pines and firs. Pansy, my stal-

lion, snorted with pretended fear and shied violently when a
falling leaf fluttered too close. In battle, not even a heavy
blow would cause him to step to the right or left without my
request, but outside of serious work, Pansy loved to play.

The shortest path to Atwater's farm skirted the edge of the
mountains where the land was too rocky to plow. The farm
was isolated in a hanging valley away from the other culti-
vated fields of Hurog. That isolation had lured bandits into
thinking it was a target before, but none of them had ever
managed to take anything from Atwater. I didn't think that
was going to change today.

The turf was still soft enough that the steady trot I'd set
was unlikely to cause the horses much stress. People were
another matter entirely.

"We need to hurry," said the boy for the third time. I'd
had a gentle mare found for him, but I needn't have. He sat
her bareback (his choice) and was impatient with the rest of
us for holding him back.

"Never arrive for a fight breathless," snapped Tosten.

"If they overran your farm, we'd smell smoke by now," I
reassured the boy, shooting Tosten a repressive look. "They
might not have seen the farm, or your father may have driven
them off or killed them. Either way we don't have to hurry.
There can't be very many of them, or I'd have heard about
it before they made it this far onto Hurog lands."

"Don't worry about Tosten, boy," said Oreg cheerfully.
"He's as impatient as you are."

Tosten sank into silence. Oreg, in contrast, was unusually
lighthearted, teasing the boy until he smiled—at which point
my brother let his stallion speed past us. With a glance at
me, the boy sent his mare cantering after my brother—obviously hoping I'd hurry after both of them.

"I wish you wouldn't bait Tosten," I murmured to Oreg.

Oreg just smiled, though his eyes didn't light up the way
they did when he was really amused. "Your brother has had
plenty of time to decide that I'm no threat to him. Time he
grew up. If I choose to tweak his tail a bit—that's between
him and me. He doesn't need your protection anymore,
Ward."

I rolled my eyes. "You encourage him," I said.

"I frighten him," Oreg corrected, and even his mouth was serious. I must have looked unconvinced, because he shook his head and said, "I'm no threat to his relationship with you, and he knows that. It hasn't been about that for some time." Oreg smiled again, but this time it was a genuine one. "Poor lad's fighting dragons."

It was an old Shavig saying about someone who was displaying rash bravery impelled by fear. The ironic twist to Oreg's tone was because in this case it was literally true. Oreg's father had been half-dragon. Oreg could take dragon form when he wished, and considered both the human seeming and the dragon his true forms. *Reason for living*

I weighed what Oreg had said. Tosten was the only one who knew the whole story about Oreg. As my heir and as my brother I thought I owed him that. Perhaps it would have been better if I'd stuck to half-truths.

Atwater's boy waited for us at the top of the trail, though Tosten was still ahead.

"Tosten told me it is magic that lets you see there's nothing wrong at my home. There's a lot of folks who are frightened by magic."

It sounded like a personal observation, and I looked at him sharply. He colored up, but his eyes met mine squarely.

"Most folks know you can do magic, my lord," he said firmly. "Most of us are grateful for it. Father says that they'd never have found my brother and his hunting party caught out in the blizzard if you hadn't joined in the search."

I smiled at him and he dropped in beside us. Tosten, when Oreg is not around, usually knows how to charm people into doing what he wanted them to. It came from being a bard, he claimed, but I thought it might be a bit the other way around. Charm, good voice, and clever fingers made for good bards.

As we neared Atwater's farm, the land told me death had visited here recently. Death was no stranger to Hurog—its mortal residents came to an end on a regular basis—but I had to assume that this death had something to do with my being summoned here. Whoever had died was not of the earth of Hurog, which meant it wasn't Atwater or his people. It must be the bandits.

Nevertheless, when we passed the boundary at the edge of the farm, I drew my sword. Tosten (who'd let us gradually catch up to him) and Oreg drew steel likewise. The path we'd taken approached the farmhouse, which from the rear was more of a fort than a house, but a lookout spied us riding down into the valley and let out a series of notes on his hunting horn—Atwater's own call. The tightness eased in my shoulders.

A moment later the unmistakable form of the holder, himself, came around the corner. Seeing us, he whistled an all clear, so I sheathed my sword.

The boy heaved a great sigh of relief and nudged his mare into a gallop.

When one is a grizzled old war lord or the younger son of a holder, one may gallop as much as one wishes. Since I was a young lord who was trying to live down various reputations, I slowed my horse to a walk.

Mounted on my father's old war stallion, walking was sometimes adventurous. Pansy knew better, but I let him snort and huff and generally announce to everyone watching that he was dangerous and would be much faster than that little mare if I would just let him go.

Atwater nodded at me when we got close enough to talk. "Thank ye, my lord, for coming. But the problem of bandits has been dealt with. I've the bodies if you'd like to look at 'em."

Atwater was a mountain of a man, approaching my height and build. His pale blond hair fading unnoticeably to gray was braided in old Shavig style—unusual now, but not worth commenting about. His beard, however, was a magnificent thing. Fiery-red, it covered his face and a fair bit of chest. A little barbaric by proper Kingdom standards, but my Hurog folk were beginning to exhibit a pride in our Shavig heritage.

Like many of the older men at Hurog, Atwater had fought to put down the rebellion in Oranstone at my father's side. Sometime during the campaign, Atwater had conceived a dislike for the previous Hurogmeten. I hadn't been fond of my father for my own reasons, but even I had to admit there weren't many men who could fight as well as he had. Most of the men who fought under him wouldn't hear a word against him. I don't know what my father had done to Atwater, but it had taken me the better part of two years to make him see that I was not the man my father had been.

Tosten, Oreg, and I followed Atwater and his son around the building into the chaos of children and relatives who helped him farm and protect the land. At the center of the fervor were three dead men, covered decently for the sake of the children.

I dismounted, handed my reins to Oreg, whose gelding Pansy tolerated, and pulled the blankets aside to look at the dead men's faces. I took care to keep the blankets arranged so the children couldn't peek. I'd seen one of them before, but it took me a moment to remember where.

"Mercenaries from Tyrfannig," I said, dropping the cover over the last man's face. Tyrfannig was the nearest seaport town half a day's ride to the south. Hurog bordered the ocean, but her shores were too rocky for ships to harbor in. "They must not have caught jobs with the merchants going south and decided to become self-employed." Sometimes mercenaries didn't see the difference between looting on a battlefield and looting from anyone they could. "I'll see if anyone in Tyrfannig wants the bodies. Otherwise we'll bury them ourselves, eh?"

"Yes, my lord."

I started to turn away, then realized something about the wounds I'd seen on the bodies. "Who took them down?" Atwater was famed for his bow work and could use an ax on people as well as wood, but he'd never have taken on these bandits armed with nothing more than a knife. Yet the two bodies with the most obvious death wounds had been killed by a short blade, not an ax. I didn't know about the third—and wasn't about to examine the bodies more closely with all the children milling about.

"No, sir. My oldest boy, Fennel, saw them coming in time to warn us. I sent Rowan to you, and we waited. After a bit I tracked Fennel's trail to where he'd seen the bandits. And

I found them three dead, sir. And I found what killed 'em, too. You'll never guess."

As we'd spoken, Atwater's wife had come out of the house with a little sprite of a girl about six.

"It was a girl," the child caroled in satisfied tones. "A girl killed them bandits all by herself."

Atwater's left eyebrow buried itself in his hairline. His wife shrugged.

"My aunt could have killed them," I said. "Why are you so surprised a woman took care of them?"

Atwater shook his head. "Maybe Stala could at that. But I'd be surprised if a *man* in this woman's condition could have walked from where we stand to my home, let alone killed three healthy men with naught but a puny knife. Would you come look at her?"

Bemused, I nodded at Oreg. "Stay out here and keep the babes out from under Pansy's feet, please?"

Tosten gave his reins to Oreg, too.

Atwater's house was dark and close, insulated for winter with dried grasses and straw. I had to duck my head to avoid rubbing the ceiling.

The fire in the hearth was more for light than warmth—that would change as winter approached. One of Atwater's older daughters sat on a nearby bench sewing, a bucket of water by her feet should a spark fly out and touch either fur or straw. She nodded at me, but turned shyly back to her work. I didn't know how she could sew in the dim light. Even with the fire so near, I could barely tell there was a person buried in the furs in front of the hearth.

But I could smell the distinctive odor of rotting flesh. I knelt beside the furs and touched the skin on the back of the unconscious woman's neck, feeling the dry heat.

"She hasn't moved since I found her, my lord," said Atwater. "Her weapon's on the table. After seeing the bodies, I thought I'd better get it out of her reach."

I got up and looked at the knife on the table. Not a hunting knife—the blade was too short, not even a full finger-length. A skinning knife, I thought, but not a common one at all. The metal was worked like the finest sword, the pattern of its folding visible even in the darkness of the house.

Tosten whistled softly. "She took out three mercenaries with that knife?"

"They underestimated her," I said, setting the knife back on the table. Stala said that men tended not to take her seriously because she was a woman, and that gave her an advantage that more than made up for the difference in size and strength. "Tosten, would you go hold the horses and send Oreg in to look at her wounds?" I'd done some field surgery, but the smell of flesh-rot told me we'd need more than that here—and Oreg, among other things, was an experienced healer.

Tosten nodded and turned on his heel without comment.

When Oreg appeared in his stead, the atmosphere in the house changed. No one in the house acted like they were afraid of Oreg, but they set him at a distance due the Wizard of Hurog.

Oreg's dark hair made him stick out among the fair-haired Shavigmen, but his purple-blue eyes, duplicates of Tosten's, proclaimed him a Hurog born and bred. In the past few years, unbound by the spells that had held him, he'd begun to look more like a man and less a boy, but he, like Tosten was slight of build. He didn't look like someone to be afraid of. Still less did he look like a man who had arisen from the dead.

I'd told everyone that Oreg had been ensorcelled and that by killing him I'd broken the spell. They seemed to accept it and Oreg—but they gave him space when they could.

Oreg held up his hand as he approached the hearth, and light reflected from his curved palm and lit the little house as if the roof had come off and allowed the sun into all the dark corners. He tossed the ball of light up and it hovered above him while he pulled the furs off of the woman to get a better look at her.

In Oreg's light, her cheeks were flushed with fever and her eyes were sunken. But then, even at her best she had never been beautiful—not by conventional standards.

"Tisala," I said, stunned.

Oreg stopped his examination to peer with momentary interest at her face. "So it is," he agreed mildly. "Good thing they took her knife away from her."

"Do you know her, my lord?" asked Atwater as if it surprised him not at all. He'd gone from thinking I was as brutal and irrational as my father to expecting miracles ever since that night last winter when I found his son.

"Yes, I know her," I said. It didn't seem enough, so I added, "I fought with her at my back." And there wasn't a higher compliment any Shavigman could give.

Atwater nodded, content that his lord was still odd, worldly, and all-knowing.

The last time I'd seen Tisala, her curly dark hair had been shorter than my own, but now it hung in lank tangles down to her shoulders, making her skin all the more white.

Oreg's hands were gentle, but when they touched her left hand, her whole body stiffened and she moaned.

"She's been tortured," he said matter-of-factly.

I nodded. It was hard to miss: both hands, left worse than right, both feet. No telling what other damage had been done: She wore an old pair of trousers, patched and baggy, and a shirt whose arms were too short over the rest.

"They hadn't had her long," he said at last. "She'll live, if the fever and the putrefaction don't kill her. But we ought to take her to the keep, where my medicines are."

Magic, that meant. I'd told Oreg not to tell people exactly what he could do. He couldn't really cure her, but he could kill the infection and let her body heal on its own—which was more than any other mage I'd ever heard of could do. It would be safer for him if all of Shavig didn't start whispering about how powerful the Hurogmeten's wizard was. Better by far to avoid all notice so we didn't get another Kariarn looking for power.

I took one of the larger furs and rolled Tisala in it. Then I scooped her up and stood, forgetting how low the ceilings were, so I rapped my head a good one.

Atwater winced in sympathy.

·　　·　　·

AS SOON AS WE WERE WELL AWAY FROM THE FARM,
my brother guided his horse next to mine and said, "What
was Tisala doing here?"

Oreg gave a snort of laughter. "Why do all strays end up
at Ward's door?"

"I don't know," I said. Had she been running to me? It
would have seemed unlikely to me this morning—I hadn't
seen her in a long time and had only known her briefly. I
wouldn't even have thought I would have left much of an
impression on her—I had been nineteen and full of myself,
while she had been her father's right hand for several years.
Moreover, I was nothing out of the ordinary—well, except
for my size—while she was the only female warrior I knew
of other than my aunt Stala, who served as my arms master.

I looked down at her again. Undeniably she was here.
She'd fled whoever had hurt her, and come to me. I remembered hearing that she'd been estranged from her father. It
bothered me that the only one she'd had to turn to was someone she'd known a few days several years ago.

"I'd like to know how she got into this condition," I said.

"The mercenaries?" hazarded Oreg, who'd ridden up to
my left. But he shook his head almost instantly. "She'd have
gutted them long before they could bring her up here."

"Her father, Haverness, disowned her for taking up with
a bunch of dissidents in Estian last year, didn't he?" Tosten
mused. "People who wanted his half brother Alizon on the
throne rather than Jakoven?"

King Jakoven's name made me pause. If it had been Jakoven, then Tisala did indeed have a reason for coming here.
There weren't many nobles still powerful enough to thwart
the High King of the Five Kingdoms, but my family was.
Hurog was an ancient keep and carried more power than its
lack of wealth should lend. The Shavig were a long-
memoried people, and Hurog had ruled Shavig in the days
before the Tallvens had eliminated their competition.

"I wouldn't rule it out," I said. "That would explain why
she fled here, rather than to her father or one of her cocon-
spirators."

"We'll keep her safe," said Tosten, his jaw set. My family would be a long time forgetting that the king had killed my cousin during one of his political games. Tisala had chosen wisely; no one would betray her here.

I couldn't be certain it had been Jakoven, not until she woke; but I had to plan for it.

"Oreg, will you ride ahead and let my aunt know what's happened here? Be discreet, but make sure she understands that we may have royal troops here soon."

"Right," he said.

I waited until his sprinting horse was out of sight before I turned to my brother. "You're my heir. If the king finds out I've sheltered an enemy, he's likely to declare me a traitor. I'd like you to ride to our uncle and explain to him what's happened."

He gave me a small half-smile. "You don't have the right to protect me anymore, Ward. I'm older than you were when you took on Kariarn of Vorsag. You can quit giving me that look—Stala does it better. If it comes down to making sure Hurog stays in Hurog hands, I'll run. But it's highly unlikely that Tisala would have led them here, and there's no reason for the king to think she'd come. I've not seen her above a dozen times in the last four years. The way you stay away from court, I doubt you've seen her at all."

Only in my dreams, I thought. I might not believe I'd made much of an impression upon her, but the reverse was certainly not true. "I would feel better with you in Iftahar with Duraugh."

"Too bad for you," he muttered. I don't think I was supposed to hear. He cleared his throat. "I always liked Tisala—Mother spoiled me for delicate women."

I LAID TISALA FACEDOWN ON THE TOP OF THE TABLE IN the library because it was one of the few finished rooms in the keep that had a window to let in the light. Tosten had mumbled something about being useful elsewhere, turned on his heel, and left. He seldom stayed in the room while Oreg worked magic.

I cut her clothing and pulled it out from under her until she lay bare. Her back had whip marks laid out so evenly that there wasn't more than a thumb's worth of skin left on her whole back. Some of them were almost healed, but in many places the scabs were broken and wept clear fluid.

I heard an indrawn breath behind me. I turned my head and saw Oreg stare down at her back. Then he began to pace rapidly and rub his hands together, not usually a good sign.

I sat down on a bench hoping that my own restfulness would allow him to calm.

"Oreg," I said to catch his attention. Sometimes he had relivings that could be harrowing to all concerned. Soldiers had them, flashes of past battles that seem, for a moment, more real than the present—but Oreg could make the visions real. I'd never seen anyone but Oreg be harmed by them, but they were frightening all the same. "Tisala needs you."

He stared at me, breathing hard, looked away for a moment, and then gave me a tired smile. "Right."

We started by cataloging the damage. It was not pleasant, that half hour, I was glad more than once that Tisala was unconscious, both for her dignity and her pain. It was her left hand that was the worst—the initial damage, which was considerable, compounded by infection. Upon closer examination several of the broken scabs on her back were puffed up with pus. Bruises abounded on her hips and inner thighs; she'd been raped.

Oreg growled and muttered as we continued checking her carefully. Her feet were a mess. Oreg said finally that the damage was from walking so far in ill-fitting shoes rather than a torturer's knife.

He set her foot down and turned to the smaller table that held various herbs and salves, hot water, and bandaging. "You think Jakoven did this?" With a wave of his hand he indicated Tisala's damaged state.

I nodded. "I can't think of any other reason she'd run all the way here."

"She liked you." Oreg used a clean knife to open one of the putrid places on Tisala's back, sponging up the fluid that escaped with a clean wet cloth.

"True enough," I agreed. "But I haven't seen her since I was last in Oranstone."

I'd helped Oreg heal before, and we worked as a team. Most of what we did was ordinary stuff, clean wounds, cover with mixtures of salves and powders that Oreg hoarded, then bandage.

But her left hand was swollen to twice its normal size and it was the source of the putrid smell. He soaked it first in hot seawater. Tisala must have really been in rough shape, because she didn't even protest. When Oreg was through, he poured alcohol over it, and again she had no reaction. He reexamined her now-clean hand.

Healing was the most difficult of all magics to do because the mage must know as much about the body as he does about his magic. And even a little healing sucked up such power as most mages can only dream about.

In power I was the equal of many and better than most, with such ability as four years of Oreg's tutoring could bring, but I would not have even known where to start to save the mess that remained of Tisala's left hand.

"She might lose her fourth finger anyway," commented Oreg, shaking his head. "There's too much dead flesh."

"She fights right-handed," I said. "Would it be better to cut it off now?"

Oreg frowned and turned her hand this way and that. "I always hate to cut something off I can't put back on. Let me try and heal this. If it doesn't take, there will be plenty of time to cut it off later."

He set her hand down and pulled up a three-legged stool next to the table. When he was comfortable, he took her hand up again and poured magic over it.

Oreg had been part of Hurog since there was a Hurog to be a part of, and I was Hurog-bred sensitive to the magics imbued in the land and in him. When Oreg worked magic around me, it felt almost erotic—like a hand touching me intimately. It was disturbing, but I shrugged off the uncomfortable feeling with the ease of long practice.

There is an art to working magic, and Oreg was very, very good at his art. His touch was focused and powerful, eerily beautiful to watch. When his power began to flicker, I rested my hands on his shoulder and gave him what I could of mine, all the while watching what he was doing to Tisala's hand.

Flesh peeled back and burned away in bright purple flame, leaving healthy pink behind. Oreg left other bits of flesh that looked no more healthy than the flesh he'd destroyed—he must have seen things I did not.

When he was finished at last, her hand looked more swollen and bruised than it had when we started. I hauled Oreg off to rest on the padded bench against the wall, then turned back to Tisala with clean bunting.

"Don't wrap that hand," Oreg said. "The air will help it heal, and she won't be doing much for a few days to get it dirty."

I looked to the wounds we hadn't dealt with yet. "I think she's got a rib that's cracked or broken," I replied. "Do I bind her ribs, or will that hurt her back?"

Oreg pushed himself off the bench, and moving like an old, old man, examined the place I showed him. "Bruised," he grunted, shuffling back to the bench. "Don't wrap it."

I left Oreg, pale and sleeping, in the library and took Tisala up to my own room to rest. She looked oddly fragile in the bed built for me, I thought, smiling because she would have laughed if she'd heard anyone call her fragile.

A MIDDLE-AGED MAN WITH SWEAT FROM THE FIRE coating his bald head looked up as I came into the forge and nodded at me before turning his gaze back to the bar he was shaping.

"Good 'noon, Hurogmeten," he said. "What can I do for you?"

"Hinges," I said. "And a portcullis door to go with the gatehouse we don't have. Bars for all the windows. A thousand blades and the warriors to use them."

The armorer gave me a brief smile. "The same as usual, then." He shaped the iron with the same swift skill he showed with steel. It was a real concession on his part when he agreed to shape iron with the blacksmith. Blacksmithing was a step down from the work he'd usually been called upon to do.

"Stala said we might have a visit from the king soon," said a quiet voice from the back.

I walked around to see the blacksmith pulling shoes off a horse. He was a little younger than the armorer, with long blond hair he pulled back to keep out of his eyes.

"We might," I agreed. "But we'll not be fighting if I can help it. For one thing, the gate in the curtain wall will come down at the first hit of a battering ram. He'll be looking for the woman we brought in today, and the trick will be not to let him know she's here."

The blacksmith set the horse's leg down and tossed the old shoe into a barrel. "I had heard you'd gotten another stray." He grinned. Unlike the armorer, he liked to chat while he worked.

"Hardly a stray," I said, then reconsidered. "Well, she needs help for a bit—but she'll not be staying."

"We've gotten most of the bars for the windows done," he said, "and bolts and brackets for the doors inside the keep. Hinges, too, for that matter—but we haven't started on the hinges for the keep door yet. So far we're ahead on nails and fasteners of various kinds, but the carpenter sent his boy in to check today—so I imagine we'll be doing nails again in the near future."

The heat of the forge felt good in the cool air, so I stayed and talked a bit, helping with bellows and fetching water from the well.

Tisala's state had left me melancholy, and work was good to dispel it. When I left the forge's warmth, I wandered along the curtain wall and touched a rough-hewn granite block to remind myself of how much we'd accomplished since Hurog had fallen.

The inner curtain walls had been the first thing I'd had rebuilt after Hurog fell. And it was a good thing, too—between the death of my father and the invasion of the Vorsag, bandits from hundreds of miles around had come to see if Hurog was ripe for the plucking. The Blue Guard, under my aunt's direction, fended them off—but had there not been the curtain wall to hide my people behind, the bandits would have laid waste to the farmers who worked the land.

The wall was as tall and as solid as the one that had withstood many centuries of Shavig weather. On the bottom it was almost fifteen feet thick, good stone block on the outside, and filled with rubble (of which we had plenty). On the top it narrowed to less than nine feet across, but was still amply wide to allow the guardsmen to walk. It was a good wall, even if it looked odd with the granite stones outnumbering the blackstone.

Inside the wall, the bailey was oddly barren now that the miscellaneous small buildings my ancestors had added were gone. It had taken a great deal of work to level the bailey, since the earthen mound the keep had sat upon had settled after some of the caves beneath it had collapsed.

The new guards' quarters were built against the wall near one of the six towers, the only stone building in the bailey except for the forge. The quarters were a neat, rectangular building that took up half the ground of its predecessor with twice the usable space. There was stabling in the bailey for a few animals, but most of the horses were outside, between the inner wall and where the outer had once stood.

I sighed, thinking of the outer walls, and decided to continue to work on the floor of the main hall—something that might be finished before I died of old age. Tosten was working alone on the floor and I joined him. Tiling was mucky and nasty, and the lime in the grout found its painful way into every little cut.

"Why did you rebuild Hurog so large?" Tosten asked, fitting a tile into the pattern we'd decided upon. "It doesn't need to be this big anymore. Hurog isn't rich and this seems pretentious. We could have had a hall half this size, two stories instead of three, and half the bedrooms."

I could have argued the large. It only felt big because he and I and Oreg were the only Hurogs left to live in it. My sister, Ciarra, had married our cousin Beckram and lived at Iftahar, my uncle's estate. Iftahar's keep rang with the sounds of children and seemed much smaller than it actually was.

I said, "There is little expense involved—the granite is

ours and only needs quarrying. I'd be paying the Guard anyway, they might as well do something for it."

Tosten snickered, "I'd like to hear you say that in front of Stala."

I widened my eyes and dulled the expression on my face. "Do I look stupid to you?"

"No one," he said, fitting a tile against the grout he'd laid down, "is as stupid as that."

I laughed and looked around at the keep. "It's not that large; you could fit our keep into the king's palace at Estian a dozen times over. The trade with the dwarves isn't much yet, but Axiel tells me that the mysterious illness that had afflicted his people is over. There are dwarven children now, after so many years, and soon there'll be more time to spare for the making of luxury goods for trade."

Tosten nodded. "Good for him. I haven't talked to him since he came here last winter and helped finish your room."

"Neither have I," I said, "but Oreg visits him now and again."

"How is Tisala?"

"The only thing we're still worried about is her left hand, but she'll live even if Oreg doesn't manage to save it."

He nodded again and turned his attention to the floor. After a little while he began humming a ballad. When he began singing, I joined in, too. After a bit we began to attract a group of children, so we hammed it up a little. Tosten found a song with male and female roles. He took the male in a high squeaky voice, and I sang the female in bass. We entertained the children and worked on the floor until it was time for dinner. Even Tosten was hoarse, but the cook brought in hot-mulled cider and kissed his cheek in gratitude for keeping the children at bay while their mothers cooked and cleaned.

3
WARDWICK

Rejecting properly sent invitations is impolite and can cause lasting harm to one's future.

AFTER I FINISHED EATING, I VENTURED UP TO check on my guest. One of the maidservants had told me she'd brought soup and bread up but Tisala had been sleeping.

The Lord's Chamber at Hurog would show well against any room I'd ever seen, including the royal chambers at Estian. It had been a gift from the dwarves who'd snuck in while I was away at Iftahar working out some business with my uncle.

The wood trim was some exotic southern hardwood, full of swirls and rich color. The dwarves had taken advantage of the complex grain and carved fantastical shapes in odd places. The walls were layered in plaster drawn into soft patterns gleaming with powdered gemstone. High above, skylights let in slits of sunshine through narrow strips of thick, clear crystal. It was luxury I still could not accustom myself to—and it was distinctly odd in the spare style of Hurog keep.

"You live well for a poor northern barbarian," commented Tisala hoarsely.

Her eyes had been closed when I came into the room, but she was awake now.

I waved an arm at the whole room and said, "A gift from the dwarves."

She grinned suddenly. "Save a race from extinction once, and have to live with it forever. I killed a couple of bandits and passed out—I didn't expect to wake up in luxury. It's certainly not what I expected from Hurog." The grin disappeared as quickly as it had come—it must have hurt the purple bruise that had bloomed on the right side of her face since I'd last seen her.

"One of my people found you," I said. "We brought you here this morning. I believe there's some soup and bread around somewhere if you're hungry."

Ignoring my offer of food, she looked at her unbandaged left hand, which looked significantly better than the last time I'd seen it, and her face registered astonishment. "Just this morning?"

"Oreg is a good healer," I said. "You came to the right place—your hand had gone septic. Anyone else would have had it off."

She was silent for a moment, flexing her fingers slowly. Still watching it, she said, "I'm so sorry to show up here like this, but I couldn't think of anywhere else I could go."

"My home is your home," I said, meaning it.

"He'll look for me," she said, "because he thinks I am the key to two things he wants very much."

"Jakoven?" I asked.

She nodded, and met my eyes. "He thinks I know the names of the nobles who are giving aid to Alizon."

"Do you?" I asked.

"Not all, but enough to hurt a lot of people who are doing nothing but protecting a man from unlawful, unjustified prosecution—unlawful at least until Jakoven officially declares Alizon a traitor."

The king's half brother had disappeared almost a year ago, about the same time the royal armies descended unexpectedly on his estates. Alizon had escaped with little more than the clothes he was wearing—and a large number of allies who were willing to hide him. The king had pressed no charges, saying he preferred to wait until his half brother could defend himse!f.

Tisala sat up, her face tightened in pain but her chin rose to stifle any hint of sympathy. "I needed a place to hide until I recovered. I'm sorry I've put you at risk—but I don't think he'd ever consider looking for me here."

"King Jakoven doesn't like me much anyway, nor I him, for that matter," I said wryly. "You are welcome here as long as you like, and know that you are not hurting my standing with the high king."

"I didn't come empty-handed," she said. "The second thing Jakoven wants from me is the means to convict your cousin Beckram of being a traitor." She flexed her hand again and continued, "It seemed to be a matter of some importance."

I noticed that she didn't say Beckram wasn't involved.

I turned away and stared at a dragon carved into the mantelpiece. According to my uncle, who was seldom wrong when it came to matters of court affairs, King Jakoven was angry about his half brother's growing support, but he didn't appear to take it as a serious threat to the throne. A view I thought, regretfully, that was fully justified.

"How did you escape?" I asked. "Torturer's victims are usually carefully guarded."

"I wasn't held in the castle," she said. "Jakoven had me secreted away in the basement of a building in town."

Jakoven always played games, intrigues within intrigues. Some things, though, made sense—of course he'd secreted her someplace other than the castle. He'd lose a lot of support if it became known he'd tortured Tisala—a woman of high birth. "Correct me if I'm wrong," said Tisala thoughtfully. "But Jakoven's murdered several of the queen's other lovers. And he was trying to kill Beckram and got Beckram's twin instead four years ago. It would be easier for Jakoven to have Beckram killed than to pin a charge of treason on him."

I shrugged and sat on the foot of the bed, leaning against one of the elegantly carved posts. "You're right. But when the king killed Erdrick, I don't think he realized just how much power the name Hurog still holds on the heart of Shavig. Politically, it is smarter to have Beckram proved a traitor and executed than to have someone kill him. Besides, then the punishment would fit the crime. My uncle forced the king to back down for Beckram's sake—a charge of treason would humiliate Beckram equally." I slouched a little, sliding down the bed, and Tisala casually pulled away from me.

"Though Jakoven failed with you, you are hardly the only person the king could torture a confession out of. I need to get word to him. Do you know if Beckram is in Estian now?" I asked. I didn't keep an eye on my cousin's travels. Iftahar was much nearer to Estian than Hurog was, and Beckram went to Estian on a monthly basis.

"No," she whispered. "I don't know. Do you think Jakoven took others to make them accuse Beckram?"

I had been thinking about it from the angle of containing the threat toward my cousin, but, prompted by her question, I realized that anyone Jakoven had taken was likely to have been at least an acquaintance and probably a friend of Tisala's.

I sat forward and Tisala jerked back from me. When she realized what she had done, she flushed with embarrassment—but she didn't relax.

I'd fought side by side with Tisala. The thought of what it would take to make her flinch from anyone made me want to hit something. I wanted to say something to comfort her—but the closed look on her face told me she wouldn't talk about it.

"Do you think Jakoven has taken someone else?" she asked again.

"That depends upon what he really wants," I said finally. "If he's really trying to break Alizon's support, he'll go after the lower born first. Build up cases against the nobles from the confessions he gets from the ones he can attack with impunity."

"What do you mean 'if'?" she asked.

"I told you," I said. "On the run the way he is, Alizon's no threat to the king now. He has no access to his wealth or lands—both of which have been padding the king's purse nicely. Alizon might have had a chance four years ago, if Kariarn had been a little more successful in his attempt to take over Oranstone—and if Alizon weren't illegitimate. When Alizon's caught, Jakoven will make a fool of him and confine him somewhere convenient—like the asylum next to the king's younger brother, Kellen—where Alizon will die from choking on his dinner some night after everyone has forgotten about him. Jakoven's too smart to make a martyr out of his half brother either by a long trial or by killing him."

"So what do you think King Jakoven is doing?" asked Tisala after a moment. I thought she sounded bleak—had she really thought Alizon had a chance of oversetting his brother?

"I think Jakoven's moving against my cousin," I said. "Though he's taken quite a risk in doing it."

"What do you mean?" Tisala wasn't sitting up quite so straight anymore, and her face had gone from pale to gray. She tried to lean back against the headboard of the bed, but desisted as soon as her raw back touched the wood. I could have moved away and allowed her to lie back comfortably, but I didn't want her to feel as though I was making allowances for her fear. *I* hadn't done anything to her—she just had to force herself to remember that.

"Taking you could have precipitated a scandal," I said. "Even with your father disowning you, you are a highborn lady—and as such entitled to a certain amount of respect to your person. The Tallvenish are very protective of their aristocratic womenfolk, and it is the Tallvenish who are the heart of Jakoven's seat upon the throne."

"Not that protective," she protested. "They wouldn't change their allegiance over a woman—especially not an Oranstonian who fights like a man."

I raised my eyebrows at the bitterness in her words and I wondered how uncomfortable she'd found life in Estian after the freedoms her father had allowed her.

"You're right," I said, "at least in that most of them wouldn't have run to your rescue. But it would be as bad for him as if he were caught having relations with one of his hunting dogs. They would lose all respect for him, and that would be dangerous. My cousin's downfall must be important to him in order for him to risk being found out."

"So he won't stop with me," she said. "And he probably didn't start with me, either."

She sounded a little frantic, and I wondered if there were a man in particular she was worried about.

I shrugged. "I don't know. It would take more than the word of a peasant or merchant to give King Jakoven a clear shot at Beckram. Someone that everyone knows is one of Alizon's supporters. Have you been missing anyone who fits that bill?"

She shook her head. "No—not when I was taken. I don't know about now."

I shifted forward slowly, to give her time to control her initial recoil, and put a gentle hand against her shoulder. "There's nothing you can do from your sickbed. Rest."

She held still under my touch, but made no move to lie back until I got off the bed.

"Do you need help?" I asked, letting my hand drop casually to my side. "I know what your back must be feeling like."

"No," she said. She hesitated for a moment, then sank back beneath the woven blankets and turned painfully onto her side to take pressure off her back and sore rib. "I can't think," she muttered.

"Don't panic," I said. I'd been healed by Oreg a couple of times, too: I knew how it felt to have exhaustion pull my consciousness away from me. "It's just the magic."

Her lips curved up as her eyes closed. "They call you a wizard—the Shavig Wizard, as if there were no other mages to come out of Shavig—or Hurog, for that matter. Did you really pull Hurog apart with your power?"

"No," I answered. With my soul, perhaps, mine and Oreg's, but not my magic. "Rumor exaggerates. Oreg's our wizard here. On a good day I can light the fire in the hearth." I was a bit better than that, or had been before Oreg decided last month that I needed to learn to use my own magic rather than Hurog's to power my spells.

The smile fell away from her lips and she struggled up on her elbows and forced her eyes open. "I shouldn't have come here," she said, her voice slurring the words. "It's too dangerous."

"What would have been dangerous," I said, "would have been not knowing that Jakoven was moving against my family. For that you are welcome to stay here until you grow old and rot." My words eased her and she allowed me to pull the covers over her again. I waited until her breathing slowed before I touched her cheek.

She wasn't objectively beautiful—she had her father's hawklike nose for one thing. On her father it was distinguished. On her it was . . . intimidating. Her face was all angles except for her slightly slanted eyes and overlarge mouth. She was too tall as well, and not in the slim-fragile manner of most tall women. Instead, she was lithe yet muscular, stronger, I daresay, than many men.

To me she was glorious, even battered as she was. For the past four years I had measured every woman I met against her, to their detriment. Now she was here, in my bed.

TISALA PROGRESSED RAPIDLY FROM INVALID TO cranky and bored. Sympathetic, I brought out a chessboard to help her pass the time.

"My father taught me," she said apologetically as I stared at the board as if that would explain how she beat me faster than Oreg ever had.

I gave her an annoyed look, sat back on my chair, and shook my head. "You never apologize for winning, that just increases your opponent's humiliation."

A slow smile crossed her face. "I know."

I shook my head again. "No. When you win, you want to crush your opponent, not just humiliate him. A humiliated opponent just gets vicious, a crushed opponent crawls off and never bothers you again. Watch."

I took a deep breath, then hit the table with sudden violence, scattering hapless chess pieces on the floor. "Hah!" I bellowed. "*Do* you call that a *game*? My grandmother's dog played better on its deathbed. *Fifteen* moves! Teach you to believe it when someone claims to play a *little* chess!" I subsided slowly.

Tisala had flinched at my first move, but it had been reflex only, and even when I loomed over her, she was relaxed in her chair. It had taken me weeks to get my father's warhorse to trust me that much—but Tisala had only been abused for a short time.

"Subtle, Hurog, subtle like a battle-ax," she said. "My father taught me better manners than that—but I suppose we must take into consideration that you are a Shavig barbarian and given to fits and starts."

I collapsed back into my chair and put my hand over my heart as if she had wounded me.

She'd been here for five days and looked much better than she had at first. Her left hand was healing well. Though it would never be as strong as it had been, she'd be able to hold a shield or use a bow with it.

Giving up my pose, I reset the board, having to scramble under the bed to find the dark rook, and we started again. This time I was playing for death. Lunch came and went, and the early shadows of the shorter winter days necessitated the lighting of candles before the game was over. I beat her this time, but I'd had to work at it.

"Hah!" I bellowed, hitting the table, and she laughed.

Better than the healing of her body was the easing of her spirit. She hadn't talked about what had happened to her, and I hadn't pushed. I knew from experience that some wounds heal best in silence. Later, when the experience wasn't so fresh, I'd press her on what had happened, and in the meantime I worked on helping in other ways. She didn't even flinch at my aggressive gloating.

When she quit laughing, she said, "Not that I don't appreciate the game, but don't you have other duties here that call for your attention?"

I picked up the scattered pieces from the floor again, and said, "The harvest's in and stored. My aunt needs no help keeping the Guard busy. I could help lay the floor in the main hall, but it's not necessary."

As I set the pieces back in their case, I asked her something that had been bothering me. "What were you about in Estian? I thought your so-public fight with Haverness was staged, but I've never figured out the reason for it. What did your exile to Estian accomplish?"

"What was it supposed to accomplish?" she asked.

I scowled at her. "No one who plays chess like you would do such a stupid thing without reason."

"How was it stupid?" she asked. "I fought with my father. He tried to tell me how to think, and when I refused to agree with him, I was asked to leave—I think he believed that would make me give in. So I left."

"And went to Estian," I said.

"Where else?"

I laughed. "That might work with Tallvenish folk, my lady. But I've seen how your father dotes upon you. Like me, he might understand that Alizon's rebellion hasn't a chance of succeeding, but he'd never toss you out for that. What took you to Estian?"

She was silent, but it was a challenging silence. I'd grown up with a sister who couldn't speak and communicated by expression. *Figure it out yourself,* Tisala's folded arms and superior expression said.

What makes Tisala unusual enough that Alizon's cause would pull her to Estian? I wondered.

I smiled at last, getting it. "A man, even a man of high rank, whose support of Alizon became common knowledge would be taken in for treason."

She smiled back, but didn't say anything.

"But a highborn woman would be safe because of Tallvenish custom—at least you *should* have been. They would need a single woman—otherwise her husband would be expected to stop her. But to what purpose . . ." I stared at her and she stared back blandly.

This woman, something whispered deep inside my heart, *this woman is for me.*

The bruises on her face were yellow and green. She was too thin, making her nose stand out even more. She wore one of my oldest robes and one of the pieces of chicken we'd eaten at lunch had left a greasy spot on the material over her arm. And none of it mattered at all.

"Perhaps," I speculated, hoping she hadn't read what I was thinking in my face. "Perhaps there is a nobleman who would like to see Jakoven fall. Maybe this nobleman has money to support Alizon, perhaps it is information, or even just a message. Perhaps he wants to be completely anonymous. If there were someone who could be trusted to pass things on, an anonymous servant or even a street child could be sent to this supporter of Alizon—if people knew who he—or rather she was."

She raised her eyebrows. "Truly you have an active imagination, Ward."

"Accurate, too," I said. "How did you contact Alizon?"

She opened her mouth, then shut it. When she spoke, she said, "I'm not a fish to rise to your bait. Suffice it to say that your casting is in the right area and we'll leave it at that."

BUT IT WASN'T SO EASY TO LEAVE THE INFORMATION I'd gotten from Tisala alone. Jakoven was moving against Beckram, my cousin—my responsibility. The king's gambit with Tisala had failed, but he had many other arrows in his quiver.

Over the next few weeks as the first snows left the mountains white and frosted the air, I pondered Jakoven's next move. But the only thing I settled upon was that it would be disastrous to wait for Jakoven to play his own game. I'd have to make a move of my own.

"I'M GOING TO ESTIAN," I SAID OVER SUPPER.

The guardsmen ate in their quarters, but there was enough tile done in the great hall that my family took our meals there, my family and our guest. Tisala had been mobile enough to take the stairs for the last week, so she'd begun to join us for meals. We sat close to the great fireplace that tried to make up for the open doorway, where soon the great doors would hang. The armorer's first attempt at hinges had been beautiful, but not strong enough to hold the doors, so he was trying again.

"Estian? You *are* mad," said Oreg with conviction, though not disapproval—more as if he were delighted with the discovery. He'd finished eating and was settled back watching the rest of us.

I grinned at him.

My aunt Stala, seated next to him, shook her head—but I think it was at Oreg and not at me. She was my captain of the guards and my mother's baseborn sister, a Tallvenish woman who'd taken her destiny in her own hands and shook the world. She bore the scars of those battles gracefully and there was not a man in the Blue Guard who would not die willingly for her, including me. "You forced *me* to stay here," said my brother, "by following me to the capital every time I tried to go, threatening to expose yourself to the possibility that he would decide to enforce his own writ and have you caged in his zoo for unwanted nobles—"

Tosten had been intent on supporting Alizon—something I'd determined was both dangerous and useless. But Tosten was still young and hotheaded; he'd been very close to both of the twins, and Erdrick's death had hit him hard.

"Unwanted *crazy* nobles," I murmured, taking a bite of stew and relishing the taste of fresh carrots. By the end of winter we'd be out of vegetables. I glanced at Tisala and she sent me a strained smile in return. She obviously agreed with Tosten.

"Unwanted crazy nobles," Tosten snapped with a wave of his hand. "Now you want to hie off and see what Jakoven's been up to? You might do well to remember that the last Hurog who stuck his nose in Jakoven's business got his throat slit."

"He killed Erdrick," I acknowledged. "And now he's after Beckram. I need to find out what's going on, before we end up with Beckram dead as well."

Tosten's fists came down and made the table jump. "And you can look after Beckram's business so much better than he can?"

It wasn't the words that got to me, it was the tone of voice that implied simultaneously that Beckram was competent and I was an idiot.

I bit back several things that would have been unforgivable—foremost was reminding everyone that it was Beckram's affair with the queen that killed his twin, Erdrick. I took hold of my temper and told them the truth as I saw it. "I am Hurogmeten, guardian of Hurog. Beckram is of Hurog blood and thus under my protection. If I cannot or will not protect my own—I am nothing."

"That attitude would surprise the two other Hurogmetens that I've known," said my aunt dryly, referring to my father and grandfather.

"*Meten* means guardian, and Ward is Hurogmeten," said Oreg before taking a bite of bread.

"What can you do that Beckram can't?" protested Tosten. "I say warn Uncle Duraugh and Beckram and let them deal with it." But the heat was gone from Tosten's voice. He knew all of Hurog's old songs and stories better than I did. He knew the duties of the Hurogmeten. If Oreg's firsthand experience had robbed the old lays of veracity, it hadn't robbed the ideal of its power.

"I need to have a better feeling for what's going on in court," I explained. "Jakoven's abduction of Tisala is just the start. Something ugly is about to happen, and I'm afraid Hurog is going to be caught up in the middle of it."

"Who are you taking with you?" asked Aunt Stala, and the matter was settled.

We planned the trip over the last of the meal, and if Tosten didn't eat much, he didn't protest again, either. We had just stood up to let the kitchen staff clear the dishes from the table when we heard the clatter of racing hooves.

The armsman who ran in was white-faced. "My lord," he said. "There's royal troops riding in."

My mouth went dry. Were they here after Tisala? Thoughts flew through my head. But I'd decided after I heard Tisala's story that it wasn't likely that Jakoven would come after her here—too many people to silence with too little gain. He wouldn't want anyone knowing he'd tortured Tisala.

That left only one answer that would send a royal troop: the writ.

Should I run? Oreg would take me—but that would leave Hurog and those who belonged to her vulnerable—and my family open to charges of treason. My uncle couldn't prove he hadn't helped me, could he? Nor could Beckram, if that was truly whom the king was after.

We could fight. It would start a civil war. Shavig would fall behind us. Oranstone might as well—but they had to worry about the Vorsag invading again as they had four years ago. Except . . .

I shook my head as I dismissed the thought of civil war. It might have happened if the king had attacked us next year instead of this. Today, Hurog would fall in a day, and presented with that accomplishment, Shavig would moan and groan, but ultimately submit to Jakoven's hand.

We were ready to hold off bandits, but the king's army was another thing entirely. Maybe if we had a real gatehouse and portcullis on the curtain wall we could have withstood for long enough. Instead we had nothing but an outer wall with a stout wooden door barred against intruders—the keep had no door at all.

"No need to go to him, he's come for you," said Stala, confirming my thoughts.

The pulse of fear beat heavily in my throat. I didn't have much time. "Tisala—go to my room now and stay there. It'll be death for everyone if the king's men find you here. I'll make certain they don't search the keep, but I'm not sure I can keep them out of here altogether."

Blessed woman turned on her heel and made quick time up the stairs without argument. I waited until she was out of hearing and turned to the others.

"Stala, you keep the Guard from fighting, do you understand? They, and you, must stay here to protect Hurog. Keep Tisala safe as long as you can. As long as the troops say nothing about her—we don't, either. I don't think the king will try and force the issue—it would leave him with too much to explain."

Grim-faced, Stala nodded.

"Tosten, stay out of sight, too. As soon as we are gone, ride for Uncle Duraugh. Make certain he knows that Beckram is in trouble. I would have expected to hear from him sooner than this—maybe something happened to our message."

"You're going with them?"

"Yes, I have to. Don't worry, I'll get out of it. Oreg, can you find your way to Estian and to me in secret?"

Of us all, only Oreg didn't look worried. "Of course."

The sound of hoof on tile made us all jump. But it was only the guardsman's horse. He hadn't taken time to secure her and she'd wandered through the open doors and come to see what the fuss was about.

I ignored the man's embarrassed apology and set my foot in the stirrup. His stirrups were too short. From the mare's back I said, "Luck to you all," and rode out of the great hall without a backward glance, afraid that I'd lose my nerve if I didn't go.

I dismounted at the gates and tried to send the armsmen there to their quarters, but I made the mistake of letting them know just what I thought the king's troops wanted. They were reluctant to leave me alone.

"Begging your pardon, my lord," said Soren, dropping to his knees on the cold ground. "But you took my family and me in when we would have starved to death last winter. I'll not leave you alone with an unfriendly troop of men."

There was a murmur of agreement; the man who'd stayed on the wall called out as the king's troop approached. They were making good time, I thought, if they followed so close on the heels of my lookout.

"If I'm here alone," I explained, "they'll see no need for violence. But they've come looking for a fight—and they'll find reason for it if they can."

"If you are given an order, you will obey it," said my aunt's voice coldly. "Ward, you know better than to explain your orders." She looked at Soren and the defiant men, and sighed pointedly. "And if you have to explain your orders, make certain you do so clearly. Gentlemen, Oreg will accompany the Hurogmeten at a distance and retrieve him if it

looks as though the king intends to harm him. In this way
Ward is safe and Hurog won't suffer under an attack we
cannot win. So go now before you endanger him further."

Her clear voice carried to the tops of the wall and the man
who was there scrambled down the ladder and started for the
guards' quarters without a word. His action inspired the rest,
and Soren jumped to his feet and retreated with them, leaving
me standing with my aunt.

"What'd you do, tell them you were going to let the king's
men take you in order to save everyone here?" she said dryly
after they'd gone.

I flushed and she shook her head. Then she leaned forward
and pulled my ears until I bent down and she could kiss me.
Without another word, she followed the path the men had
taken and I was alone in the darkening bailey.

I walked to the gates, but before I could touch the bar to
open them, something hit them with a reverberating crack
and they bounced and flexed against the bar. The king's men
were using a battering ram before parlaying with the guards
that should have been on the walls. It made me even more
sure what they were here for: They didn't parlay, because no
man would give himself up to be taken to the Asylum unless
he was truly crazy. For a second a humorless grin twisted
my lips.

They hit the gates again. I wondered a minute where
they'd found a timber to use as a ram, then remembered the
rubbish pile just outside the wall. There might have been a
broken timber or two large enough put to use.

The cups had bent around the bar until only a crowbar
could have released it. Not having one handy, I moved out
of the way and waited for them to open it from their side.

When the doors fell, the king's men swarmed over and I
was glad I had decided not to fight. There must have been
two hundred men. *Flattering,* I thought sourly.

With no one to offer them a fight, they stopped, casting
alert gazes at the arrow slits in the third floor of the keep
and the guard towers along the walls. I was standing next to
the doors behind the men and they didn't notice me at first.

The Blue Guard would never have made such a mistake—

but these men weren't trained by my aunt. A harsh blow of a battle horn from beyond the walls stopped them, but they looked only in front, missing me entirely. If I hadn't been so frightened by what I intended to do, I would have grinned. Standing head and sometimes shoulders above most people, I didn't get overlooked very often.

Their ranks parted reluctantly and three men on horseback rode between them: troop commanders. The man nearest me was one of the king's pet sorcerers riding a big piebald mare with blue eyes. Vanity on his part, I thought. He preferred not to share his real name and was known as Jade Eyes. I'd never met him, but I'd heard him described. His face was extraordinarily beautiful, but it was his eyes that clinched it. They were a pale green rarer for humans than his horse's blue eyes were for a horse. The color stood out more in the context of the deep wine-red of his hair.

Beckram had told me that Jade Eyes was one of the king's lovers, though that wasn't the reason for his rank of king's sorcerer. I could feel his power washing over me as he searched my home for something. Whatever it was, he did not find it. Not even the most powerful sorcerer in the Five Kingdoms could invade Hurog with magic, not as long as Oreg was here. I doubt Jade Eyes even knew he'd been stopped.

Most days, Oreg was just Oreg, and I took the power he had for granted. Only once in a great while, like when he fooled the king's best sorcerer, did the knowledge of how good Oreg was awe me.

I turned my attention to the second of the two men. I did not know him, but, by the markings on his armor, he was one of the king's generals.

The third man was Garranon. There was no mistaking the slender build and curly brown hair, even though he rode on the far side of the other two men. His presence surprised me.

For well over a decade he'd been the king's favorite, until he chose to try to save his native Oranstone rather than cater to the king's whims. I understood he was still a power in court, but Jade Eyes had mostly replaced him in the king's bed.

I liked Garranon, which was odd, since he'd been the one to bring the original writ that robbed me of my home. But he'd had reason enough for it then. I did not like it that he'd come a second time.

When they'd ridden to the front of their army, the sorcerer and the general stopped—but Garranon rode his horse a few paces forward.

"Wardwick of Hurog," he called. His voice echoed against the stone of the keep; it would have carried easily over the clash of swords on a battlefield.

"Welcome, Lord Garranon," I said, trying to sound relaxed and a bit amused. I'm not sure I succeeded, but I really scared two or three of the men closest to me. I was unarmed, but they moved back to give me room anyway.

Garranon turned his horse and rode it back to where I stood and handed me a much folded sheet of vellum. His face was carefully expressionless, but his eyes told me he wasn't here willingly.

In a voice that carried clearly to anyone in the bailey who cared to listen, he said, "The king has discovered that his will was not done concerning this, his writ. He desires you, your brother, Tosten, Lord Duraugh, and his son Beckram to come before him and discuss this matter."

"I see," I said, handing the writ back to him. I wondered what I would have thought about that little speech if I hadn't talked to Tisala first, knowing that the king was still angry with my cousin. Would I have thought King Jakoven had chosen to hold a real, legal hearing? Perhaps—but probably not. I wasn't as stupid as I sometimes looked.

"None of the others you have named are here now." I wouldn't hand them my brother if I could help it. "I am always my king's humble servant and am willing to join him in Estian. Would you come in to eat your evening meal?" Tosten had enough sense to stay out of the way as I'd requested.

Garranon glanced at the general—I was going to have to find out who that was, as he was apparently in charge of this mess.

The general shook his head. "Our king desires your presence as soon as possible. We leave now."

I raised my eyebrows. "It will take me a moment to pack and gather my retinue."

"My orders were that there was to be no retinue. We have a spare horse. You will come now and bring Lord Tosten. We were informed that your brother was in residence."

They weren't even going to let me pack. So much for the polite fiction of a "discussion" before the king. I couldn't see what Jakoven was gaining by this, other than the enmity of all of Shavig, but I would find out eventually. Moving against the Hurogmeten was something entirely different than moving against Beckram, the half-Shavig son of Lord Duraugh of Iftahar. It had to be something bigger than simple vengeance—though with Jakoven it was hard to say for sure.

"Ah," I said. "Tosten has a lady friend whom he is visiting. He hasn't been completely forthcoming on where she lives— I believe it is somewhere within a day's ride of here. He's quite enamored of her. You know how young men are." Due to a beating my father had once given me, I speak very slowly. It was making the general restless, so I continued talking. "Still, he usually only spends a couple of weeks at a time with her, so he should be back next week some time. Would you like to wait?"

"No," snapped the man so quickly I heard his teeth click. "The king may send someone else for him if necessary." All polite fictions aside, I was a prisoner and he wasn't going to give me a chance to escape. He also was impatient enough that he wasn't going to search for Tosten. Something in me relaxed knowing my brother and Tisala were safe.

Garranon was still closer to me than the general, and no one but I could see his face. He gave me a wry smile. He knew me well enough to understand what I was doing to the general, but he made no attempt to interfere.

"Well then," I said with impatience, as if it had been the general who was keeping us waiting. "If you are in such a hurry, what are you waiting for? Where is this horse you have for me?"

The horse they brought forward was solid enough to bear

my weight, but clearly wasn't going to outrun anything anytime soon. Maybe fifteen years ago it might have picked up a canter.

Garranon clearly expected me to object, but I didn't. I didn't need to escape on the road, because Oreg, as fanatically loyal to me as if the ancient platinum ring I wore still bound him to my service, would find me in Estian.

With a shrug, I checked the cinch, tightened it, and mounted. I rode out of the broken gates without waiting for them. I would have lost the pose of an uncaring, slightly silly lordling if I had looked back—so I didn't. The stupider they thought me, the easier it would be for Oreg to get me out of this mess.

We rode until full dark. We didn't make it to Tyrfannig, which was the nearest town, so they drew up camp in a relatively flat field. I protested mildly when my wrists were tied, but allowed it without active resistance. While the men cursed and stumbled about putting up tents, I sat by the fire and watched.

The soldiers had dismissed me as a threat, so the ropes around my wrists were loose and comfortable. They all knew the reason that the writ had been issued in the first place was that I was stupid. Very stupid. If they'd heard rumors that I'd recovered, the information was more than countered by my size (which had initially alarmed them), my slow speech, and the pretense I kept up that I believed I was going to a genial discussion despite the ties on my wrists. Garranon could have warned them, and I found it most interesting that he didn't.

I put my forehead against my knees and tried to get used to being off Hurog land again. My head ached, my bones ached, and my muscles felt without strength. It would ease in a couple of days, but only being back on Hurog land would make it leave entirely.

When I lay down to sleep, my arm was tied to the general's wrist and that rope was well-tied. He was taking my continued presence very seriously. That was all right—I didn't intend to escape tonight anyway.

As I closed my eyes, I could feel Jade Eyes watching me.

He hadn't yet uttered a word, but his eyes had followed me constantly. The surveillance bothered me, but it was the knowledge that he was a wizard that really gave me pause. Oreg was in a nearby copse of trees not a hundred yards away.

I knew where Oreg was because *finding* was my best talent. It was the only magic my father hadn't stolen from me the day he tried to beat me to death. I could work magic now, but *finding* was second nature.

I wish Oreg hadn't stopped so near us. In his dragon form he oozed magic. He covered it well, but I didn't know if he was aware how good Jade Eyes was. Dragons, I had learned, were arrogant creatures.

WHEN I AWOKE, THE FIRST THING I SAW WAS THE mage's ice-green gaze.

"What is it," Jade Eyes asked in a voice like honey, "that you do when you dream?"

It was an odd question and I couldn't see what he wanted from my answer.

Without conscious decision, I fell back upon my old habit of sounding stupid when I was defensive. "I sleep when I dream," I said. Had I done something while I slept?

"I could feel your magic beside us in the woods all night long," he said. "It tastes of you as your home tasted of you. But when the sun began to rise this morning and you awoke, the magic went away. Why is that?"

He had it backward, I thought. Oreg and I both tasted of my home, not the other way around. I realized that I'd been worried for naught. No one would believe in a dragon—Jade Eyes found it much easier to conjure up a new power from his imagination than to believe there were dragons at Hurog again. There was desire in his eyes that had nothing to do with sex and everything to do with the lust for power.

"I can't work magic anymore," I said. People who lusted after power were dangerous; one of them had destroyed Hurog.

"But that doesn't mean that the magic went away," he

replied. "Magic doesn't do that. It came to us here and watched over you all night—I could feel it hover. You have given your magic an intelligence of its own. Did it happen when your father beat you?"

"If there is magic here, it is not mine," I said. I knew what must have happened: When Oreg had fallen asleep, he'd forgotten to mask his power. But Jade Eyes had certainly come up with an entertaining explanation.

He ignored me as if I hadn't spoken, rocking back on his heels and humming a bit to himself. When he stood up, he murmured, "I'll have to tell the king about this. How interesting."

Garranon's eyes met mine, worried. I shrugged. It wasn't a good thing to draw Jade Eyes's attention, but there was nothing I could do. Oreg was supposed to meet me in Estian, but he'd followed instead, and I had no way to tell him not to.

Ah, well, I thought, *at least Jade Eyes thinks it is just me he is feeling.* Nothing that would endanger Hurog.

Jade Eyes didn't speak to me again during the remainder of our journey, but he watched me all day, and when I awoke each morning, he was seated by my side staring at me again. The desire to cross my eyes and stick out my tongue at him grew almost overwhelming. But I was Hurogmeten and I had my dignity.

I was a model prisoner, joining in dicing games in the evening, and rowdy songs during the day. The general, whose name I finally discovered was Lawin, eventually only tied me at night. I didn't play stupid—as I once had—but I didn't go out of my way to discuss philosophy and battle strategies, either.

Garranon kept to himself, like a man who'd betrayed a friend. I'd have told him not to fret, but it would have looked odd for me to search him out. I knew he'd had little choice. Jakoven liked to watch people writhe. Truth was, I wasn't precisely Garranon's friend; men in his position couldn't afford to have friends. But I liked him, and always had.

On the evening of the third day of the journey, Garranon sat down beside me. He squinted his eyes and looked at two of the men who were putting up a tent with swift efficiency.

"Gods, I'm sorry, Ward," he murmured in a voice that wouldn't carry farther than my ears.

"No need," I said back. "I know whose decision this is."

We sat for a while more in a surprisingly companionable silence.

"He can't decide what to do with me," said Garranon with bitter amusement. Someone else might have thought the comment came out of the blue.

"Jakoven?"

"Jade Eyes is his new favorite."

I nodded my head. "Does it bother you?"

Garranon laughed. "Not if he would let me go. I have a son, did you know?" He continued without waiting for my nod. "He's three and I've seen him twice. When I request leave to go to my estates, Jakoven says he can't do without me."

"Jakoven's still punishing you for joining Haverness to run the Vorsag out of Oranstone?" It wasn't really a question.

He shrugged. "I don't know what he's doing." He buried his head in his knees. "I'm not entirely certain he does, either."

I disagreed. I thought the king knew exactly what he was doing to Garranon, but I didn't say so.

We stayed there in silence until it was time to sleep. I hope I helped him as much as he helped me keep my panic at bay. Oreg was nearby, but I couldn't see any way out of this without putting Hurog at war with the king. Maybe my uncle would do better.

IT GREW HARDER TO KEEP UP THE "HAIL, FELLOW, WELL met" image as we got closer to Estian. The last morning of the journey, General Lawin put iron manacles on my wrists.

"Sorry," he said, half apologetically, and handed me a water skin.

Feeling sympathy for him, I drank his peace offering. I gave it back to him and he took it gingerly.

He met my eyes squarely and said, "I am very sorry, my lord. I must do my duty."

Foreign magic, tainted and foul, burned through me, and I realized he hadn't just been talking about the manacles.

"The water," I said hoarsely. "Something in the water." Something more than the herbs my mother had favored.

Two guards, eyes lowered and faces grim : . . I blinked my eyes and they were replaced by two fire demons that clutched my manacles in their clawed hands. I spun, and the demons fell away from me to lie broken on the ground.

The pain of the magic elixir made my arms shake. Sweat ran into my eyes and distorted my vision until everything I saw was blurred in hues of red.

Someone called, "We need help!"

"I am helping," said a monster with glowing jade eyes. "If I don't keep this barrier up, his magic guardian in the woods will destroy us all. That's why I had to wait until now, during the day, when it is at its weakest. You go fight him—that's what you do."

They came with clubs and swords, and I hurled them into the ocean that somehow yawned behind them. After the first few, though, the demons were ready and their weapons began to find their mark.

"I thought the king wanted him alive," someone exclaimed harshly. For a moment I knew it was Garranon, but then that understanding left me.

It was hard to fight with the manacles on, so when I'd won myself some space, I pulled. The links bent, but not enough.

Someone swore, then said, "Look at what he did to that chain."

Something hit me in the back of the knee and I stumbled. My vision exploded in a flash of light as I was hit again.

I WOKE ON A PILE OF STRAW IN A SMALL ROOM DIMLY lit by a window high above. Garranon sat on his heels beside me.

"The demons didn't get you," I whispered, because I was certain I could hear the rustle of their feet just outside.

"I think they did," he said, sounding sad.

There was something I'd wanted to tell him, but I couldn't quite . . . "I have a secret," I said.

"Don't tell anyone," he replied, looking a little worried.

"It's for you—Ward wants you to know." *? his Ward*

"Ah." He looked a little confused, but made no other sound.

"Isn't your fault," I said. It was harder to talk than usual, my tongue felt swollen. "Jakoven would have done it anyway."

"Would you have come if I hadn't been there?" he said bitterly.

I nodded. "Hurog's not completed. Not prepared to take on the king. Ward had to come, he knew it was a trap."

He knelt down. "Ward?"

But when he knelt, he turned into my father and I curled into a ball. Father was angry with me, and I knew that his anger always hurt.

After a while the door opened and shut, and I was alone.

If I burrowed under the straw that covered the floor, the demons couldn't find me. Terror was my closest friend; my room was rank with the smell of it. The only hope I clung to was that if I could hide long enough, I knew the dragon would come and save me.

4
TISALA

Some stereotypes are useful. Certainly I've never met a dishonorable Oranstonian, nor a Shavigman who wasn't happy to fight.

TISALA PACED THE CONFINES OF WARD'S ROOM. Waiting here while someone else dealt with her problems was harder than the role she'd accepted in her father's little plot—which was just what Ward had thought it to be.

It had been her father who proposed it. Alizon had been none too happy about her knowing everything—*his* plans were more than Ward had guessed. Enough more, she hoped, for her father and others she cared about to triumph over Jakoven. But Ward had been brutal in his dismissal of Alizon's rebellion, and his recital had had the ring of truth about it.

She'd been too long among men who grasped every straw as a great hope and built a house of it. Everything she knew of Ward told her that he saw the world as clearly as any. If he saw disaster, she was afraid he was right.

It was too quiet.

A keep always has noise: people going about their lives, the clash of weapons as the Guard trained, the creak of wagon wheels. With the king's troops here it should have been louder than ever. But there was no sound here at all, not since the tremendous booming cracks of wood on wood, and Tisala was growing even more nervous.

She sat down abruptly, fighting the dizzy exhaustion that claimed her at unexpected minutes. Some aspect of the magic Oreg had used to help heal her, Ward had explained.

The soreness was mostly gone, though her left hand ached. Oreg warned her it might not ever have much strength, but he'd been pleased that she could open and shut it completely. She'd been pleased that it was still on her arm. She remembered distinctly wondering whether she should try to cut it off herself before the bandits attacked her. She hadn't realized she was so close to Hurog.

She pushed back her hair wearily and clung to the carved post of the nearby bed to stand, knowing that if she stayed in the chair she'd fall asleep no matter how anxious she was.

Ward's tunic hung over the end of the post. There was a salt-sweet smell that clung to the fabric, a smell that lingered in his bed as well.

Would she have come here if it weren't for that compelling memory of an afternoon spent riding and joking?

Ward probably had such afternoons often. But no man before had ever teased Haverness's daughter, who could outfight, outride, and, mostly, outwrestle anyone. No man had ever flirted with her before. Perhaps she'd misinterpreted, perhaps he'd just been polite. But at least he didn't see an abomination when he looked at her.

Well, she wouldn't embarrass him by hanging all over him. She knew how to be a comrade in arms, someone men were comfortable with. She wouldn't make a fool out of herself. She pulled the fabric of his shirt against her nose and breathed in deeply, all the while sneering at herself for acting like a silly girl half her age.

The door opened and Tisala dropped her hold on the shirt, adopting a defensive stance as Stala strode in. Tisala relaxed as she realized the woman hadn't seen her sniffing Ward's shirt.

"Ah," said Stala briskly. "We've much to discuss. Lord Duraugh will be here in a few days and we need to decide what to do with you. I expect Duraugh will strip Hurog of every soldier here and take them to Estian, but we've got to keep you safe as well. How are you feeling?"

His aunt's voice was quick and biting—from habit, thought Tisala, and not any particular irritation.

"Better than I should be," she answered. "What has happened that Lord Duraugh needs Hurog's men? Where's Ward?"

"The king's troops took Ward with them to Estian to stand trial—no, no, girl," snapped Stala impatiently, "don't look like that. As far as I could tell they didn't have a clue you were here, and Ward kept them out of the keep. It had nothing to do with you." She gave Tisala an assessing look. "Do you know why Ward was fighting in Oranstone five years ago?"

"Four years," corrected Tisala before she could stop herself. Clearing her throat she continued before Stala could wonder why Tisala would keep track of how long ago it had been since she'd seen Ward. "Because the king threatened to imprison him in the Asylum—he and Tosten were just talking about it." The thought of Ward in one of those barren little cells she knew all too well made Tisala feel ill.

Gods, she thought, *he won't last long.*

Stala said, "Ward won enough acclaim for stopping Kariarn's invasion, the king couldn't very well declare him mad, not then. But time has passed and Ward hasn't done anything else remarkable. People forget. Unlike the general populace, though, Jakoven has a long memory, and a grudge against the family of Hurog. It's not your fault they took him. If anything, from what Ward told me, it sounds as if you are a victim of the king's ire with Hurog rather than the other way around."

Tisala took a step away from the bed, impatient with the weakness that caused her to sway unsteadily. "You can't let them take him to the Asylum. Have you ever been in it?"

Stala shrugged, but Tisala could tell she wasn't happy. "I didn't *let* them do anything. Ward decided he'd go with them and gave the rest of us our orders. I'm to make certain you're safe." She narrowed her eyes and grabbed Tisala just as her knees gave out. The older woman's firm grip propelled her back into her chair.

Stala's voice softened. "He'll be fine, lass. Our Oreg is trailing them. He won't let them do anything to Ward—gods help them if they try. Oreg doesn't have Ward's fine political sensibilities. Tosten's gone for Duraugh—and that man is as sly a politician as ever was bred from this family. If Duraugh can't get him out by negotiation, Oreg can get him out with power. Ward's safe enough. Don't fret. We just need to decide how to keep you safe."

Keep her safe? Would Ward have gone with them if he hadn't had to worry about her? Tisala shook her head firmly. "I came here because I was hurt and needed a place to hide while I healed. I can keep myself safe. Give me some food and I'll be fine. You don't have to do anything more for me—but"—she leaned forward—"maybe I can do something for you."

"Oh?" Stala pulled a chair up and sat close enough for soft conversation. "What can you do for us?"

"Much of my work these past years for Alizon has been with people not in favor with Jakoven, such people who have a tendency to end up in the Asylum." There, that was as fine a line between lie and truth as she'd ever trod. "As a result, I know a lot about the Asylum and how it operates. If politics don't work, and someone has to break in to get him out—I can help."

If the Hurogs were more loyal to the royal house than Tisala believed, she might just have signed away everything she'd worked for. The Hurog family had strong ties with tradition, and tradition had them supporting the king no matter how he treated them. Tisala was betting that Stala and Ward's uncle loved Ward more than they loved tradition.

"Most of the people imprisoned there are people of little consequence or power," commented Stala. "At least now."

Tisala forced a smile. "Most of the people who support Alizon are people of little consequence. But there are a growing number of them."

Stala let out a breath. "Right. I won't stop you leaving as soon as you wish, but waiting for Duraugh might be better.

He knows when a mouse sneezes in Estian; he'll know how to use your information."

"When is he coming?"

"Tosten set out to find him as soon as Ward left. Perhaps as little as four days."

Surely Ward could survive a short time in the Asylum. It would take days of travel before he was actually in Estian. She knew a man who'd lived there for years.

Tisala stretched her stiff neck. "I'll wait for Lord Duraugh."

TISALA SLEPT MOST OF THE DAY, AND AWOKE THE following morning feeling much better, especially after she ate the enormous breakfast that had been left to cool by her bedside. When she finished eating, she stretched out gingerly. Sweat poured off her forehead anyway, but when she was finished, most of her stiffness was gone.

Ward's staff, which she took from its place against the wall near his sword, was too long. Her left hand, as Oreg had speculated, wouldn't grip right, so she had to alter some of the steps accordingly.

Stala came in without knocking as Tisala was in the middle of turning a slow cartwheel using the staff as an extension of her hands. If the ceiling had been lower, or the room smaller, it wouldn't have worked.

"Not a particularly useful move," Stala observed dryly.

Landing lightly on her feet, Tisala smiled neutrally. "I've found it *very* useful in my line of work. In the middle of the second act, the warrior goddess teaches the hero how to defeat the emperor's evil wizard. It doesn't bring in much, but it pays for my room and board."

"You've been acting?"

"Ward's told you about what I was doing in Estian," said Tisala. It was a safe enough guess. Now that she wouldn't be able to go back to it, there was no harm in Ward's aunt knowing about her role. "As Haverness's daughter I couldn't work—not and keep my status as a lady, but being a spy is an expensive lifestyle."

Her father had sent her money once, but she'd told him not to do it again. The chances of someone making the connection were too great—and Jakoven would love to have an excuse to take Haverness for treachery.

Tisala continued, "One of the men at the inn where I stayed was an actor; he got me the part. I wear a mask, and the theater's in a district not overrun with nobles anyway."

Stala nodded her understanding. "Ward told me that you can use a sword—high praise. Can you use a staff as well?"

Tisala shook her head. "Not right now. This staff's too long, but I suspect my left hand's not up to it even with one the right size."

Stala examined the hand in question, turning it this way and that.

"The sooner you start pushing it, the sooner it'll recover," she said at last, returning Tisala's hand. "I think we can find a better fit for you than Ward's weapon. That boy could use a tree trunk. The Guard is working with staff today in the bailey. I've a Seaforder, several Tallvens, and a few Avinhellish men, but we've not had an Oranstonian here in my memory. It would do the men good to see the difference between Oranstone style and ours."

Tisala felt a real smile spread over her face. It had been so long since she'd been in a sparring match with trained men. "Fine."

STAFF FIGHTING GAVE WAY TO SWORD OVER THE next few days, then hand-to-hand and bow.

Tisala was in her element as she'd never been. Here the men weren't afraid to lay into her just because she was a woman. There were better fighters among the Guard, but she was far from the worst, and Stala taught her a few tricks. What lingering weakness she felt began to fade hour by hour. When she put her head down to sleep, exhaustion gave her dreamless rest instead of the nightmares she'd been plagued with since she left her torturer dead in Estian.

By the end of the morning workout, three days after Ward had left, she felt well enough that she decided to set out for

Estian that afternoon on her own rather than wait for Lord Duraugh.

While Tisala wiped off sweat and exchanged friendly insults with the Seaforder she'd been sparring with, she decided what she'd need to ask Stala for: a horse, supplies, and money for bribes.

The sound of a horn's staccato blast from beyond the newly repaired gate brought everything to a standstill.

"Lord Duraugh," said Stala. "It's about time."

Stala put her fingers to her lips and blew a sharp whistle that was answered by a horn. At that sound the men guarding the gates scrambled to open them. A second whistle had the Blue Guard in formal formation. Tisala stepped in beside Stala and watched Ward's uncle ride through the gates with half a hundred men, including Tosten and Beckram.

Their horses were stumbling tired, and Stala sent a group of her guards to help the grooms with the animals.

Ward's uncle was a big man, too, though not so extraordinarily large as Ward. The Hurog blood was easy to see in the shape of his face and his coloring. Like Tosten and Oreg, his eyes were a luminous blue very close to being purple. They swept over the men in the bailey, touched briefly on Tisala, then settled on Stala.

He dismounted and yielded his gelding to a groom without comment. "The king's men are close on our heels. I dared not take too many men from Iftahar—Ciarra is due to give birth to my grandchild any day. Without us there to bargain with, like as not they'll leave her be, but I needed to give her a force to fight with if the king decides he really needs all the Hurogs, rather than just the men in Estian."

Stala frowned. "What do you mean, all the Hurogs? And why are the king's men chasing you?"

Beckram answered her, "The day before Tosten reached us, I had word from a friend that the king was going to summon us all to him. Tosten told us that the king has already taken Ward."

Tisala, standing unnoticed behind Stala, had forgotten how effective a weapon Ward's cousin had in his voice and face. The rich baritone caused a pleasing flutter of her heart, and

his face combined the best of Hurog features with unusual
golden skin tones and reddish hair. Unlike Ward, Beckram
was very handsome—she'd heard somewhere that he'd married Ward's sister. *first cousines*

"We decided to lead them away from Ciarra and find out
if Hurog were still safe, before we let them catch up with
us," said Duraugh. "Have you had any word from Oreg?"

Stala nodded, though Tisala hadn't seen any messengers
come or go, nor any sign of a carrier pigeon coop. Maybe,
being a wizard, Oreg had other means of communication—
although her father's wizard had not.

"He says they're two days out of Estian. Ward is fine. Oreg
says he's already won over the general, though none of them,
possibly with the exception of Garranon, have a clue what
they're dealing with."

"He's not trying his stupid act again?" exclaimed Beckram.

Stala rolled her eyes. "Of course not, but you know how
he is. Even without the act most people think he's not too
swift."

"It's the eyes," added Tisala, deciding it was time to make
her presence felt. "They're lovely, but not the eyes of a clever
man."

Tosten grinned at her under his dirt. "Nope, it's that it
takes him so bleeding long to say anything. Uncle Duraugh,
Beckram, allow me to introduce Ward's warrior-maid and
Haverness's daughter, Tisala. Tisala, you already met Beckram, though you might have forgotten." His tone made it
clear that he was well aware that no woman, having once
met his cousin, would ever forget him. "And this is my uncle,
Lord Duraugh. Though he's Shavig to look at, he holds his
estate in Tallven, which gives the king's chamberlain ever
so much trouble at formal dinners—does he sit with the
Tallvens or the Shavigmen?"

Lord Duraugh set aside his weariness and bowed with au-
tomatic courtesy. "Lady."

Tisala smiled. She bowed in return. Women who topped
six feet looked ridiculous and awkward bobbing up and
down, so she avoided curtsies when she could. She remem-

bered meeting Lord Duraugh and his son any number of times in Estian, though she doubted they could say the same.

"Lady," said Beckram.

"I congratulate you on the upcoming birth of your child, Lord Beckram."

A glorious smile lit his weary face. "Yes, and I'd give my right arm to be with her now, but I wouldn't sacrifice Ward— no more than Ciarra would let me. My mother's there, and she's devoted to my wife. Ward's troubles aside, we'd have put her in more danger by staying—the king's men won't fool around at Iftahar when they're looking for us." He turned his attention to Lord Duraugh. "Father, we don't have much time. What are we doing?"

"Stala," said Lord Duraugh, "I've got to leave you here. No sense rescuing the boy and having Hurog overrun while we're about it. How many men do you need?"

"You've fifty men with you, and we can mount that and fifty more on trained, well-rested horses," Stala said. If she felt any resentment at being left behind, Tisala couldn't see it. "That leaves a hundred here—more than I need. If you'd like, we can pull a few more horses off pasture . . ."

"No," said Duraugh. "I don't want to feed and house more than a hundred in Estian anyway. It's too expensive and unnecessary. I need to make a showing, but if the king decides to take us, it wouldn't matter had I twice a hundred."

"As to expenses," said Tosten, "I know you didn't bring much extra from Iftahar. Hurog can help support this army— I know that Ward has some gold stored away. I'll bring it as well."

Duraugh nodded. "It would help. I have some banked in Estian, of course, but I wasn't planning on feeding an army there."

"I'm coming, too," said Tisala. "I know the Asylum and I owe Ward a favor."

Duraugh hesitated, obviously wondering why Haverness's daughter would know anything about the Asylum. A shrewd look passed over his face. "We'd be delighted to have you."

That fast he'd made the connection Stala had missed; Tisala could see it in his eyes. Haverness's daughter, with a known sympathy for Alizon's rebellion, could have only one reason to know the Asylum so well: The Asylum had been built to hold the king's brother. In Stala's defense, though, it had long been rumored that Kellen was dead.

"Good," she said, half surprised that Lord Duraugh's speculations bothered her not at all. Being at Hurog had obviously made her less wary. "I'll stay out of sight in Estian. You don't want the Hurog name tied to that of a known rebel."

He nodded and turned back to Stala. "Can you get my men settled? They need the rest. We'll start at first light tomorrow—we've that much lead over the king's men."

IN THE MORNING IT WAS TOSTEN WHO ORGANIZED the distribution of fresh horses, while Stala dealt with men and supplies. Tisala helped where she could, saddling horses and running messages. She'd just gotten back from such an errand when Tosten led a sizable liver chestnut mare with a wisp of white on her forehead and handed her the reins.

Tisala knew that something was up from the expressions on the various faces of the guards around her, but the mare didn't bolt or show any signs of bucking when Tisala lowered herself onto her back.

"That's Feather," Tosten said, stepping into the saddle of his own fresh mount.

"What's wrong with her?" asked Tisala, indicating the watching crowd with a sweep of her gaze.

Tosten grinned. "She's Ward's remount—no one else rides her, except our sister, Ciarra, in her wilder days. Don't worry, he'd want you to have her. You'll just have to sit on her a bit to keep her back with the rest of us."

Tisala was taken aback, knowing how Ward felt about his horses. Had her feelings for Ward been so obvious? She didn't allow anything to cross her face, but she was afraid Tosten saw it anyway. He grinned at her, then rode over to help direct the last few mounts.

Stala stepped up beside her and put a hand on the chestnut's shoulder. "When this is over," she said quietly, "visit us again. Ward would enjoy sharing Hurog with you."

Stala grinned suddenly, doubtless at the expression on Tisala's face. "He's recounted to me every blow you struck against the Vorsag and every word you spoke to him. You're not so obvious, but I'm an old woman. I've seen how you touch things that belong to him. Come back."

Tisala glanced around quickly to make sure no one was listening. "I am older than he by five years, and hardly a beauty to make a man's heart beat faster. He'll do better finding a pretty Shavig maid."

Stala smiled and stepped away from the horse. "You make *his* heart beat faster, and five years is less than nothing to a man's soul. Come back."

THE JOURNEY TO ESTIAN SEEMED LONGER THAN THE one Tisala had taken here. Her hand ached in the morning and she was grateful Feather's soft mouth allowed her to use only one hand on the rein.

By evening they'd ridden by a small trading town and were in the lower hills that marked the barrier between Tallven and Shavig. They camped near a creek that night. To Tisala's relief, they'd left the snow behind in the mountains of Shavig.

The morning of the second day dawned without a sign of the king's men. Tisala tossed an icy handful of creek water over her face, hoping to wake up. While she was wiping her face, several horses cried out a warning—then it sounded as if every animal in the camp went mad.

Feather, she thought. Even if she hadn't seen Ward with his horses, the guards' attitude would have made it plain that Feather was precious to him. The last thing Tisala wanted to do was to explain how she'd let the mare get hurt.

She found Feather at her picket rolling her eyes at the other animals, though not unduly alarmed. The rest of the horses were kicking and fighting as if they were dragon-frighted. Feather'd broken out in a light sweat, but calmed at a few soft words.

The worst disaster averted, Tisala turned to see what had

caused the fuss, expecting to see a bear or even one of the great mountain cats.

The blood rushed from her head and she swayed against the mare. Dragon-frighted, indeed. There in the midst of their half-packed tents and scrambling men stood a creature that could only be a dragon.

It was a huge and glittering creature in every shade of blue and violet she'd ever seen. The dark midnight blue on its extremities faded to violet-rose glinting with iridescence like a sea-pearl. The bony structures of its half-furled wings were black and shiny with faint patterns of gold that carried through on the lavender scaled membrane that made up the bulk of the wings. Light purple-blue eyes contrasted the irregular, dark blue scales of its face.

Tosten stood alone in front of it, his fists clenched as he shouted at it. As soon as Tisala realized that everyone else was fighting horses or scattered too far away to help him, she drew her sword, leaving Feather where she was tied. The dragon's attention was on Tosten, so Tisala advanced at a walk. It hadn't done anything yet and she didn't want to incite it.

She'd crossed half the distance between them when she heard what Tosten was saying.

". . . not here!" Hot anger threaded his voice, though she hadn't misread the fear on his face. "No one is supposed to know! It's too dangerous: You know what Ward says. There are a hundred people here—someone will talk. Do you want to be hunted by a thousand want-to-be mages who are after your magic?"

Tisala stopped where she was. This was, it seemed, a private conversation for all that Tosten was shouting at the top of his lungs.

The dragon's head snaked forward with deadly swiftness and Tosten's hair parted from its breath. Ward's brother paled but held his ground.

"I'll ride out to meet you as soon as I find my horse," he said. "Which might take a while, thanks to you. Go away."

The dragon took an enormous breath and huffed it out, twisting its head and glancing at Tisala briefly. Then it heaved itself onto its hind legs and up into the air, vanishing over the edge of a ridge of mountain to the west.

Tosten turned to her with a look on his face that was almost pleading.

Before he said anything, Tisala answered that look. "*Hurog* means dragon." *I've seen a dragon,* she thought giddily.

"And when the rest of the world finds out we have one, they'll be camping at Hurog's doorstep waiting for a chance to kill him," said Tosten, running a worried hand through his hair. "Damn it. He knows better than that."

She nodded. "I'd pass out the word that Ward will be unhappy with anyone who tries to seriously pass around this tale if I were you. Not being a Shavigman myself, I never claim to see dragons."

Tosten smiled wearily, and she remembered he'd ridden twice as far as Lord Duraugh and his men.

The runaway horses were caught and rumors flew about what had spooked them. (From what Tisala heard, only a few people had actually seen the dragon—they, like she, had been trying to calm their mounts. Most of them had had significantly more trouble than she'd had.) The cold night with just a hint of frost ensured that everyone was gathered around the small fire where Lord Duraugh's cook was handing out bowls of warm mush.

Tosten cleared his throat and avoided his uncle's eye. "It surely was a strange windstorm we had this morning."

"Strange indeed," answered Duraugh solemnly.

Tisala could tell by the expression on his face that Tosten had not thought his uncle would say anything. Tosten had known about the dragon, thought Tisala, watching their faces, but his uncle and cousin hadn't until this morning. Hurog blue eyes met in a soundless argument, Tosten pleading for time. It occurred to Tisala that the dragon had had Hurog-blue eyes as well—just like Oreg, who'd gone to watch out for Ward.

"Frighted the horses but good," said Beckram. "I dare say that a storyteller would make up something about a great monster who scared the horses—but that might make it harder for us to get the Hurogmeten out of the Asylum. These

1. Dragon guardian

lowlanders are greedy for things they don't understand; they might think that Ward had something to do with a mythical beast."

Tosten gave his cousin a grateful look.

Lord Duraugh glanced about at his own men. "I would be very unhappy if a rumor were to make it more difficult to free my nephew. Very unhappy." He sounded it, too.

"What windstorm?" said one of the Blue Guard, a man named Soren. "It was Bethem's snoring that startled the horses."

Bethem, whom Tisala knew as one of the best swordsmen in the Guard, spit on the ground. " 'Twas naught but your wife—she's scared the hides off braver animals than our horses."

"It was a giant sea turtle a hundred feet long, blowing flame from his nose," said another man. "Would have ate us all, but for Bethem's snoring. It thought he were another giant turtle, even larger and more ferocious, so the monster turned and fled back into the sea."

After a while the camp settled into a more normal atmosphere. The men cleaned their dishes and packed camp, saying nothing more about the incident, but there was a subtle, understated glee in their faces as they worked. Dragons, said each cheerful whistle, each blithe look, were a good thing for Hurogs.

Tisala finished her packing and walked to where Tosten was huddled with his uncle and cousin.

"We're ready to ride," she said.

Lord Duraugh looked at her, and with the air of a man ending an argument said, "I'll get them started. Tosten and Beckram have an errand to run, and I'd like you to go with them."

"But—" said Tosten.

"She already knows enough to ruin us if she wants to. If he came for the reason we all think he did, she might be able to help him. Now go, before he gets impatient and creates another incident."

Tosten and Beckram mounted without another word. Tosten set out away from camp at a trot, not looking to see if Beckram and Tisala were following him.

As soon as they were out of sight of the camp, Ward's wizard, Oreg, stepped out of the trees.

"I've bad news," he said.

Tisala looked into his eyes, which were purple-blue, just as Tosten and his uncle's were. Just as the dragon's had been. And her speculation solidified—somehow Oreg and the dragon were one.

"It must be important," said Beckram, sounding not at all like his normal self. His horse shifted uneasily, looking for whatever had disturbed its rider. "What happened?"

"I'm sorry," said Oreg, looking from Tosten to Beckram. This was not the reserved, somewhat intimidating man Tisala knew from Hurog. This man was shaken and worried—and was apologizing for appearing in the middle of the camp in the guise of a dragon.

Not a guise, she thought, remembering Tosten's reaction. *Oreg was a dragon. A dragon who was supposed to be watching over Ward.*

Tisala dismounted and gave a huff of disgust at the two Hurogs and the wizard. "Oreg, you have just shown me the most beautiful thing I've ever seen in my life, but if you don't tell us what happened to Ward, I'll kill you myself."

Oreg raised both hands from his sides and said simply, "I can't find him. He was there when I went to sleep last night, but when I tried to find him this morning, he was gone. Their camp was pulled up and their tracks lead to the city. I checked out the Asylum and the king's castle, but I couldn't find him. I can feel him but I don't know where he is. I always know where Ward is."

"The king had his wizards build a place in the Asylum to contain mages. Could something like that keep you from finding Ward?" asked Tisala.

Oreg stared at her for a moment. "It might."

"The king said he was taking Ward to the Asylum," she said. "We have no real reason to doubt that. When we get to Estian, I know people who can get me in so I can look for him."

"He's frightened," said Oreg, his eyes almost blank. "I can feel his fear. He doesn't scare easily."

"All the more reason to believe he's at the Asylum. We'll find him," she promised. She glanced at Tosten and Beckram. "Let's get going. The sooner we get to Estian, the sooner we get Ward."

"YOU ALL HAVE THE WRONG IDEA," SAID TISALA TO Tosten, who had taken up a post by her side for the day.

"What's that?" he asked.

"I am not now, nor ever will be Ward's woman." It was baldly put, but Tisala didn't know any other way to fight the assumptions that Ward's people were making. Riding Ward's mare was only adding to the problem.

"Hmm," replied Tosten gravely, though a faint smile tilted the corner of his mouth up. "You don't like my brother?"

She didn't know how to answer that without lying or giving the wrong impression, so she closed her calves against Feather's sides and the big mare increased her pace and left Tosten behind.

He waited the better part of an hour before approaching her again.

"I don't know how much you've heard about my father," he said when they were close enough for conversation. "But, being an Oranstonian, you've probably heard the worst of it. Ward, when he speaks of him, will tell you that he was mad. But I've always believed he was evil."

He stopped there and rode with her until she thought he'd said all he'd intended. At last he continued, "When I was a boy, we had a kitchen maid, the daughter of one of the stablemen, whom everyone was in love with. I was thirteen and thought she was the most beautiful woman I'd ever seen. It was more than her face and form—though those were remarkable—it was . . . joy, I suppose is the right word, though happiness would work as well." Tosten gently dissuaded his gelding from snatching a bite of grass. "I don't think that she and Ward were lovers until the night my father tried to rape her."

"Ward stopped him?" she asked.

"I used to think it was Stala," he replied. "But I've thought about it since, and I think Ward sent Stala there. The maid was carrying trays from my mother's rooms when my father walked by her. I was hiding from him—under a piece of furniture in the hall—and when he stopped I thought he'd found me, at least until she screamed.

"She fought him hard—and he let her. If he'd wanted to, he could have stopped her struggles easily. He was almost as big as Ward is." Tosten stopped speaking again.

They ate lunch in the saddle and Tisala made no move to push him. When Tosten resumed his story, he did it as if there had been no break in their conversation.

"My aunt Stala came in running." Tosten closed his eyes. "I think she heard the screams. No one else in the keep would have gone to rescue a woman trapped by my father. Stala knocked him away from the maid, then slapped her, I think, because the screams stopped. I couldn't tell, since my view was limited by the hall table I was hidden under.

"Stala helped the maid up and sent her to my brother's rooms." Tosten let out a huff of air that might have been a laugh. "I think now, that night was the first she spent in my brother's bed. But at the time I felt truly betrayed: by my own inability to face my father down and rescue the maiden, and by my brother's relationship to the woman I, a thirteen-year-old, thought I was in love with. I couldn't deal with my own shortcomings, so I blamed them all on Ward. I listened to Stala and my father fight—both verbally and physically and then have sex in the hall—and I thought about the maid and my brother doing the same thing and I hated them all."

There was a smile on Tosten's face when he turned to look at Tisala, but his eyes were flat. "So when the castle laughed at my stupid brother's devotion to his little serving maid, I laughed, too. He followed her around all day at her chores, carrying the laundry baskets or the serving trays for her, and at night she slept in his bed."

Tisala didn't want to think of anyone sharing Ward's bed, but she set the feeling aside and listened to the story.

"Ward would have been about fifteen or sixteen during

that time, and already a big man. My father had begun to avoid him—I think he was afraid of what Ward could do. So he did nothing about my brother's unseemly devotion, which went on for a little over a year before she married someone else."

Tosten's breathing was erratic, and Tisala could tell that this story was not without cost. "One day I walked by my brother's room and stopped because the door swung open by itself. Hurog was haunted, so it wasn't that uncommon to have doors move on their own. I wasn't frightened until I heard Ward crying. He would have married her, I think, if she'd have had him. But she knew her place, if he didn't. She left for Tyrfannig and a marriage with a merchant her father knew." Tosten rubbed his gelding's neck. "She had a miscarriage a few weeks later—the day I heard Ward in his room. I think it was Ward's child. I wish I'd gone to him when I heard him crying instead of closing the door.

"I didn't know if I was going to tell you the whole thing or not," said Tosten. "But it seems the right thing to do. None of us have seen Ward like this since then. He doesn't have casual relationships. He doesn't flirt, he doesn't light up with eagerness when other women come into the room—just you." He gave her a quick grin. "I wanted you to know that I don't just think of you as—how did you put it? Ah, yes, Ward's woman. I believe it's much more serious than that."

5
WARDWICK

Ciarra had a nursemaid who told stories of horrid monsters living in the Hurog sewers that ate bad children. Far from being horrified, Ciarra liked to pretend she was a monster. Once she jumped out from behind a door and terrified the nursemaid. Aunt Stala, when told of the matter, said that the monsters that scare us the most are the ones we create ourselves.

TWO GUARDS CAME TO TAKE ME FROM MY HAVEN of straw. Their eyes glittered weirdly and snake-tongues of fire rippled from the top of their heads. I couldn't understand what they said, but I understood that they grabbed my arms and sought to drag me away from safety.

"Don't kill them," advised the quiet voice in the back of my head where a small part of me hid from the drugs and magic.

I left the men where they lay and curled up in my nest with the cool stone reassuringly firm against my back.

More guards came and removed their limp comrades. After a while Jade Eyes brought in a small metal brazier and set an herbal concoction burning.

"Something in the smoke," said my voice. But it wasn't able to coax me out of my safe cubby to knock the fire out. Finally it left me alone.

The smoke was acrid and at first it stung my nose. But after a few minutes the terrible fear seemed to dissipate. The straw became a warm blanket.

When someone came for me, I allowed him to pull me to my feet and support me when the floor heaved and buckled.

I was brought to a large chamber lined with shelves of pottery. In the very center of the room was an odd piece of furniture, waist high and flat like a table, but heavily padded with straps hanging from it.

Jade Eyes was talking quietly with the king's archmage, Arten. I didn't know him personally, but anyone who'd been to court knew who he was. Truthfully, it took me a moment to recognize him without his colorful, glittery court robes, for, like Jade Eyes, he wore only plain black.

"Be careful," said my secret voice. Even though I was no longer frightened, I was glad it had not left me.

"Ward," said Jade Eyes, "how are you feeling?"

I smiled and spread my hands out. "Better."

"I'm going to help you stay that way, all right?"

"Careful," murmured the voice, but no tinge of worry or fear could touch me while I suffered the effects of the herbs they'd burnt in my cell.

Jade Eyes led me to the table and indicated that I was to lie on it. Something about the straps frightened my little voice, but I was anxious to please the man who would help me, so I ignored it. I lay still while a collar was affixed to my neck to hold my head. They pulled and they prodded and strapped until I couldn't move at all.

"Ward," said Jade Eyes at last, "I'm going to help you— but first I want you to help me."

That sounded fair. I tried to nod my head, but had to settle for talking.

"Yes," I said. It was hard to get the word out, just as it had been after my father had hurt me very badly. Fear began to tighten my belly at the memory. But the man had said he would help. I remembered that and relaxed again—though I couldn't remember why I needed help.

"I thought we were to break him, not conduct an inquisition," said Arten. His voice was harsh and it made my stomach tighten again.

"The king's wizard." My silent voice supplied the iden-

tification, and I remembered that I had reason to fear the king.

"Jakoven says we have two weeks. I want to find out how he set up the magic to guard us all night first. I've never heard of such a thing."

"Are you certain it was he?" said Arten. "I've heard the only thing he could do was *find* things."

"He destroyed an entire stone keep," said Jade Eyes, defending me from the contempt in the older mage's voice. "Pretty impressive for a *finder*. And, yes, I'm certain he set up the magic guardian. There was a taste to the magic—a signature, and his aura has the same feel. I'd show you what I mean if you could read auras."

Jade Eyes stepped into my line of sight. In one hand he held a staff that glittered with gold and precious gems. On the very top of the staff, looking out of place, was a battered claw the size of my hand.

"Dragon," I said. It came out easily and that took away from the sick feeling in my stomach that tried to insist there was something wrong.

Jade Eyes smiled. "Yes, it's a dragon claw. I'm told that Seleg himself gave it to his king as my king gave it to me."

"Seleg had no right!" The voice was so loud, I expected Jade Eyes to hear. *"His duty was to guard dragonkind. Betrayer."*

"Hurogmeten," I said, the strength of the voice leading my speech. But I forgot what I needed to say, and so fell silent.

"Yes, he was Hurogmeten. Just like you." Jade Eyes bent his head closer to me. "Seleg was a mage, Ward. Are you a mage?"

I frowned at him. Everyone knew that story. "I used to be, but my father broke me."

"Can you work magic now?"

I couldn't remember, so I tried.

"Oh, yes," said my voice, eagerly. *"Fire is easy, almost as easy as* finding. *I can do fire even without Hurog's magic to help, remember?"*

As soon as the voice said that, I knew it was easy. There was so much here that would burn. I could feel the oils in the clay pots. They went first, bursting into flame in violent explosions that shattered pottery on all four sides of me. It was fun.

I heard vague shouts echoed by the sharp pops of the pots, but for the most part I was lost in the joy of working magic. Candles melted to stubs, oil-soaked wood sought my magic more than my magic sought it. Power began to loosen the hold of smoke and drugs, almost I could begin to plan.

Cold hands touched my forehead with white-hot fury. There was no warning, no period of going from bad to worse; just shivery bands of pain that wracked my body and caused me to twist helplessly, caught between it and the leather collar that would not let me move away.

But I knew all about pain.

I knew that when it stopped, you closed your eyes and played dead, because sometimes my father would stop if I quit moving.

So I lay limply while Jade Eyes vented his anger at the damage I'd done to his lab, the precious items it had taken years to collect burnt to ashes in an instant.

When he saw what I'd done to his dragon's claw, he hurt me again. He hurt me until Arten dragged him off. "He's unconscious. Damn you, man, leave off."

I was willing to let them think me senseless. It had saved me before. But the pain had been worth it. The dragon claw was destroyed, its magic scattered unused (though I could have brought down the building with its power) and no one would get any more benefit from Seleg's betrayal. Without the magic pouring through me, I couldn't remember why that was important, just that it was. Sweat dripped into my eyes and I thought at first it was blood.

Jade Eyes snarled at the other mage, "Tell the king he'll have what he wants. Tell him I can do it in a se'night." Then he hurt me again.

Men came to put me into the cell at last. They brought in food and water and set it near me. When they were gone and wouldn't see I was awake, I grabbed the carafe and drank until I noticed that the world was beginning to grow eyes in the shadows. I set the water down, though I still thirsted. The food was easier to ignore. I wondered for a minute that my skin was unmarked and not split from the all-consuming pain, but then the shadow-things began to creep out of the corners and I hid in the hole in the straw.

"YOU ARE A DIFFICULT MAN TO FIND, WARDWICK of Hurog."

I huddled away from the voice because it wasn't my voice. My head hurt and my lips were cracked and dry. When I closed my eyes, all I could see was the strange color of Jade Eye's irises.

"Hurogmeten?"

The voice called me back from memories. It belonged to a woman, but it had a bass rumble no female tone should ever carry. I opened my eyes fearfully and saw brightly mottled fur of orange and yellow, bright eyes above finger-long fangs. Somehow the fur seemed to give a little of its light to the room and drive the shadows back to the corners where they belonged.

"Hurogmeten? How long since you've eaten?"

The Tamerlain, guardian of Aethervon's temple, sat in front of me. Another hallucination, I thought, so I didn't answer her. She lived on the hill of Menogue in the ruins of Aethervon's temples outside the city of Estian. She could not be in the Asylum.

Closing my eyes, I waited for her to go away. After a moment I heard the bowl they'd given me skitter across the floor as she inspected it.

"Good lad, you didn't eat tonight," she said. "Garranon said he thought you were drugged rather than magicked, and that's harder to combat."

It was the water that was dangerous; I felt very clever for knowing that much. I had sweated a great deal earlier and now my thirst was great—but I knew the water had held as much danger for me as the wizard. I held a straw in my mouth and that had helped keep my mouth moist, but it wasn't working well anymore.

"Wardwick," she coaxed (I could tell by the change in her

voice that she was coming closer), "look at me, lad. You know me."

I pulled my eyes reluctantly away from the wall, and stared into the face of the beast. She was as large as a small northern bear, and her head looked ursine, except for the large golden eyes that were more suited to a tiger. Her thick fur covered a body that was not as bulky as a bear's nor as lithe as one of the big cats'. Her tail curled around her front paws and she purred when my eyes met hers. I thought the sound might have been meant to be reassuring.

The air suddenly felt clearer, like my thoughts, but I knew it was a continuation of my delusions, because the guardian of the ruins of Menogue had no business in my cell.

I sat up straighter and brushed straw off my shoulders, to give myself time to think. The movement exacerbated the remnant pain that lingered after Jade Eye's rage.

"Leave me," I said. The last time I'd met her, her god, Aethervon, had taken over my sister's body and tormented Oreg. No one hurt my people if I could help it.

"Hold your anger," she said. "I come as a favor for a friend. Garranon was worried about you. He asked me to see you if I could. So I took his request to Aethervon. My master has been interested in you since he awoke to your presence when you visited His temple at Menogue."

"Go away," I said again. Aethervon could hang for all I cared. He had used my sister without her consent and hurt my friend. Granted, the Tamerlain had little part in either—but I despised her master.

"I can help you," she said.

I gave a short laugh and tried to hide how much even such a slight movement hurt.

"You tell me Garranon is your friend," I said.

"Garranon is my friend," she agreed.

I stared at her and she met my gaze steadily. I hadn't really considered the Tamerlain as anything except a servant of a weakened, treacherous god. That Garranon was a friend of the Tamerlain was beyond belief. Had he had such a powerful ally, surely she would have shown herself sooner—saving his brother, destroying his enemies. Something. If my life had been hard at the hands of my father, Garranon's had been worse.

"How long have you been friends?" I asked.

My disbelief stung and she jerked her chin up, a low growl in her throat. "He has been mine since he came here to Estian, a child, alone and afraid. He saw me—as no one from that place has ever seen me—and he feared me not. Since that night when he slept curled against me, a child even by your short-lived reckoning, he has been my friend."

I believed her suddenly, but it didn't improve my opinion of her. "A friend who watched as the king raped a child."

"It was never rape, that happened before he was here. The king used herbs . . . magic." Even in her inhuman face I could read anguish. She'd known that herbs and magic don't mean it wasn't rape.

While we'd talked, the last of Jade Eye's drugs had left me. Without their aid, my terror of the Asylum, my claustrophobic anger at my inability to fight back effectively against Jade Eyes had been growing in my belly. The addition of bone-deep anger at the pain of a child—for all that he was now an adult well able to take care of himself loosed the ties on my spiteful tongue.

"And now I'm supposed to allow you to help *me*?" I asked.

She shot to her feet as if I'd hit her, and for an instant the rage in her eyes made me think my worries about my current situation would be over even sooner than I'd believed possible—though I'd been hoping for Oreg rather than death.

She snarled soundlessly, then stalked away from me. Facing the wall she said, "You know *nothing* about it. I was constrained, as was my master. I had to watch and do nothing." The tension left her in a rush and when she turned back to me, there was only sorrow in her eyes.

"So much damage had been done to the fabric of this world, it was all my master could do to hold it together. Do you think He wanted to let His temple fall to foreign armies He could have destroyed with a touch? But even so much might have been enough to burst the dam built to keep humankind alive. He . . . I couldn't even save one child."

I had been ashamed of my words almost as I'd said them. "I'm sorry," I said.

"So am I," she whispered, but I don't think she was talking about the past few minutes.

She sighed and shook herself like a wet dog. " 'Tis done now. Know you this, though: I was not the only one chafed by the little we could do. Aethervon was constricted to giving visions and hoping that they allowed the humans to whom He gave them to make better choices. Then you came to Menogue."

"He gave me back my magic," I said.

"He saw in you the chance to mend one of the greatest rifts—so He did what He could to help you," she replied. "When you cleansed the land of the great evil done at Hurog, you released some of the constraints He has to work through. There are monks now at Menogue for the first time in centuries. Through me he can do a little more to help you."

"I thought Aethervon vowed to support the Tallven kings," I said. "It was a Tallven king who put me in here."

"He has sworn to serve the Tallvens, in so much as a god serves man," she agreed. "It is only that He chooses which Tallven to serve."

I let one eyebrow creep up. "Aethervon supports Alizon?"

She veiled her eyes with pleasure and purred. "It pleases me, this turn of events. Oh, not you here like this—but that Aethervon stirs Himself against that one, that one who hurts my Garranon. Oh, yes, that pleases me. If it were allowed I would tear the flesh from his bones and leave him to rot . . ."

Her tail twitched like a hunting cat's. Deliberately she stilled it and wrapped it around her front feet. "But that may come in time. The gods still must leave it to humans to determine their own fate. You might bear it in mind that Aethervon will be inclined to grant favors if He is properly petitioned." She purred. "Garranon, my friend, asked me to see you, and I will tell him how I find you. But it pleases Aethervon for me to help you as well.

"The king is waiting for your relatives to come so he can present you and them to his court," she said. "Word has come from Iftahar that your uncle is at Hurog. It will take them time to travel here. When you stand before them, I will take their poison from your flesh—so much I can do. It is for you to keep them from destroying you until then."

She left. Just vanished, and I thought I might have imagined her except that my thoughts remained clear.

So, I thought. *The Tamerlain means to help me.*

The king would see me broken. He wanted a madman to present to his court. This was more than just a power game between the king and my uncle, more than a simple attack upon me. But my abused mind couldn't work through the convolutions other than to know that Jakoven was working against my whole family.

The Tamerlain promised a way to save myself. I just had to keep sane until my uncle came. Or until Oreg found me and rescued me.

The thought of Oreg brought me relief so strong, I shook. He knew where they were taking me—he'd get me out. Taking a deep breath, I decided I had to act as if he weren't coming. Prepare for the worst, my aunt said.

So I thought of how to let Jade Eyes think he'd broken me.

Over the past few years, Oreg had managed to teach me a little about the magic that was still coming back to me, like drops from a bucket. I lit a dim magelight, just enough so I could see clearly, and I looked at my body. It hurt to move. It was worse than when Stala set out to teach me a lesson and beat me into the ground in an all-out while training. But there wasn't a bruise anywhere, as if Jakoven had ordered his mages not to leave a mark on me.

So if Jade Eyes continued in the way he had begun, all I had to worry about was pain. That was fine, pain and I were old friends—my father had seen to that. I could take anything they could give me as long as I knew there was no real damage taking place.

But they could find another way to break me, unless I let them believe their methods were working. A small, arrogant part of me wanted to object, but Stala had taught me better than that. Anyone could be broken. All I could do was convince them that it had already happened before it really did.

The pitcher of tainted water sat upright on the floor—I could reach out and knock it over; but then I'd have to pretend to be overcome by the drugs. I could do that, but I didn't know if I could do that while I was in enough pain that even the memory of it made me sweat. And who was to say that they would give me the same herbs every time? What happened if they switched them?

The first nineteen years of my life had been a contest between my father and myself. I won it because I'd learned control at the hands of a master. Control, Stala said, was the thing that kept you alive. Control your emotions, control your body, and you were more likely to survive a battle than a man who could not. Control had become something of a religion for me—a means of survival and a way to differentiate myself from my father.

I stared at the worn pottery pitcher.

To survive, I'd have to throw away that control and trust my instincts. Trust that even drugged, I wouldn't fight the pain.

There was a murmur outside my door. ". . . take four men this time, Jerron won't be using that hand for a month."

Guards.

I took the pitcher in my hand and remembered the sour taste of fear, knowing that I had to deceive two wizards into believing they'd broken me completely. Or I would lose.

Drinking that water was one of the most difficult things I had ever done. Only losing would have been harder.

Writhing monsters came into my cell. One had yellow snakes with black eyes growing out the sides of his head. They stared at me with dead eyes that laughed at my struggles to break free of the myriad hands that gripped me.

The monsters took me to see the green-eyed mage. He did things to my head and to my body, things that left me shaking and nauseated, things that didn't leave so much as a bruise.

He used magic to hurt me, but it was only pain. I knew its nature and its name; it had nothing more to teach me. When the wizard brought agony in liquid waves over my body, I accepted it and became it. My body cried out and fought, but my mind rode the fiery demon and was untouched. I had my limits. I could tell that eventually the pain would devour me, but for now I was safe.

The wizard didn't *see*. He observed the surrender of my body without seeing the patience that waited beneath.

After a few days the demons who dragged me from cell to wizard's den and back quit being frightened of me. When I cried, they seemed sad.

"He was a rare fighter," said one. "I'd have liked to have him at my back."

"You want an insane man fighting at your back," bleated a little sheep—

"*Lad,*" corrected my little voice. "*Just a boy, not a sheep.*" As always the pain had made the voice closer to me—if I wanted to, I could see as the voice did. Later the remnants of the session would make it difficult to hear my silent, hidden self. I blinked carefully and saw a boy, younger than Tosten.

The monster under my left shoulder grunted. "If you think this place holds the mad, you haven't been paying attention, boy."

There was fresh water waiting, and after the monsters left I picked it up in shaking hands.

"*Drink,*" urged my little voice, already growing fainter. I pressed the clay rim against my lips and drank it until the pitcher was dry.

6
TISALA

My aunt says that if common goals make good friends, common enemies make better ones.

TISALA SAT IN THE PRIVATE ROOM OF THE TAVERN and watched the door. She'd sent out a message over an hour ago, but there was no telling when Rosem would get it. She sipped at her drink and then leaned her head against the wall. The hood of her cloak shielded her eyes from the candlelight and she fell asleep.

"I thought you were dead," said a quiet voice, waking her. "Let me see your face."

Tisala blinked at the man standing beside her table. He was shorter than she, but broad through the shoulders. A scruffy, bright red beard hid the features of his face except for the wide nose that had been broken more than once.

She pulled the hood away from her face. "Hello, Rosem."

"Gods, girl," he said, sitting across from her. "When the house you were rooming in burned down, I waited for you to turn up for a full week. Then I wrote to your father."

"The house burned?" she said. "Did everyone get out?"

Tight-mouthed, he shook his head. Tisala swallowed and rubbed her face, as if that would wipe away the faces of the people she'd lived with for the past few years. Jakoven must have had the house burned to cover her disappearance.

Rosem reached out and caught her hand, pulling it into the dim light of the tallow candle.

"Who took you?" he said.

She pulled her hand back. "Jakoven." She explained how she escaped and where. "So you see that I owe the Hurog-meten. Can you get me into the Asylum?"

THE ASYLUM WAS A BEAUTIFUL BUILDING ABOUT A mile from Jakoven's castle. The pyrite-flecked marble of the facade made it look more like a temple than a holding pen for society's embarrassments. There was even a pond just big enough for the two swans in the small but meticulously groomed lawn.

Tisala's flesh crawled as she shuffled in beside Rosem. It had taken him a healthy bribe to the woman whose place she took to get Tisala in again. No one would notice the switch because the cleaners were practically interchangeable. The woolen robes they wore were designed to let them fade into the background as they went about their work. They talked only to one another, never to the inmates or the guards. It was a system designed to keep the cleaners ignorant of what went on in the Asylum, but it kept the guards ignorant of the cleaners' world, too.

They crossed the marble entrance hall quietly, keeping to the left-hand side near the velvet wall hangings. Doubtless had there been another entrance to the Asylum, they, as lowly cleaners, would have taken it; but there was only one way into or out of the building.

Past the entrance hall they walked through the model cells. Six largish apartments, three on one side, three on the other, were displayed for perusal. Each cell was carpeted, with a padded chair and a brocade-covered bed. Furnished with nothing an inmate could hurt himself with, but with subtle luxury nonetheless. Four of the cells held actors paid to pretend to be mad, but mildly so—nothing that might disturb the family who came to see if the Asylum was safe for their old uncle or mother who had become difficult. Two were left empty in case a family wanted to visit a patient. He or she would be cleaned up and drugged or magicked into some semblance of happiness and settled into one or the other cell an hour or so before their visitors arrived. Unscheduled visits were not allowed.

Tisala wondered how many of the people who'd incarcerated their problems in the Asylum really believed in the fiction they were presented with. How many of them, when Alizon shut the place down, would exclaim in horror, knowing that as long as they pled ignorance, no one could blame them?

Silently, Tisala stepped shoulder to shoulder with her guide through the wooden door into the real Asylum. As always, the first thing to assail her was the smell: feces, urine, and covering it all the strong, spicy scent of the brew the cleaners were given to scrub the cells with.

Without speaking to her confederate, Tisala turned left and entered a small room filled with buckets and mops, and grabbed one of each. Then she moved back into the hall to stand in the silent line that waited to fill their buckets.

Not that the hall itself was silent. Shrieks and groans echoed wildly from behind the barred doors. Eventually, Tisala knew, she would even get used to that. But always, the first few minutes of it were difficult. She wanted to plug her ears, but that would draw attention. At last she filled her bucket at the stone font that was full of something Jakoven's wizards had brewed up. There was nothing magic about it, herbs and alcohol mostly, or so she'd been told.

The guard who was in charge of the cleaners gave her the cell numbers she'd expected as he always did. She didn't know if he was one of the rebels or if it was some little trick of Rosem's, and she didn't ask.

She trudged through the next set of doors with her bucket and mop and shuffled through the maze of halls. She'd memorized a map before the very first time she'd come here, and now she didn't even have to count hallways. She didn't pause when she passed the dead-bolted doors leading into the mage's wing where Ward must be, though she wanted to. That wasn't her assignment today.

At long last she stopped in front of the solid door of a cell that looked just like the one next to it, except for the number over the door. Setting her bucket down, she pushed the bar up out of its cups. Several doors from her, a guard watched. As long as she didn't scream, or the patient didn't barrel out of the door, he wouldn't interfere.

She left her mop beside the bucket and got a flimsy wooden hay rake down from the wall in the hallway and entered the cell. The little room had nothing a patient could hurt himself on, but that was the only resemblance between it and the "show" cells near the entrance. The floor was strewn with straw rather than carpets. A hard wooden bench was attached to the wall. It was, barely, wide enough to sleep on if the patient were careful. There was no discreet chamber pot under the bed here.

Tisala, her nose already hardened to the smell of the Asylum, raked out the foul hay. She found little difference between this and mucking out stalls—though she knew that the man who lay on the bench with his back to her didn't feel the same way. Rosem made certain that everyone who came to visit this cell knew how this inmate felt, and behaved accordingly.

She did a good job, piling the soiled hay in the center of the hallway, where she or another cleaner would collect it later. That done, she took her mop and bucket and shut the door behind her while she wiped down the floors. She heard the dull thud as the guard barred the door, sealing her in.

The man didn't stir, so she started to scrub the floor, ridding the room of the smell of human waste. Finally he sat up, but she didn't stop cleaning until he spoke.

"Tisala, I was glad to hear that you weren't dead."

She put the mop down and dropped to her knees before the bedraggled, rag-clothed, painfully thin man who sat cross-legged on the bench.

"Your majesty." This man was the truth of the rebellion. It was Jakoven's younger brother, Kellen, whom Alizon worked to put on the throne.

Though he was sitting, she knew from previous visits that he was half a head shorter than she, and in better times his build would have been stocky. Her father would have said "built like a wall." His hair was curly and dark with a light frosting of gray. He was barely twenty-six. He'd been fifteen when his much older brother had incarcerated him in the Asylum.

The public story was that Kellen had been struck by a mysterious illness. Although he recovered physically, the pain had driven him mad. Jakoven built the Asylum for his brother, a peaceful resting place where the aristocracy could safely stow their unwanted members. For the past decade Kellen had been in this cell—but some people had not forgotten him.

Kellen had once told her that one of Jakoven's wizards had gone to Menogue and received a vision that if the king killed his brother, Jakoven himself would die a hideous, painful death. So when the king decided having a charismatic younger brother was too unsettling, he created the Asylum.

"Tisala," said Kellen again. "Rosem told me you were taken by my brother?"

It was not really a question, but she told him her story, including as many questions the torturer had asked as she could. She told him why she'd run to Ward of Hurog—not just the danger to Beckram, but the more personal reasons as well. When she was finished, he was quiet. She waited patiently.

"You appear well." It wasn't a casual comment, the years in the Asylum had made him distrust most people.

"Sire, the Hurogmeten has a wizard skilled in healing. Though he could not repair all the damage, the healer's work seems to have hastened my recovery." She showed him her hands with the nails partially regrown and turned her left hand so he could see the ugly new scar tissue.

He smiled his rare smile. In all the times he'd called her here, she'd only seen him smile once or twice. "So there is still magic in Hurog. I was told it was so, but I am glad to hear of it. We have need of all the magic we can."

"Sire, Ward is not sworn to your cause." It hurt to make

the warning, but it was her duty not to mislead him.

"I know, Tisala, but Jakoven will take care of that for us—if his killing of Erdrick has not already done so." He paused. "I rather liked Erdrick, you know. But Ward . . ." Kellen shook his head, eyes lost in the shadows. "Who would have thought that his stupidity was feigned? I knew him before his father ruined him—I would not have though he had a duplicitous bone in his body."

"Survivors can't always choose their methods," she said.

He nodded his head, the smile dying. "I suppose I should have remembered that Ward was the only person I ever met who could beat me at chess . . . Speaking of which, we have a game to finish."

Tisala stood up and sat on one end of the bench. Kellen scooted back until his back was against the wall.

He'd carved a chessboard on the bench with a sharp rock, and from a bag he'd hidden on his person he withdrew finely carved jade and jasper chess pieces. He set them up quickly, remembering the moves that they'd made the last time she'd been there months ago. Rosem had told her that Kellen played chess with a lot of the people who visited him, remembering each game as he did hers. It gave him a hobby, kept him sane.

They had time for three moves each before Kellen stored the pieces back in his bag.

"I enjoy playing with an opponent as good as I," he said pensively. "There aren't many who play as well as you."

"My father taught me," she reminded him.

"Yesterday, Rosem said you were here looking for Ward," he said.

"Yes, sire."

"No one I know here has been able to find out where they have him. But there's something going on in the mage's section. Jade Eyes has been here every day, and the archmage as well."

"I thought that's where he might be. His wizard can't find him."

"Ward is mageborn," said Kellen. "I remember that Ward could find things that were lost." He stared at the empty board on the bench for a moment. "I'll see if we can't get you into the new section in the next few days. What do you intend to do when you find him?"

"His wizard thinks he can get Ward out if I can find him."

"He'll lose Hurog," said Kellen softly. "If you are not very careful, Lord Duraugh and Beckram will lose their lives over this. I can't afford to lose Hurog—I've been counting on their support."

"If you tell me so, sire, I will tell them that I could not discover where he is." She knew as she said it that she lied— she'd never lied to Kellen before. "If Jakoven holds Ward, Duraugh will support any party that opposes him."

Kellen thought of it for a bit but shook his head. "You can't cage an eagle for long without destroying it. Get Ward out. I'll think about how to use this; it will give me something to do. Go ahead and see what you can do to get Ward out. I'll tell Rosem to give you what aid we can." He gave a nod of his head in dismissal and she bowed and finished mopping the floor while he lay back down on his bench and turned his back to her again.

After she'd knocked on the door to let the guard know she was finished he said softly, "I liked Ward."

"Me, too," she whispered back. And then the guard drew the bar and opened the door.

"Took you long enough," he said shortly.

He wasn't supposed to talk to her so she just bowed her head and nodded. It took her five trips to the straw room to cover the entire floor of Kellen's cell with a thick layer of straw. She finished and without a look at the still man on his bench she shut the door and bolted it behind her.

TISALA STOPPED AT A PUBLIC BATHHOUSE TO STRIP away the odor of the Asylum before her meeting with Oreg. It was just full dark when she got to the designated tavern, about the time she'd told him to expect; but from the empty mugs in front of him, Oreg had been there for quite some time.

He took one look at her face and turned away to gulp down the contents of a mug.

"I'm going back tomorrow," she murmured. "I can get into the mage's wing then. I'll find him."

"It's bad," he said, almost to himself. "He's hurting."

Tisala felt herself pale. She knew some of the things that went on in the Asylum—but usually they picked their victims carefully from those whose relatives wouldn't care. She'd assumed that Ward, with Lord Duraugh and Beckram awaiting audience with the king, would be safe enough—even with Jade Eye's attention.

"We'll get him out, Oreg. I promise."

He gave her a look and his eyes were far, far older than his face. "You are in no position to promise anything. And I am too old to believe in promises. We will do our best and only the gods know if our best will be enough. Come, Lord Duraugh will be expecting us."

"Us?"

He nodded. "The king is going to make us wait while his 'healers' examine Ward more closely. Lord Duraugh decided to rent a house rather than stay in the allotted rooms in the Residence, since it was made clear that there wasn't enough room for Duraugh's men. We've managed to shed the king's guards and spies. As long as we're careful getting in and out of the house, you should be able to stay there. Lord Duraugh wants to keep on top of this."

She'd been staying at Rosem's, but Duraugh's would significantly reduce the risk to Rosem. If someone looked too hard at Rosem, they might realize that the meek man who'd worked at the Asylum for the past decade was Prince Kellen's man, his body servant and guard.

"Give me the address of Duraugh's house and I'll find it," she said. "I have to stop by and let the people I was staying with know that I've found somewhere else to stay."

"Do you want me to accompany you?" he asked.

She shook her head. "I'd rather go alone. The people I stayed with don't like strangers."

He rattled off an address in a genteel district close to the Residence. "There's a park nearby with an oak tree the children climb on. Meet me there and I'll see that you get in unobserved."

"It may take me a while," she warned.

"No matter. Come when you're ready." He settled their tab with a few coins on the table, then left.

Rosem's home was a fair walk from the tavern, but when she got there, she continued to walk past it. She had a pilgrimage to make.

The buildings on the streets grew smaller and less well kept. Businesses were mostly run out of single-room dwellings without public licenses or signs. Here an old woman sold bruised fruit purchased at a discount from a regular merchant, while across the street a younger woman advertised her trade with bared breasts and fluttering eyes.

Tisala pulled up the hood of her cloak as if she were cold and turned down an alleyway to find the place where she had lived. It had been a small building built behind a narrow two-story house that faced the street. The only way into or out of it had been through the alley, and even then it was easy to miss behind the tall, old stone structure that had once been a part of an outer city wall.

She stepped behind the wall and stared at the scorched timbers that were all that was left of her home and the people who'd lived there. She'd sent a message to tell Haverness she was alive, but he wouldn't get it for a few weeks yet.

Death hung over the blackened ruin.

She'd lived with nine other people here, mostly actors and whores. They had shared cooking and cleaning—the small chores of living together. Tisala's nose burned and she rubbed it furiously: She would not cry for them. Their deaths would not be a small deed—little remembered—but another crack in the wall that held Jakoven on his throne. Her determination gave her little comfort.

Cold and depressed, Tisala walked back to Rosem's home, a basement apartment below a chandlery. She opened the door without knocking and found him in front of the tiny fireplace stirring the contents of a pot hanging over the fire.

"Find your man?" he asked without looking up from his task.

"No, but he said he'd get me into the mage's section to-morrow." They didn't use Kellen's name outside the Asylum.

Rosem nodded. "He enjoys your visits." He stopped stir-ring and set his spoon aside. "Do you really think that this mage of yours can get the Hurogmeten out?"

"He seems to think so," she said.

"Would he agree to get someone else out, too?"

Her heart picked up, but she said, "Is this the right time? I thought that we needed to wait until things were properly supported. Wouldn't want the whole structure to fall for want of underpinnings." Like Kellen's name, the rebellion was only referred to indirectly. Scrying spells could be set to activate at key words—like "Alizon" or "Kellen"—if there were a wizard who wanted to waste so much effort on a poor man who worked as a cleaner at the Asylum.

"We are supposed to get word when the time is right," she said. Alizon swore he'd tell Rosem as soon as there was any kind of hope for a rebellion against Jakoven.

"I don't think he'll last much longer in there," said Rosem heavily.

In all the time she'd known Kellen's man, she had never seen him nervous before, but the blunt-nailed hands that used toweling and pulled the hob out of the fire were shaking. "Until last season I used to get him to wrestle with me, but he won't do that anymore. I don't think he believes he'll ever get out. I think he's just humoring me because he can't bear to hurt me. He's lost more weight, did you notice?"

She nodded her head. "Ward's man would do it, I think. But he'll need to know what he's getting into. I won't have him unaware of the magnitude of what we want."

"Let me meet your wizard," Rosem said.

"After I get out of the Asylum tomorrow," agreed Tisala. "I'll talk to him."

"Just ask him to meet me. Don't say anything else. I want a look at him before I trust him with this."

TISALA FROWNED AS SHE WALKED. BRINGING OREG into this made her feel uneasy and she thought until she pinned down the cause.

Oreg liked to bait people. She'd seen him do it with Tosten in particular, because Tosten rose to the occasion. Ward mostly enjoyed it. But if Oreg tried it with Rosem, as uptight as Rosem was now, he'd would try to kill Oreg.

Rosem was good with any weapon at hand, but Oreg was a wizard—a dragon.

Tisala sighed and rubbed her forehead.

OREG WAS WAITING BY THE OAK TREE IN THE PARK when she got there. His face was peaceful in the moonlight, all the signs of stress she'd seen in the tavern were gone as if he'd donned a blank mask.

"Oreg," she said when she was close enough. She'd decided to approach him here, rather than in Duraugh's house. "My contact at the Asylum wants to meet you tomorrow."

"Why does he want to see me?" The wizard's eyes were hidden in the shadows. For a moment she felt a shiver of fear. Around Ward and the other Hurogs, Oreg went out of his way to appear boyish—but she was too skilled a hunter to believe his camouflage.

"I can't tell you," she said. "But you are free to refuse what he asks. Just don't play games with him."

"Play games?" He smiled at her, showing his teeth. "Why would I do something like that."

No, she thought wryly, she was not imagining the menace he projected. He wanted her to be afraid. "I care for him and I don't want to lose friends. Rosem doesn't have much of a sense of humor. If he believes you'll betray us, he'll try to do something about it."

"You think I'd deliberately mislead him?" His hand came out and touched the rapid pulse on her neck.

"Yes." The touch made her lose her temper. "I think you'd enjoy it. You may have everyone else fooled, but I know what you are."

"You do," he agreed.

She waved her hand in dismissal. "Not the dragon part. Ward treats you as if he needs to protect you—just like he treats everyone else. Stala thinks you a bumbling wizard, powerful but shy. And Tosten . . ." She considered a moment. "Tosten's worried you're going to hurt Ward."

He'd been watching her complacently until her last statement. "Hurt Ward?"

She nodded. "He knows that Ward sees you as one of his strays—like me, that young girl with the birthmark across her face, and the little boy with the crippled foot whose father is in the Blue Guard. But he thinks that means that Ward doesn't know what you are, what you're capable of doing."

"I'd never hurt Ward," Oreg said, his voice low.

"I know that," she said. "Tosten does, too now, I think. No one could miss how you felt about Ward when you came to tell us you'd lost him."

Oreg took several strides away from her. After a moment he came back, his face and body relaxed once more.

"So you know me better than anyone?" The threat was back in his voice.

She raised her chin and smiled coldly at him. "You are a predator—like me. I think you would give your life for those at Hurog—but you care little or nothing for anyone else." She could feel the menace gathering around her. A chill wind cut through the trees, rustling the old leaves that waited for spring budding to fall. "It worries me to take you to Rosem," she said. "You are too careless with other people. But I want what he wants enough to risk exposing him."

He laughed suddenly, sinking bonelessly against the oak tree. "I'll make a deal with you. You find Ward and I'll listen to what this friend of yours has to say. I'll be a sincere, innocent half-mad wizard for you. If"—he held up one finger, "if you don't subject me to any more speeches."

She considered him warily. Probably, she thought, there had never been any danger at all. "What if I promise to try not to subject you to speeches? I have a weakness for them, which I'll try to curb in your presence."

He grinned at her, showing his teeth. "Let us in to the dragon's lair, then, and let Lord Duraugh know what we know, hmm? He'll be expecting us."

She half thought he would work some wizardry that would transport them into the house, but he merely extended his elbow in invitation. When she tucked her arm in his, he patted her hand and let out another snort of laughter.

"If you think I am so dangerous, why are you so easy with me?"

She smiled. "Because I am no threat to Ward and you know it."

They walked into the alleyway that ran behind the house and through the garden gate. The back door was unlocked, which Oreg corrected as soon as they were through.

The house was sparsely furnished with good pieces. Tisala let her hand trail over a small table. The house had an impersonal look, as if it hadn't been a home in a very long time.

Oreg led her silently up the back stairway and down a dimly lit hall. There were several doors, but only one with light shining under it. Oreg stopped there and knocked.

"Come in," said Ward's uncle, and they did.

The room had been meant for a library, but books were expensive and the shelves that lined one wall were empty. A few modest but tasteful vases and a smallish carving or two tried to make the room less empty.

Lord Duraugh and his son, Beckram, were seated before a long table. Beckram looked distinctly relieved to see Oreg and Tisala.

The warrior who'd traveled from Hurog was gone: Duraugh wore the elegant court clothes like a second skin, and it made him look almost effeminate. Beckram, though even more elaborately arrayed in court fashion, wore a leashed purposefulness like a cloak around his shoulders. No one would mistake him for a simple court dandy.

"Did you find Ward?" asked Duraugh.

Tisala shook her head. "No. But I found out for certain that he's not in the regular part of the Asylum. Tomorrow my friend will get me into the section built to hold mages. If he's there, I can find him. It's not very big, just a few cells and a laboratory."

"They wouldn't need it to be very big," said Beckram. "How many mad sorcerers could there be?"

"Too many," replied Tisala somberly. "And they all work for the king."

"Where's Tosten?" asked Oreg.

Beckram answered. "He was restless and decided to do some exploring. Since he took his harp with him, I imagine that means he's going tavern hopping."

"Oreg told me the king refused to let you see Ward," said Tisala, taking a seat on an empty bench that spanned one wall of the room. She leaned back against the wall and closed her eyes. It had been a long day.

"The king said he'd heard that Ward had recovered his wits and he wanted an expert opinion before he trusted such an important keep to a boy whose own father thought him to be addled," said Duraugh.

Beckram snorted.

The door opened and Tisala opened her eyes to see Ward's brother stroll in, his harp case slung over a shoulder.

"The king knows Ward is fine," Tosten said, revealing he'd been listening for a while before entering. "Ward followed me to court the last two times I came, worried I was getting myself into trouble. I should never have told him that someone sounded me out—"

"Sounded you out?" asked Duraugh.

Tosten nodded and took a seat at the table, setting his case on the floor. "Someone told me Alizon had good things to say about me—it was before Jakoven moved against his brother, so the comment was safe enough. Then he asked me how my cousin was, wasn't it terrible how an assassin killed Erdrick in the king's garden and shouldn't the king be doing something to ensure the safety of his loyal subjects . . . things like that. I sent him away—gently."

"Who was it?" asked Beckram.

Tosten raised his eyebrows but didn't answer. "I sent him away so that I wouldn't have to know any more than I already did. When I told Ward about it, he worried that I was as likely to get attacked by one side as the other. When I wouldn't stay at Hurog, he followed me here." Tosten's voice tightened, though his expression didn't change. "He knew that flaunting himself in front of the court would force the king to either acknowledge him as Hurogmeten or move to fulfill the writ, and he used it to blackmail me into staying away from court."

Duraugh nodded, but said, "Frankly, I'm surprised Jakoven didn't just leave him be. Ward's reputation since the Vorsag king died at Hurog should have made him politically invulnerable. Just how he managed to pull down Hurog around King Kariarn's ears has been a well-kept secret—but everyone knows Ward was responsible."

"Maybe he's worried that Ward has already thrown himself in Alizon's camp," said Tisala slowly, sitting up straight. "Jakoven has many ears in court, he might have known that Tosten had been approached. Afterward Tosten goes to Hurog and brings back Ward. Twice. He might think the rebellion is closer to breaking out than it is, and that Ward is a part of it."

Beckram shook his head. "Hurog's not that important. It's personal. Jakoven wasn't able to get to me, so he went after Ward instead."

Tisala almost held her tongue, but she didn't want them going to court unprepared. "Alizon thinks that all of Shavig will follow Hurog's lead. The king was almost apoplectic when he received his due from last harvest. A number of the Shavig lords included veiled references to Hurog with their tribute. Colwick of Cornen went so far as to sign himself 'Hurog's liegeman.' "

Duraugh nodded. "I heard about that. They're trying to protect Ward, I think, by letting the king know Ward has their support. Shavig hasn't had a hero like Ward since old Seleg, and that was a couple of centuries ago. They don't intend to lose him."

Tosten gripped the table with both hands. "So the king thinks Ward's opinion carries Shavig, which is true." He glared at Beckram. "But he also believes that Ward has already leaned into Alizon's camp—which is probably what will happen eventually. So he has to get Hurog out of Ward's hands."

"So," breathed Tisala, terror robbing her of a stronger

voice, "he *investigates*. For the safety of his subjects he calls the Hurogs to court."

She looked at the men in the room blindly, as the pieces fell into place. "His wizards will examine Ward. Then he presents you with what his wizards have left. The court will only see that Ward's body is healthy, but you know him. You'll see what the king has done to him even if his body is untouched. Unprepared for Ward's condition, you give Jakoven an excuse to declare you all traitors—he doesn't need much, just a drawn sword or a misspoken word. Then he can set whomever he wishes over Hurog. It would antagonize Shavig—but not unpardonably. A king has the right to defend himself. Shavig loses Ward and Lord Duraugh in one blow and retreats to lick its wounds. Without Ward it is unlikely that the Shavig lords will fight against the king."

The Hurog men were all staring at her with various degrees of horror, but it was Oreg who whispered, "What are they doing to Ward?"

"Until just now," she said, "I thought Jakoven would want to keep Ward in good condition for fear of you acting against him—but that is exactly what he wants. There are bodies carried out of the mage's wing wrapped in canvas and burned. I know the two that I, personally, had the opportunity to see were . . . changed. One man had no face, no skin, no . . ." She had to quit speaking, it was probably for the best anyway, because Oreg's eyes were beginning to glow in the shadows of the library. "And the other?" Tosten's voice was no louder than Oreg's had been.

"She was dead," Tisala said. "But she still moved. We saw her because the cleaners who were supposed to take her to the crematorium dropped the bundle and ran. She was dead. There was no intelligence in her, but magic allowed her body to move."

"I know that spell," said Oreg, who looked as if he wished he didn't. "I thought it had been lost when the last emperor was killed."

Lord Duraugh turned to Tisala. "Find Ward tomorrow. Once you have him, we will get him out—one way or the other. If Hurog has to declare rebellion against the king, so be it."

7

TISALA

Confidence is as much a weapon as a sword. But, like a sword, it can shatter on an opponent's blade.

THE SECTION OF THE ASYLUM WHERE MAGES WERE kept was not very large, and Tisala found Ward in the second cell she cleaned. He was huddled in the corner of the room, half covered with straw.

She said his name tentatively because even with the skylight, it was dimmer in the cell than it was in the torch-lit corridor; and because, though it was hard to believe that there were two blond men of such stature in this particular section of the Asylum, it was harder to believe that Ward would ever cower from anything.

She shut the door and he came instantly to his feet with the speed and grace that always surprised her in such a large man. The maneuver put his face in the light briefly and she couldn't deny it was he. He wore little more than a loincloth and in less than two weeks he'd lost a stone of weight.

"Ward," she said a second time, realizing he must have been putting on an act. She'd never seen him act a part before, though she knew he was very good at it. The extreme weight loss worried her, but at least he was still whole. Her own recent experience in Jakoven's power sent her gaze to his hands, but she counted five fingers on each hand with one dirty nail apiece.

But he still didn't say anything, just stared at her. Gooseflesh crept up her neck, and she knew he wasn't acting. The fear she read in his eyes was real.

Ward was afraid of *her*. The realization stunned her into tears. *Her* Ward wasn't afraid of anything. Instinctively she stepped closer to him.

He held up a hand that shook slightly, but the palm-up gesture was universal.

"Tis." He said, his voice a slow grumbling growl that held more than a touch of menace. "Stay back." Then in a soft voice, almost a whisper, he added, "Please?"

For an instant she was hurt, but then reason took over. Whatever they had done to Ward, it had not made him slow of body. His rush to stand up had been quick. She'd been in too many fights to miss the heavy breathing and vibrating readiness. Whatever the cause, she'd frightened him. She had him cornered. She didn't really believe he would hurt her, but she backed away.

She took her eyes off his face because eye contact could feel threatening. Some visceral part of her protested the move, recognizing the danger he presented. But, out of the corner of her eye, she saw him relax marginally.

As she cleaned the cell, Ward slid back down the wall until he was crouched the way he had been when she'd come in. He drew the straw around him until it covered his legs and was scattered over most of the rest of him.

Tisala was careful to wipe her eyes and blank her face when she left Ward's cell. The other inhabitants of the wizard's block were more recognizably hurt, showing cuts and missing pieces. In one of the cells, the guards held the prisoner, who alternatively laughed and cried, while she cleaned.

There were many things that she despised about Jakoven, things that had authored the painful decision creating the distance between her father and her. But though his sins were legion, she had never hated him before today.

·   ·   ·

TISALA STRODE THROUGH THE DARKNESS OF THE TAV-
ern toward the back corner where Oreg waited for her.

She sat across from him and leaned forward. "You've got
to get him out of there."

Oreg lowered his eyelids so she couldn't read his reaction,
but his voice was mild. "If you found him—I can get him
out."

Relief washed over her. Oreg would get him out. Of course
he would.

"I didn't think anyone could lose so much weight in such
a short period of time," she said. "He's lost at least a stone."

"Working magic can do that," said Oreg. "Tell me about
what you saw."

With a handful of questions he got more information out
of her than she remembered noticing, the way Ward's eyes
had appeared black rather than brown, his swift coordinated
movements contrasting to his slurred, labored speech.

Finally, Oreg tossed a silver coin on the table—too much,
but Tisala didn't protest. She just took the arm he offered
her and strode out of the tavern by his side.

He walked with controlled violence. Tisala didn't disturb
him with talk because she felt the same need for action, the
same fury. She hadn't forgotten that they'd met at the tavern
so she could take Oreg to meet with Rosem, but she didn't
want to take him there in this mood.

They walked through a small area shopping district, and
he paused in front of a building with a mortar and pestle over
the door, an apothecary shop. It was locked up tight at this
time of night, of course, though there was light above where
the proprietor doubtless lived.

"Herbs," said Oreg abruptly. "There are herbs that can
make a person overwrought and confused. You said that he
was not otherwise hurt."

Herbs suggested that the condition Ward was in was temporary.

"I told you the cell wasn't well lit," she said, "but I would
have noticed any sizable wound or bruise. They're keeping
whatever damage they're doing from showing." *Maybe it
was all herbs,* she hoped.

"I'll get Ward out tonight," said Oreg. He resumed walking. His pace was still quick, but it was no longer urgent.

The air smelled of horse manure and other, even less savory, city smells, but it was clean and pure compared to what she'd been smelling all day.

"Tell me," said Oreg, "about the Asylum wing where Ward is. You said the king's wizards have a laboratory in the mage's wing."

"Yes, but I didn't see inside. It's kept locked."

He questioned her about little details, which side of the corridor Ward's cell was on, how many cells there were, about how big each cell was. Some things she knew, others she guessed, and a few she could only shrug about.

"Do you have time to see my friend?" she asked when she thought he was through questioning her.

He looked vague for an instant and she knew he'd forgotten.

"I wouldn't ask if it weren't important," she said.

"Fine," replied Oreg abruptly.

They walked a few blocks before Tisala found a street she knew, and it was well after full dark before she located Rosem's home.

She knocked at the door, three times in rapid succession so Rosem would know who it was, then entered without waiting for him to come to the door.

Rosem was seated at his table in front of the fire eating stew from a wooden bowl. He looked up once, a single sweeping glance, and gestured at the bench that spanned the length of the table across from him.

She took a seat and Oreg sat beside her. Rosem ate his dinner and didn't speak a word until he'd sopped up the last of the stew with a piece of dried bread. Tisala knew that he'd been using the time to assess Oreg, though he'd appeared to give his full attention to the wooden bowl he held.

He set his bowl aside and folded his arms across his chest. Without looking directly at Oreg, he addressed Tisala. "He's Hurog-bred."

"The old lord fathered a lot of us," said Oreg. "As did his father before him."

"Ward was the first wizard born into that family in living memory," continued Rosem. "Are you the second?"

Tisala frowned at him. What was he doing? She'd told him that Oreg was a mage.

Oreg smiled with boyish charm. "So they say."

"Rosem wants to know if you can get another person out of the Asylum," said Tisala before Rosem had time to really antagonize Oreg or vice versa. "He's not in the same wing as Ward."

Oreg's smile didn't change, so Tisala added, "Remember, without Rosem, I wouldn't have been able to find Ward."

The smile went out like a candle and Oreg said, "I can get another person out—if Ward agrees. But when I get Ward out, we won't linger here. Have your man put this on." Oreg opened his belt pouch and set a wooden bead on the table.

It was the size of a prune pit, painted with yellow and red designs and strung on a leather thong. Tisala had seen a number of barbarians—*Shavigmen,* she hastily corrected—wear such charms for luck while she had been at Hurog.

Rosem shook his head. "He won't be allowed to keep it."

"Can he hide it in his chambers, then? That's the only way I'll know where to get him, unless you want me to wait until you, yourself, are with him?" Oreg's voice was unfailingly courteous.

"I'll find a place to hide it. Don't you want to know who we want you to get out?" Rosem's voice was level with suspicion.

Oreg shook his head. "It doesn't matter. If I get Ward out of the Asylum, anyone else we get out can't worsen his position with the king."

"Kellen," Tisala said. "Jakoven's younger brother."

"I was wrong," said Oreg after a bare instant. "Rescuing Kellen Tallven will definitely take Ward off Jakoven's list of who is to be invited to important social events—except, of course, Ward's own execution."

Tisala couldn't help a quick grin.

Not knowing Oreg or Ward, Rosem said, "So your answer is no."

"I didn't say that," said Oreg. "It'll be up to Ward, but

since he has a wide band of stubborn stupidity that would do credit to a mule when the question of right and wrong is concerned, I expect he'll agree. You understand I can't say for certain until I have Ward out. Once I have him, I'll get Kellen out immediately so security doesn't tighten."

"I'd rather you not use his name so freely," said Rosem. "Being a wizard, you know about scrying."

Oreg snorted. "Being a *competent* wizard, I can keep Jakoven's pets from listening to any of my conversations. They'll not learn of your plans for Kellen from me."

"Tell me where and when to meet you after you've gotten him out," said Rosem.

Oreg hesitated. "Menogue," he said at last. "At the path before it begins the climb to the hilltop. I'll meet you there the evening after your man escapes. It should be very soon— so make sure he gets that charm."

"First thing tomorrow," agreed Rosem, closing his hand over the little bead until his knuckles turned white.

TISALA CLOSED ROSEM'S DOOR BEHIND THEM AND hugged her arms together as the chill night breeze cut through her clothing.

"He's not usually so abrupt," she said, setting out for the mansion where Ward's family would be waiting. "He's just worried."

"Jealous," correct Oreg, a hint of mischief in his voice.

"Jealous?" she asked.

"Rosem has Tallvenish body servant written all over him. His duty and honor is to protect his lord, but he has to go to a mage for help."

She thought about that for a moment. "Maybe a little," she said.

Rosem had engineered an escape once, years ago. It had failed, and the resulting chaos made it perfectly clear to everyone involved that if the king believed there was a real chance of his brother escaping, he'd forget about oracle warnings and kill Kellen. If Oreg wasn't successful, Kellen would die and it would be Rosem's fault. But Kellen was already dying in that little cell.

"I still think it's mostly worry," she said.

WHEN TISALA FOLLOWED OREG INTO THE LIBRARY at Lord Duraugh's rented manor, they found Tosten waiting for them. Dark circles shadowed his eyes and he rubbed them wearily, setting aside the battered harp he'd been fingering.

"I found him," she told Tosten in a voice suitable to a house where people were sleeping.

"How was he?"

She looked away and said, "Oreg thinks they are using herbs—he wasn't himself." The image of Ward trying to bury himself under the straw haunted her, and she didn't see any reason to share it with his brother—especially when the effects were, she hoped, temporary.

Tosten turned to Oreg. "But he'll be all right?"

"I'm getting him out tonight," said Oreg in oblique reply. "Help me move this furniture, I need a clear space on the floor."

By the time they'd cleared the floor, Lord Duraugh, looking more tired than Tosten, had come up to see what the noise was.

Oreg produced a sheet of vellum and made Tisala stand over his shoulder as he drew the section of the Asylum where Ward was. When he was finished he had a fair map. Then he picked Tisala's memories to pieces again. She found she remembered details she couldn't possibly have: how many stone blocks there were between each doorway, where the paint was scratched on the inside of Ward's cell door, the shape of the lock.

When he was finished with her, Tisala sat down abruptly on a bench and realized he'd used some magic on her—she could feel its absence now that it was gone.

Without a word, Oreg took a piece of charcoal and began marking the polished wooden floor.

"What are you doing?" Tosten's voice startled Tisala. She'd forgotten he and Duraugh were in the room, too.

"Transportation spells without a definite destination are difficult in the best of times." Oreg replied. "This"—he paused in his drawing to gesture at the marks he'd made on the floor—"will help me return here if something goes wrong. Hopefully I'll be able to get myself to where they've stashed Ward, and then I can get us both out."

"They have the area magicked to prevent someone doing just that," said Duraugh. "I've asked a few friends about it—discreetly."

"Jakoven's pet wizards don't have the power to ward it against me," said Oreg contemptuously.

Tisala had watched her father's mage use symbols to work magic before, but there was something different about the way Oreg moved—like the difference between watching an artist and a talented amateur. Oreg never stopped to look something up in a book, never paused in the detailed lines he placed on the floor, though she could barely see the marks in the dim light. He never had to stop and go back to redraw anything. Even so it took him quite a while before he was satisfied.

After setting aside the charcoal, he jumped lightly over his artwork and sat, cross-legged, in the unmarked section he'd left in the middle. He closed his eyes and became still.

Nothing happened for such a long time that when the first few sparks sputtered from the marks on the floor, Tisala thought she was imagining things.

Then between one breath and the next the temperature in the room shot up from winter-cool to unbearably hot. Blue and gold sparks spewed from the black marks and lit the room, forcing Tisala to bring up her arm to protect her eyes.

When she lowered her arm, the room was thick with smoke and a dragon curled around itself where Oreg had been, filling the room.

Then Oreg stood in the dragon's place, staggered a few steps forward, and fell to his knees. Duraugh rushed to his side and helped him to a chair.

"Oreg?" he said. "Are you all right?"

The wizard nodded his head, breathing heavily. "I can't get to him," he said in a voice that shook. "I haven't seen wards like those since . . . It's warded with dragon magic. I couldn't get through. If I were inside, with him, I might have been able to get him out—but not from here."

"They have a dragon?" asked Tosten tightly.

Oreg shook his head. "More likely some remnant piece—a tooth or scale would be enough."

"Are you sure you could get him out from inside?" Tisala asked.

Oreg smiled grimly. "Yes."

She rubbed her hands over her eyes. "I'll see what we can do. There is only one cleaner for that section. It'll be difficult to remove her again without arousing questions—not to mention the prevalence of mages who might notice a wizard strolling through their doors, for all that he's dressed like a cleaner."

8

WARDWICK

What you do when no one is watching reveals your true character.

DAY BY DAY I WAS FAILING, HOUR BY HOUR IT WAS harder to ride the pain. The greater portion of the panic gripping me had nothing to do with the herbs in the water I drank; I lost hope.

Oreg, where are you?

Sometimes the demons brought me back to my cell when the morning sun trickled through the small, grated window far above me. I would stare at the pale light on the straw because the window hurt my eyes. In my more cognizant moments I realized they weren't letting me sleep.

At some point I quit eating the food they left, but I managed to remember that the water was important, and I gagged it down before crawling to my straw cave.

I COULD TELL IT WAS ALMOST TIME FOR THE MONSTERS by the relative clearness of my thoughts. The door opened and I tried to pretend I wasn't there, burrowing into the straw until they couldn't find me.

But it wasn't the usual monsters, because the door shut, leaving the intruder caged with me. The break in routine was frightening and the resulting adrenaline rush sent me to my feet.

A woman stood just inside the door in a plain woolen robe. In her right hand she held a wooden rake.

"Tisala." The small voice spoke for the first time in a long time, but it was virtually lost in the sea of terror that drowned me. It hadn't taken long to learn that anything new was bad.

She walked in tentatively, a horrible creature with seven heads who was going to poison me with the tears that tracked down her face. I scuttled away from her as far as I could, but she kept coming.

"Tis," I said, though I hadn't planned on saying anything at all. "Stay back. Please?" If she tried to touch me, I knew I would die. But the little voice had been forced out of hiding for fear *I* would hurt *her.*

She backed away then, and left me to my safe haven while she raked out the straw that didn't belong to my nest. I stood glued to the far wall, shaking.

When she left, I wept as she had, but I didn't know why. I didn't stop until the monsters came again.

THEY HELD MY HEAD UNDER WATER THIS TIME, BUT I didn't struggle because Jade Eyes told me not to. I held my breath until I passed out. Then they—and I—did it again.

This was something new, and in my drugged exhaustion it seemed perfectly sane to peer through the depths of the water and look for . . . safety, sanity, I don't know what. It seemed to me that I could see it just on the outside of my vision.

"See what?" Jade Eyes asked, after I awoke coughing and choking the second time.

I blinked at him like an idiot; even after four years, the mask of stupidity I wore throughout my youth was more at home on my face than not. Tosten liked to tease me about it.

Tosten. Hurog.

"Something to fill the hole in me," I said, realizing after I said it that it was true. I rolled off the wet bench and back into the water without help this time.

Hurog, I thought. *Dragon, come take me.*

Dragon claws snatched at me, dragon magic, filled me for a moment. I knew this dragon.

"Oreg!" I screamed underwater.

Then between one instant and the next it was gone, and the hole that separation from Hurog always left inside me was all the emptier for having once been filled. It was infinitely worse than the pain in my head, and some part of me believed that I would never be whole again. That this time they would succeed in taking Hurog from me.

A hand, not dragon claws, hauled me out of the water and strapped me down to the table in the center of the room.

"Did you feel that?" asked Jade Eyes excitedly to his fellow mage. "That's what his magic felt like on the trip over here. Have you ever felt anything like it?"

I cried for Oreg's loss. Even in the state I was in, I realized that Oreg had tried to rescue me—and he'd failed. There would be no rescue. And if Oreg couldn't rescue me, no one could.

"It was unusual," said Arten. "But Jakoven was firm that we break him. I think we've done it. The drugs should be mostly out of his system and he still threw himself into the water that last time. I suppose he might be trying to kill himself, but that flare of magic . . ."

"He was looking for something," said Jade Eyes, petting my forehead. "Weren't you, Ward?"

His voice was so soft and soothing, I couldn't help but reply. "Dragons," I said, sobbing out the words. "The dragon is gone."

Arten nodded abruptly. "I'll be back with Jakoven," he said. "Amuse yourself until I return at his convenience. Don't take him back to his cell. I'll tell Jakoven you've managed to re-create the effect you noticed bringing him here. But I think he's impatient to get on with his plans." On those words he left me alone with Jade Eyes.

Amuse himself Jade Eyes did. And it was different this

time. The knowledge that not even Oreg could get me out had broken some hard core of resistance. The thin veneer, the shadow of my old mask that I wore to protect myself, crumbled completely and there was nothing left to save me. I screamed when the pain flamed through my body, robbing me of all control. I sobbed for it to stop, then sobbed and shook when it did and the pain was replaced by caressing hands. I wished fervently for the pain rather than the sure knowledge that it would begin again, and over and over I received my wish.

It was during one of the "rest" periods that Jakoven finally came. I didn't hear him enter, didn't notice him until he struck me lightly on the face.

"Ah, Ward, my boy. Good to see you," he said.

I stared at him blankly, far past worrying about the newly familiar smells that accompanied Jade Eyes entertainments: feces and urine, blood and sweat. Nor was I concerned about the tears that continued to slide down my cheeks, though I was aware that all of these things would once have embarrassed me—especially the tears.

"Hurogs don't cry." It was not my inner voice who spoke, but an older one. It took me a moment to remember that my father was dead and I didn't need to hate him anymore.

I think Jakoven thought the heat in my eyes was directed at him, not realizing I was almost beyond recognizing who he was.

"Do you know why you are here?"

No, I thought. "Hurog," I said in a voice so hoarse and deep that it must have been difficult to understand. Then the tissues of my throat, swollen from screaming, closed up, and I couldn't utter another word.

Jakoven looked away from me and said, "Leave us. Stay, Jade Eyes."

The room emptied. I hadn't realized until then that there was anyone else in it but the king, Jade Eyes, and me, but a number of mage robes passed by my eye.

When they were gone, Jakoven pulled up a stool and sat by my head so I could see him. The Tallvenish king who ruled the Five Kingdoms including my own Shavig was, in many ways, the epitome of what a king should be. His voice was rich and carrying, the kind of voice that could encourage armies in battle. His face was regular without being handsome—the face of a general, perhaps, or a . . . well, a king.

"Arten tells me that you've amazed my Jade Eyes, who thinks you've happened upon a new form of magic." The king shook his head with a kingly smile. "He's young yet, and hasn't met many self-taught mages—as I have." He reached out with a clean white cloth and wiped my cheeks, but I continued to cry without knowing why. "When a mage teaches himself magic, he has little control, leaking power he should capture and use. Your father really should have sent you out for training. I doubt you even know when you set up your magic guardian to watch your sleep—that's what gives it the feeling of sentience he received."

"But—" protested Jade Eyes.

"Quiet, my lad. You're young yet and convinced you know all the answers. I know the guardian spell is advanced—but someone thought it up once. I imagine they did it in much the same way our young friend here did. Poor boy." He crooned to me and kissed me.

I gagged and jerked, but the king was thorough and the bonds that held me were tight. Fear shook me, sweeping up from my feet and to my head, leaving me light headed and dizzy. Fear of the king, fear of the pain, fear of what new thing they were going to do.

I heard Jade Eyes say something, but I didn't pay attention.

"Jealous?" asked the king, pulling away from me. "Foolish boy. Now get me that bag on the top shelf—no, not that one. The small one. Thank you."

I couldn't see the bag with my head restrained. And the king settled back so I couldn't hear him, either, just felt the feather-light touch of his fingers on my forehead.

"Did you know that *Hurog* means dragon in old Shavig?" said the king. My stomach wove itself another knot. "Why do you think that is?"

I didn't say anything, but Jade Eyes answered, "Because when there were dragons, they nested near Hurog, I suppose."

"Mmm," said the king. "There are stories about Hurog. That the dragons are drawn there by a magical stone, deep in the heart of Hurog."

The only thing that had been in Hurog's heart was the bones of a dragon, and I'd taken care of that when I used the bones to heal the sick earth.

"I've heard that one," said Jade Eyes.

"When I asked the Hurogmeten—the real Hurogmeten, this one's father—about it, he laughed and said there was nothing in Hurog to attract a dragon. I've since come to believe he was right—but there's a grain of truth in some old folklore. Some years ago during the renovations of the castle here at Estian, my stone mason, rest his soul, came across a curious thing. He brought it to my attention shortly before he died."

Broken I might be, but I found myself wondering why Jakoven felt it necessary to remind Jade Eyes that he could kill anyone he chose.

Maybe, I thought, in sympathy with Oreg's formerly suicidal tendencies for the first time, *maybe Jakoven would choose to kill me.* I didn't believe it, really, just hoped for it.

I heard the rustle of cloth. Jade Eyes gasped, and a cold fog of dark magic crawled through my skin, dirtying me inside and out.

"I keep it here in this special bag, so that no one would ever be curious about it—as you must have noticed, it was difficult for you to find even after I directed you to it. Do you recognize it?"

"No, sire," said Jade Eyes, fear or excitement tightening his voice. "It's very old—and powerful."

"How about you, boy?"

A hand appeared in my field of view holding a bronze staff head. Mages liked to top their staves with elaborate metal sculptures, usually just expensive toys encrusted with gems and glass beads. This wasn't even impressive, just a crude rendering of a dragon holding a small gem in its open mouth. With a body length of distance no one would have even noticed the dull, cloudy gem the size of a pea, much less that it hovered between the dragon's jaws without touching the metal anywhere. Without being mageborn, no one would have noticed the black power spilling from the gem. I could almost see the wave of misery that flowed out to cover me like thick syrup.

I knew what it was, though not how it survived. Anyone who'd ever listened to the tale of the Empire's Fall would have recognized it. Jade Eyes must not have a taste for music or old tales.

"Tell him what it is, Ward, if you know." I didn't have to see Jakoven's face to hear the smile in his voice.

Maybe if my throat hadn't closed up from screaming I would have complied. But then again, maybe if my throat hadn't closed up from screaming it would have closed up from fear. Not the nameless fear for myself that had troubled me so only moments ago, but directed, heart-wrenching fear for all that I loved.

"Ah, children. How undereducated you are. This is the Empirebane, Destroyer of Cities, also called Farsonsbane. The greatest mage ever known, Farson Whitehair, took the blood of three dragons and concentrated it into this small stone—an experiment. Years later it was stolen and enemies of the Empire used it to bring down the stone buildings and walls of the great cities and crumbled them to ashes. Farson recovered it and hid it, vowing that no one would use it again."

I'd heard that the Last Emperor, a boy of twelve, had stolen it and hidden it until he could recover it. But he and his remaining bodyguards were found. They died without revealing where it was. Either way, it made a good story.

"Farsonsbane?" Jade Eye's voice was incredulous, but not doubting—the power of the thing was palpable. "I thought it would be made of gold, and the gem was supposed to be the size of my fist. My servant has gems more impressive."

The magic gathering around the bane wasn't growing, I finally realized, it was exploring. I shuddered as the rich darkness slipped through my defenses and tasted my magic greedily. How ironic that Jade Eyes would mistake Oreg for some sort of sentient magic, and not recognize this. I'd felt magic like this before, on Menogue and at Hurog.

"Your servant's gem couldn't flatten a city the size of Estian with a word. Show some respect." The king removed the staff head from my sight but the magic stayed.

"Too bad you can't use it," said Jade Eyes. "It must be fed with dragon's blood, and there are no more dragons."

The king's stool creaked and he said, "There is an interesting thing I ran into while doing my research. It was something so insignificant, I almost didn't pay attention to it. How old is Hurog keep?"

I could almost hear the shrug in Jade Eye's voice. "It's old, maybe the fifth century after Empire? That would make it eight hundred years."

Earlier than that, I thought. *Far earlier.*

"There are books in my private library that were written during the time of the Empire, and one of them mentions Hurog. Calls it the Dragon's Keep." I could hear Jakoven's nail tapping on something metallic, maybe it was the staff head. "There is a story that the first few Emperors had a mage who was a dragon. There are also old stories that claim the lord of Hurog is a dragon. So what do you think, Ward? Are you descended from that mage? Do you have dragon's blood?"

He cut my arm, just a little. And mopped up the blood with the same cloth he'd wiped my face with. I didn't see what he did with it, but I presumed it was to wipe the red smear against the gemstone because something happened.

Jade Eyes exclaimed loudly and the king's stool fell to the ground. The power that had been examining me changed, just a little. Just for a moment it recognized me.

"Hurog?" it said, resonating soundlessly in my skull. *"Dragon?"*

And something deep inside of me answered the call before the magic of Farsonsbane was abruptly cut off.

"It's not supposed to do that," exclaimed Jakoven. "The records specifically say the stone flares with red light as it is touched by dragon's blood. But this is the first response I've gotten from it."

"Blue," said Jade Eyes assessingly. He walked near to me until I could see him. "Your blood turned the stone from black to blue." He looked across me at Jakoven. "Did you try your own blood? Perhaps mageblood affects it."

"My blood does nothing to it," Jakoven replied. "I've tried." I saw a flutter of cloth out of the corner of my eye as the king walked past me. I heard him replace the bag on the shelves.

"Ah, Ward," Jakoven said, kissing my forehead. "You have answered my most fervent wish. For ten years that artifact sat upon my shelves waiting to be awakened."

He pushed back from me and I heard him pick up his stool and set it upright.

"Well enough," he said briskly, as if the raw lust in his voice had never been. "Arten tells me you are ready, Jade Eyes. And any fool could see he is broken. But I want him stupid and happy. Make sure he can speak, eh?"

"Right," agreed Jade Eyes. "We've been experimenting with drugs to get the proper effect. We'll give him a little sorcerer's root to make sure no one could ever mistake him for normal and top it off with a few things to make him happy."

"Good. See that it is done."

IT WAS A BEAUTIFUL DAY, THE CRISP CHILL OF LATE fall drifting clean and pure into my lungs. I told the guards that as they helped feed me into a covered two-wheeled cart that was to take us to Court.

I told the big Tamerlain who sat rumbling on my feet. It bothered them when I talked to her, though, because they couldn't see her.

"Gods take you, shut up," said one. "Are we going to have to listen to this all the way to the Castle?"

Surprised, I looked up from the big animal stretched across the floor of the cart.

"Look at him," he said to his comrade. "To smile like that with tears running down his face . . ."

"Relax," grunted the other guard. "He's been shut up in the Asylum for almost a week. He's not used to the light, and his eyes are tearing up. It'll go away soon."

The Tamerlain sat up on her hindquarters and placed a forepaw on either side of me. The cart didn't shift with her movements the way it did with mine—as if the Tamerlain had no weight at all.

"I'm sorry, Ward," she said into my smile. "But it's time."

As she spoke, fire lit my blood and licked up my body, icy fire that burned impurities and nerves alike. Sweat poured from my skin and stung my eyes, mucus blocked my breath.

"Damn it, he's having convulsions," grumbled the second guard, though he made no move to come near me. "If the stupid mages did something to him that kills him—you and I know who's going to get the blame."

The worst of it was over by the time the horses stopped. I stumbled shakily out of the carriage to face a back entrance to the king's palace, truly sober for the first time since I'd drunk from the general's waterskin.

The guards hauled me unceremoniously up a narrow stairway and into a back room where a hot bath was waiting. They stripped my filthy clothes off and scrubbed me with rough cloths. Wrapped shivering in a bath sheet, I sat on a stool while one of them shaved me clean. There was some discussion about cutting my hair, but they decided it was a Shavig affectation, toweled it dry, and brushed it into a queue. The Tamerlain watched, unnoticed—Oreg could do the same thing. I took care not to look at her directly. And I smiled the whole while until my cheeks ached with the strain.

The clothes they gave me to wear were all black and plain, though expensive. The boots they pulled on my feet were my own, though they'd been polished to a higher gloss than I'd had them. They covered me with a hooded cloak and shuffled me out the door and into the hall. The hood kept me from seeing much about where I was going, but that was fine. It gave me more time to think. And I needed to think.

The king wanted me so he could work Farsonsbane. He wasn't about to give me up.

But there was something else he wanted. Today the king told Jade Eyes to make sure I was happy and stupid. The

Tamerlain had told me that Jakoven would present me before his court—no, that wasn't it.

I stopped abruptly and someone pushed me forward.

Abruptly my forehead broke out with sweat and a flash of heat swept from my feet to my head, robbing my joints of their strength as it passed. I slumped to the floor. The Tamerlain nudged me anxiously.

"What is wrong with me?" I whispered.

"Your body has begun to crave the drugs they fed you," she said. "I can do nothing for this."

Jakoven's men scrambled. From their words I understood that Jakoven had commanded me to be in a presentable condition when I was brought before the court. The only thing he wanted the court to see was that my mind was broken—not my body.

They brought a bucket of water and washed my face with cold, damp cloths, careful not to muck up the clothes. I grabbed the bucket from them and drank to assuage my dry throat. When they helped me to my feet, I let them steady me.

I was weak, so I leaned upon the men who led me, saving my strength for when it was needed. The Tamerlain walked in front of us, pausing every few steps to watch me worriedly. The halls we traversed were unfamiliar, but I was more interested in getting to the stage of Jakoven's drama than I was in observing the sights. I had acted many roles, but this was going to be the performance of a lifetime—if I could manage it.

My guard stopped before an inconspicuous door, and one of them stepped through it, closing it behind him—but not before I glimpsed the tumult of people in the formal hall. I took a deep steadying breath as I heard Jakoven's voice, only slightly muffled by the door.

"My lord Duraugh, my chamberlain tells me you have been waiting for some time. We are sorry for it. Please come forward now with your family and receive Our apologies." There was a pause, and I supposed my uncle was following the king's directions.

"Well now, Duraugh, what brings you here?"

"I am here, my king, at your bidding and to inquire about my nephew, the Hurogmeten." My uncle's voice cut through the closed door as easily as it cut through a battlefield.

And finally I realized the whole of what Jakoven intended. He wanted to present the court with a Hurogmeten who was stupid so they'd see why he couldn't leave Hurog in my hands. That would leave me in his power. The Tamerlain's magic had given me the chance to counter his plot.

But my uncle *knew* I wasn't an idiot. Without warning of my condition, he might have done something unpolitical—like accuse the king of damaging me.

But I wasn't going to go into court under the influence of Jade Eye's drugs.

"Ah, yes. Ward of Hurog." Jakoven spoke as if he had forgotten about me, as if I were of only minor interest to him. "We were reminded that at one time the boy was considered unfit. We have not seen him since you set him to run Hurog and We decided that such an important post could not be held by an imbecile."

"My brother is no imbecile," snapped Tosten. The pause before he added "my king" was too long.

Panic froze me in place. Tosten was here.

My uncle was good at court politics: As long as there was no obvious blood, no signs of torture, I could count on him to keep a cool head. My brother would take one look at me, too thin and barely strong enough to stand on my feet, and he'd do something rash.

"I'm sure you're right," purred Jakoven.

My brother let out a low rumble that sounded for all the world like the growl of a dog.

If I waited here any longer the king would incite Tosten to riot even without my haggard appearance to help. I'd have to count upon Uncle to control Tosten.

The men I leaned so heavily against were not prepared for my sudden shove. I stepped around them and through the door, which opened just below the royal dais.

"Of course I'm not an imbecile," I said cheerfully, striding into the room. "As our most gracious majesty has discovered for himself."

I bowed low before the king and then turned to face the court. The Tamerlain stood close to me and I let her brace me.

"Our king has been a very gracious host the past week." I pulled the time frame from the guard's comment as we traveled from the Asylum. As far as I was concerned, it could have been months or years since I'd left Hurog. "And I hope that I have satisfied him as to my fitness to rule. As he told me earlier today, I should have presented myself formally to him a long time ago, but I've had my hands busy rebuilding my keep. I suppose I could have left it to the dwarves"—I paused to remind Jakoven that I had allies he hadn't considered—"but it was my fault that Hurog fell. It seemed my duty to see it arise again."

I glanced over at my family, who stood tense and still at the front of the court, arrayed before the king, and smiled convincingly at them. The hard pump of battle fever and the Tamerlain were the only thing keeping me upon my feet.

The lords present, including many Shavigmen, nodded and smiled at my reminder of my role in stopping the Vorsag invasion and the cost Hurog had paid for it. I'd made mention of the dwarves, who had come from the mists of legend to reappear at Hurog. Many of the Shavigmen, at least, had seen them. I noticed that there were several of the more powerful Shavigmen who moved through the crowd to stand at my uncle's right. If this didn't play right, it wasn't only my family who'd suffer. I set the smile in my eyes and wondered how to get out of the room and take my family with me.

"I see you, Hurogmeten," growled a deep voice, and I turned to face the Warder of the Sea, the highest-ranking Seaforder, whom I knew only by sight. He seldom came to court, being needed to run his shipping empire. "It would have been Seaford that the Vorsag would have eaten after they digested Oranstone. We remember what you did." He bowed low twice. Once to the king and once to me.

I wondered if he knew that I was circumventing the king and wanted to help—or if his words meant no more than was said. Either way I was grateful, because the cheer that followed his pronouncement gave Jakoven no choice.

I turned back to the king, my face a careful blank. "I trust that I have settled any doubts that you have, my king."

He looked from me to the smiling court. "I have no doubts about you, Wardwick of Hurog," he said graciously.

I bowed once again, carefully so as not to upset my precarious balance. As I stood upright, my eyes met Jade Eyes's gaze and knew bloodlust. Child of my father that I was, the desire for Jade Eyes' death momentarily consumed me.

The king waved his hand in dismissal and called to his chamberlain for his next case as if he'd forgotten about me. But I saw the white-knuckled grip he had on his throne as I walked past him toward my family. I put a casual arm about Tosten's shoulders and whispered "Out, now" around my wide smile.

Tosten slid his arm under my cloak and unobtrusively half carried me out of the court. Beckram and Duraugh fended off well-wishers, so when Tosten dragged me into the corridor, we were alone.

"Someplace out of sight. Quickly," I said, feeling the weakness increasing in my knees.

Tosten leaned me against a wall and jerked open several doors. He hauled me through the last one, shutting the door behind us. Light came through the open windows from the garden and I could smell the faint scent of autumn roses. I sat abruptly and concentrated on breathing.

"You've lost weight," observed Tosten, crouching next to me where I'd collapsed on the floor. "But you're still too heavy for me to carry."

I nodded, but instead of speaking I wrapped my arms around myself and tried to quit shaking. He said something more, but I couldn't hear it because the sound of my heartbeat drowned it out. After a few minutes the shaking eased and I rested my head against the wall in relief.

"We can't stay here forever," said Tosten. "Someone's bound to notice."

"How far are we from your rooms?" I asked.

"We're not staying here. Duraugh rented a house—I gave him the money from the strongbox in your study to help pay for your rescue. I hope that was right."

I didn't want to sleep under Jakoven's roof, but I didn't see how I was going to get from here to a rented house without causing a scene.

"How do I look?" I asked.

"Like you've been poisoned and are waiting to die," said Tosten. "But in the dim light in the corridors of the palace, I don't think that anyone who didn't know you would notice. It's getting dark outside as well. I think we can get you out without attracting attention."

I slid myself up the wall with Tosten's help. When my legs didn't immediately collapse under me, I walked slowly to the door. "Did you bring horses, or am I going to have to crawl all the way there?"

"Horses," said Tosten, wedging a shoulder under my arm. "Uncle Duraugh, in a fit of optimism or a show for the audience—I'm never sure with him—even brought an extra for you."

When we stepped back out of the room, Duraugh and Beckram were in the hall waiting. Neither of them spoke, but I had learned to recognized the slight tightness in Duraugh's cheek that denoted white-hot rage, and Beckram was shaking with it.

"I'm all right," I said, though it was patently untrue. Beckram slid under my free shoulder and helped with the task of getting my unwilling body out of the castle.

There were things I needed to know, things I needed to tell them all, but I contented myself with staggering to the stables. The grooms tactfully didn't notice that I had to lean against the wall while my brother pointed out the horses to be saddled. They'd put it down to too much drink, unless someone questioned them, and forget about it before the day was over.

When Tosten appeared with Feather, I buried my head against her neck and let the clean smell of horse wash away the stink of the Asylum. I tried twice to mount on my own, and if Feather had been any lighter, I'd probably have pulled her over. Beckram, with a shoulder in my rump, made my third attempt successful.

I don't remember riding through the gates or arriving at

the house. I do remember being met at the door by Oreg, who picked me up and carried me up the stairs as if I didn't weigh half again what he did.

They fussed over me for a while, my brother, cousin, and uncle, while I scrubbed in an oaken tub, then sat while Oreg went through my hair with a comb to rid me of lice and nits—which the king's men hadn't bothered to do.

"Ciarra and I have a daughter," said Beckram, leaning back on his stool to keep out of Oreg's way. "Three days ago. I just found out today."

I looked out from under the clean wet hair Oreg had thrown over my eyes. For a minute we grinned at each other.

"Does she have a name yet?" I asked, stammering a bit.

"Leehan," he answered. "After the spirit of the woods."

"There are a lot of your men here. Is she at Hurog?" Surely they wouldn't have brought her all the way to Hurog when she was so near to delivering.

"No. We left half the guard there—she said she was fine. The king's men left as soon as Mother convinced them that Father and I were on our way to Hurog."

I rubbed my face tiredly. It was so hard to gather my thoughts, harder still to order my tongue.

"I think it's dangerous," I said. "You need to get her to Hurog."

"Ward," Duraugh said, "she's just given birth. She's not up to the ride to Hurog. What makes you think she's in danger?"

"Jakoven," I said. "Get all of our blood out of Iftahar— it's not a fortress. Hurog is better defended even now."

"I would think Jakoven more likely to lick his wounds and try again," said my uncle.

"No," I said, rubbing my forehead. "It's important to him now. He'll act immediately. We need to get Ciarra and the baby to Hurog."

"I'll go," said Beckram, hearing the urgency in my voice. He stood up as his father started to argue. "If Ward says they're in danger, I'll move them to safety."

Duraugh shook his head at both of us, but said only, "Sleep the night, then, and leave at first light. It won't help her if you break your neck galloping off in the darkness."

Oreg helped me stand and poured warm water over my head as Duraugh and Beckram worked out the details. Shivering even in the warm room, I huddled in the toweling Oreg brought me and wished I felt clean. Tosten handed me fresh clothes and I struggled into them.

They managed me into another room, complete with fire and bed, and Oreg bullied everyone else out. He stayed, a silent sentinel. But even his presence couldn't make me feel safe.

I didn't sleep. Didn't want to sleep. There were too many things running about in my head. I just lay still with my eyes closed.

Jakoven wanted power and he thought my blood might be the key to using Farsonsbane. My blood, or the blood of someone in my family—descended from dragons as we were. Oreg had said as much to me.

Jakoven wasn't going to let us retreat in peace for long. Gods forbid he find out what Oreg was.

Alone, Hurog could not stand against the king, but if I threw Hurog behind Alizon, some of the Shavigmen would follow me. And if the rebellion took fire before Jakoven managed to get me or another Hurog-blood in his hands again to activate the Bane, we might be able to hold the king off for a few months.

But my objections to the rebellion were still valid. Essentially, there were too many nobles who would stand behind the king. In the end we would lose.

While I tried to chart a course with a possibility of survival, I was dimly aware of the door opening quietly and a murmured argument. The door shut and I was left once more in silence with my fears, but not left alone.

Every plan I came up with led to disaster sooner or later. I was in the middle of trying to see how we could lure the Seaforders to Alizon's cause (something I wouldn't have dreamed of without the Warder of the Sea's little speech), when I experienced another of the debilitating bouts of miserable shaking. This time I itched as well.

A cool damp cloth wiped my face and then the rest of my

body as armies of imaginary bugs trooped over my skin, driven away by the clean water and Tisala's soft crooning.

She waited until the fit left me before she spoke. "Ward? Are you all right?"

"What are you doing here?" I asked. She was supposed to be safe at Hurog. Jakoven had taken her once already.

She lit a small candle from the banked fire and set it in a holder on a table near my bed. The flickering candle lit her dark hair with red tones. The darkness of the window coverings told me I'd lain with my eyes closed longer than I'd thought—or I'd fallen asleep.

"As if I would sit in safety when I could help," she said crisply. "I came to help get you out of the Asylum—though you got yourself out in the end."

The Asylum. The drugs had left me with a pitiful handful of clear memories amidst the nightmare images. I closed my eyes in embarrassment. "You came while I was there. I thought I had made it up." I thought of what a fool I must have looked like, hiding under the straw, and laughed.

"What?" she asked.

"I was just wishing I had some straw to cover my head," I said with more bitterness than humor.

Her hand, as callused as mine, touched my temple and trailed down my sweat-streaked cheek. "Oreg says that you should feel better in a few days."

"He told me," I said.

"After I found where they had you, Oreg tried to get you out." She took her hand away suddenly, as if she had just noticed she was touching me.

Though the king's men had scrubbed and soaped, and I'd done it again here, maybe the smell of the Asylum still clung to me. "I know he did." I remembered the call of Hurog magic as I tried to drown myself—had it been this morning or last night? "The Tamerlain couldn't get me out, either. The part of the Asylum I was in was designed to hold mages."

"The Tamerlain?" she said.

She would know what the Tamerlain was, of course, but I doubted she really believed in it. I shouldn't have said anything about the creature—not coming out of an asylum for crazy people. I glanced around the room, but the Tamerlain, having done what she could, was gone.

"You really saw the Tamerlain?" she asked, but more in wonder than if she truly doubted me.

"She made it possible to carry out that little farce in Jakoven's court," I said.

"Who are you that Aethervon takes an interest in your deeds?" she asked.

I wasn't ready for undeserved admiration. I felt fouled and small, so I snorted and told the truth. "A pawn. Don't get your hopes up, Aethervon has done all he intends to."

Tisala crouched beside my bed and looked hard into my eyes. "Tell me again what you feel about Alizon's rebellion."

I sat up and rubbed my face wearily. "If this is a serious conversation, would you mind lighting a few more candles so I can see you when I'm talking?" The shadows in the room reminded me of the cell in the Asylum.

When she was through I made her drag a chair over near the bed. Between the candle lighting and the rearranging of furniture, I bought myself enough time to decide I didn't have to be entirely honest with her, but I was going to do it anyway.

"The time is still wrong for a rebellion," I said. "The harvest was good this year, not only in Shavig, but Tallven and Oranstone as well. My father used to say that full bellies make for happy subjects, and he was right. Jakoven's tithe is fair. He hasn't overtly oppressed anyone who would incite the nobles. It's unlikely Alizon can draw any of the Avenhellish lords away from Jakoven, and the Tallvenish and Avenhellish lords can raise larger, better-trained armies than Shavig, Seaford, and Oranstone combined, even if Alizon could gather them all together—which he can't. In return for battling a superior fighting force, Alizon offers to replace one Tallvenish king with another, himself. And Alizon is baseborn. I suspect that your father is not the only Oranstonian who's refused to follow Alizon."

Her face was carefully blank while I talked. Toward the end of my speech she turned her face away.

I shrugged. "I'll tell you what has changed, though. Jakoven has made it impossible for me to do anything except join the rebellion."

Her eyes snapped back to me and ran over my bare chest and shoulders looking for wounds that weren't there. For all the pain I'd endured, the only blood I'd lost in the Asylum had gone to the lice—and the Bane.

"What did he do to you?"

I smiled at her, but she didn't look reassured, so I stopped. "He found Farsonsbane."

She started to look puzzled before the name registered. "I thought Farson destroyed it—or the boy emperor."

I shook my head. "Jakoven found it while he was rebuilding Estian castle. It needs dragon's blood to activate it."

"Oreg," she whispered.

I felt my eyebrows rise. How did she find out about Oreg? No wonder she'd accepted that I'd met the Tamerlain. From dragons to the minions of gods was a small step.

I could have left off there. She'd have believed that I'd throw myself behind Alizon for Oreg's sake.

"My blood did something to it," I said. "I need to keep every person who can claim Hurog blood away from him. If Alizon is ready, I'll declare for him. If not, Hurog will rebel on its own. It's that, or allow Jakoven access to the same power that brought down the Empire."

She stared at me a moment, then said baldly, "The reason I knew how to get into the Asylum is because Alizon is not the heart of the rebellion—Kellen is."

"Kellen?" I said, startled. The king's brother—I remembered a quiet-spoken, clever boy a few years older than I. My heart began to race with a shard of hope. Kellen was legitimate: moreover, he had been terribly wronged by Jakoven and had a just cause for rebellion. With Kellen, the rebellion Alizon was leading was much more likely to succeed.

"He's been in there a long time, Ward," Tisala said. "Since it was first built. We left him there because it was the safest place for him—Alizon knew we'd have to wait for success, too. But it's been too long. He's not insane, but . . ." Her voice trailed off.

"Not exactly healthy, either," I finished, inwardly shuddering at the thought of spending years in the Asylum. "How long has it been?" Kellen had disappeared sometime after my father beat me stupid; I couldn't remember exactly when. But I knew it had been a long time.

"Over ten years," she said.

What I thought must have shown on my face, because she continued, "It's not as bad as what they did to you: Mostly they leave him alone. We've been looking for a safe way to get him out. Oreg said he'd try it, with your approval."

There was a plea in her voice, and I realized she was worried that I would refuse. "If Oreg can get him out, we'll do it. We can take him to Hurog if no one has a better plan. I think the dwarves will agree to transporting him to a safer place."

I swung my legs to the floor, but was taken with a fit and couldn't do anything more for a while. When I steadied enough to pay attention again, Tisala had pressed me back on the bed and was crooning to me.

"I'm fine," I said. "Would you get Oreg and bring him here?"

She looked at me, but I couldn't tell what she was thinking. After a moment she left.

I must have slept, because it seemed like I only blinked my eyes and Oreg was waiting. Tisala wasn't with him.

When he saw he had my attention, he said, "Tisala has told you of the man they want me to get out of the Asylum."

I nodded. "It needs to be done—if you can do it without risk to yourself."

"It's the risk to you I'm thinking of," he replied frankly. "If a man disappears from the Asylum the same day you get out, the king will assume you had something to do with it."

"I'm not exactly his favorite Shavigman anyway. It doesn't matter now. In the end, if we get Kellen out, the chances of my surviving to a ripe old age increase tremendously."

I waited a moment, then said reluctantly, "I hate to ask it of you, but I think it's our only chance. Alizon's rebellion needs a hero—and Kellen, as I remember him, might just be the man to pull it off."

He gave me an odd look and said, "I don't expect you to kill me again and use my bones to destroy Jakoven, Ward. Quit feeling guilty about a deed that happened centuries before you were born. You can ask anything of me without guilt. I'm old enough to refuse if I wish."

I nodded, then said, "Jakoven's found Farsonsbane."

Oreg's head snapped up and his eyes began to luminesce as they did when he was agitated. "Are you sure?"

I described it briefly, then said, "I don't know what he intends to do with it—I'm not sure really what it does. But while he had me in the Asylum he used my blood to call it to life. Something happened, but it wasn't what he expected."

Piece by piece Oreg pulled the whole story out of me. He dismissed my belief that some of the effects I thought I felt when in the Bane's presence were from the drugs they fed me.

"Blue," he exclaimed. "And the magic changed?"

I squirmed but told him, "It recognized me."

"Blue," he muttered, and rubbed his cheek absently. "I've never heard of it doing that."

"Neither had Jakoven. That's why I'm sure he'll come after me—or some Hurog, I don't suppose it matters which one of us." I had a terrible thought. "Father and his father left by-blows all over Hurog. I'm going to have to warn them."

"How did he anoint the stone with your blood?" asked Oreg. "Did he use a ceremony—"

"No," I said. "He just cut my arm, dribbled blood on a cloth, and rubbed it on the stone."

Oreg frowned and sat down beside me. "What kind of cloth? Linen, cotton, silk?"

"I don't know," I said, but I closed my eyes and tried to remember the feeling of the cloth on my cheek. "Not silk. Linen, maybe."

"Was there anything else on the cloth? Was it clean?"

"Clean," I agreed, then said, "Or it was to start with. He wiped my face with it—and I was pretty filthy."

"Sweat," murmured Oreg, then he stiffened. "Not sweat, *tears*. Tears, Ward. Did he have your tears on the cloth?"

Oreg wouldn't think the less of me—he'd known too much pain in his long life—so I admitted what any son of my father wouldn't have acknowledged to anyone else. "Yes."

"Ha," said Oreg triumphantly, rising to his feet and fisting a hand melodramatically to the ceiling. "Take that, you bastard. Ha!" He turned to me with a grin. "Bet that Jakoven forgot he'd wiped your face—or modern mages have forgotten the power of a tear."

"So what did it do?" I asked.

Oreg, still grinning, shook his head. "I have not a clue. But it will change the nature of the Bane—you said it recognized you."

I nodded. "Almost the way Hurog recognizes me when I come home."

He was quiet for a while and then said soberly, "Farson was the grandson of my half brother, did you know?"

It's one thing to know that Oreg is ancient. It's another to understand what that means. But with a little effort I managed to keep my jaw from dropping.

"He was stupid, unthinking, and angry at being part-blood dragon with nothing but a bit of magic to show for it," said Oreg. "He was the first born of Hurog who could not take on dragon form, and was obsessed with dragons because of it. Farson killed three dragons to make his toy, and bound their spirits to the blood gem for all eternity—I've always thought it was a variant of the spell that bound me to Hurog, but Farson wasn't as good a wizard as my father was. If I held that stone, I'd be worried about how tightly the spirits of the dragons were still bound into obedience." Oreg grinned nastily. "Maybe we won't have to worry about Jakoven long."

"Can you get Kellen out of the Asylum?" I asked.

Oreg nodded. "If he's not in the same section you were in, I'll be able to do it somehow. I told his man to meet us on the road near Menogue after he'd heard Kellen was out." He paused. "You know, he's going to have the same problems proving himself that you have had."

I laughed. "No. No one has ever accused Kellen of being stupid—just insane. It's not at all the same thing. A stupid ruler is much more of a problem than an insane one."

"We'll have to wait until you're fit to travel before we get him out," Oreg said. "That will give Beckram a chance to get Ciarra out of Iftahar."

"He'll have to get out more than Ciarra, Oreg," I said. "You'll have to tell Duraugh and Beckram about Kellen. Hurog is under snow by now, and it'll be a difficult place to besiege until spring. Iftahar, though, will fall to Jakoven as soon as he thinks to take it—which won't be long after he finds out Kellen has flown."

I thought a minute. "Tell them there's grain to feed a thousand people for six months at Hurog. If Duraugh thinks we need more, Beckram will have to bring it with him."

"I'll tell them," Oreg promised. "Since we're stuck here until you can travel, they'll probably beat us to Hurog. We'll have to send a messenger to Hurog and warn Stala to expect company."

"Right," I agreed. The thought of staying longer in Estian made my knees turn to water. I tried to hide my fear and come up with an alternative, but I had no greater trust in my abilities than Oreg did.

"The king will wonder if we send Beckram off by himself tomorrow," I said. "If we all leave Estian tomorrow, he won't know we've sent Beckram ahead. We can camp on Menogue instead. No one goes there, so unless Jakoven sends out someone to track us, Menogue should be safe."

Oreg's nostrils flared white even in the dim light of the room. His memories of Menogue were not fond. "What of Aethervon?"

"It was the Tamerlain who allowed me to face Jakoven without the effects of his mages' herbs. I think Aethervon will allow us refuge. The Tamerlain told me that there are a few people there now. It sounds as if Aethervon has been recruiting for some reason."

"Don't trust in the gods," said Oreg.

"No," I agreed. "I don't expect him to help fight off Jakoven, but that shouldn't be necessary. Jakoven will be planning a proper vengeance—pursuing us won't be a priority until we break Kellen out."

I yawned and Oreg shooed me back under the covers and I sent him to his own bed. I hadn't slept much since my imprisonment in the Asylum, and I was too tired to stay awake any longer.

The dream started innocuously. *I waited in a large chamber more grandiose even than the one the dwarves had devised at Hurog. My feet rested upon a deep-piled rug that covered a malachite inlaid marble floor.*

The door in front of me opened and a pale-faced Tallvenish nobleman whom I recognized vaguely from court entered and fell to one knee before me.

"Ah," I said. "So kind of you to answer my summons promptly. You told me once of a Hurog-born whore that you frequented."

"Yes, sire," he agreed. "She died a while back."

There was no servility in his voice, and I decided it might be necessary to teach him better—but for now I had a use for him. "She had a child by the old Hurogmeten."

"So she claimed, sire. The Hurogmeten certainly visited her a time or three, sire. I saw him there myself."

"A Hurog boy bred back to Hurog should concentrate the blood," I murmured to myself before turning my attention back to my informant. "How old would the child be now?"

The man looked blank for a moment. "I don't know, sire. He was ten, maybe, when I saw him last."

A boy, *I thought,* excellent. *I liked boys.*

The thoughts that accompanied my words woke me and sent me dry-heaving into the chamber pot next to the bed. I sat on the cool floor and sweat ran down my back.

Jakoven. I'd been in Jakoven's mind. Though the scent was dissipating, I could still smell the magic that had overlaid my room when I awoke. Whose magic, I could not tell, but I decided it meant that I had dreamed true. Those thoughts could not have come out of my head, not from me.

"They did not," said the Tamerlain from the corner of my room. "You dream true dreams sent by Aethervon. They are meant to aid you."

Gods, I thought, *Jakoven is after a child.*

"I owe you thanks for your help," I said, wiping my mouth with a cloth lying on a small table next to a basin of water. "And for the dreams, if I can get to the boy before Jakoven does."

She purred and rolled over like a playful kitten. "No thanks are necessary. It is we who are the debtors."

She left before I could say anything in reply, and I stared at the place where she had been. I wanted nothing more than to slink back to Hurog and hide in the snow-shielded hills until the gods called me to my rest—but I would not leave a boy to Jakoven's clutches, nor would Jakoven leave me in peace.

It was a long time before I crawled back under the covers and tried to get more sleep.

I was troubled again with dreams, but these were more normal nightmares born of the Asylum. I dreamed of terrifying monsters that attacked me over and over while I tried to hide in straw that fell away from my fingers. But a soft voice that reminded me of green apples and clean rain drove the beasts away and guarded me while I hid in safety.

I dreamed of a gem that hovered in the air above me and dripped red blood on my chest. I tried to roll away, but I was restrained on the leather-covered table. The blood became a flood drowning me, and I awoke with a gasp.

"It's safe, Ward," said Tisala's voice from the darkness of the room where I slept. She shifted uncomfortably and I made out the outline of a wooden chair set against the wall opposite my bed. "Go to sleep."

Somehow, knowing that she was there allowed me to do just that.

9

WARDWICK

Survival is not a pretty business.

I AWOKE IN A BLACK MOOD. YESTERDAY IT HAD ALL seemed so unreal, but this morning I remembered bleakly all of the humiliations of my captivity. I didn't remember everything clearly, mostly bits and pieces, but that was enough. I remembered losing control of my body in every possible way, remembered pleading with Jade Eyes both to stop and not to stop. I felt filthy and used.

Tisala slept backward on the chair, her arms folded over the back with her chin resting upon her forearms. I didn't want her to see me, somehow certain that what I'd done under Jade Eyes's hands would be written upon my flesh.

Quietly I pulled on the covers until they cloaked my miserable self. If I'd had a knife at hand, I'd have slit my own throat.

The door opened and Oreg, whose light footsteps were unmistakable, came in.

"All right, Tisala," he said. "Time for a changing of the guard. There's a bed with your name on it on the other side of the wall.

"Ouch," she said, and I heard the legs of the chair shift on the wooden floor. "Though mind you, anyone who falls asleep on guard-duty deserves to be stiff."

"Go sleep," Oreg said, and I heard from his tone that he was fond of her. "I told you I slept just across the hall, you didn't need to stay here."

"Yes, I did," she said, yawning. "He watched over me under similar circumstances."

He waited where he was until she'd shuffled out and the door shut behind her.

"All right, Ward," he said. "Time to wake up and face the day."

I took a deep breath and pulled the covers down. "Good morning," I said, trying to sound normal.

Oreg sat on the foot of the bed. "How did you sleep?"

I opened my mouth to lie and tell him I was well-rested when I remembered that at least one of the nightmares I'd had was important. "The Tamerlain was here—I don't know if I told you her part in all of this. Yesterday is a bit of a blur."

Oreg nodded. "You told all of us that she cleared your head so you could think and throw Jakoven's plans to the wolves. It was a near thing, though. I talked to the guardsman who was watching so he could summon your uncle's men if they were needed. Even as it was, he said that but for your uncle's hold on Tosten, he'd have gone for the king right there and then."

"Well," I said, not wanting to think how close I had come to getting my entire family beheaded for treason. "She visited me last night and told me that Aethervon had a gift of true dreaming for me—out of gratitude for cleansing the land, I think she said. I dreamt the king was looking for a boy, my father's son out of a Hurog-bred whore. The boy's mother is dead, but the boy would be Hurog-born from both parents."

"Can you *find* him?" Oreg asked.

I shook my head. "I just saw the king's part in this. I need to see the boy before I can *find* him with magic." An increasingly familiar feeling of weakness crept over me. "Ah, gods," I whispered before my body began to try to shake itself apart.

An extremely unpleasant interval followed. Oreg held me until it was over, then efficiently removed me to the chair, burned my clothes and the sheets, and cleaned the room. He stepped out and returned—in clean clothes, as I had managed to dirty him, too—with sheets and clothes for me. He made the bed as I dressed.

"Efficient," I said, sitting stiffly on the bed.

"You think you are the only Hurog whose body rebelled from the poisons pumped through it?" he said. "If I weren't efficient after all these years, it would be a shame. Most of them even chose to indulge in vice. Go to sleep, Ward. Duraugh has to write orders for Beckram to take to Iftahar's seneschal, so we're not leaving until later this morning. I'll have a talk with Tisala about your newest foundling. As it happens, she has a lot of contacts in Estian. If there's a young Hurog out in the streets, she'll find him."

He left and I lay back in the bed, feeling even worse than I had when I awoke. As I stared at the ceiling, Tosten opened the door, his battered lap harp in one hand.

He gave me a measuring glance. "You look worse than you did yesterday. Oreg told me you needed cheering up— and I was to come and make myself useful."

I didn't know what to say, so I said nothing.

"I see he was right." Tosten nodded. "You need to hear *The Ballad of Hurog's Dragon*, which is even now making itself popular in the taverns of Estian."

He pulled up Tisala's chair, settled himself in it, and began to play a song that purported itself to be a story a Shavig armsman was telling to a Tallvenish audience at an inn. That it was one of Tosten's own compositions was obvious to me. I knew my brother's music.

About halfway through I surged to my feet in disbelief. "He did what?"

Tosten stopped playing. "Oreg was really worried about you, Ward. It wasn't his fault. None of the horses got hurt, and he did that thing that makes people look away from him.

I bet there weren't half a dozen of the men who really got a good look at him."

"And you're singing about this in the taverns? No one is supposed to know about our dragon."

"Oh," he said. "We've done something about that. It was Tisala's suggestion, actually, and I've refined upon it a bit. Listen to the rest."

The pair of Shavigmen used their tale to lure a Tallvenish nobleman (who sounded a lot like several of Jakoven's cronies) away from his fellows and out into the woods. Whereupon the Shavigmen stripped and bound him. They gathered his possessions and clothing and took them back to the inn with a note warning him to leave a certain Shavig heiress alone or they'd spread the story of his humiliation far and wide.

I sank back onto the bed with a laugh. "Catchy tune."

Tosten looked pleased. "I thought so. I've heard several other minstrels play it—or a version of it."

"No one will ever admit to believing there are dragons at Hurog after hearing that," I said.

"That was mostly the point," agreed Tosten. "Feeling better?"

"Mostly," I said. "Thanks, Tosten."

I HAD ONE MORE SHAKING FIT THAT AFTERNOON, though it wasn't nearly as bad. Or wouldn't have been if I hadn't been on top of Feather halfway up the steep trail to Menogue. I didn't stay on top, and for a moment I thought someone was going to force poor Feather to fall on me as they tried to move her away on the precipitous slope and she slipped.

So I recovered lying directly under Feather's belly.

"Damn," I said with feeling as I rolled carefully out from under my horse. "Good girl, that's a love. Not your fault." When I was through soothing her abused pride, I remounted with Tosten's help and didn't protest as Oreg and Tosten left their mounts for others to lead and walked on either side of me.

As Feather labored up the trail, I thought that if the king's army wanted to chase us up the steep-sided, flat-topped hill (that the flatlander Tallvenish called a mountain), he was welcome to do so. Any army that climbed up to the top wasn't going to be in fighting shape when they got there.

As the Tamerlain had told me, there were a few of Aethervon's followers camped on the site of the old ruined temple. They welcomed us as we arrived on the top as if they had expected our coming.

I slept most of rest of the day. Oreg discovered several reasons he couldn't possibly rescue Kellen until the following night. Unsaid was his conviction that I needed to rest at least another day before setting off for Hurog.

WHEN THE SUN ROSE AFTER THE FIRST NIGHT WE spent on Menogue, I ate breakfast with the two young men and the old woman who were the new followers of Aethervon, and set out exploring. There was nothing else to do until darkness fell, and lying about gave me too much time to dwell upon the Asylum.

My feet took me toward the ruins of the old temple grounds. It was a path I'd walked before, and I could see the differences that the new priests had wrought in the landscape. Grass had been trimmed and flowers planted, but the wooden hut that served Menogue as its new temple was overshadowed still by the ruined walls that rose up to hide it from the sun. The crude wood structure paled in contrast to the ancient artisans' skillful carving. Some of the fallen blocks had been cleared away, leaving patches of raw earth where the stone had lain since they fell two centuries before. Strange how Oreg made me think of two centuries as recent.

I sat down in the shade of the old ruins and shivered. It would probably be snowing in the mountains of Shavig by now. Closing my eyes, I felt outward as Oreg had taught me at Hurog. I wanted to see if the magic here was as I remembered it. I reached out, touched the morning-cold walls of the old temple, and found what I sought.

It was ancient, this magic, and, unlike Hurog's, it held

memories. I saw things for which I had no explanation, battles and great victories or defeats, but many more small memories, a man holding a black stone in his hand and flinging it to crack against the bark of a tree, a woman laughing as she ate a ripe fruit. My mouth salivated and I knew the fruit was tart and juicy. Tattoos bisected my wrists and I hated them bitterly for the symbol of thievery that they were—though part of me was certain that I'd never heard of anywhere that tattooed thieves. These were the memories of the people who tended this temple in times past and shaped the magic here with the help of Aethervon, binding the magic until it would protect His temple unless Aethervon himself restrained it—as he had when it had been overrun. It was this part of the magic of Menogue that reminded me of the oily black magic that had oozed out of Farsonsbane. It had been magic without direction, yet strong and aware.

I pulled my hand away from the wall and realized that the shadow I'd sat in was gone—as was the darkness the Asylum had laid upon me. For the first time since I left Hurog, I felt at peace.

"Oreg was by a while ago," Tisala said. She was reclining on one of the massive stones that had formed the arch of the dome. Close enough to keep watch, I thought, but not so close that she'd disturb me. "He said you were 'daydreaming,' and to get him if you didn't wake up by noon." She glanced at the sun straight over our heads. "He also told me to ask you if you learned anything."

I nodded my head slowly. "I learned that sitting still all morning is not a good idea—give me a hand, would you?"

She grinned and came over to pull me to my feet. I let her work at it a while before I stood, groaning as my joints protested.

"Getting old," she pronounced with a shake of her head. "I could hear your back pop."

I laughed, and it felt good. Kissing her felt better. When I pulled back, her eyes were dark and her breathing quick.

I bent back down until my forehead rested against her hair, warm from the sun, and sweet-smelling. When I stepped back, she stared at me fiercely, as a falcon measures its prey.

"I am older than you," she said. "I am too tall, too strong, too used to having my own way. I am Oranstonian, born and bred to secretly despise Northlanders as much as we fear the Vorsag. I am scarred and plain. My nose is too big."

I waited, but that seemed to be all she had to say. "My father tried to kill me off and on until he died—that makes a person old before his time. I am taller than you, stronger, and used to getting my own way. But the trees are taller yet, and in strengths that surpass that of thew and bone, we are well-matched, I think. I'm Shavig born and bred, which makes me arrogant enough to laugh when Oranstonians try to make fun of my big horses and yellow hair. I'll match you scar for scar with some left over." I hesitated for effect, fighting to hide my exultant feelings because if I laughed I wouldn't get said the things I needed to. "So, let's see"—I ran a finger lightly over her lips—"that leaves only your last two complaints. Tisala, don't you know that there is such beauty in you that leaves men trembling? It is not the beauty of a flower in the king's gardens, but that of a tigress with sharp fangs and—"

She laughed suddenly. "Whiskers?"

I smiled. "If your nose were any smaller, it would be too small." Then I kissed her sharp, arrogant nose. "Will you marry me?"

I pulled away to look into her eyes, but she kept them closed.

She shook her head slowly. "No. You rescue people, Ward." She opened her eyes hoping, I think, to convince me of her earnestness. "You rescued me. It's natural for us to feel this connection—but it's not real. One day you'll look up and see me, and wonder where the woman who needed your protection went. Men don't marry women like me, Ward."

I started to open my mouth to argue with her, when several things occurred to me. The first was that words were not going to convince her that what I felt was real. Only time would do that. The second was that she felt something, too—both her words and her response to my kiss told me that much. Knowing she cared gave me the hope to be patient.

So I smiled at her and started back for camp.

Unless she told me to leave her alone, I would pursue her unto the ends of the earth.

KELLEN'S MAN ROSEM HAD THE LOOK OF A SOL-dier about him. Something in the way that he stood spoke of long hours in ranks and parade rests. Stala wasn't big on fancy marching, but I knew what the results looked like. He was wary of me, and unhappy at having to trust someone else to rescue Kellen: very unhappy at how we were going about it.

"Why does he have to go off alone—why can't he work the magic here?"

I shrugged, not about to tell him that Oreg intended to fly to the Asylum under the cover of night and take a good look at what spells were put on Kellen's cell. "For," as he'd said to me, "Kellen is too rich a prize to leave out with the common discards. They'll have other safeguards about him even though he's not in the wizard's wing."

"Oreg knows what he's doing, Rosem," said Tisala patiently for the third or fourth time. "Trust him."

"Do I have a choice?" he said finally. The edge of desperation clung to his tones.

"No," said Duraugh. "But Hurogs pay their debts."

"The Hurogmeten got himself out," replied Rosem.

Duraugh shrugged. "Maybe so, but you risked a lot to help us—we can do no less."

The atmosphere of Menogue after dark didn't help, I thought. If we'd been back at camp with the men, the familiar noise and bustle would have drowned out Rosem's realization that he was standing on a place reputed to be haunted. No good Tallven would have been caught dead on Menogue after dark—unless he was awaiting the rescue of his liege lord by a pack of wild-eyed Northmen.

It affected everyone. Duraugh had been careful to lean up against a tree so that nothing could sneak up behind him. Tosten stared off into the darkness of the woods as if he expected to see something there. Tisala played with the hilt of her sword.

I closed my eyes and took up a more comfortable perch
on the waist-high boulder I'd found to sit on. If something
out there meant harm to us, the Tamerlain who was curled
up, unseen, behind me would give warning.

A wind came suddenly out of nowhere, strong enough to
make the aspen saplings clatter together. Tosten half drew
his sword and turned to face the wind, but when I put my
hand on his elbow, he slid the blade back into its sheath.

"It's Oreg," I said. If Rosem thought the wind was
magic—well, dragon wings are magic, too.

The wind died abruptly and Oreg walked out of the trees
in human form. "Ward, you have to come with me."

He could have meant a dozen different places, a meadow
where he'd brought Kellen or drawn up a spell he needed
me to help power, but my gorge rose in my throat because
I knew. He wanted me to come to the Asylum.

After so long in his cell, Kellen was unlikely to trust
strangers. He needed to see someone he knew.

Rosem would have done—but that would have meant
trusting him with Hurog's secret. And I wasn't ready for the
world to realize that there were dragons still.

Tisala could do it, but I needed to face my fears.

"Very well," I said, hoping my voice didn't tremble.

"Where are you going?" asked Rosem, sharp distrust rais-
ing his voice half an octave.

"To help Oreg," I said, and strode after Oreg into the trees.

When we'd covered a sufficient distance to hide what we
did, Oreg transformed himself into the dragon. The darkness
hid him, but even in my fear I felt the familiar sense of awe
that a creature so beautiful still walked the earth.

"Up," he whispered like the rustling of the yellow and red
leaves of the autumn trees.

I had only ridden dragon-back twice before. It seemed a
highly personal thing, so I never asked, only went when he
offered. With the adrenaline of the knowledge of where we
were going adding to the excitement of such a ride, I was
afraid I was going to be sick.

I set my hand against Oreg's cool and surprisingly soft
neck scales and swarmed up his shoulder, carefully avoiding

the delicate skin of his wings. After I'd settled into the narrow grove between neck and wing, Oreg gathered himself and launched into the air.

I'd never flown at night, and the yawning darkness below worried me more than seeing tiny dots of buildings and patchworked fields had. There was something unsettling about darkness, and I was glad when we reached the city.

The first time Oreg'd taken me flying, I'd asked him about someone seeing us. He'd said that no one sees a dragon unless the dragon wants to be seen. The guards at the city gates didn't look up as we flew above them.

Estian glowed with a thousand torches as we approached. Seen from above, the confusing twists of the main streets spiraling away from the palace took on a pattern. I could see where streets had been closed off in ages past or new ones opened, but the original layout of the streets had circled a place not far from the current castle where there was an open market now.

I could see the low stone walls of the market, where children perched to eat their meat pies or baked apples in the daytime. From above the pattern of the walls looked like a three-towered keep, and I wondered how long ago it had been brought down.

Oreg swooped suddenly and brought us to ground just behind the Asylum in a small park that belonged to a wealthy merchant's house. I slipped off his back and he regained his own form.

"I'll have to transport us in," he said.

I nodded. He stepped behind me and put his hands on my shoulders. Hurog magic, dragon magic flooded me and blocked my senses from everything but its presence. When I could see again, we were in a cell in the Asylum. The smell of the place raised the hair on the back of my neck, so I concentrated on other things.

A cold crystal magelight hung suspended from the ceiling, too far away for the cell's occupant to reach it and cover the light to give himself some privacy. Guards could look through the slit in the door at any time and see the whole small cell. Abruptly I recalled that the laboratory had been lit the same way.

"Ward?" said Kellen, seated on the bench.

I turned away from the door and dropped to my knee. Oreg, I noticed, remained standing. "My lord."

Kellen came to his feet and strode over to me. I bit my lip to keep from voicing my dismay—I've seen healthier people die from starvation.

"So they did get you out."

I could hear nothing in his voice, but I wondered how it would feel to be caged for a decade and then released. A man who'd been a prisoner for so long would know how to hide fear very well, but that didn't mean he didn't feel it.

"Yes, my lord. And we have come here to free you as we should have a long time ago."

He waved away my apologies and began to pace, muttering to himself. Each moment brought the chances of drawing the attention of the guard, but I said nothing.

Finally he turned to Oreg and said, "From what Rosem told me, you must be the wizard Oreg. Can you destroy this board?" He waved his hand to the board that served him as a bench—and a gameboard. "I don't want to leave it behind."

Oreg nodded and walked over to the bench. With his knife he cut a sliver of wood and held it in his hand. He closed his fist and then wiped the dust out of his palm while the bench crumbled into a dark gray mulch.

Kellen stared at the mess as if the crude board had meant a lot to him. His breathing was heavy and I could see the pulse pounded in his throat. "I'm ready."

"I can't take you the way we came in," said Oreg. "Transporting people is nigh impossible if the person I'm carrying doesn't trust me."

"So what do you suggest?" I asked, rising to my feet since Kellen wasn't paying attention to me anymore.

"Flying." Oreg waved an arm at the stone wall between us and the outside. I could feel him draw on the fear that the Asylum's captives had impregnated in the walls. Oreg took the wordless desire of every prisoner and gave it form as the wall popped and the great stones fell to the ground below.

It was a good thing Kellen's cell was on the highest floor, I thought, looking over the edge to the ground below, otherwise Oreg might have collapsed the whole building.

The hole in the wall was more than large enough for a dragon, though Oreg had had to take out the wall next to us as well. Either the other cell was empty or its occupant had been crushed by falling stone. I gave it a closer look and felt relieved that there was no straw on the floor.

I turned back to say something to Kellen, but he was crouched in a corner as far from the broken wall as he could get. I looked at Oreg, but he shook his head and gestured for me.

My old stable master had never liked keeping horses in stalls for longer than a day or two. He told me once of a horse he'd seen who'd been kept in its stall from the moment it was born until it was ready to be trained for riding. It had taken four men to drag the horse out of its stall.

The rockfall had been loud; someone was bound to come here soon to check on Kellen.

There wasn't time to coax Kellen out. I remembered how unsettling I'd found the darkness below Oreg's wings, and I used my knife to rip a strip from the bottom of my shirt.

"Shh," I said, wrapping my makeshift blindfold around Kellen's eyes. "It's just the shock of it. Let my dragon and me get you out of here to safety and you'll be fine."

Oreg took his cue and shifted into dragon form. I heard the noises of guards in the hallways, doubtless drawn there by the sound of falling stones.

As it did with horses, the blindfold steadied Kellen. He didn't say anything when I told him of the dragon. I think he was concentrating too hard on surviving his rescue to be concerned about legendary creatures.

With my guidance, Kellen scrambled onto Oreg's back. I sat behind him to hold him on. Oreg shuffled awkwardly to the edge of the room and launched.

I thought we were going to have to land, but three quick wing-strokes had us aloft.

As we neared Menogue, I said, "Oreg, can you take us

somewhere for Kellen to recover a bit before we meet with the others?"

Oreg dipped his wings in answer. He took us to the far side of Menogue and landed in a small clearing where long-ago people had encased a small pond in stone. The clearing was surrounded by trees and lit by the full moon.

I took the blindfold off Kellen and slid down Oreg's shoulder to the ground. After a brief hesitation, Kellen followed. When we were safely dismounted, Oreg curled up and laid his great head on the ground, looking as harmless as he could.

"So Hurog has dragons," Kellen said. He was stiff with stress, but was clinging with his fingertips to sanity—I knew how that felt.

"One," I agreed.

"Where is your mage?"

I gestured to the dragon. "He is not full-blooded dragon. He tells me he's equally comfortable in either guise."

Kellen nodded slowly and gestured to the pond. "Is it safe to wash in this?"

"Yes," said the Tamerlain from the opposite side of the pool. "Welcome to Menogue, Kellen Tallven."

Kellen looked at her, then at the dragon, and abruptly laughed.

"I'm no dream," she said, catching the edge of hysteria in his merriment. "I have been here serving the kings of Tallven for a long time. The world has changed since you were bound in stone, Tallven, though most people don't know it yet. Dragons fly, the old gods stir, and mages grow in power because an old wrong has been righted."

The expression on Kellen's face was oddly blank, despite his earlier laughter.

"Go away, Tamerlain," I said, staring worriedly at Kellen. "Time enough for this later." The Tamerlain shot me an amused look and disappeared with a needlessly theatrical crack of sound. "Let's wash the stink of that place off our skins and eat before we start thinking further ahead. Oreg?"

The dragon head lifted and Oreg looked at me mildly.

"Go tell the others Kellen is safe and bring his man here—

only his man—with clean clothes, please. Take enough time
for us to bathe." If Kellen felt like I had, it would take a
while before he felt clean. I'd only been in the building for
a few minutes this time, but I felt as though the smell of that
place clung to me.

Oreg stood up, yawned, and shook himself before resum-
ing his human form. "Sounds like a good idea." He bowed
his head to Kellen once, a gesture of respect he didn't make
often, and retired into the trees.

Kellen made no move to go into the water, just stood staring at me as if he didn't know what to do. Or as if he didn't
trust me. I don't suppose being locked in a cell by my own
brother would have made me very trusting, either.

"Rosem's coming soon," I said. "You can wait for him if
you want—but I'm not." I pulled off my clothes and walked
into the pool.

It was not cold, as the water in such a pool should have
been, but lukewarm. I felt no particular welling of magic
here, so it must have been fed by underground hot springs.
In the dark it was hard to tell how deep it was going to be,
but I needn't have worried, for the drop-off was gentle when
it came. I swam away from Kellen, letting him decide to
follow or not. After a few minutes there was a splash from
that end of the pool, so I supposed he had.

When I heard nothing more I swam back to Kellen.

He stood waist-deep in the warm water and trembled.

"Do you know," he said, watching his shaking fingers, "I
hated Aethervon as much as ever I hated my brother for
locking me away in the Asylum. If it hadn't been for the
vision Aethervon gifted Jakoven's mage with, my brother
would have just killed me."

He was ready to break, and maybe he needed to pour out
what he was feeling to someone. But if he broke now, he
might not be able to put himself back together again. Wait,
I wanted to urge him, wait until a little time has made you
something more than a boy who has no more past than a cell
in the dark. I wished for Beckram's clever tongue, but had
to make do with my own.

"I'm pretty ambivalent on Aethervon, myself," I said, ignoring the agitated state Kellen was in. "Last time I was here, he took over my sister without so much as a by-your-leave or 'excuse me,' and used her to babble prophecy that was not even very helpful."

"If I had told you more, you wouldn't have done as you were needed to," said a soft, sexless voice.

I looked around and noticed the old woman who was one of Aethervon's people, sitting on a rock—but I had no doubt that the voice belonged to a god rather than an old woman.

"So why did you say anything at all?" I asked.

"Because my prophecy was not unsought." As before, the voice changed from moment to moment. "I am sworn, so long as mankind seek me here, to tell them somewhat of the future."

"Who sought prophecy and gave you a chance to meddle in my business?" I asked.

The old woman's mouth smiled, though her eyes remained blank. "Meddle? I suppose that is as good a word as any." The sound of the young girl's voice in the old woman's mouth made the hair on the back of my neck rise. "Your dragon worried that you were not as he believed. He asked for my wisdom and then flinched at the cost. I gave you the opportunity to break through the barriers that had been placed between you and your magic."

I was Shavigborn and served no gods but Siphern, He whose justice ruled the Northlands. Though Aethervon was being helpful now, I didn't like Him.

My lip curled. "You used Oreg's wishes to punish him. He asked for reassurance and you took my sister, whom he was sworn to protect, forcing him to endure the pain of his broken oath. Oreg had enough pain, you didn't need to give him more."

"It reminded him who he was—your slave and not your master."

"Oreg belongs to no one," I snapped. "And never should have."

The god's voice was a deep rumble, larger than the old woman. He sounded irritated. "Oreg is yours as much as Hurog is yours. If he had not been reminded of it, your will

would have bowed before his as the sapling bows before an
ancient wind, and the evil that twisted the world would yet
remain."

"You play games with people's lives," I said, remembering
my sister's eyes, blank like the old woman's, and Oreg writhing on the ground at the base of the stone wall she'd stood
upon. "You forget that they are fragile."

The god laughed, soft as thistledown in the night, and
answered me with the rich velvet of a whore's trained voice.
"Fragile does not describe you, Guardian of the Dragon.
Thrice forged in fire you are and the stronger for it—as is
the king who shall be. As the boy he was, he had no chance
of outfacing his brother. But with the strength of his forging
at Jakoven's hands, he shall carve a path through the bodies
of his foes—or shatter like a blade that has been hardened
too much."

The woman got up and bowed shallowly, as Stala taught
me to bow to my opponents. Then she turned and disappeared into the foliage.

I swore and then turned to Kellen. "Do you see what I
mean? Siphern save me from the whims of Tallvenish gods."

Kellen gave me a wry smile touched with real amusement.
"I don't feel strong," he said. "But, unlike you, I'm not in
the habit of arguing with the gods. So I'll wash up and see
if I feel better in the morning."

That's it, I thought. *Give yourself time to reinvent yourself.
And if that fails, do it again.* Just like I had.

Just as I was.

Resolutely I pushed back the sick, formless fear that
welled up from my time in the Asylum.

"My lord," I said. "I'd appreciate it if you would keep my
dragon a secret for now. Hurog's already had one power-
mad man attack us hoping to find dragon bones—no telling
what they would do to find a real dragon."

Kellen raised an eyebrow, but nodded. When he had
scrubbed as well as he could, he put his head low in the
water and began swimming. I kept a watchful eye on him
because he was in no condition to do much, but he stopped

after one lap when Rosen and Oreg, carrying clothes and toweling, entered the clearing.

I dried quickly and dressed, leaving Kellen with his man. It looked as though they had a lot to talk about. Menogue wasn't so big that they'd have trouble finding the rest of us when they were ready.

Late as it was, there were few people sleeping at camp. The story of what we were attempting had traveled through our men and sponsored a great deal of discussion, though no dissent. King Jakoven was not much liked among our men since Erdrick had died at his hands. My own capture, it seemed, had cemented the feeling.

When I approached the central fire where Duraugh was holding court, Tisala brought me a cup of tea. She ran her eye over me as if to make sure I wasn't missing any parts, and then strode back to the fire without saying a word.

Kellen and Rosem came not long after I did. Dressed and clean, Kellen looked better, but my uncle made sure that he had a wooden platter of travel bread and cheese as soon as he sat down.

"So you think Hurog is the best place to store me?" Kellen asked. Obviously Rosem hadn't wasted any time when I'd left them.

My uncle nodded. "Even if Jakoven knows that we're the ones who got you out, he'll expect us to take you to my own Iftahar or to one of the Oranstonian lords who are supporting your uncle."

"I've seen to it that Alizon knows where we take you," Rosem said. "He'll probably be there before us."

Kellen's eyebrows lowered as he stared at Rosem. "I may go to Hurog, Rosem. Indeed, it sounds as if, for the moment, that would be for the best. But if I go, it is not because I have been taken there." The frightened prisoner shaking in the water had given way to a man who had been raised as royalty.

Forged indeed, I thought, pleased.

"There are problems with Hurog," said Tosten. "You ought to know that the keep is in the process of being rebuilt.

If the king discovers where you are, the walls will not hold
him out."

Or at least the gates won't, I thought, remembering how
little time it had taken Jakoven's men to open them.

Suddenly Kellen smiled. "I have to admit that part of the
reason I'm inclined to go to Hurog is to see it for myself."
He turned to me. "Rosem kept me informed about things,
and I heard much of what happened when you brought the
walls down on the Vorsag."

"If we can manage it," said Duraugh slowly, "we can pull
a lot of the lords of Shavig behind your standard while you
are at Hurog. If the Hurogmeten follows you, they will as
well."

"You assume I want the throne, then?" Kellen said, a hint
of bitterness in his voice.

Everyone froze—even Tisala, who'd been staying out of
the conversation by sipping her tea, halted mid-sip.

"No," I replied sharply, when it appeared no one else
would. "We assume that you will do as you were born to
do: protect your people as Jakoven has failed to do. But if
your time in the Asylum has rendered you unfit to rule, I
would rather you stop now than continue what your brother
has begun."

Oreg stared into the night, smiling at nothing.

Rosem put his hand on his sword and would have stepped
between us had not Kellen put a hand on Rosem's shoulder.
"Peace, old friend, he's right." Kellen nodded respectfully to
me. "Locked up in a cell," he said, "it's too easy to forget
what I have been fighting for. I want everyone here to understand what that means, though. Rather than injustice, there
will be war. Civil war. Brother fighting against brother." He
gave an elegant hand movement that asked us to include
himself in his last statement. "The ties that bind us together
might be ruined forever, leaving the Five Kingdoms broken
before her enemy's sword. And, from what Alizon's letters
and messages have told me, we probably will not win. Make
certain before we start what cannot be undone that Jakoven's
sins are such that they are worth the cost you will pay."

I shrugged my shoulders and said before my uncle could

speak, "Jakoven has declared war upon Hurog and we must fight. With your banner before us, we have hope of winning; otherwise we fail. I would rather fight a war for my rightful king than a war for survival. But for Lord Duraugh, Tosten, Beckram, my sister, myself, or any who have the blood of Hurog strongly in their veins, we have no choice." I opened my mouth to tell them why, but Oreg got there first. Just as well, because my slow tongue was making my audience restless.

"The cost of doing nothing may be higher yet. Jakoven seeks to bring upon us a cataclysm as bad or worse than the one that destroyed the first empire." Oreg's voice was full of the mysteries of the ages. He could do that when he wanted to, pull the cloak of his years around him until the weight of time beat upon his audience like a mallet. "He has been trying to pull the secrets of the Imperial mages out, and he dabbles in things he knows nothing about. Farsonsbane destroyed civilization on this continent until the people deserted their cities for the wastelands. For nine and a half centuries the Bane was hidden, but Jakoven has found it again. If he lives long enough to unlock its secrets, we'll wish the Vorsag had invaded and sold us all as slaves."

Oh good, I thought, glancing around at the faces reflected in the firelight. *They really needed something more to be frightened of.*

"He doesn't know how to use it yet," I said. "But he's convinced that the answer lies in the blood of Hurog. So you see that it is not some notion that you are the rightful king that sways Hurog to your support. Nothing so tenuous as honor or the belief in a cause. Hurog fights for survival— which makes us your staunchest supporters."

Kellen smiled at me. "Your sword will cut my enemies as well as any zealot's. I just wish I had a hundred more lords with cause to fear Jakoven."

"Ward can bring you most of Shavig and a fair portion of Oranstone," offered my uncle with unfounded confidence.

Kellen looked at Duraugh with interest. I looked at him with disbelief.

"Shavigmen have long memories," Duraugh said. "They

fought against Oranstone in the Rebellion because Fen, Ward's father, fought. Most of them will fight shoulder to shoulder with Ward because he is the Hurogmeten—and because no Shavigman worth his salt ever turned down a good fight."

"Myth," I contradicted Duraugh flatly. It was dangerous to allow Kellen to believe that. "Shavigmen are men like anyone else. They fight when they have to and are not about to follow a callow boy blindly. You've been to the same Shavig council meetings I have."

Tosten smiled blindingly and laughed. "When you hear respectful tones from a Shavig lord, it's time to run," he quoted smugly. "Ward, don't you know you've given Shavig a hero for the first time since old Seleg died and the dragons died with him."

"Hero?" I choked. "If Orviden calls me a puppy one more time, I just might bite him."

Kellen stared at me for a moment. "The council meets, I believe, next month. Can you get them all together sooner?"

"You are well-informed," said my uncle approvingly. "But my son Beckram and Ward's sister, Ciarra, just had a new baby girl, the first of her generation. Reason enough to hold an informal celebration at Hurog."

"Fine," I said. "To celebrate my niece's birth I'll see to it that the lords of Shavig attend. If they understand what Jakoven holds, they'll see that they have no choice."

Rosem said, "Alizon has the support of most of Oranstone—but they are tired of warfare there. Things are better since the Vorsag were driven out, but there are still many Oranstonian lords who have very little power over their own lands."

"Avinhelle is behind Jakoven," said Tisala. "But there are a few men I believe will support Kellen where they haven't supported Alizon." She turned to Kellen. "Remember, we haven't told them that we intend to put you on the throne rather than Alizon, yet. Seaford will split, I think, from what my people have overheard. And there are several powerful Oranstonian lords who are making noises of support for Alizon, but may not support Kellen."

Kellen raised his cup to me and said, "May we all outlive this year."

Soberly cups were raised and drunk.

I DREAMT I WAS BACK AT THE ASYLUM THAT NIGHT, but fortunately I woke up before I woke anyone else. The camp was quiet when I got up and went for a walk.

When I got to the broken wall that looked out over Estian, Tisala was already there.

"What keeps you up so late?" I asked, careful to keep my face in the deeper shadow so she couldn't see the remnants of my nightmare there.

She glanced at me, and then returned her gaze to the city below us. She shook her head. "Have you ever felt like you've stepped into someone else's story?"

"No," I said, intrigued. "Whose story have you stumbled into?"

"I'm not sure right now. Kellen's? Oreg's? Yours?" She looked at her hands where they lay on a broken stone block, capable hands that could wield a sword with rare skill.

But she wasn't seeing what I did. She was looking at her left hand. The scarring was bad—even in the dim light of stars and moon I could see that.

I took her hand in mine; it was damp and tasted salty when I kissed it. I didn't think she'd been sitting in the dark sweating.

"It took something away, didn't it," I said to her tear-wet hand. "I didn't really understand before."

"What did? What didn't you understand?" she asked, trying to get her hand back.

I held on tighter. "Being strapped down while someone hurts you. Being helpless. Even out of the walls of that cell, I'm not free of the Asylum—any more than the torturer's death freed you of his tormenting."

She stopped struggling and stared at my face. Finally she reached up and touched my cheek, tracing the path of my tears, invisible in the darkness.

After a moment she turned back to look at the lights.

"It makes you feel filthy and small," I said, then laughed painfully. "I'm not used to feeling small."

"And guilty," she whispered. "As if you should have been able to stop it like the hero in one of Tosten's songs."

Her damaged hand gripped mine and the strength of that grasp was a testimony to Oreg's healing skills. Together we watched the night and felt a little better for each other's company.

WHEN I SLEPT AT LAST, I DREAMT I WAS SMALL WITH dirty hands and ragged clothes. Hunger spurred me to dig through the trash that covered the cobbled alleyway, hoping that there was some scrap of dry bread that the rats and wild dogs had left behind. I was so intent on my quest that I didn't hear them until a large hand grasped the back of my neck.

They dragged me kicking and screaming before a harsh-faced man who said, "Purple eyes. This is the one."

I awoke in the early hours of the morning and used the dream to *find* my brother.

10
GARRANON IN ESTIAN

Only as adults do we understand our childhood.

THE SKY WAS YET DARK WHEN GARRANON AROSE from his temporary quarters, walked the corridors of the castle, and entered the rooms that had been his since he first came to Estian. His things had been moved out yesterday at the king's orders—Jakoven thought they'd been placed in a different suite, but Garranon had sent them home to Oranstone.

The malachite floors gleamed in the light of the torch he carried from the corridor. The floor was older than the walls, one of the few things Jakoven had left when he rebuilt the castle. Green, thought Garranon, green for the king's favorite, the color of Oranstonian whores plying their trade. Appropriate.

The king had dismissed him from these rooms, the rooms that belonged to the king's whore.

All alone in the suite that had been his, Garranon closed his eyes. He was so tired. For two decades Garranon had been hostage for his brother, for his homeland, and now he'd outlived his usefulness. When the time was right he would

retreat to his home like Haverness had, and not return to
court. Surely the king would allow him that, after all these
years.

He felt hollow and useless. All of the sacrifices he'd made
had ended at nothing. He was no longer of importance to the
king, and because of it he was no longer of importance to
Oranstone.

The suite where he'd lived for the past two decades felt
curiously abandoned without his things. Garranon supposed
he ought to open drawers and wardrobes to make sure the
castle servants had gotten everything, but instead he wandered from one room to the next watching the flickering
torchlight reflect in the polished floors.

The king had found a new favorite. Someone more important to him than Jade Eyes—who had been as much a
weapon to be used against Garranon as he had been a serious
rival for the position of king's favorite. The king had been
very angry with Garranon for choosing to fight for Oranstone
after Jakoven had determined that Oranstone should fall to
the Vorsag before he mounted a defense. That Haverness's
Hundred had managed to throw back the invasion had rubbed
the king's wounded pride with salt.

Jade Eyes had been a punishment for Garranon and a
warning. This new favorite was something else—Jade Eyes
had not been triumphant when he'd delivered the message
for Garranon to vacate his apartment.

Garranon's reign as the king's favorite was ended, and
with it any hope he held to help his people. Not that he'd
been able to do much these past few years. It was time to
go home and leave Jakoven to his new plaything.

Why did that hurt?

He touched an embroidered couch absently and a memory
came to him. He'd been in the garden chatting quietly with
the queen, so it must have been before the young Hurog's
death a few years ago had driven her to living in solitude on
her family estates.

A servant had dropped a tray of food, distracting him from
his conversation. When he'd looked up his eye caught the
face of one of the lesser nobles, a man he'd seen any number

of times over the years, and for an instant Garranon was once again a terrified young boy being raped in the remains of his mother's gardens and the insignificant Avinhellish nobleman was holding his wrists.

Unable to deal with the unexpected memory, Garranon had turned without a word and retreated to this embroidered couch. He hadn't noticed the king in the garden, but Jakoven had followed him only a few moments later.

At the king's insistence, Garranon had, haltingly, told him what happened that long ago day while the king held him until he was finished. Their lovemaking that night had been sweet and gentle.

Garranon jerked his hand away from the couch as if it had burned him.

Garranon hated Jakoven. He knew he did. Had hated Jakoven secretly since he'd been brought to the king's bedroom as a terrified boy. Hated him more every time he went home to Oranstone and then was forced to leave his wife, his child, and his lands again to serve in the king's bedchamber.

Garranon lay on the bed, which was made up with unfamiliar ticks and bedcovers, and stared at the painted ceiling two stories above the floor.

It was only pride, he told himself. Oranstone would survive without him to soften the king's orders, but it was natural to fret that it could not survive without him. He would not miss Jakoven. His hands clenched in fists.

When the bed sank underneath the weight of another occupant, he put out his hand to pet the soft pelt of the Tamerlain without looking away from the star-and-moon-covered ceiling.

"Thank you for helping Ward," he said. "He was magnificent—I thought Jade Eyes would drop dead of flouted spite."

She purred and rubbed her broad face against his shoulder before settling against him. "What troubles you?"

He laughed without humor. "I do." He rubbed his hand over the unfamiliar coverlet. To her he could say what he could not admit to himself. "I hate him, so why does leaving him hurt so much?"

She was quiet for a minute and then said, "You've been Jakoven's lover for twenty years."

"Nineteen."

"More than half your life. It should feel strange to leave it behind."

He smiled at her.

"Perhaps," she said slowly, "you need to find out who he is putting in these rooms. It might help you either way. Yes, I think that might be a good idea."

The Tamerlain rolled off the bed and said, "Come."

She led him through the familiar passage between his rooms and the king's, stopping before the panels of wood that opened into the king's chambers.

"Shh—they won't see us, but noise is harder to mask," she said, and huffed at the panel, which shimmered and then dissolved before her. When she stepped forward, Garranon followed.

The passage opened into the king's receiving room. The only furniture it contained was the king's chair, which sat on a dais so the king, when he was seated, was the same height as a standing man.

Jakoven sat in his chair, while Jade Eyes, wearing only a sea-blue night wrap, leaned against it. On the strip of carpet in front of the dais, a guardsman held a struggling boy. All were apparently unaware that Garranon and the Tamerlain were watching them.

The child was tidy, but there was only so much soap and water could do to the dirt of years. His skin was gray and his hair was so neatly trimmed it had to have just been done. It was cut almost to his scalp—most likely to get rid of the pests that infested the lower population of Estian. Hunger gave him the face of a much older person, though Garranon reckoned his age to be around ten or twelve.

He hadn't felt as young as this boy looked when he was twelve, and one of the king's soldiers had presented him and his younger brother to the king in a scene very similar to this one.

"Hold him still," ordered Jakoven. The excited tremolo in his voice brought Garranon to alert as the guardsman wrapped an arm around the boy and gripped his jaw, forcing the boy to stare at the king.

"Hurog blue," said the king, satisfaction in his tone. "Your lord will be rewarded as I promised. Jade Eyes, take the boy for me."

The king's mage took the boy ungently by the arm and the guardsman left. The boy jerked once, then cried out and went still when Jade Eyes shifted his grip.

"A little scrawny, isn't he?" said Jade Eyes distastefully.

"We'll feed him up," said Jakoven, leaving his chair.

"Boy," he said in a velvet tone as familiar to Garranon as his own voice. "Give me your name."

"Won't," said the boy, spitting on the floor.

Jakoven smiled and touched the boy's thin cheek. Garranon saw nothing, but Jade Eyes dropped his hands and stepped away.

Magic, thought Garranon.

The boy stood still, held captive by the touch of Jakoven's finger. His face was blank and empty.

Vekke's breath, thought Garranon. He remembered that, remembered the king holding him with nothing more than his touch. He hadn't realized it was magic Jakoven had used. Not until he saw the king use it on another boy.

"Give me your name, boy."

"Tychis." His consonants were thick with the accents of the Estian slums.

"Who was your mother?"

"Illeya of Hurog."

"Do you know your father?"

The boy's body began to vibrate with tension, shaking as he fought not to answer. "Fenwick of Hurog."

"What relation was he to your mother."

Tears spilled down the boy's face. "My mother was his uncle's get."

Jade Eyes lip curled in contempt. Jakoven saw it and smiled. "It may be incest here, but in Shavig, next cousins often marry if there is no weakness in the family. The old bastard probably saw nothing wrong in sleeping with his cousin—and he left us this boy with the blood of dragons running through his veins from both sides. It wasn't strong enough in the young Hurogmeten—that's why the Bane only turned blue instead of red. I think this boy's blood is the key to loosing Farsonsbane."

The king smiled pleasantly at Jade Eyes and shook his head. "You will not allow your attitude over his parentage to trouble this boy."

Jade Eyes read the king's tone as well as Garranon did and nodded obediently. Jakoven turned his attention back to the boy.

"Tychis, you will be loyal to me above all else and serve me."

"I will be loyal," said the boy dully.

"Some things that are done to you, you will hate. Others may give you pleasure. But you will serve me and do as I command."

"I serve you."

Gods, oh gods. Garranon found the memory of those words in his soul. *How long have I followed those commands? Do I still?*

The king pulled his hand away. "Take him into the green rooms, Jade Eyes. Go with him, boy, you'll find a bed there. Sleep until I awake you."

Garranon glanced at the passage doors behind him to see that the passageway looked as solid as if the Tamerlain had never dismissed it. He stood to the side as Jade Eyes and the boy walked past him, opened the door, and entered the short passage without seeing Garranon or the Tamerlain, though Garranon could have reached out and touched Jade Eyes's robe.

"I've only been able to get that spell to work on a dog," commented Jade Eyes, returning to the audience chamber without the boy. He closed the door to the passage behind him. "I quit using it because the dog's devotion became so annoying, I had to kill it."

Jakoven smiled. "You'll notice I didn't tell him to love me. Hatred is so much more entertaining."

Garranon stared at Jakoven and knew that the king meant him. And that knowledge took his understanding of the whole of his life and twisted it. He didn't hear what else Jakoven and Jade Eyes said before they entered the king's private chambers, closing the door behind them.

"Garranon," said the Tamerlain impatiently, though softly, so her voice didn't carry into the room beyond.

He turned to her.

She said, "The spell isn't as strong as he thinks it is. It would not hold an adult as it does a child who is weak and frightened—or hurt as you were. But the remnants of the spell might make you sad at leaving his service, even after all this time."

Garranon thought of his most terrible secret and shuddered. "Did I tell him anything—is that why Callis fell?"

"He didn't ask for information from you," she said. "You told him nothing because he asked nothing of you. The concept of using children as messengers never occurred to the Tallvenish. Oranstone simply never had a chance against the armies Jakoven's father brought against it."

Garranon nodded and went through the passageway that led to his former rooms. The boy slept on top of the covers, his face peaceful.

"What will you do?" asked the Tamerlain.

"How long was I in thrall to Jakoven?" Garranon asked.

"Four years," she said. "Almost five."

He deliberately stared at the boy, because the answers to the next questions mattered greatly to him, and he didn't want her to know how much.

"You heard what the king wants him for?" she asked. "Jakoven has found Farsonsbane and, in this child's Hurog blood, he has found the key to using it."

"Farsonsbane?" Garranon stared at her a moment. "I suppose my part in your game is to rescue the boy and take him to his brethren. Tell me, what about this spell of Jakoven's?"

There was a pause before the Tamerlain answered. "I can break it."

"You could have freed me?"

She didn't answer.

He turned on his heels to look at her. "Do you think that I have survived this long in court not to realize when I've been manipulated?" he asked bitterly, her betrayal worse than the knowledge that he'd been the king's puppet everyone had always thought him. For nineteen years she had been his only friend, his only confidant. "How kind of you to show me, after all these years, that the king held me in thrall. I assume you will break the king's spell so I don't have to drag this child kicking and screaming all the way to Hurog?"

The Tamerlain stepped back. "It would be better to wait until you're on the trail. He won't be safe in Estian, and given a chance, he'd try and run. He'll sleep until I break the sleep spell the king laid on him as well." She hesitated. "I would have taken the magic off you, but Jakoven would have noticed. It would not have helped you, and Aethervon is limited in how much he can do that is contrary to the king's wishes."

It might have been the truth. Garranon shrugged. "It doesn't matter now. We have no time for this if I'm to get him out of the castle before everyone is awake."

He wanted to ask her if she understood what this task she'd given him meant to his estate and to his wife and son. The king would know who took the boy away as soon as he noticed that Garranon was gone as well. But it wouldn't matter to her, and his wife would not thank him if he left this child at risk because Garranon was afraid for her and for Buril, his home.

The boy didn't awaken when Garranon picked him up and carried him back through the rooms that had once been his.

Garranon traveled the servant corridors. When he passed a few maids, they curtsied to him and averted their eyes from the boy. Garranon had removed a number of children from the play of the higher nobles, and the servants wouldn't go out of their way to report him until they learned whose bed he'd removed this one from.

A stable boy brought his horse without comment, its saddlebags already filled for the journey to Oranstone he'd planned on making tomorrow. When he asked, they brought a second horse for the boy when he awoke.

The stable master held the sleeping boy until Garranon was mounted, then handed him up.

"Poor little tyke," said the master. "He'll be lucky if they haven't drugged him to his death, as fast as he's sleeping."

Garranon nodded; it wasn't necessary that the stable master know that it was magic, not narcotics, that kept the boy quiet. Although his own mare was well used to the company of the Tamerlain, the second mount snorted and sidled when he was led up for Garranon to take the reins.

The stable master frowned. "I'll ride with ye for a bit, if ye need a spare hand. I have an aunt in the south who could take a turn for the worse at any moment."

Garranon settled his burden in front of him and organized his hands until he could control both horses, then shook his head. "Best if you are not caught up in this any further. I'm not sure I'll survive this one with my head on my shoulders."

"Jade Eyes," said the stable master firmly. "He's evil, he is. Don't see what the king sees in him."

Garranon gave him a faint smile and walked his horses out of the stable. The guards at the entry towers opened the gates without challenging him—as they had on other such occasions. Garranon nodded at them and hoped no one would suffer for the ease of his departure. The Tamerlain kept her distance and didn't speak until they were out of the city.

"There's no need to travel all the way to Hurog," she said. "The Hurogmeten has been camped at Menogue since he left Estian, to give him time to recover from his imprisonment. Aethervon gave him dreams so he would know to look for the boy."

Without a word, Garranon turned his horse's head down the less traveled way leading to the old temple.

"It doesn't matter where you go," she said. "He's a Finder. He'll locate you."

On the tail of her words a red mare cantered into view bearing Ward of Hurog—looking much better than he had when he'd confronted the king in court. When he saw Garranon, he stopped and waited for the Shavigman to approach.

"Hurogmeten," acknowledged Garranon. "I have a gift for you—I believe he's your half brother. He calls himself Tychis."

The big red mare flared her nostrils at his horse and ignored the Tamerlain. Ward rode close and touched the sleeping face with a look of relief.

"That's two my house owes yours," he said.

Garranon shook his head. "I think the debt still lies in the other direction. My actions have hurt you more than I've been able to help. Take him." He glanced down at the Tamerlain, but he couldn't tell if Ward could see her, so he said, "I think he'll wake in a little bit," rather than explain her part in the boy's recovery. Even now he protected her secrets. "He might be a little disoriented and a lot hostile, but you need to get him away from Estian."

"He is my brother," answered Ward peacefully. "My brother Tychis. He belongs at Hurog." He looked at Garranon a moment, and the Oranstonian had trouble seeing behind the affable mask to the thoughts running through the Hurogmeten's head.

"How stands your favor with the king?"

Garranon shrugged. "About as high as any man who might accuse Jakoven of being a pedophile. No. Lower than that, since I stole the boy who would be instrumental—I don't want to know how—in allowing Jakoven to use Farsonsbane."

Ward didn't flinch, so Garranon knew that the Hurogmeten knew about the Bane.

"About where I do, then," said Ward. He watched Garranon for moment and asked softly, "How stands the king in your favor?"

Garranon looked away. "As always," he managed finally. "You'd better take him and ride—I have an extra horse for him. I don't know when the king'll think to send someone to find him. You may have half a day, maybe only half an hour."

Ward shrugged and said, "What would you do if you had a knife and found the king asleep in a back alley with no witnesses?"

Garranon didn't answer, but Ward smiled, and rode his horse around to take the reins of the extra gelding, leaving the boy in Garranon's arms.

"Then come with us to Hurog," he said. "It'll confuse the

king a bit—I imagine he'll expect to find you on your way
home to Buril. But the king won't hurt them until he has you
where he wants you. They'll be safer if you're not there.

"So come with us," Ward said again. "And on the way I'll
try to show you why your fate—and mine—might not be as
black as you think. Dark, yes. But not hopeless."

"Go," said the Tamerlain, and Ward glanced down at her.

Garranon looked at her a moment, too, then started his
horse in the direction Ward had been riding.

11
WARD

Home heals the heart.

I WATCHED GARRANON CLOSELY AS HE LOOKED AT THE packed camp, glanced through the faces, and drew in a shocked breath when he saw Jakoven's brother. "Kellen?"

As I dismounted I watched expressions run across Kellen's face too fast for me to interpret, but the one that stayed was sheer pleasure.

Garranon's eyebrows rose and he turned to me and said with mock awe, "And I thought Jakoven was going to come after *me* with branding irons and skinning knives. All I stole was his new play toy—you took his brother."

Kellen had taken a few steps forward, but stopped cautiously at Garranon's words.

Garranon shook his head and grinned. "I thought the king might have bitten off more than he could chew when he attacked the Hurogs—but I didn't dream this big." He dismounted without disturbing his burden and handed the boy to me. "What are your plans, Kellen? Are you going to run from Jakoven and hide in the wilds of the north?" There was nothing but curiosity in Garranon's voice.

I looked down into my half brother's sleeping face and wished I'd known about him sooner—and that the only reason to keep him at Hurog *was* that he was my brother. It would have made his absorption into the Hurog household easier on everyone. I noticed also that there was a bandage around his wrist, and I worried about how much blood Jakoven had already taken from him.

Kellen said, "I plan on dethroning Jakoven and becoming king in his stead."

Garranon stretched his neck, first one way, then the other. I was standing close enough to hear the cracking of his spine. Then he stepped forward and fell to his knees before Kellen in a graceful, humble gesture.

"I am your man," he said.

Kellen looked momentarily taken aback, glancing at Rosem, then Tisala before pulling a regal air out from somewhere and cloaking himself in it.

"Arise, I ask no one to humble himself so before me until I hold the throne."

Garranon stood and took a good look at Kellen. "You could use a few hundred meals, my friend. But you still look much better than the last time I saw you."

Kellen glanced about. "Garranon comes—came once a week to visit me, in spite of Jakoven's disapproval. We played chess."

I remembered that all-important chessboard Oreg had destroyed, and smiled as I laid the boy on the ground. I caught Oreg's eye and he came over to check on the sleeping child. I'd begun to worry about what Tychis had been given to make him sleep this deeply. Whatever they'd done to him, I hoped Oreg could rectify it.

"Allow me," said the Tamerlain, appearing on the other side of the boy. "I know what was laid upon him, so it'll be easier for me to break it."

I felt her power rise and cover the boy, but I couldn't tell exactly what she did. The results, however, were obvious. The boy rolled to his feet, the whites of his eyes showing as he looked around them. Then, sprouting appalling Tallvenish gutterspeak that effectively stopped Kellen and Garranon's conversation and directed the attention of most of the people in the vicinity toward him, he reached down and grabbed a chunk of rock in his hand.

"Impressive," I said dryly in Tallvenish—which we'd been speaking out of courtesy to Kellen anyway. As I remembered from before his imprisonment, he could get by in the Shavig tongue, but was more comfortable in Tallvenish. "What do you think happens after you've hit one of us with the rock— assuming you can throw it hard enough to matter?"

He stopped swearing and glanced fearfully from me to Oreg and on to the rest of the men (Tisala was some distance away saddling a horse) who were watching him. A couple of them stepped forward, hands on their swords.

I shooed them with a wave of my hand. "Finish packing camp. I need a little time to explain matters to my brother here." I said it first in Shavig, for the men, and then again in Tallvenish for the boy.

Turning back to Tychis, I nodded my head in greeting. "I am Ward of Hurog—your half brother. Next to me is my mage, Oreg—also a relative of sort. Your uncle Duraugh and Tosten—another of your half brothers—are over there. Tosten is the one over by that oak with his hand on his sword. Duraugh is that one," I said, pointing behind Kellen, "the one frowning at me."

"I'm not your brother," Tychis said fiercely in broken Shavig. Then he repeated it, with a few more filthy words, mostly adjectival, in Tallvenish.

I shook my head sadly and settled myself on the ground where I was on more of a level with him, not so threatening. "I'm sorry if it pains you—but your father was Fenwick of Hurog, as was mine. You've half a dozen other half siblings in Hurog. Some of them, I'm sure, won't be all that you could wish for, either."

The rock was getting heavier; I could see his hand droop. Neither Oreg nor I gave him reason to throw. I was safely distanced by being on the ground, Oreg leaned negligently against a trio of sapling aspens. Everyone else was farther away. The Tamerlain, I noticed, had disappeared somewhere.

"You might as well drop the rock," said Oreg. "He'll sit

here all day until you do." He caught the boy's eyes. "If you don't believe in futility, you might as well give up the hostility, too. It's as easy to stay angry with a puppy as it is to be angry at Ward. Ask Tosten someday if you don't believe me."

The rock dropped at last, and the tough front cracked a bit as tears welled in the boy's eyes. "What do you want with me?"

I sat up and pinned him with my eyes. "I want you to be safe. I want to bring you back with me to Hurog—as my father should have."

"I'm a bastard. The son of a whore and your father," he spat, then added the bit he certainly seemed to think damning. "And the whore was your father's cousin."

Oreg made tisking sounds with his tongue. "The Tallvens have certainly done a job on you, haven't they. In Shavig, cousins marry all the time." That was overstating matters, but for a good cause. "Duraugh's son is married to Ward's sister—your sister, too—and no one thought a thing about it."

Tychis begun to look faintly alarmed—which was better than the fearful defiance he'd displayed before.

"No one says you have to marry a cousin," I soothed. "But you do have to be polite around Beckram and Ciarra—that I will insist upon." Since politeness was the last thing he was worried about, it succeeded in distracting him.

"Do you know how to ride a horse?" I asked, changing the ground under him.

He shook his head. I stood up and held out a hand. "Well then, come and meet your mount and I'll get you started. By the end of this trip, no one will ever know you weren't born in the saddle."

The bait was too great. Soon he was sitting on a bay gelding, newly named Death-Bringer. I'd given Tychis several choices of names. From the size of the horse's barrel I'd have called him Hay-Mower. But Death-Bringer pleased the boy, and the height of the horse gave him the illusion of safety.

As I was coaching Tychis in the proper manner to sit (preferably on top of the horse), steer (mostly let him follow everyone else), and stop (pull back), my uncle, who'd been in an animated conversation with Kellen and Garranon, gestured to me. I handed Death-Bringer's reins to Oreg and joined the discussion.

"Garranon says it's possible that Jakoven will launch an attack on Hurog immediately," said Duraugh. "Is it really safe to bring Kellen there? The gate was off the curtain wall when we overnighted in Hurog on our way to rescue you."

"Right," I agreed. "I've two good men working on the ironwork for Hurog—I suspect that the gate and a gatehouse or at least a portcullis will have climbed to the top of their list of things to do. Stala was left expecting the worst. I trust she'll have something devised by the time we arrive. Were this summer we'd be in trouble, but by now the snow is knee deep there. With your men from Iftahar, we can hold off a besieging army for a week—and southern-bred men in tents won't survive a week at Hurog."

"I can help, too," murmured Oreg, who'd led the boy close enough to overhear.

I shot him a repressing look. "*Mages* are always useful in such situations."

Duraugh said, "If the weather's not bad enough at Hurog, you're going to have to see if your dwarves can transport Kellen away. They may not want to involve themselves in a human dispute."

"Dwarves?" said Kellen, startled.

Tosten grinned. "They owe Ward a favor or two."

MY UNCLE GUIDED US THROUGH A FEW HARVESTED fields and onto a track I'd never taken to Hurog.

Stala's second, a Shavigman by the name of Ydelbrot, led the men and organized the march. At my uncle's request, I trotted Feather over to Ydelbrot and told him we needed to make as much speed as possible since the king might be "just a wee bit miffed that we took off with Kellen and Tychis."

He grinned and nodded. "Wouldn't want to be overrun by a Tallvenish army on Tallven soil."

I smiled, but in truth I was more worried about how much

blood Jakoven had taken out of Tychis's wrist and just what he could get Farsonsbane to do with it.

The whole column broke into a trot. I held Feather as it passed me, swinging in to ride next to my brother—who happened to be behind Tisala. She was riding next to Tychis.

"He looks like Tosten at that age," said Oreg, coming up to us and pointing at Tychis—who bounced so much, I winced in sympathy. Tisala leaned over and talked to him and he stood up in his stirrups. I could almost hear his horse's sigh of relief.

"I was never so scrawny," disagreed Tosten stoutly, but with such good humor, I turned in my saddle to stare at him. He and Oreg seemed to be getting on much better since they'd organized my rescue.

It is difficult to talk while trotting, so for the next hour or so we were mostly quiet. I watched Tisala and savored the fresh air. At long last we walked the horses. They weren't too tired yet, but by the time we stumbled them into Hurog, they wouldn't be good for much for a month or more.

I dismounted when it was time to walk to save Feather as much as possible—I weighed half again what some of the other men did.

"Huh," said Tisala, still mounted—though a number of others were walking their horses. "If you had some Oranstonian horses, you'd have another league or more before you had to pull up."

"No." I shook my head solemnly. "If I had an Oranstonian mount I'd always be walking because my feet would drag off either side."

She laughed and we spoke of everyday things—gratitude for the recent frost that killed most of the flies, though it had made the past two nights of camping chilly; hope that the clouds over our heads would wait for a few days before raining—or snowing. Anything but what lay ahead of us. Such talk made the journey shorter.

"How's Kellen doing?" I asked. "I haven't talked with him much today."

"He's giving a good performance," she said, nodding her

head toward a place a little distant where Kellen rode beside my uncle.

"Sometimes," I said, "if you can hold the role long enough, it becomes part of you. I'll give him my room at Hurog—not only is it the only room in the keep fit to put him in, but it's as far from a cell in the Asylum or even one of the royal rooms at Estian as a pack of dwarves can make it."

"It is rather cluttered," said Tisala.

I grinned at her in appreciation of her acerbic tongue. "There still aren't all that many places in the keep with doors that lock and roofs that don't leak," I said. "A lot of things get put in there for a bit and stay for a few years."

WE SET UP CAMP JUST BEFORE DARK. I STARED AT THE stars from beneath my blanket to remind myself where I was before I closed my eyes—it didn't help my dreams.

I stood in the laboratory room of the Asylum once more, but this time I wasn't strapped to the stained leather table. Instead I stood before one of the other tables, the ones that held flasks of potions and implements of torture. I held a velvet bag in my hands, a bag I had to force myself to look at. Pulling back the velvet, I took out the staff head called Farsonsbane and set it in a stand on the table.

I think it was the way I saw the Bane that made me realize that I was looking at it through Jakoven's eyes. The cloud of darkness that I'd seen in it was not there, though my hand, Jakoven's hand, still vibrated with its power.

I took out a flask and dropped a very small drop of blood on the black gem. The stone flared red and when I touched the dragon's head lightly, I took the power and created a magelight from it—and I still had magic left over.

I took a clean boar bristle brush like those used by artists and painted the stone with blood. Momentarily power filled my body as it had the night I, Ward, destroyed Hurog keep. I reached out with a hand and the leather table, its iron manacles, and metal base disappeared, leaving behind only a bare spot on the stone floor.

"So the Hurogs are descended from dragons," murmured

Arten's voice behind me. "Do you know what happened to the boy?"

My lips curled as I answered the archmage. "Garranon happened. Rode out of the stables and through the gates this morning with the boy and an extra mount, heading north."

"North?" Arten's question held no urgency.

"Where else would you take a Hurog brat and be certain they wouldn't let me pay them for his return? Garranon's not stupid."

"Really? He betrayed you."

"The spells don't hold him as well anymore," I said, staring at the power that bled through my hand, not noticeably diminished from the energy expended from the destruction of the table. "It was always so much fun seducing the body while the boy writhed in guilt."

"You'll not find Jade Eyes writhing in guilt," said Arten dryly.

I laughed. "More likely to find him writhing in blood. Jade Eyes has his own charms, don't get me wrong. But I always thought when the spell I kept to insure Garranon's loyalty faded, he'd break."

"Maybe he still will," suggested Arten. "I wonder how he feels betraying the man he's loved for so long."

I smiled at the thought. "I hope he weeps and hates himself for it as he did when he was a boy. I hope he thinks of me as he futters his wife. I . . ."

"Jakoven?"

"I have just had a marvelous idea," I said. "Tell my guardsmen to bring me the stable master who let Garranon ride through the gates."

"Ward!"

I sat up gasping and saw my breath gather in front of my face in the predawn light. Tosten crouched before me with a cup of something hot in his hands.

"Were you dreaming of the Asylum?" he asked.

I shuddered and took the cup of weak tea he offered, and sipped it to warm my body and soul. "Yes. True dreams, I think. I'll be glad to get far enough from Menogue that Aethervon leaves me alone."

I shared the dream later with Oreg, hoping he could tell me how much power Jakoven could glean from a half cup of Tychis's blood.

"I don't know," he said finally. "I never saw the Bane, you understand—only felt its creation and the disturbance it wrought. It's been such a long time. After so many years the memories fade, faster because I never wanted to look back and see how long I'd been enslaved. I can no longer remember what was history and what was story told over a cup of ale."

"It doesn't really matter," I said, rubbing Feather's nose as I walked beside her. "We need to get Kellen to Hurog, get Shavig to support him, and then get him out to a safer place. We can't risk sending someone to try and get rid of the Bane or the blood . . ." I hesitated. "I'd be able to *find* the Bane," I said—as I spoke I could almost hear it calling me. "If I could break it—or destroy Tychis's blood . . ."

"Don't be stupid," snapped Oreg. "*I* couldn't get into that part of the Asylum. All that would happen is that you would find yourself Jakoven's guest—and this time he would not underestimate you."

"Right," I said. "So we'll hope Jakoven doesn't have as much power as it appears."

I knew the stable master slightly. He'd seemed like a good man. I hoped he'd die quickly, but I didn't really expect that would be the case. I wouldn't tell Garranon. There was nothing he could do about the poor man except feel guilt. As I was. But I could not risk going back.

A hunting horn blew three crisp notes and I tightened Feather's cinch and swung back into the saddle. There was another part of the dream that bothered me. I wrestled with it as Feather trotted over the flat Tallvenish landscape.

When we walked again, I stayed in the saddle. My time in the Asylum had robbed me of endurance. I would just have to depend upon Feather.

By chance I found myself riding beside Garranon. He was walking beside his mount some distance from anyone else. We traveled in silence for a few miles, Feather as content to match her walk with Garranon's as I was to match his silence.

Apparently it was more restful on my part than his because he said, abruptly and angrily, "Aren't you afraid to catch it, too?"

Bewildered I wondered if I had dozed off and missed part of a conversation, or if my exhaustion had made me stupid.

"Catch what?" I inquired.

"The desire to sleep with men instead of women," he said with great bitterness.

Confounded I stared at the top of his head. I cleared my throat and ventured an answer. "No."

My reply seemed to stymie him and he walked on a little faster. Obligingly Feather increased her pace as well. Despite Garranon's obvious desire to get away from me, I didn't slow Feather because I realized what Garranon's problem was.

"My uncle doesn't dislike you because you sleep with the king," I said. "He dislikes you because you served the king's writ on me while I was under his protection—and he couldn't do anything about it. Tosten has a similar problem. The rest of them," I jerked my chin at the Blue Guard, "they might just not like you because you're an Oranstonian. But, more probably, they think homosexuality is catching."

Garranon turned his head away for a moment, then relaxed and laughed.

"Now as for me," I continued, "I have my eye on a woman and could really care less what bed you spend your time in."

He looked up at me to say something, but changed what he was going to say when he got a good look at me. "I've seen people look healthier than you on their funeral pyre."

"So I've been t-told." I'd been stuttering a lot since I left the Asylum. I took a small sip from the water bladder I carried on my saddle and tried not to think about the touch of Jade Eyes's hands.

My experiences in the Asylum had left me with a couple of questions and it occurred to me that Garranon might be able to answer them.

"In the Asylum," I said struggling both with the words and

getting my stubborn tongue around them. "Jade Eyes . . ." My throat froze and I looked away.

Garranon's hand rested on my knee. "Rape is rape," he said, "whether your body responds or not."

I flushed scarlet and shook my head. "He didn't actually . . ."

Garranon waited for me to finish, but when I couldn't he said, "Rape is one person hurting another because he can. Sometimes a rapist hurts your body, sometimes your soul."

After a while he said, "Making love, to a man or a woman, is about caring, passion, and joy; not just physical pleasure." When I looked at him, he grinned and continued lightly, "But done right it feels good, too."

The signal for mount-up broke through the crisp air. Garranon got on his horse.

"Thank you," I said.

He smiled at me and bowed in the saddle, before we set our horses off at a trot.

BY THE NEXT AFTERNOON I GAVE UP ANY PRETENSE of conversation, and that evening Oreg pried my fingers loose from the reins and led Feather himself. Mornings were better, but in the late afternoon I was barely staying in the saddle. Tosten gave the order to open the packs and distribute the woolen riding robes among us. Oreg made sure that I put mine on. Tisala rode next to me, talking quietly with Oreg.

I didn't see much of Kellen, probably because he couldn't be in much better shape than I was. I asked and Tisala told me Rosem was taking care of him.

When it snowed, I was too far gone to do much besides turning my face toward the sky, because I knew we were getting closer to home. I suspect I was the only one in the whole, cold mass of men (and Tisala) who took quiet satisfaction when the night's bitter temperatures made Feather's feet squeak on the snow in the morning. I told Tisala as much while she examined my hands for frostbite—I was too clumsy by then to get my gloves off and on by myself.

"It's true what they say about Shavigmen," she said, turning my hand over in hers.

"What? That we're tough?" asked Tosten with a grin as he checked Feather's cinch for me in preparation to hoisting my uncooperative self into the saddle.

Tisala shook her head sadly and finished with my hands. "Stupid. Only a stupid person would enjoy this weather."

The horses felt the nearness of home, too, and lifted their weary hooves faster. The snow was up to their hocks when, in the very late afternoon, we saw the walls of Hurog in the distance.

Feather whinnied and quickened from trot to canter, then when I didn't slow her, into a full-blown gallop. Power surged through me, swept away my tiredness, and welcomed me home.

As I neared the gates, I saw they were properly hung and reinforced so that they could keep out an army if need be. There were two guards on the gates and when they saw me, they started down the stairs to open them, but it was unnecessary.

Hurog opened to me all by itself.

I stopped Feather without entering, staring at the gates. It hadn't been me. Working magic is just that, work. I hadn't even thought about opening the gates, though I felt the surge of power that had accomplished it. Directed by Hurog.

Hurog wanted me home. It should have frightened me more, but how can a man be afraid of his own home?

Feather and I walked somberly through the gates. The guards on duty welcomed me formally—with a little touch of awe that told me they thought I'd been the one to fling the gates open with magic. I let them keep thinking it.

A few questions ascertained that my cousin and his wife had arrived from Iftahar only this morning. Ciarra was resting comfortably with her new daughter in one of the lower storage rooms where a temporary bed had been erected. I dismounted and began giving orders, the fatigue of the journey held at bay by the euphoria of being home. I sent a runner with orders for the keep. Kellen and his man would share my room. I gave Tisala the room next to it, the only other finished room on that floor. Garranon, Oreg, Tosten, and I would share the library. My uncle would join my aunt in their customary room.

I sent another man to gather grooms to take care of the spent horses that were just beginning to filter through the gates.

"So is it war?" asked Stala after threading her way through the confusion to my side.

I hugged her once, tightly. "Not immediately," I said. "But yes."

"With all of Shavig behind us, we will still lose," she said, teacher to student, not as if it bothered her. "But we can make him hurt."

I shook my head. "We might do better than that. I don't know if Beckram told you—I come bringing a royal guest to Hurog. We've rescued Kellen out of the Asylum so that Alizon can put him on the throne."

She drew in a breath, then laughed. "That does change things, doesn't it."

"Maybe not enough," I answered.

"We'll make it be enough," she said. "Now give me that horse; I'll see she's taken care of. You go in and get warm."

I SPENT THE NIGHT ON A PALLET IN THE LIBRARY WITH Oreg, Tosten, Garranon, and a wary street rat with Hurog eyes. I was going to have to find something for Tychis to do, something that would make him feel like one of us.

I was still thinking about it when I fell into a (thankfully) dreamless sleep. I awoke at first light, feeling like myself for the first time in a long while. I breathed in Hurog air and felt the familiar currents of magic that flowed through me, filling the terrible emptiness I'd felt away from Hurog and cleaning away the lingering effects of the potions Jakoven's mages had fed me.

I stepped around my sleeping comrades and snuck out of the library without awaking anyone.

There was a council to call and rooms that needed to be prepared. But first I needed to ride.

The big paddock had four horses in it. A moon-colored mare with gentle eyes, two chestnut matrons whose years of foaling showed in their widened rib cages and loose-jointed stance, and a mud-dark, big-boned stallion who bugled and charged when I whistled at him.

"Miss me, Pansy?" I asked, opening the gate and haltering him. He shoved me with his convex nose and ran his fluttering nostrils over me as if to check for damage.

"Nothing that shows, Pansy. Nothing that shows," I assured him as I led him to the stables where saddle and bridle awaited us. *His* scars were visible, white hairs on his ribs and flanks, and ripples in the soft skin on the corners of his mouth.

He lent me his enthusiasm as we charged the mountain trails. In the last few years these wild rides had grown less frequent; my need of them lessened by the satisfaction of turning Hurog into a prosperous land once more. But Pansy's memory was sharp and his feet didn't hesitate as he powered up the steep, snow-covered game trail. Hurog had *real* mountains.

Standing by the broken bronze doors on the mountainside, we stared down onto Hurog. It wasn't as impressive as it had once been. The stark black lines were softened by granite and the places where the stonework had not yet been replaced. But the air of decay that had clung to it was gone.

Pansy cocked an ear back, so I turned him around to see what he'd heard.

The dragon that stared at me was not Oreg. Its scales glittered green and black instead of purple, and it was less than half Oreg's size.

Pansy, conditioned by long rides with Oreg, didn't flinch when the dragon's head darted suddenly past us so its right eye was even with mine.

"Hurogmeten," he said in a voice that could have belonged to Tosten when he was ten.

"Dragon," I said. Oreg had told me that he wasn't the only dragon around here, but I'd never seen another one until now.

He tilted his head, butting my shoulder painfully with a bony ridge. Then he pulled his head back. "It sings in you," he said. "They said it did, but I didn't think magic could sing to a human."

"This is Hurog," I said. "And I am Hurogmeten."

"Hurog," he said after a moment, "means dragon."

"Yes," I agreed, smiling.

That seemed to satisfy him. After two running steps down the mountain he took awkwardly to flight.

"A fledgling," I said to Pansy, feeling lighthearted. I hadn't really believed Oreg when he told me that there were more dragons—no one had seen one in a very long time.

"TOSTEN IS INCENSED," ANNOUNCED CIARRA'S voice on the other side of my horse. "He said they almost put a rider up behind you in the saddle yesterday—and yet this morning one of the stablemen sees you taking flight up the mountain."

I set Pansy's brush on the rack and turned toward the open door of the stable. My sister, wrapped in winter clothes and backlit by the morning sun streaming behind her, looked like the spirit her new daughter was named after. Her pale hair looked the same as it had when she was a toddler.

I hugged her and lifted her gently off her feet for a spin. "How are you? I hear that you and your baby made the trip in better shape than Beckram."

She kissed my cheek and I set her down.

"Beckram fussed," she agreed, "but Leehan slept most of the way. Are you all right?" There was more concern in her eyes than a tiring ride from Estian would have called for. But she knew me as well as I knew her. She wouldn't pry unless I wanted to talk.

"I'm fine," I said. "Really. A bit stiff when I awoke. Tosten wasn't exaggerating—the last two days he and Oreg had to hoist me in the saddle—but I felt much better once I was in Hurog."

"I heard about your triumphant entry," she said. "Did the gates really open for you? And what's this about your newest stray? Tosten says he's our father's get."

I nodded, since it sufficed for most of her questions. For

a woman who had been mute for most of her life, words often cascaded from her in an effervescent flow. Her words, though, reminded me that I needed to do something with Tychis—and looking at my sister, I suddenly knew exactly what that was.

"What?" she said, no doubt seeing the sudden satisfaction I felt on my face.

"A new mother needs help," I said. "I believe I'll give you someone to fetch and carry for you and Leehan."

She rolled her eyes. "Oh please, not you, too. You'd think that I just got off my deathbed. Not that birthing is easy, mind you, but I don't need any more coddling."

"Perhaps not," I said, smiling at her. "But we have a newly discovered brother who was raised on the streets of Estian, and he needs to coddle someone. I think I'm going to give you and your baby to him."

12
WARDWICK

I'd have thought that persuading people to do what they wanted to do would have been easier.

IT TOOK US TWO WEEKS TO ORGANIZE A MEETING OF most of the Shavig Council. Two weeks of lightening my purse to hire every laborer and idle farmer in the area to work on Hurog had given us three more usable rooms and seen the great hall finished to the extent that our meeting was unlikely to be interrupted by wandering horses.

My uncle's people worked hard as well. Some of them stayed in the keep, but most sheltered in the holding's farms so there would be room for the Council when they came, which they did, despite the snowstorm that preceded them. Shavigmen knew how to travel in winter.

The councilmen, mostly nobles with an odd wealthy farmer or guild master thrown in, all came bearing gifts for my new niece, but the carefully worded invitations had been carried by messengers instructed to tell the recipient of Kellen's escape and Jakoven's seizure of Iftahar—Beckram told me that they'd left only hours ahead of Jakoven's troops.

Though they knew that even to be at Hurog was likely to invite Jakoven's wrath, almost everyone came, and the few who didn't were ill or snowed in. We feasted and hunted and listened while Tosten provided bardic entertainment, and no one mentioned Kellen's escape or Jakoven's attempt to imprison me in the Asylum. Kellen and Rosem stayed secreted in my rooms, waiting for the most politic moment to present them to the Council.

On the evening of the second day, when the night's meal had been taken away, I stood on the dais (newly built along with most of the tables and benches in the hall) and waited for the after-dinner talk to quiet down. Everything—down to the clothing I wore—had been carefully orchestrated by my uncle.

I wore formal Shavig dress as had been out of fashion for a number of decades. Close-fit breeches, loose-sleeved shirt covered with a knee-length tunic split down the sides—all of several shades of brown. Over my left shoulder a Hurog-blue dragon crawled.

"My lords, tradesmen, farmers all, we've welcomed you to Hurog, and given thanks for the gifts you brought. It is time now to speak on more serious matters." I took a deep breath.

I'd protested that the speech Duraugh and Rosem had put together was too wordy. The original one would have taken me an hour to get through. Duraugh cut it down, but it was still long. I hoped they'd all stay awake through my speech to hear Kellen's.

"You all know the reasons why I have stayed here at Hurog these years past. You probably all know that Jakoven recently called me to Estian. He claimed I was incapable of ruling Hurog and intended that I should prove him right and open a way for him to claim Hurog for the Tallvenish crown."

I paused to let the growl of several of the nobles be heard. Hurog was Shavig, and belonged in Shavig hands, never should it be held by Flatlanders—things like that. I continued before the tide of indignation had a chance to fall.

"It didn't work out as he had planned," I said, and my voice carried over the other men talking in the room.

Colwick, one of the eastern Shavig holders and the only

Shavig lord younger than I, laughed, jumped up from his seat, and said, "I was there. Jakoven sat waiting complacently for his men to bring a stupid lunatic in to display before the court. Ward came in dripping guards off him, leaving them lying about like plucked flowers. He bowed like a courtier and thanked the king for his hospitality." Colwick had something of a case of hero-worship for me; I think he listened to too many hero-songs as a young man.

The smile left his face. He looked around the room, then at me and said, "It was obvious that the king thought he was presenting an idiot before the court. Why was that? What did he do to you?"

The anger in his voice was hot. I pictured in my head what would have happened to Colwick if matters had proceeded as Jakoven had planned. I wondered how many other Shavig lords had been in that crowd, slated to become traitors and die.

I smiled sunnily and said, "Oh, the king has his methods, I'm sure. But I was trained by my father and I've had a lot of years of making people believe I'm something I'm not." Telling them the details would have made them pity me. Let them fill in what they would.

"So you decided to get a little of your own back, Pup?" suggested Orvidin from the back of the room. His voice was a soft thrum that penetrated the shadows of the hall, and everyone turned to him. The aging warrior leaned heavily on a cane. His snow white hair fell unbraided to his waist, a sharp contrast to the iron gray of his short beard. Orvidin was a contemporary of my grandfather's.

"So you took the king's brother home with you to worry Jakoven and lost Iftahar for your uncle," he said.

I nodded my head slowly. "I suppose you could say that Kellen's rescue had something to do with my uncle's loss— yes," I agreed. The tension in the room was taut enough to sing. "Or perhaps after several people had risked everything to help me, the only repayment they asked was to spirit Kellen out of the Asylum where he never should have been in the first place. When they asked this of me, I felt ashamed because I had never thought to demand his release before, even though I knew as well as you that he did not belong there."

Silence echoed in the room. How many of them had given thought to Kellen over the years? Kellen, who had been a quiet, good-natured boy, sentenced to life in a small, dark cell. Had they lied to convince themselves that the fit of *illness* that Jakoven used to justify his imprisonment of Kellen had been real?

When I felt they'd had time to feel such guilt as they would, I continued. "Both reasons for rescuing Kellen are true. But it is also true that I know Jakoven will not let me or mine hide in peace again. I no longer have the luxury of hiding here in Hurog and hoping the king will forget me again."

"Alizon's rebellion is doomed," I said. I let my gaze sweep across the room and saw agreement in some faces and repressed anger in others. "Or so I thought. But as it turns out, it has never been Alizon's rebellion—it is Kellen's."

I let the murmur of conversation swell for a beat or two, then continued. "So by helping Kellen out of that hellish place—" Someone smiled and I stopped.

"Don't any of you believe the fictions that Jakoven spouts about luxury and good treatment in the Asylum," I said. "I've been there and I wouldn't leave a dog I cared about in the 'gentle' keeping of the men who run the King's Asylum for Noble Embarrassments and Inconveniences."

I'd put too much feeling in it. I would rather have left them believing that all that Jakoven's wizards had done was question me while I played stupid.

I swallowed and continued on in deadly seriousness, my carefully memorized speech forgotten. "So as Orvidin has already speculated, it was entirely self-interest that led me to help Kellen and join in his rebellion. But I believe that it is a self-interest that all Shavigmen share."

I took my tankard off the table and let the sweet water pour down my throat. My uncle gave me a small smile of encouragement that would have been invisible to anyone farther away. I set the empty tankard down, and turned back, trying not to notice the way the sound of the metal tankard hitting the table echoed in the silence of the room.

They want to be convinced, my uncle had said. They'll listen as long as it takes you to do it.

"Let me tell you why it is imperative to your survival that you help us here," I said. "It is the reason that Jakoven will not let my family alone."

I took a deep breath and plunged on. "While I was in the Asylum, I saw Jakoven produce an artifact he found while renovating his castle at Estian: a staff head bearing a dragon with a black gem."

"Are you telling us you think Jakoven found Farsonsbane, Pup?" asked Orvidin.

"I'm telling what I saw," I said. "And I'll tell you that Jakoven told me he found Farsonsbane and I, a wizard, believed him."

"Even so," said someone else. He sat near the eastern Shavig group, but the room was shadowed and I couldn't tell for sure who it was that spoke. "There are no dragons left to activate it."

"Jakoven managed to get the Bane to do something with my blood while he held me," I said. "As soon as I left, he went after one of my half brothers—whom Garranon spirited here."

"You're claiming to be a dragon?" asked Orvidin incredulously, standing up again with such force that the bench he'd sat upon rocked back. "You don't expect us to believe that. I tell you, Pup, I came here ready to throw my support behind Kellen—but I will not abide following a man stupid enough to try to make me swallow a story about a mythological artifact and then compound it by seriously declaring that he bears the blood of dragons." He turned on his heel and gestured to his supporters, who rose noisily to follow him.

I'd hoped no one would draw attention to the reason my blood awakened the Bane. I had planned on spinning some connection between the Hurog name and the legend that the Bane drew its power from dragon's blood. But Orvidin was too quick. He gave me a choice of lying outright or spinning them a truth that was unbelievable—and I would not lie to the Shavig Council.

The role I'd been assigned this night had been a deliberate attempt to remind those here of our Shavig heritage. I'd come before them as Hurogmeten and not wizard. Duraugh's speech did not mention the Bane at all. As I talked, I'd come to believe that the Council had to know what it was they were facing. Too late I realized that the Hurog warrior I'd shown them was so prosaic it made it impossible for them to accept the Bane and dragons. Myths belong in the darkness, in wild woods, in mages dressed in fantastic garb—not to a too-large man dressed in plain clothes.

"I never claimed to be a dragon," I said, my voice still audible even over the clatter. "Only a Hurog."

But it wasn't my voice that stopped Orvidin. Out of the flickering shadows left by the torchlights, a dragon coalesced in the large walkway that ran from the lord's dais where I sat to the outside doors on the far side of the great hallway.

I glanced at the table where Oreg had been, and sure enough, he was gone.

The lavender scales looked purple in the dim light and the dark violet on his muzzle matched the black on his wings. He lifted onto his hind legs until his head rose to the braced vaulting in the ceiling: I winced a little, hoping he didn't knock any of the stonework loose. His wings spread, knocking tables and their occupants carelessly aside. Slowly, he set his forefeet onto the ground. He sat motionless for a moment, then stretched his head forward until his muzzle was only inches from Orvidin's face.

"Don't you know your own language?" asked Oreg softly. He'd let an ancient accent fill his voice so no one but I, who'd heard him speak like that before, would know it was he. "*Hurog* means dragon—did you think that was chance?"

Some of the people in the room began moving closer to Oreg. I watched their faces carefully, but no one made a move to draw sword or knife. Before Oreg drew my attention back to him, I caught a glimpse of the narrow face of Charva, who had the distinction of holding the northernmost keep in Shavig. That he was a very capable wizard might have had something to do with his ability to hold lands where no one else had. The northern reaches of Shavig were infested with a number of interesting creatures who dined on humans when they could. On his face I saw an expression of awe that reminded me of how I felt the first time I saw Oreg take on his dragon shape.

"I am an ancient of my kind," said Oreg. I don't know if he was telling the truth or not. I'm not certain how long dragons live—or if Oreg even considered himself more dragon than human. But it sounded impressive. "I was here when the family Hurog was born of the unhappy marriage of dragon and human blood, before the fall of the Empire," he said.

He let the quiet build and raised his head, sweeping his gaze over the Shavigmen who occupied my hall. When he spoke, his voice was even softer than it had been, but there wasn't a person there who could not hear him. "I was here when the Empire of Man covered the land from western sea to eastern, from the northern mountains to southern glaciers, while wizards wielded powers that you consider legend. I was here when Farson brought his Bane to humankind and the Empire was destroyed. I witnessed the few humans who remained living in scattered, hidden populations that had lost the trappings of civilization and were little more than animals fighting to survive."

In the fire-lit darkness of the hall, some of the beauty of his coloring was muted, but nothing lessened the impact of what he was, of what he said. His body had to coil upon itself to fit in the space between Orvidin and the doorway. Abruptly he folded his wings in, hiding their lighter, reflective undersides and leaving the impression that darkness had descended upon the hall in the darker scales of his body.

"Once again I smell the foul magic emanating from the Farsonsbane. And I tell you to beware." While he spoke, his scales had darkened gradually until it was hard to see him. When he uttered the last words, the shadow that was the dragon dissipated slowly into the scintillating light of the torches.

"How do we know that this is not just an illusion?" asked

Orvidin—but there was a reluctance in his voice as he turned back toward me that told me he wished with all his heart to believe there had been a dragon here. His voice firmed as he said to the room at large, "Ward's a mage."

"Does it matter?" said Kellen, stepping out of the passageway where he'd been waiting for his cue—which I hadn't managed to get to yet. "You all know what my brother is. In your hearts you know that he must be stopped. It is only that the need is more urgent than you know."

"May I present to you, Shavigmen all, Kellen Tallven, late of the King's Asylum," I said.

He bowed shallowly to me and after he had straightened, I stepped off the dais and dropped to my knees before him. This was important, my uncle explained to me in private. The biggest problem was not to get the Shavigmen to rebel, but to get them to support Kellen instead of me. Yet another reason for my plain clothes—I had the sinking feeling that Oreg hadn't helped in that area at all.

Kellen was fitted in the richest fabrics we could scavenge, mostly velvet and fine wool. The green and gray of his house colors looked good on him, and the past few weeks, spent largely outdoors, had lessened the pallor of prison. He looked just as a king should, and he carried himself the same way.

"Gentlemen," he said, touching my shoulder and signaling me to rise. "You have before you a story of which legends will be made. But as with all such legends, there is a core that is as basic as right and wrong."

I stood up and stepped behind him, noticing that Orvidin had bent down to pick something up from the floor. I saw it glint in the uncertain light and thought it was his knife, dropped when Oreg had made his sudden appearance.

"My brother has no care for his kingdom. He collects tithes that are supposed to go to his armies, that he might defend the kingdoms. Where were those armies when the Vorsag attacked Oranstone? What has he done to help the nobles recover after they fought the Vorsag off themselves? Has he allowed the Oranstone nobles to return to their lands? Haverness holes up in Callis because if he returns to Estian—as by the king's law he was supposed to—he knows he will fall afoul of the king's assassins. Why? Because he saved Oranstone when the king would not and made my brother look foolish in the bargain. Haverness's Hundred will be remembered in the history of our people long after our grandchildren are telling the story to their grandchildren. And my brother cannot tolerate that."

The land tugged at my attention, like a small feather of magic running up my spine. A person had crossed onto Hurog land, a person ill-touched. I sent my magic out for a closer look and knew that it was a lone foot-traveler. The ill-magic he bore was small—he would not cause much harm, if any. As long as he passed through Hurog, I wouldn't trouble him.

Kellen gathered his audience in the palm of his hand and I turned my attention back to him.

"My brother," continued Kellen, "has failed in his duties and I must oppose him—as Aethervon warned him would happen a decade ago. He has chosen to walk dark paths, and so I must stand in opposition to him. Ward of Hurog stands behind me, who of you will do likewise?"

It wasn't just the words he spoke, but the way he said them. At his last words, men stood and fell to their knees. Until only an old man stood alone in the hall. Orvidin walked up the center aisle until he was only a few feet from Kellen. I saw Rosem's hand twitch surreptitiously toward his sword.

"I don't know you," said Orvidin, his voice thick with some emotion. "But I know this pup, here." He threw a jerky gesture toward me. "And I know that what you say of Jakoven is true. And I know that this"—he held up the glittering thing he'd picked up off the floor, which was not a knife after all, and I saw tears slip slowly down the worn skin of his face—"this scale is no illusion. If there are dragons in Hurog, I will follow the Blue as Shavigmen have done as long as there has been a Shavig. And if the Hurogmeten follows your banner, I can do nothing else."

THE DRAMA OF THE MOMENT COULDN'T LAST, OF course. But it seemed to satisfy everyone. All of Shavig, as represented by the men under my roof, would support Kellen's bid to take his brother's throne whether in the cause of right, in search of a place in legend, or just to have a reason for a good battle.

The kitchen produced more food, mostly small cakes and sweet bread, and the servants brought in ale. Tosten took a seat before the fire and spent a while spinning music. With his usual good instincts, he avoided legendary tales and stuck to romance and war. We all needed a good dose of the normalcy a few sobbing tunes about dying lovers and soldiers could provide.

My uncle Duraugh set about charming and cementing the details as he drifted from one small group of Shavigmen to the next with Kellen by his side. Beckram clapped me on the shoulder in congratulation and then slipped away to tell Ciarra and Tychis what had happened.

When I'd first sent Tychis to be Ciarra's errand boy, he had been less than enthusiastic. But Ciarra had a touch with fragile spirits, and he was now her loyal slave—as were most of the other male Hurogs, including Oreg.

Hurog's dragon slipped back into the room in human form sometime after we'd all sworn to Kellen's cause. I hadn't seen him do it, so I hoped that no one else had either. I needed Oreg beside me, but I didn't want anyone exploiting what he was. What help he chose to give was enough.

Tisala stayed beside me. As I had noticed once before, she was as at home in feminine frippery as in hunting leathers. The dress she wore was one that Oreg had made her—I recognized the embroidery style. Oreg liked to embroider bright-colored animals on sleeves or shoulders. The making of clothes was a hobby of his, and he shared the results with only a few of us. The colorful tigers that ran up the black silk sleeves suited her, fierce and strong. The dress clung to her curves and celebrated the strength of her body, but I was too smart to tell her so.

Over the past few weeks she'd been pleasant and helpful, but any hint of passion sent her scurrying away. So I didn't tell her that I loved the way the firelight touched her hair, or that I dreamed of her naked in my bed. But I thought it a lot, and made certain she knew it. I'd learned from my sister, who'd been mute until a few years ago, that there were other ways than speech to convey information.

"Impressive," said Garranon quietly on my other side.

"What?" I asked.

He shrugged. "Dragons and legends . . . It would have been difficult for any man not to want to fight beside a dragon."

"I'd have rather kept him secret," I said. "But if Orvidin had walked out, we'd have lost most of the rest. However, it was Kellen who took them and made them his."

Garranon gave me an odd smile. "Ah, yes. They are Kellen's men. As long as you are—" he broke off as magic flared wildly, and I drew my short ceremonial sword in reflex to the attack on Hurog. It was the sword that cut off Garranon's words, not the magic, for the gates that were torn apart were on the curtain wall, too far away to hear.

The crowd, most of whom felt nothing at all, looked at me and fell silent—I think they thought I was going to attack Garranon. Even Tosten stilled the strings of his harp.

"Away from the door," I said. When I opened my senses to Hurog, I knew the curtain gates were wide open, and the bars that held them closed were splintered.

The man my Hurog magic had warned me of earlier was even now approaching the keep while the guardsmen on duty tried to reclose the gates. Magic, Stala'd told them, was best dealt with by mages, not soldiers. They were to stay at their post and let Oreg and me deal with it.

I could detect no sign of the power that had opened the outer gates of the walls surrounding the keep, nothing but the residue of ill-magic and the remnants of the spell that had thrown open the outer defenses.

I felt the man touch the keep doors lightly, and they sprang away from his skin as if they had been hit with a battering ram. They hit the walls hard, knocking dust from the stones. If anyone had been standing next to the door, they would have been crushed.

I could see the man quite clearly as he stepped into the room. I don't know what I expected, Jade Eyes, or Arten, or even one of the lesser court wizards—not Jakoven, surely. But it was none of them.

Instead I saw a man, neither large nor short, clad in rags and boots that were more hole than leather. The air that blew in was chill, but he seemed not to feel the cold. He walked hunched over and he moved strangely: not loose-limbed like a drunkard, nor with the clumsiness of exhaustion, but near to both. His skin, where it showed through the rags, was mottled dark with bruises, frostbite, or maybe dirt; but the dark patches seemed to grow as he drew closer. For he looked neither right nor left as he shuffled down the aisle toward me.

I didn't recognize him.

"Can I help you?" I said at the same time Garranon pushed around me and took several steps forward.

"Valsilva? What are you doing here?"

Once Garranon used his name, I could see that the shuffling figure was indeed Jakoven's stable master, but so changed from the jolly man I'd met that he could have been a different species. Abruptly I remembered dreaming of Jakoven calling for the stable master who had let Garranon ride out of the castle with my brother.

I caught Garranon's shoulder when he would have continued forward. "Wait," I said. "There's something wrong."

Other people started feeling the wrongness, too. The space around the stable master grew larger as he continued up the walkway toward Garranon and me. Something fell from his hand and rolled into a brightly lit area so I could see clearly it was a finger. Someone swore.

I pulled Garranon back a few steps.

"Valsilva? What do you want?" asked Garranon.

It stopped where it was, close enough for me to see its face clearly. The dark spots weren't dirt or even bruises, but rotting flesh, the smell of which began to seep from the body into the air of the hall. I heard someone gag.

"Garranon," it said clearly.

Garranon's shoulder stiffened further under my hand because he heard it, too. I don't know that I would have recognized the voice of the king's stable master, but I would recognize the voice it now used anywhere.

"Jakoven," Garranon replied steadily.

I caught sight of Tisala, someone's sword in her hand (she hadn't been wearing one), stalking around behind the thing. Her sword looked more useful than the ceremonial short sword I held.

The body of the stable master shook its head dolefully, and as I watched, the rot began to spread across its left cheek. "Twenty *years,* Garranon. I gave you *twenty years* and you betray me."

I watched its eyes carefully. It saw only Garranon. I doubted if Jakoven even knew where his creature was.

"Yes," agreed Garranon.

The thing began shuffling forward again, saying, "See what happens to those who betray me? See what you have done to this man?"

Before it could touch Garranon, I threw up a shield of magic. After seeing the trick with the door, I shouldn't have been taken by surprise at what happened—though in my defense, watching the accelerated rotting of the stable master was distracting me.

The pulse of magic that hit my shield was stronger than anything Oreg had ever hit me with. Red sparks flew up and ignited small fires on the great timbers that arched three stories over our heads. Tankards of alcohol burst into flame around us, lighting the hall as if it were daylight.

I cried out with the flash of pain it caused and lost hold on my spell. But Tisala ran the creature through with her sword and knocked it off balance, so it stopped short of Garranon. Instead, it stumbled to its knees and gasped in pain.

She'd struck right through the spine, but it began pulling itself toward Garranon anyway. Tisala jerked her sword free for another try, but stopped when it began speaking again.

"I'm all right," it said in another voice that must have been the stable master's own. "I'm just very hungry. I'll eat and be just fine." As it talked, great clumps of hair fell off with bits of scalp still clinging to it.

I tugged Garranon back onto the dais because he stood frozen in horror or guilt. I could feel that breaking my shield changed something with the creature. The magic that held it wasn't quite as focused. It stopped to eat a crust of bread that lay in its path. Crumbs fell like snowflakes out the sides of its face where the muscles of the jaw had rotted away. If I lived to see this finished, I'd have other things to dream of than the Asylum.

"Stay back," commanded Oreg from the far side of the room, near the open doorway, and the men who'd drawn their weapons as Tisala attacked halted where they were. "If you touch it, your flesh may well rot way as quickly as his is. Let Ward and me deal with it."

"What is it?" I asked Oreg, but it was Orvidin who answered, his face gray and drawn.

"A golem," he said, spitting on the floor to ward off evil spirits, a habit that leads the Oranstonians to call us Shavig barbarians. "I haven't seen one of these since my father offended the Acholynn in Avinhelle, and I hoped to never see another."

"Perhaps," said Oreg, who'd circled the thing and took his place beside me, staring all the while at the remains of the stable master, which finally finished the food on the floor and started to slither forward with legs dragging behind it.

"Garranon?" The thing sounded bewildered, but its advance was steady, if slow. "The king said I shouldn't have let you go. Did I do wrong?"

Tisala lifted her sword again, but Oreg waved her off.

"Fire, Ward. Not the kind you use to light the kitchen fire, but what you did at Silver Fells."

What I'd done at Silver Fells was to call down Siphern, God of Justice, to carry away the souls of the villagers slaughtered by the Vorsag. Not something I'd repeated often enough to know how to do it at a moment's notice.

I tried calling the god as I flung my magic at the stable master. Flames leapt off the animated corpse as if it had been doused in brandy, but I knew that nothing had answered my call.

Alight with the fire eating away at the flesh that remained

on the skeleton, the creature hesitated. It shook its head and muttered—this time in a broken whisper. "Hungry," it said.

Tisala stepped in and thrust her sword past the flames and through the blackened head where it slid through the temple and into the eye and stuck there. It was a metal-handled sword and she had to let go as my magic-fueled flames shot up it as if it were a branch of wood.

The golem shifted away from Garranon for the first time. It looked right at Tisala with its good eye.

"Hungry," it said.

"Jakoven's lost control of it," said Oreg, adding his fire to mine, but it continued after Tisala. Tisala backed down the aisle way, keeping her face toward the thing. The golem, far from being affected by the sword sticking out of its skull or our fire, moved faster until Tisala was trotting backward as Oreg and I followed.

The crowd of Shavig nobles swirled in tension, barely held in check by Oreg's command. I caught a glimpse of Rosem's firm wrestling grip holding Kellen back, and I blessed him for it. All that was needed was for Jakoven's plaything to run amok amongst all the Shavig nobles. There was none—except maybe Charva, the wizard, who even stood a chance against it.

Orvidin, who'd managed to get one of the decorative pole arms off the wall, pushed through the crowd and shoved the pike under the crawling stable master and flipped it on its back. It twisted around as quickly as a snake and began to stalk Orvidin.

"Gods," muttered Garranon beside me—I'd thought he'd stayed sensibly behind on the dais.

"Valsilva," Garranon called, trying to attract the creature's attention.

Floor coverings smoldered near the burning monster. A spilled mug of ale poured fire like water down the side of a table.

"Ward, that's not working!" snapped Oreg though his magic poured through me to aid my efforts.

I called out to Siphern and *reached*—Hurog, not Siphern answered my call.

Power flooded into me and had not I immediately sent it away it would have reduced me to ash the way it consumed the poor thing that had once been a man. Still frantically dumping the magic I doused the fires in the hall.

"Oreg!" I called and, bless him, he saw what was happening. His hands closed over my shoulders and he began to absorb the magic I had no good place left to send.

The power stopped as quickly as it had come, leaving my limbs as weak as water. The smell of rotting flesh was gone, leaving only a sour smoky smell and a strange quiet that Orvidin broke.

"Siphern bless him," he said, leaning on the old pike. He spat on the floor again. "I knew Valsilva."

"Jakoven sent him all the way from Estian," said Oreg. "To give a message to Garranon—and kill him if possible. A punishment for saving Ward's brother."

Kellen pushed forward looking angry and ruffled, followed by Rosem, who had seen to it that Hurog's hope of salvation had not thrown himself onto the first of Jakoven's monsters. I owed Rosem.

Garranon looked at the ashes that were left on the floor and swallowed hard. "He was a good man," he said, then turned on his heel and left the room.

The anger left Kellen's face as swiftly as a slate wiped by a cloth. "I'll go talk to him," he said. "He might listen to me. Ward, talk with your wizard and be ready to tell me what just happened before we, any of us, seek our beds tonight."

Kellen followed Garranon and I silently wished him luck.

Oreg released my shoulders with an absent pat and said, "I don't need to consult—I know what this is."

"Golem," I said. "But why didn't a normal fire kill it?"

"Not a golem," said Oreg. "At first I thought so, too, but it breathed—did you notice? A golem is, by definition, nonliving. It was a geas."

"A geas that could cause a man to walk all the way from Estian and cast aside barred doors in the process?" said Charva the wizard. He sounded tired and I realized that some of the power Oreg had fed me had been Charva's. "He sounded like Jakoven. Geas doesn't provide for that."

Oreg smiled, "If you'll excuse me for disagreeing with you—I'll tell you that geas can do all of this, if there is sufficient power behind the spell. And right now, Jakoven has sufficient power to lay waste to cities if he chooses."

So Jakoven has managed to activate the Bane, I thought, chills shaking down my spine.

"So you say," said Porshall, a western landholder I didn't know well. He seldom came to Councils, as his lands were in disputed territory and he needed to protect them. "I say that the timing of this attack was interesting."

"Are you accusing my nephew of this?" said Duraugh with icy politeness.

Porshall held his hands out as if to forestall offense. "I merely observe that as your nephew has so clearly demonstrated, he is a wizard. And that, if any Shavigman here was harboring thoughts of supporting Jakoven, this demonstration would cement their support of Kellen."

Orvidin, still playing with his pike, let out a bellow of laughter before saying, "Only someone who didn't know Ward could even think that. Half the problem we've had with the pup in the Council is that he's too honest . . . No, that's not quite the word." He narrowed his eyes at me. "Too honorable. He'll lie if it furthers his aim, but his aim, *and* his means, never lie in foul waters. He might create an illusion of a dragon, but you'd not catch this pup hurting an innocent man."

Porshall abruptly shook his head. "I still say—"

"Enough," said Charva. "This was no magic of Ward's. Those of you without magic will have to take my word that Ward's magic has an unmistakable signature—and this was done by someone else. Jakoven is the most likely source." The wizard looked around the room. "I'd pay attention to this, all of you. If we don't stop Jakoven, the stable master's fate might be kinder than anything we face."

13
WARDWICK

Action is the best cure for despair.

"I THOUGHT YOU SWORE YOU'D NEVER FIGHT AN-other war, Orvidin," said someone just beyond my view.

Holding a pair of horses, I paused inside the stable to hear what Orvidin would reply. With most of the Council leaving at the same time, my stable master had seen me standing around and handed the horses to me with orders to find their owners who were wandering around in the bailey.

"A man says a lot of things in summer he doesn't mean in winter," Orvidin said. "Winters are a good time to make war. The fields are barren, so the crops can't be burnt out. And there's nothing else to do for fun."

Laughing inwardly, because I knew he was serious, I led my charges out, nodded to Orvidin and his man, and finally ran down the men the horses belonged to.

For a while longer the noise and confusion pervaded my home, and then they were all gone. I shivered in the cold air and glanced at the new green timbers that were being fitted to bar the curtain gate. In his smithy, I knew our blacksmith was working on yet another set of brackets.

The bailey hardly felt empty, with the extra people from Iftahar filling the keep and its surroundings to capacity, but with the Shavig lords gone, it was certainly quieter.

"I didn't get a chance to thank you," Tisala said, breaking my reverie. Her breath rose in the cold morning air, and I caught a faint whiff of flowers from her hair.

"For what?" I asked, inhaling deeply, as if I could breathe the scent of her into my soul—then hoped she hadn't noticed me doing that. It wasn't polite to sniff people, even people who smelled good.

"For not rushing to my rescue last night."

My brows went up in honest surprise. "You were doing fine by yourself," I said. "Although I think Orvidin was brighter than either of us for grabbing a pike. For the most part it was after Garranon, so I guarded him and let you take the offensive."

"But he's a man," she said.

I stared at her and she grinned at my puzzlement. "You're right, we adopted the most logical plan of attack. I had a sword and was behind that poor thing. Garranon was far too stunned to defend himself and was weaponless besides. But I'm a woman and most men would have thought me even more defenseless than Garranon."

I pictured what she would have done if I had abandoned Garranon to protect her and laughed. "So, did you reduce the last man who tried to protect you to a pile of humility with your tongue? Or did you just run him through with your sword?"

She raised an eyebrow. "What do you think?"

I shook my head. "Poor misguided fool."

"Ward, did you hear Kellen this morning at breakfast? He's really upset with Rosem for holding him back."

" 'A girl and an old man fought it off, and you think it was too dangerous for me,' I believe is what he said, though fortunately he and Rosem ate rather later than most of the Council," I replied.

"I've never seen Kellen this angry," she said.

"Rosem was right," I said. "We can't afford to lose Kellen.

He's not ready to go fight monsters. He doesn't have the stamina yet."

"I was hoping you could do something about him." She stepped closer to me as she talked, and I took another deep breath before I caught myself; lilac, that's what she smelled like. "It's not just the physical danger he put himself in—but the time in the Asylum has left him suspicious and wary. If he quits trusting Rosem, who can he trust? A king who trusts no man is weak."

I asked, "Why come to me? He's more likely to listen to my uncle—and Beckram was close to him once, too. Or Garranon."

"I haven't seen Garranon this morning—but I don't think talking will do. Someone is going to have to show him that he is not ready for a serious fight."

"You want me to attack my future king?" I asked incredulously. "In the hopes that proving Rosem was right will make Kellen trust Rosem's judgment?"

She flushed the same color she'd turned when I'd taken off my shirt last week when she'd joined us in Stala's daily training. It had been cold fighting without a shirt—but seeing Tisala's blush had been worth it. This time it wasn't discomposure but anger that heated her face.

"Beckram could beat him—*I* could beat him," she snapped, bringing my attention back to the matter at hand. "But that would only humiliate him. Being beaten by a man of your reputation and size humiliates no one—but it might humble him enough to listen to what you have to say."

Put like that it made more sense.

"I'll do what I can," I said.

WHAT I COULD DO WAS HUNT DOWN MY AUNT. Stala would know when and where Kellen practiced. If I found him, then it would be away from the people who might try and stop me—like my uncle.

I found Stala in her rooms in the newly constructed housing for the Blue Guard. The hide-covered windows made her rooms cooler in the early winter morning, but the fire in the stone fireplace was warm.

"What do you think you can do about him?" my aunt asked me without looking up from her needlework.

"Teach him the same kind of lesson you'd teach me," I said. "I'd let you do it, but his ego is flattened enough. Being beaten by someone a head taller and several stones heavier won't hurt him much—being beaten by a woman half his size who's old enough to be his mother might."

She grinned at me and set aside the skirt (Ciarra's) that she'd been mending. My aunt taught all of her men to sew—me included—saying you never knew when you'd need the skill on harness or skin. "He usually practices twice a day, morning and night, but not with the Guard. He's been using the training ring by the stables and fighting only with Rosem. He doesn't want an audience."

I didn't ask how she knew. "But he didn't fight this morning."

She shook her head.

"Thank you," I said, and impulsively took her hand in mine and kissed it as if we were at court.

She stood up, pulled my head down, and kissed my cheek. "For that I'll give you a word of advice you won't like. You have to beat him quickly and mercilessly. Make him understand that it would have been his death to fight that thing you faced last night. Then you pick apart his fighting style . . ." She told me some things to look for.

"That's not much."

"Tell him that, too. His problem is that he sat in a box for a year and didn't move. Kellen's fault—he was in good shape until then, from what Rosem told me."

"Rosem talked to you?" That surprised me; from what little I'd seen of him, I'd heard even less.

"Rosem started in the Blue Guard," she said. "He fought in Oranstone under your father—one of the reasons he doesn't like you much. Kellen is well-schooled, he knows both Shavig and Oranstone style in sword and hand-to-hand. Try fighting him with Axiel's dwarven moves."

"They're really better for someone a little shorter than I am," I said.

She snorted. "Maybe so—but you still managed to set me on my butt with them a time or two. Now go find him. I think he's still sulking in the east wall tower."

The east wall tower was the only place in Hurog you could see the sea. Other people spent time there, staring at the waves where the White River met the ocean, but Kellen was alone when I found him. From the look he turned on me, I thought he preferred it that way.

"Come practice with me," I said.

"No." He returned his gaze to the open window. "Thank you all the same."

Since we'd left Estian, his face had tanned. Hair dark as rich earth had been tamed and trimmed. Only the thinness of the body beneath the rich tunic and over-robe gave any hint of what he'd been a short month ago.

But inside . . . I knew how deceptive the outer coverings could be. If he weren't strong and we weren't careful, we'd have nothing to put upon the throne. Tisala was right, *Rosem* was the crutch that would let him survive. Kellen needed someone who cared for him because he was Kellen and not their only hope to defeat Jakoven.

"It wasn't a suggestion," I said mildly. "You need to hit something and so do I. There's no one in the training ring by the stables." We only used the ring for a few months in the spring with the young horses. "And you can't afford to let your sword arm weaken any further."

His eyes flashed hotly. "You overstep yourself, Wardwick of Hurog."

I raised my eyebrow. "Do I?"

Anger swept over me that I had not been able to avoid putting the fate of Hurog in the hands of this man. He was so badly damaged he might take the rest of us down with him. He *had* to be strong.

I bent down and set my face close to his, so he backed up involuntarily.

"I think you are weak," I said. "A weak man cannot save Hurog for me. I won't have my people destroyed because I was worried about stepping on royal toes. Now get yourself down those stairs and take your attitude into the ring." I almost didn't recognize the voice I used as mine; I sounded so like my father in one of his killing rages.

His eyelids fell until his lashes veiled his eyes, but it was anger, not fear, that made his shoulders tremble as he preceded me down the stairs. I shadowed him through the bailey, out of the inner gates, and past the stables to the training ring.

The fence was solid so a young horse wouldn't have anything to distract him, and taller than I so a frightened animal wouldn't be tempted to try and jump over it. It made an excellent place to fight if you didn't want to be observed.

The ring had been scraped after the heavy snow, but there was a new skiff on the ground, and I could see the evidence of Kellen's previous practices in the frozen earth.

Kellen pulled off his heavy over robe and tossed it over the top of the fence. Slowly he pulled his gloves off and drew his sword. He walked to the center of the ring before he turned to face me with the relaxed air of a man who had been in many similar battles.

I had no over-robe to cast aside, no gloves to pull off casually to intimidate my opponent, so I just drew my sword and stalked the man I wanted to serve as my high king.

Take him down fast, Stala had advised me, and hard. So I did.

The dwarves were short, but their strength, like mine, was tremendous. I've heard men say that dwarves are slow—but that's what comes from listening to too many minstrels' songs. No man who'd ever faced a dwarf with an ax or sword ever said they were slow—and no more was I. I had adapted some of their moves—beheading a man a foot taller than I was, for instance, was singularly useless to me, but with a few changes it was effective against a mounted opponent.

Axiel said he thought I was better with a battle-ax than a sword, but I preferred the sword because it made me feel less barbaric. When I fought, part of me loved it, loved flesh parting under my weapon, loved the sounds of metal on metal and bellowing men. And what hitting people with an

ax or morningstar made me feel was more than I could comfortably live with afterward. The sword is a cleaner weapon.

The first time my sword hit Kellen's, it struck sparks. If
he hadn't turned his blade and dodged, I'd have broken his
sword then. As Stala had warned, he was well-trained. I
could see it in the line he maintained with his body and
sword, could see it in the way he managed to save his blade
against my longer, heavier sword.

But the weakness of his imprisonment kept him from the
edge of speed that he might have otherwise held over me.
My use of dwarven techniques kept him from settling firmly
into his style. I controlled the fight from the first blow and
he was swordsman enough to know it. I allowed eight clashes
of blade before I knocked his sword across the ring. Too few
for him to adjust to the strangeness of my style. One solid
hit from my shoulder and he was on the cold ground with
my sword at his throat.

I left him there while I took my aunt's observations and
lectured Kellen on what he needed to work on in a dry tone
I also stole from her. And as she did to her new recruits who
resented serving under a woman, I left him without a shred
of pride. He lay in the dust beaten and raw.

When I stepped away, Kellen rolled to his feet and stalked
to his sword, which he sheathed with trembling anger.

"My father's man was the half-human son of the dwarven
king," I said mildly. "He taught me dwarven style, which
works very well for me. That's why you felt like you
couldn't quite get your balance."

"What was this for?" he asked around his rage. He stayed
half the ring away from me. Probably so he wouldn't act
upon his impulse to separate my head from my body—I
sometimes have that effect upon people. "Why the lesson?"

"There's not much wrong with your style or technique," I
said. "The list I gave you is very short for my aunt—who
provided it to me when I asked. What you do not have is
strength or endurance. The only way to gain either is time
and hard work. Rosem was correct in holding you back last
night. We didn't know what it was or what it could do."

"So I was to let an old man and a woman take it out?"

I raised an eyebrow and let my voice grow cold. "That old man is the toughest raider Shavig ever produced. He's a veteran of the Oranstone Rebellion and has fought in a hundred lesser battles—would you have thought of grabbing a pike? A peasant's weapon, when there were swords about? I didn't think of it, either. And as far as Tisala goes, I've fought with her and she's better than half the Blue Guard. Did you see her slice the man's skull in half? That takes skill and strength."

"So I'm supposed to stay in the background while you all fight my battles?" The rage was leaving him, I could see the emptiness of defeat in his eyes.

I shook my head and allowed my tone to sharpen. "No. You are supposed to be smart. Use that. Use the people around you. Rosem is not stupidly overprotective." Not if Stala trained him. "He'll not get in your way when you are ready to stand on your own. But when he tells you to stay back, listen to him. We, none of us, knew what that thing was capable of. If Tisala had died, it would have broken my heart, but not the kingdom's soul. If I had died, my uncle would have served you as Hurogmeten as well as ever I could. Keep your goals in mind. There will be battles enough in front of us."

"So you think I should forgive Rosem for holding me back?" There was no temper in his face or voice, but the tones were acidly polite.

I narrowed my eyes. "No. I don't."

He stared at me a moment and then the mask of royalty dropped from his face and he grinned sheepishly at me. "You think I need to apologize."

I nodded slowly. "I think you owe him."

"I think you're right." His smile fell away and left him looking tired. "Thank you."

"We are demanding a lot of you," I told him. "If you aren't strong, we are all ruined. We need you to be a hero who can face Jakoven and triumph over his power and his games in a way that we have not been able to. But Rosem loves you more than he loves us. He will keep us from destroying you with our demands. Keep him by your side."

He stared at me, an odd look on his face. "You sound humble," he said. "You're big and you talk slowly—it leads people to underestimate you. But somehow we always do what you want us to do."

I grinned. "I'll be glad to knock sense into you whenever you feel you need it."

OREG WAS WAITING FOR ME IN THE LIBRARY.

"King Lorekoth will meet with you tonight," he said, looking up from the book he was reading to hand me a note.

I'd sent Oreg to the dwarven king.

Jakoven had proven that he could attack Hurog despite the winter as long as he controlled Farsonsbane. He'd sent this creature after Garranon for spite, but the Bane was capable of far more harm. So Kellen had to leave Hurog, and the fastest way to do that was through the dwarven waterways beneath the earth. For that, I needed the dwarven king's permission.

The hidden stair that led to the dwarven ways was still half buried in rubble. There weren't very many entrances to it from above ground; I knew of only one other in Shavig and three in Oranstone, though I could make an educated guess at four or five more—the keeps that had traditionally been famous for their dwarven trade.

As we neared the dwarvenway, the sound of the water became deafening, proof that a delegation awaited to escort us to the Dwarvenhame where the king held court. Without dwarven (or Oreg's) magic, the water was still and quiet. Only when a raft was hurtling through the tunnels did the water roil.

The door opened before we had quite reached it and a slender-built man stepped through. His beard and hair were dark, with only a hint of gray threaded through it, though I knew that he had been born before my grandfather.

"Axiel," I said, and picked him up in a bear hug. "It's good to see you."

He laughed and slapped my back. "Put me down, you

overgrown runt, before you infect my brother with your poor manners."

I set him down and turned to his companion, who had watched us with wide eyes.

"Ward, this is my brother, Yoleg. Yoleg, Wardwick of Hurog."

The man he introduced me to was a hand shorter than Axiel, but he outweighed him by five or six stone. Axiel could pass for human when he wished, but this one could only be dwarven. He wore no beard, so he wasn't much over a century old, just a lad for the long-lived dwarves. Yoleg, I knew from conversations with Axiel, was the heir to the throne.

I bowed. "Prince Yoleg, good of you to come and offer me escort."

He bowed to me as well. "Hurogmeten. It is our honor to ride the ways with you and bring you to our father."

Royalty or not, the craft we seated ourselves on looked no more seaworthy than any other I'd seen in the ways. Axiel told me that most of them had been made before the illnesses had plagued his people—so at least two hundred years ago.

I sat on a seat not meant to accommodate a man of my size and pulled the leather harness tight around my middle. Riding the ways was rough, and falling off the raft meant you had to swim for a very long time.

I could feel the pulse of ancient magic as it caught our raft and flung it wildly down a narrow tunnel so fast it was hard to catch my breath. Spray hit my face and left small bruises, like the first touch of frostbite. Sometimes the tunnel was lit with a million stars—dwarvenstones spelled to light the way. But the dwarves had been weakening for hundreds of years, and in some places the magic had faded and we were engulfed in absolute darkness. There, the sound of the water hitting the rock became almost painful.

There were chambers in the ways, crossroads where Yoleg decided which tunnel to follow. We had to wait until the water calmed and the magic died down before we could set off again. I'd traveled these ways before, but each time the sight of the chambers rendered me dumb.

One chamber was coated in crystal gems. Backlit by dwarvenstone, emerald columns rose from the ground to cross over our heads. It was difficult to judge distances in caves, but the columns looked colossal, the base of the nearest one longer than our raft.

Another chamber held gray stone carved in countless shapes. Small statues crowded the water's edge and climbed over the tunnel. I could have stayed there a whole day, but we were off again with a rush of water magic.

As we waited in a place that smelled of mint and glittered with gold, something large bumped our boat twice. Yoleg looked concerned, and Axiel held up a hand for silence. We all crouched motionless until whatever it was gave up and swam off in waves of midnight fins.

The raft came to rest gently against one of a series of docks in a cave I hadn't seen before—although I had been to Dwarvenhame several times. Our raft was alone in a port obviously built for a hundred, and the dock we tied to was the only one I'd have trusted with my weight.

"This is the formal dock," said Axiel, answering my unasked question. "Before we took you as a visitor to my family. But you come tonight as Hurogmeten to petition the king, and that requires we tie up here."

Axiel organized us so that Yoleg led, followed a half-step later by me on his right. Axiel and Oreg flanked me on either side.

Yoleg brought us into a large chamber, irregular in shape but flat floored and walled. Gold and gemstones were conspicuously absent because dwarves don't mix pleasure and business. That this hall in the Dwarvenhame was barren except for mounds of stone to serve as seats told me that this was very serious business indeed.

Plain-clothed dwarves packed the room in a way that reminded me forcefully of my own great hall yesterday. But there was a stillness that lay over this room that would never be a part of a gathering of wild Northmen. It felt as if the dwarves had internalized some part of the stone of the room into themselves.

On the far side of the room, Axiel's father, Lorekoth the

dwarven king, rose from his seat and looked at me as if he'd never laughed at my table or dug through the broken stones of Hurog to pull books tenderly out of harm's way.

He was young to be king, only four hundred years old, but his father had been one of the first to die of the series of plagues that had nearly destroyed the dwarves. His mane of red hair swept the ground. It was loose because a dwarf only braided his hair to go to war. In his neatly trimmed beard there was a bare hint of gray. King Lorekoth wore plain gray robes trimmed in black. Only the fabrics, silk and linen, reflected his rank.

"Who comes?" he asked slowly, the only person I'd ever heard with a voice deeper than mine. Axiel said that he could use the deeper tones to conjure fear in anyone listening to him, a useful trick on the battlefield.

I bowed, one ruler to another. "I am Wardwick, Hurogmeten of Hurog Keep, where dragons once more fly."

"Why do you come before me, Hero of Hurog?"

I didn't flinch in embarrassment at the title, but it was a near thing. "I ask repayment of the debt your people owe me. We fight a war above. A great evil has been unearthed to work its magic among mankind. Jakoven, High King of the Five Kingdoms, holds Farsonsbane in his hands."

"Does any person here deny him his debt?" the king asked. Silence answered him.

"What do you wish of us?"

"I need an army," I said. "What human army could stand against the dark men, the stone men?"

And so the negotiations began. Dwarves, perhaps because they are a long-lived race, do nothing in haste unless dire need forces them. My tired bones told me that the sun had risen again high in the sky before someone mentioned the dwarvenways casually. Another hour passed before I brought them up again.

Stories were told of dwarven bravery, and Oreg and Axiel told tales of my life to match them that were so blown up that several times they bore no resemblance to any memory I had of past deeds. Not that the stories were false . . . just exaggerated. I *had* carried a horse two miles in a blizzard—

but it was a newborn foal. Blood and severed body parts played a role in most of the stories, each storyteller becoming more and more graphic as the hours trailed by.

In the end I had an agreement that I could transport no more than ten people at a time through the dwarvenways. The list of people who could use them was not long—no one wanted the ways to be common knowledge—but Kellen and his man, all those of direct Hurog descent whom I deemed trustworthy, Alizon, Haverness, Tisala, Stala, and Garranon were among them. Axiel was to come with me because he knew how to use the ways.

"Most gracious king," I said with a bow that was more jerky than I would have wished, but at least my stiff muscles allowed me to rise. "I have a small gift for you, in thanks for this audience."

A gift, the king's note had said, would make it impossible for his courtiers to complain about human manners. An exotic animal, he'd suggested, as his menagerie was famous among his people. It had taken me about five minutes to come up with the perfect animal.

"I have in my lands," I said, "a basilisk, sometimes called a stone lizard. Oreg, my wizard, has enchanted it truly to stone in order to keep it safe. If you have a sanctuary for it, I will have it brought to you. Oreg can dispel the enchantment when and where you wish it."

Silence fell upon the dwarves. Shock rather than contemplation, I thought. The basilisk was the dwarven royal family's animal, a totem second only to the dragon who belonged to no one family, but to all of dwarven kind. Axiel had told me that during our trip here when I explained what I intended to do—I was not such a fool as to give the king a gift that might be an embarrassment, so I checked it out with his son. The king even had the perfect place to release the basilisk, a huge island without a harbor that was reachable only by the dwarvenways.

A slow smile spread across the king's face. "A generous gift, Lord Wardwick. I am honored to accept."

I bowed once more and left before I did anything to undo what we had accomplished today.

"I didn't think that even my father could get them to agree to allow humans to travel freely in the dwarvenways," commented Axiel as we waited for the waters to calm in one of the crossroad chambers. His younger brother wasn't with us because the raft was to await passengers at Hurog.

"He didn't think he would, either," said Oreg with a pleased smile. "I suggested to your father that if Ward started with a big enough demand—one that really would cancel the debt owed to him—then the rest of the dwarves would be more than ready to give him this small concession."

"The best part," I said, "is that your father will be taking the basilisk off my hands and Oreg will quit asking me where we can release it."

TYCHIS WAS WAITING FOR US AT THE BOTTOM OF the first flight of the stairs to the dwarvenways where Oreg's wards to keep out casual visitors held him at bay. Even fleshed out a bit he looked like a half-starved wolf—a cold, half-starved wolf. I don't know how long he'd been there, but he was pale and shivering.

"What'd Ciarra do?" I asked, briskly wrapping him in my cloak. "Tell you to find me and then let you fend for yourself?"

He bridled at my criticism of Ciarra, though he pulled my cloak around him. "She said it was necessary for you to come as quickly as you could."

"Tychis?" My sister's voice preceded her. "Are you down here?" She turned the corner and saw the four of us. Ciarra looked more respectable than she had as a young girl, wearing dresses now instead of torn-up hunting leathers—but I suspected that when she was eighty-five she would still light up a room with her energy. "Ah, there you are, Ward. Nice of you to tell people where you're going. If it hadn't been for Tosten and me, Uncle Duraugh would have been sending out search parties."

I scowled at her a bit. It had been a long time since I had to tell anyone where I was going. Seeing my expression, Tychis shuffled over until he was between Ciarra and me.

Ciarra bounced down the stairs and hugged him. "Don't worry about that one," she said to Tychis as she pointed at me rudely. "He hasn't raised a hand to me since I lost his favorite hunting knife when I was about your age."

I huffed with indignation. "What she doesn't tell you was that she lost my knife climbing up a tree to see if the eagle in the nest had any hatchlings. Stupid bird almost knocked me out of the tree when I went up to get her—I still have scars from the talons on my back. If she'd bothered to ask, I'd have told her that eagles don't have hatchlings in the winter."

I'd done the right thing by giving her Tychis. He had a place here—and someone to take care of.

"Tychis, go tell Beckram that we found Ward and he'll be up shortly." Ciarra pulled off the wrap she was wearing and tugged my cloak off of him. "Here, take this. It's not as warm, but it won't make you fall down the stairs, either. After you've found Beckram, go sit by a fire until you're toasty."

Tychis bowed correctly and then barreled up the stairs, clutching Ciarra's wrap so it didn't fall on the floor.

"I have to watch him," she said when he was gone. "He's so anxious to please, he won't tell me when he's had enough."

I kissed her forehead. "Thank you. I knew you'd handle him if anyone could."

She smiled and shook her head. "I'll be happy when I convince him that we have every intention of keeping him fed, and all that the hoard of food he's hidden does is attract rats. Oh, that poor boy, Ward. He doesn't talk much, but you can see the life he led 'til now."

Ciarra turned to Axiel and stretched out her hands and caught his. "How lovely to see you again, Axiel."

After the greetings were done, Ciarra turned to me. "Alizon arrived last night on a boat from Oranstone with a small cadre of Oranstonians." She laughed when I groaned. "Serves you right, you old hermit."

•   •   •

OREG TOOK HIMSELF OFF TO SLEEP. AXIEL ACCOMPA-
nied Ciarra to check in on the new baby, while I trudged up
the stairs toward one of the newly finished rooms next to the
library where Alizon was holding court. When I got there,
the door was shut and my cousin Beckram was leaning casually against the wall facing Tychis.

I stopped and stood quietly where I was, recognizing the
relaxed pose Beckram used to defuse tense situations. One
glance at Tychis's defensive stance told me who the tension
was coming from.

Beckram saw me, but gave no outward sign; instead he
explained obliquely what the trouble was. "So you think I
should have let that Oranstonian lord in there yell at you for
doing as you were told?"

"I'm a bastard," Tychis said.

"You aren't the only bastard here," replied my cousin.
"That's no reason to let a man cut down a boy."

"There are other bastard Hurogs here," Tychis agreed. "I
seen 'em. They work in the stables, or fight in the Guard.
They don't live in the keep—except maybe for Oreg, and
he's a wizard. So what do you want from me?"

"You and I have fourteen brothers and sisters who were
not children of my mother," I said.

Tychis didn't start, just moved until he could keep an eye
on Beckram and me. I half expected to see tears, but he was
just pale. I suppose children who survived the streets learned
not to cry.

"I was unable to do much for my family until my father
died," I continued. "By then most of them were adults." One
by one, I named them off to him and told him what Hurog
was doing to help them. Most I'd given money to, several
I'd given land. I'd paid for schooling and doweries, for a
fishing boat, for arms and a good horse.

"Of them all," I said, "you are the only one I know of
who was not born on Hurog. You were abandoned to fight
for yourself on the streets for the king to pick up on a whim.
My father owed you more than that. Later we'll talk of what
you want out of life. But know this, Tychis. As long as I
hold Hurog, no blood of my blood will ever stand alone.

When you are a man, I expect you to stand up for your family as Beckram has. Now, Ciarra is in her room with Axiel, who is a half-dwarven prince. As a matter of fact, I think he might be a bastard, too. If you are quiet, Ciarra'll get him telling stories for you."

When I waved my hand at him, he dodged past me and escaped down the stairs—Ciarra and Beckram were sharing a room in the lower levels of Hurog that was half full of this season's grain. If I were married, I would have a good reason to find some nook or closet away from everyone, too—instead of being crammed in with a host of other men.

"He doesn't believe you," said Beckram, watching Tychis run down the stairs. "He waited until we were out of the room before he informed me that I shouldn't have defended him in there when old Farrawell snapped at him for interrupting the meeting. He didn't want me to get into trouble."

"He will understand," I said. "Give Ciarra a little time and he'll be strutting around here arrogant as an Avinhellish lord."

The polite social expression Beckram wore gave way to a grin. "She does have that effect on men, doesn't she?"

14
WARDWICK

My father said that if the Oranstonians had liked fighting against the high king half as much as they liked fighting each other, they would have won their rebellion.

SIX ORANSTONIAN LORDS HAD ACCOMPANIED Alizon. Farrawell, the one who'd yelled at Tychis, I knew by reputation though not by sight. He was the only one of the Oranstonians I hadn't met, so I had no trouble fitting the name to the man.

Farrawell had accounted himself well in the wake of the Oranstonian Rebellion, surviving not by diplomacy, as with many of the older Oranstonian lords—like, say, Haverness— but because he'd been imprisoned when the Oranstonians broke. I'd heard he was a man of hot temper and little insight. He'd been one of Haverness's Hundred and, like Haverness, had taken the defeat of the Vorsag as a signal that he could stay at his estates—which were vast by any standards.

Beckram's friend Kirkovenal was there, a generation younger than the other Oranstonians. He sat next to Garra-non, who wore his usual bland court-face. Only the shadows under his eyes showed the strain of Jakoven's attack.

Danerra, Levenstar, Revenell, and Willettem had all fought in the Rebellion and the Hundred—which was all I knew of them. There was an empty seat between Willettem and Kirkovenal, and Beckram slid into it. I leaned against the wall. If I sat down now, I'd be asleep in five minutes unless someone did something more interesting than talk.

Alizon, when I'd known him at court, had been famed for his outlandish clothes and dyed hair. Today his hair was streaked with gray and cut short in no particular fashion. If I'd walked by him in a market, I wouldn't have recognized him.

Kellen and Rosem were noticeably absent, but my uncle sat on Alizon's right, watching the faces around him intently. Tosten wasn't there, either.

My uncle greeted me with a glance and then launched off into speech with the air of a man repeating something for the twentieth time.

"You say that you want to attack Estian," he said, looking from one Oranstonian face to another. "Which at this point is utterly foolish."

"Fighting in the streets of Estian, where every hand might be against you, will only lose men," agreed Alizon. "We have to pick our target."

"If not Estian, then where?" asked Kirkovenal. "Would the Shavig lords attack Avinhelle? Then we could attack Tallven while Jakoven was concentrating his efforts in the north."

Garranon shook his head. "Correct me if I'm wrong, but I doubt you'd get more than a tenth of the Oranstonian lords who would be willing to send armies to fight in Tallven. It leaves us too vulnerable to attack from the Vorsag on our southern border."

Revenell shifted forward on his seat and said, "If we split our forces and left half the army to defend our homes . . ."

Beckram shook his head. "Jakoven's men already outnumber us. If we spread out our troops like that, he'll cut a swath right through the Oranstonian armies while the Shavig are busy fighting the Avinhelle armies—which will be defending their homes, not just obeying orders to fight. Then when Oranstone is cowed, he'll come back and support Avinhelle, and they'll sweep back over Shavig before spring. The Avinhelle have their mountain folk who know how to wage war in winter as well as we."

Duraugh nodded. "He's right."

"Tallven is all grasslands," said Farrawell. He was strangely hairless except for the salt-and-ginger moustache that covered his upper lip. "There are only two or three cities of any size. The keeps can't protect the land, just the people. Easy to run over that with an army. That's why the Tallvenish worked so hard to take over the other four kingdoms, so they'd have barriers to protect their grain fields."

"But we're not fighting a war to break away from Tallven, gentlemen," said Danerra, who would have looked more at home in a library than in a meeting of war—during the Rebellion his men called him the Badger. He said mildly, "We're trying to replace Jakoven with Kellen, not destroy the main food supply for the Kingdoms."

"I wasn't talking about burning the fields," said Farrawell. "That would be stupid—at least until spring."

"It would be just as stupid in the spring," said Levenstar hotly. "Kellen will want to feed his people after we're through."

The meeting began to dissolve into chaos, with stools shoved aside as men bellowed while Alizon and my uncle tried to bring it to order. Only Garranon seemed immune. He closed his eyes and tilted his head back to rest against the stone wall.

I moved around the fight (which so far was only vocal) until the wall I propped myself up on was next to Garranon. "Where's Kellen?" I asked.

"He gave up and told them to let him know when they had a plan."

"What did he want to do?"

Garranon shook his head. "He wanted to wait and meet with all the Oranstonian lords like we just did with your people. But Oranstone doesn't have anything equivalent to your Council, and hasn't had since the Rebellion. Alizon has a good idea who is against Jakoven, but the problem is most of them won't be interested in replacing Jakoven with Kellen: To them, one Tallven is as bad as the other." He paused as someone hit Farrawell—I couldn't be sure who because I'd been looking at Garranon.

Garranon raised his voice and said pointedly, "Some of them don't know whom to fight." But none of the combatants paid him any attention.

"Does Haverness still have enough power to get the most important people together at Callis?" I asked, keeping a weather eye on the escalating battle.

Garranon shook his head. "Sure he has the power—but he's the leader of the faction that doesn't support war against Jakoven."

"Are you sure?" I asked. "Where's Tisala?"

Garranon raised his eyebrows in surprise and shook his head. "I don't know. What does Tisala have to do with this?"

The door to the room opened and Kellen stood in the doorway and watched as Beckram and Kirkovenal dragged Farrawell off of Danerra.

"Well," Kellen observed in icy tones. "When we get tired of fighting my brother, we can just kill each other instead."

A sheepish quiet fell on the room, and my uncle helped Danerra to his feet while Beckram and Kirkovenal released Farrawell gingerly. Only after everyone had taken their seats again did Kellen step all the way into the room with Rosem and Tisala flanking him.

"This is what we are going to do," said Kellen. "Tisala's father, Haverness, will call a meeting of the Oranstonians. She thinks he can get most of them to his keep at Callis without alerting Jakoven since the Oranstonian lords have grown good at keeping my brother's spies from following them. Haverness, Tisala tells me, keeps pigeons. She thinks he can have them together in two weeks."

"She exaggerates her father's importance," said Farrawell. "Why would we listen to a woman?"

"I have no idea," I said. I don't know what they heard in my voice, but there was a general shift away from me in the room. "Maybe it's because she knows what she's talking about—unlike most of what I've heard this afternoon." I looked at Farrawell. "And she's competent. For instance, if she'd hit Danerra, he would have stayed down until he woke up. But she wouldn't have hit him unless it served some purpose other than self-aggrandizement, *gentlemen*."

Farrawell's hand went to his hip where his sword would usually be.

Kellen leaned toward me. "Enough."

I bowed. "As you ask, sire." As I straightened, I caught Tisala rolling her eyes at me.

He turned to the room. "Tisala tells me that Haverness has been avoiding the more radical lords—such as yourselves—but I believe that Alizon and Tisala can persuade Haverness to cooperate."

Alizon nodded, a slight smile on his face. "I believe the Old Fox will be willing to help negotiations."

"Thank you," said Kellen.

"You won't get a majority support, sire," said Kirkovenal, his face sober. "Most of Oranstone would as soon that the royal house of Tallven disappeared off the face of the earth. They don't want a different Tallvenish king."

"I think I can change some of that," said Kellen. "I understand what they want—thanks to my uncle." He nodded at Alizon. "I can convince some of them that they'll be better off following me—and every man in this room knows that even a thousand more men might make the difference between winning and losing. I'm going to bring the Hurogmeten"—he gestured at me—"and that will help as well."

Farrawell's mouth dropped open. "*He's* the Hurogmeten? *He's* too young to be the Shavig Giant."

I bowed to the room in general. "You were busy when I came in—allow me to introduce myself. I am Wardwick of Hurog."

Danerra gave me a thoughtful look I saw echoed in several other faces. "That just might work," he said. "I wouldn't have thought so until I met him—but the Shavig Giant's a hero in Oranstone."

Garranon watched my face and grinned suddenly. "We Oranstonians are a musical people," he explained to me. "There are twenty or thirty popular songs about Haverness's Hundred—most of them praise the Shavig Giant who brought a mountain down on the Vorsag. And as Danerra has just pointed out, you might as well have *hero* written across your forehead."

I could feel my face flush with embarrassment.

Kellen smiled tightly. "He's charismatic," he said. There was something in his gaze that made me wary.

"But where should we attack first?" asked Farrawell.

"We don't," Kellen said. "If Jakoven attacks first, it will scare some of the Oranstonian lords. They know that Jakoven has just been waiting for an excuse to destroy what power the Oranstonian aristocracy still holds. He has a slew of landless Tallvenish noble lordlings who would give him utter loyalty in return for Oranstonian keeps.

"We wait," said Kellen, "and then we destroy him."

MY BROTHER COMPOSED SEVERAL SONGS ABOUT THE Shavig Giant that he sang at night after dinner. I threatened the head of whoever had told him about the name the Oranstonians had adopted for me—but no one confessed. It was probably Beckram—but it might have been Kirkovenal, who seemed to get on well with my brother.

Alizon stayed another day to rest his horses, then left with his Oranstonian lords. We left Hurog twelve days after Alizon—we being Kellen, Rosem, my uncle, Garranon, Oreg, Tisala, Tosten, and me with Axiel as pilot. Beckram remained at Hurog to supervise the keep.

"How many know of this?" asked Kellen as he fastened himself on the gently bobbing raft.

I shrugged. "I don't know. Not very many."

There were more people than the raft had seats; I planned to sit on the floorboards and hold myself on by the straps fastened to the raft for that purpose. Tisala had found a seat in the rear. I started toward her, but Kellen, in front, touched my arm.

"Stay here with me," he said. "I have need to talk with you."

So I seated myself between Kellen's seat and the one Rosem had taken.

Kellen gestured toward the tunnel we would travel down.

"Even one person knowing about this is too many." He spoke
softly, but not so quietly that Axiel didn't overhear.

"Only the dwarves can take vessels through here. In another couple of weeks the spells will be finished, and only a
man of dwarvenblood who bears the mark of the king will
be able to cross the wards and let anyone here. Then it won't
matter who knows," said Axiel.

I raised my eyebrows at him.

"Why do you think the Council allowed you access?" he
asked, checking to see that Rosem and Kellen were fastened
in properly. "They knew they had the ability to control what
uses you put our ways to."

"You mean that you control it," I pointed out.

Axiel smiled slowly. "Ah, but they think that is the same
thing."

"Meaning it isn't?" asked Kellen.

Axiel grinned at Kellen companionably. "Meaning that I
trust Ward somewhat more than my father's Council does."
He stepped past me to check the next pair of seats.

"Ward," said Kellen, in a pleasantly casual voice that carried no further than Rosem, who occupied the seat on the
other side of me. "Your Shavigmen made it clear that they
follow you, not me. You have the dwarves and the dragons
as your allies. And you have the eye of Haverness's daughter.
The Old Fox would throw away Callis for his daughter if he
could. So why don't you take my brother's throne for yourself?"

I choked. "Gods save me from that fate, begging your
pardon. Except possibly for the bit about Tisala." The
thought of being responsible for all of the Five Kingdoms
made me blanch. "It's enough to care for my own folk, let
alone all of yours. No, thank you very much."

He shifted. "I'm afraid I need a better reason than that,
Ward."

"Well, then," I said, "the kingdoms of Tallven, Avinhelle,
and Seaford would never stand for a Shavig High King. Nor
would Oranstone—they think we're barbarians."

There was safety in the truth of my words. If I'd been in
Kellen's position, I'd be looking for someone else to throw

the Five Kingdoms to, and I was grateful it couldn't be me.

"Then why not let Shavig be independent under you," he said. "You could demand it as a price for your support."

I shook my head, relaxing against the side of Rosem's seat as if I hadn't noticed that his hand was on the haft of his knife. Rosem worried that I'd take offense, since Kellen was all but accusing me of treachery. But I'd been expecting this conversation since the night the Council agreed to follow Kellen.

Because that night, I'd discovered that my uncle was right; I did have power.

"Shavig wouldn't survive on its own," I explained. "The reasons for uniting the Five Kingdoms are stronger now than they ever have been. Together we can weather early winters in the north by sending Tallvenish grain and Avinhelle cattle to Shavig. We can use Seaford fish and Oranstone rice to fill in when the crops fail in Tallven and Avinhelle. Oranstone ore mixed with Shavig iron makes a fine steel for swords. Our weavers use Avinhelle wool and flax for cloth. Together our armies can run off conquerors from across the sea or the Vorsag in the south. Alone, Shavig is nothing but meat for raiders."

"All very nice, I'm sure," said Kellen, implying by his voice that he meant just the opposite. "So you have no aspirations to the throne, and Shavig is not pursuing independence. Then why did you bring in the dragon? Once it showed itself, you knew that they would follow no other but you."

My patience for this round of questioning was thinning. He'd been in the hall that night and knew very well why Oreg had come.

"If"—I bit out the words—"the dragon had not shown itself, Orvidin would have left and taken most of the Council with him. It has been too long since great magic was done in our land for easy belief. They had to see one legend to believe in another."

My temper was rising. Questioning me to ascertain my motivations was fine, but the last question implied that he hadn't believed my answers. I looked over my shoulder and saw that Axiel was just seating himself.

"If you'll excuse me," I said, "I have a lady to mind." I stood up and bowed, as if we were at court, and strode back to sit on the boards next to Tisala.

I hadn't made any particular effort to be quiet at the last, and Tosten must have heard something of our conversation, because he patted my leg as I stepped over him where he sat on the boards between Garranon's and Oreg's seats.

"Hold on," I told Tisala as I sat down beside her. "This is a wild ride."

When we stopped in a cavern where odd formations of rock crystal wept from the roof to the walls and down to drape wearily over dark stone on the shore, Kellen sat forward with an exclamation of surprise at the oddity of the grotto.

Under the cover of the ensuing conversation, Tisala touched her hand to the top of my head and said quietly, "Don't take offense at his questions. It is only that he has been betrayed so many times. It makes him question everyone."

I raised an eyebrow and said, "Did you hear it all?"

To my surprise, color bled rapidly over her cheeks as if she were an untried maid. I shifted so I could see her better, putting my back toward Oreg as I tried to remember what we'd said that would cause her to blush.

When I remembered, I almost let it go, but something told me that it might be time to push my suit a bit—maybe because she didn't deny Kellen's claim that she was interested in me.

As she stared out blindly at the crystal-laced cavern, I said, "He had one part of it right enough. I wouldn't mind tying my house with your father's."

Expressions crossed her face rapidly before she covered them with a polite mask. When she spoke, it was with the inflection of someone repeating a rote learned speech. "I'm flattered, Ward. But you need to look for someone younger— a Shavig maiden who will run your keep—"

"Bah," I interrupted with a rude disgust I certainly didn't

feel. That she had worried enough to memorize such a speech surely was a good thing. If Tisala had wanted to dismiss unwanted flirting, she would have done a much better job of it. "Do you have quarrel with the way my home runs? I certainly don't feel any pressing need to find a wife who will run it any better. The food is eatable, and the keep is tolerably clean. I don't need a delicate flower. My father married one of those and when her children needed her to protect them, she turned to her dreamweed and sleepsease to hide from her duty."

Suddenly, unexpectedly, I had a vision of the first time my father had drawn my blood. I didn't remember what had caused him to hit me so hard. I just remembered staring at the blood on my hand and realizing that it had come from my ear. My mother looked at my hand, too, and ran out of the hall—away from me. That vision was the reason I forgot my vow to be patient and spoke with sudden passion. "I don't need a pretty maid, Tisala. I need a mate who can protect her children with her sword and with her wit. One who will not let her daughter live in terror because she didn't have the ability to cry out if attacked, or allow anyone to cut her son down until he thought the only way out was to slit his wrists, thereby missing his chance to fight for Siphern in the Afterworld. And when the bastard she married struck his son with the flat of his sword, I need a wife who would rend him limb from limb before he could do it again."

I returned from the intensity of my feelings with the same sensation I remember from falling unexpectedly out of a tree: out of breath, startled, and horribly aware that the murmur of other conversation had ceased and everyone was looking at me. I hastily sat down and looked at the dark water that lapped gently at the edge of the raft. "How old were you?" Tisala asked her voice guttural.

"Eight," said Oreg when I didn't answer. "At least I think that was the first time. It got much worse later." His quiet voice was loud to my hot ears.

"I didn't know it was so bad," said my uncle beside me.

"Sorry," I said in utter embarrassment. Then I realized I wasn't the only one I'd left exposed. "I'm sorry, Tosten." He didn't like talking about his attempted suicide so many years ago.

"If she lets you go," he replied obliquely, "she's a fool." I felt Tisala's fingers touch my shoulder in a quick caress and she leaned closer to whisper, "Maybe you do need me as much as I need you."

I took her callused, damaged hand in my free one, and my eyes met Kellen's considering gaze as Axiel gave me respite by beginning another course of the wild ride through the tunnels.

THE DOCKS IN THE UNDERGROUND CAVERN AT CALlis lit at our arrival, but there was no one to greet us.

"Perhaps Alizon was unable to communicate how we were traveling," murmured my uncle as he helped Axiel tie the boat off.

"My father would have guessed," said Tisala worriedly, stepping out of the craft and onto the ancient stone dock. "Even if he didn't intend to support you, sire, he would have left an honor guard to greet you here."

Oreg stood flat-footed in the raft and I reached out to steady him as a wave bumped him off balance. He didn't turn his attention to me, just stared into space.

"Do you feel it?" he asked me.

Of course, once he said something, I did. It was just the remnant, like smoke after a fire, but the scent of a Great Magic was in the air.

"Is it the Bane?" I asked, though I sensed the same flavor of magic I'd tasted in Jakoven's Asylum. Apprehensive certainty suddenly sponsored a hundred terrible things that could have caused Haverness to need his men at his side.

Oreg nodded. "But what has he done with it?"

"My lord?" said Kellen to me.

"Jakoven's used the Bane," I said.

"I remember the flavor lingered centuries where Farson loosed it. Some places I can still feel it," said Oreg dreamily as I helped him onto the dock. "There's no telling how long ago the Bane's magic was used."

"Oreg," I said sharply, and he refocused on my face.

"Oreg left just before the dragon appeared," said Garranon suddenly. "I wondered where he was going. Is Oreg your dragon, Ward?"

I looked around and realized that he was the only one who didn't know what Oreg was. Too many people were finding out, but there was nothing I could do about that now.

"A dragon and my friend, my brother," I said. "But never my dragon."

Garranon laughed abruptly. "No wonder you escaped from me so easily when I tried to hold you at Hurog after your father died."

"Actually, that took Oreg *and* Axiel" I explained at the same time that Oreg said, "He did that on his own."

Tisala's anxious focus on the open metal doors that led from our landing to stone steps rising to Callis proper recalled me to more important things.

"Best we set the past where it belongs and find out what caused Haverness so much distress that he would forget to welcome visiting royalty," I said, but on the tail of my words, Haverness and a panting guardsman came through the entranceway.

"Lord Kellen," he said smoothly. "Welcome to Callis. You must be Rosem, welcome sir. And you as well, Lord Duraugh. Garranon, it is good to see you again, my friend. And you, Lord Wardwick, Lord Tosten, and Oreg." I was impressed that he'd remembered Oreg's name after four years. "I'm sorry to be late, gentlemen—but you arrived on the heels of some other guests and it took me a moment to break away when my guard told me you were coming."

He turned to his daughter. "Alizon tells me that you and the young Hurogmeten have decided to escalate our careful plans."

She took his hands and held them tightly for a minute. "Father, it's good to see you." She stepped back and said formally, "Matters have escalated it for us, sir. As Alizon doubtless also told you."

"Indeed," he said, glancing at Kellen thoughtfully. "But

now come and allow me to extend my hospitality. Time enough this evening for politics."

I noted as we climbed that the passage here at Callis was rougher than the one leading to the Dwarven Way at Hurog. Did that make Hurog's older?

CALLIS WAS LARGER AND MORE LUXURIOUS THAN Hurog. Kellen and Rosem were given a large suite near the family apartments, of course. But I was given a room to myself—though it was small and spare. I realized with wry humor that I hadn't had a private place since I'd left the King's Asylum. The room came complete with a cold lunch set on a low table—the only furniture in the room aside from the bed.

I ate as I walked the space and figured measurements, and thought it might be possible to make a small addition onto the south side of Hurog and give us six extra rooms to put guests. Then I'd still have to share if the Council descended again, but any small group of noblemen—

"If you put an extra door in the side of the great hall, you could put a few of these on the south side without making the keep less secure," said Oreg from the doorway as he munched on an apple.

"Reading minds now?" I said, licking grease off my fingers. "I thought you said that wasn't one of your talents."

He grinned. "I saw you pacing the room off. It wasn't such a leap. I came by to congratulate you on your successful stalking of the warrior maiden."

I laughed. "The only thing I succeeded in was making an idiot of myself."

He smiled like a cat and shook his head. "I disagree. You convinced Tisala that you knew what you wanted, what you needed, and that she was it."

"Do you think so?" I was skeptical. "I was more of the opinion that I sounded like a pitiful sad-story hero who languishes and dies in the final refrain, leaving everyone feeling sorry they hadn't treated him better."

"Trust me," said Oreg lightly. "It wasn't pity I saw on her face, it was revelation."

I stared at him and saw that he was serious.

"If so," I replied slowly, "then I don't mind embarrassing myself in front of everyone. I'd suffer a lot worse than a little humiliation to win Tisala."

Through the arrow-slit window in the side of the room I heard a commotion outside. It was probably only the arrival of one of the men Alizon and Haverness had summoned to Callis, but I started for the door anyway.

I had a moment of anxiety when I stepped into the corridor and realized I didn't know which way to go.

"Which way to the great hall?" I asked Oreg.

"I haven't the slightest idea," he answered with a grin.

So I turned right and, with Oreg unhelpfully following, explored the twists and turns until I found a section of keep that looked familiar. Doubtless there were several paths I could have taken that were shorter, but we made it to the great hall before the new guests were welcomed.

Haverness was already in the room, seated by the fire where a scattering of chairs and benches made an impromptu conversational area. He was shaking his head as Alizon leaned forward and spoke with an earnest air. Garranon had draped himself against the wall, listening expressionlessly.

My uncle was leaned back in a wooden chair, elbows braced on the chair arms and his hands folded thoughtfully under his chin. I knew that pose and wondered when he would loose his first attack in whatever conversational battle they were engaged in. Axiel stood with his back to them all, watching the fire dance. Tosten was seated a little apart with his battered harp, playing a bit to keep anyone from over-hearing the discussion. I'd used him that way before—no sense making things too easy for the king's spies that doubt-less infested both Hurog and Callis.

Tisala sat on the flagstone of the floor, her shoulder resting against Haverness's knee. I met her steady gaze and saw something that made me think that Oreg might be right. Nei-ther she nor I smiled, but some connection was made any-way. My heart picked up an exalted rhythm as I realized it

was no longer a matter of *if* she would agree to marry me,
but *when*.

"How stupid do I look?" Haverness asked gently, in reply
to some statement by Alizon that I'd missed while exchanging glances with Tisala. "You and I know that the stories of
the Empire are greatly exaggerated. You've heard what minstrels have done to the battles of the Rebellion and it has
only been a few decades since then. If the Bane ever existed,
which I question, it was likely no more powerful than something our wizards could conjure up."

"If *I* could level my keep with magic," I said mildly, "then
why couldn't the ancients create a tool that would do the
same?"

Haverness rolled his eyes, reminding me forcefully of his
daughter. "I'm just trying to convince the old fool that he'd
do better not to mention the Bane to the people who are here.
Tell them Jakoven's a mage if that's true—and my daughter
tells me he is. But if you tell them he's got Farsonsbane, then
you'll lose them."

"He has the Bane," said Oreg quietly. "To maintain otherwise is a dangerous lie. They need to know what they
face."

Haverness shook his head. "Yesterday, after Alizon told
me the tale you've concocted, I spoke to my own wizard. If
he doesn't believe it, how do you expect to convince my
Oranstonians?"

"Oranstonians believe in magic," replied Oreg. "They worship Meron the Healer, who asks for sacrifices of magic."

"Peasants worship the Lady," corrected Duraugh gently.
"Haverness is right. We had trouble getting our Shavigmen
to accept the Bane."

"I heard about your convenient dragon and walking dead
man," said Haverness dryly.

"He was alive," said Garranon shortly. "He was a good
man and he suffered and died because of my carelessness."

"He died because of Jakoven," corrected my uncle. "Don't
you forget it, Garranon."

"I apologize," said Haverness. "I had only Alizon's tale to
go by; I hadn't realized you knew the man. I wouldn't have

spoken lightly of it if I'd thought it was anything more than an illusion like the dragon."

"Oh, the dragon's quite real, Father," said Tisala without looking at Oreg. "Just like the Bane."

"Have you seen it?" asked Haverness. "Can any of you doubt that if Jakoven decided to fabricate an ancient artifact, Farsonsbane would be the perfect one? It would inspire fear and awe."

"The Bane is real," I said. "I *have* seen it and felt its power. And only an idiot would try to re-create the Bane's semblance just to impress people. Too many people would refuse to serve a man who wielded it unless they were convinced of its power and terrified of it."

"And are you going to produce a dragon to convince the men here of that?" asked Haverness impatiently.

"If necessary . . ." began Duraugh as a guard opened the doors to the hall, letting in light, fresh air, and a bedraggled woman with a toddler on her hip. She entered attended by a handful of lightly armored guardsmen who appeared no less tattered than she.

Garranon lost his casual pose and strode rapidly across the floor toward the lady, who stood hesitantly as her eyes adjusted to the dim indoor light.

"Allysaian of Buril," the guardsman announced at the same time that Garranon exclaimed, "Lys."

I compared the image I held of Garranon's wife with the woman whose pale and plain face was tight with strain. I didn't recognize Garranon's wife, but I had only met her twice, and both times there had been other things taking my attention.

"Garranon," she said with such utter relief in her voice that I knew whatever had brought her here had been very, very bad. Something, I was afraid, that had to do with Farsonsbane and the residue of its magic, which I could still taste in the air.

Garranon walked soberly to her side and she collapsed into his arms.

The expressions on the faces of her guardsmen showed no less relief than his wife's had. Remarkable trust, I thought, for a man who was able to spend so little time at his estates.

Haverness moved as if to get up, but stopped abruptly. "Best wait," he said. "We'll get little information before she calms down. I hope she didn't run afoul of bandits after leaving Buril. I thought we were rid of most of them along the road between here and Garranon's estate."

Garranon stiffened at whatever tale the armsman was telling him in quiet tones that didn't carry over Tosten's quiet music.

Garranon bent down and said something to his wife and took the sleeping child from her arms. She nodded and stepped back, wiping her eyes. She took his arm formally and they headed toward us.

"My lords," said Garranon, his face a blank mask I recognized from court. "Jakoven has successfully tested the Bane—I think that there will be no need for dragons and dead men to convince my fellow Oranstonians that it is a threat that needs to be fought."

"What happened?" asked Haverness.

"Yesterday afternoon," said Garranon, "my wife took my son and a few guardsmen to check on outlying farms. When they got back to the keep, everyone was dead."

"Every armsman on the wall, every servant in the hall, every horse in its stall," said Allysaian in a monotone, the rhyme adding an eeriness to her quiet words. I saw her knuckles whiten on Garranon's arm. "All the plants were withered and dead."

Alizon looked at Haverness, who was shaking his head in disbelief, though the expression on his face argued that he was reconsidering even as he shook his head.

"Gods," said Duraugh. "I'm sorry, Garranon."

"How much blood does he have left? Could he get power from all that death, Oreg?" I asked Oreg quietly.

"I don't know," he replied, his arms wrapped around his middle as if he'd been punched in the stomach. I wondered what I'd feel right now if I'd already witnessed the Bane destroy civilization once. "I don't know how much it takes to use the stone. I would guess it would take more because the blood is impure. But he may have found someone else of Hurog blood to use. As for the other, he can't power the stone with death magic, but he certainly could gain power himself. I doubt it in this case, because it usually takes some sort of ceremony and the bodies collected. It would have taken days, not hours."

Garranon turned to Oreg, apparently having overheard—and the eyes in his blank face were wild with rage. "How close would he have to be to use it?"

Oreg shook his head. "I'm sorry, I don't know. I was in Hurog while the world fell, but I was young and . . . it was not a pleasant time. My memories of the Fall of the Empire are not entirely intact."

Alizon and Haverness turned to stare at Oreg.

"At this rate there won't be a soul in the Five Kingdoms who doesn't know Hurog's secrets, Oreg," I said, exasperated.

He turned to me, his eyes caught in the past, and said in an abject voice I'd hoped never to hear from him again, "I'm sorry, my lord."

I shook my head. "No matter, Oreg. It's your secret to keep or not." I looked at Alizon. "I mean that. You'll have to ask *him* about it—later."

Garranon swung abruptly to Alizon. "This gives you the attack you claimed you needed to pull Oranstone together. I hope that my people's deaths buy Jakoven's destruction."

"Kellen will see to it," Alizon promised.

The whole time we'd been talking, Allysaian had been standing beside Garranon with her arms wrapped around herself, muttering something sotto voice. When Garranon put his free arm around her and walked her past us, headed for somewhere private, I heard what she was saying.

"The children, the children . . . oh gods, so many children dead."

Bile rose to choke me.

"Excuse me," I said, "I don't feel well." I turned abruptly and exited behind Garranon.

15
WARDWICK

My father taught me that vengeance is meaningless. All that matters is surviving your enemies.

UNNOTICED, I FOLLOWED GARRANON THROUGH the maze of halls that led to the guest rooms. Unlike me, he had no problem negotiating his way to the room he'd been given, three doors down from my own.

I walked on to my room and closed the door behind me. Chills crept down my spine and stayed there. Not because of Buril's fate, though that was certainly part of it. Not because of fear, though what I was planning scared me spitless.

I'd been thinking while the others had been arguing downstairs in the hall.

Jakoven's first two attacks had been aimed at Garranon. The king had been seeking revenge, I thought, because Garranon had left him at long last. They'd also been experiments, to see what the Bane could do, successful experiments. Jakoven wouldn't have wasted his last drop of Tychis's blood on experiments, so I had to assume he had enough to power the Bane for at least one more attack—a real attack this time. Only if a weapon tested well, my aunt said, should it be used in battle.

My father had respected Jakoven's grasp of strategy. And good strategy would send Jakoven to attack Hurog next. Jakoven, like my uncle, would have seen the power of Hurog over Shavig. If he took Hurog right now, before the first battle, Shavig would lose the united front against Jakoven. All the dragon-blooded people who lived at Hurog made it an even more inviting target, more power for his Bane. And by now, he'd know we were keeping Kellen there.

We'd been counting on the winter to keep Hurog safe until improvements to the gate and walls could be completed, but we'd left the Bane out of our calculations. Jakoven would need no besieging army to take out Hurog with the Bane—not if he killed every person in Buril in a matter of hours.

If I were Jakoven, I would take Hurog next. Since I was the Hurogmeten instead, I had to stop him—and Garranon had just told me how I might do it.

Garranon had asked how far away the Bane had been from Buril. I'd come up with an interesting answer.

Magic doesn't work well long distance. My own pain every time I left Hurog taught me that over and over again. Jakoven hadn't had to be at Hurog the night his creature had attacked—a geas had done the traveling for him. There were other ways to work magic over a distance. Runes sometimes worked—or a jewel could carry a spell almost forever until it was loosed. Oreg had once transported himself a day's ride to a place he'd never been—but, as he'd later explained, he'd only done that because the magic that had bound him to me pulled him far more strongly than his body did. So there were exceptions, but I didn't think that Buril was one of those.

I believed Jakoven had brought Farsonsbane to Buril—and I had the means to test my theory.

Sitting on my bed, I closed my eyes. I wouldn't look for Jakoven. *Finding* takes magic, and there was always a chance that a wizard might feel the magic I used to *find* him. So I sought Farsonsbane instead.

I thought of the Bane as I'd last seen it, an age-darkened bronze dragon, poorly wrought and crude. It was unremarkable except for the unmistakable power that hung about it and the small jewel that hovered in the dragon's mouth.

I *found* the Bane half a day's ride away to the north.

I opened my eyes and could barely breathe over the possibilities of what I had discovered. A chance.

As I'd tried to explain to Haverness, no man would want to announce he was using Farsonsbane—not in the position Jakoven found himself. He wanted a world to rule, not a barren wasteland. So he had to keep the Bane secret until people were so cowed by it, and him, they would not fight against it—say after he laid waste to Hurog, for instance, something more spectacular than the mere death he'd left behind him at Buril. But for now he had to keep it secret or his own men would turn against him.

If Jakoven had brought an army with him, they'd have turned on him the moment he brought out the Bane and used it. If he'd brought an army, his use of the Bane to destroy Buril would not be a secret. I knew with absolute certainty that Jakoven wasn't stupid enough to have brought an army with him.

He'd come in secret, and was leaving the same way. And I knew that Jade Eyes would be with him.

The chill in my spine was anticipation. A part of me salivated at the thought of sinking ax or blade into Jade Eyes' flesh. Blood lust was a portion of the legacy of my father, and not something I was proud of. But I preferred the hunger for Jade Eyes's death to the bone-deep fear the rest of me felt.

If I were to go after Jakoven, I couldn't let Kellen or the Oranstonians know what I intended. The Kellen who'd fought to engage the poor geas-driven thing Jakoven had sent after Garranon in my hall would never stay behind given a chance to face Jakoven one on one. That was something I wouldn't allow to happen. If the attempt to wrest the Bane from Jakoven failed, Kellen would be Shavig's only hope.

Jakoven had the Bane. With it he could slay any army sent against him if he had sufficient warning—warning that the sounds of an approaching army would bring. A stealth attack could work, though. If Jakoven were a half-day's ride away from Callis, traveling to Estian, it would take us at least two hard days to catch him.

I couldn't go alone. Jakoven couldn't have an army, but I had no doubt he'd brought his core of wizards and guardsmen he trusted. I'd bring Axiel . . .

There was a soft tap at my door.

"Who is it?" I called, still wrestling with whom to take and how to contact them.

"Tisala," she said. "Are you all right, Ward?"

"Come in." Part of me would have left her behind, given the choice, but the rest of me was smarter than that. Our love would never survive if I tried too hard to keep her safe. Either I'd cripple her spirit until she wasn't my Tisala, or she'd leave me. So I was glad she'd come to my room, because I might not have asked her otherwise.

But I had a few things to say before I told her about Jakoven.

"You didn't look well," she said. "But I see you're doing better now. My father isn't expecting to have all the nobles here until the day after tomorrow—so I thought you might like to ride with me. It's better than waiting around."

She didn't meet my eyes as she said the last, pretending to look out the window. As if I didn't have far better reasons to ride with her than as an escape from boredom.

"I'm glad you came here," I said. "I need to tell you some things."

She turned back to me, her face carefully neutral.

I had never been a man of easy words, and the look on her face all but locked my throat.

"Look," I managed. "I've been trying to give you time, but I don't think I can do so any longer."

It somehow didn't seem fair that I should have to declare how I felt when she was standing across the room from me. I thought longingly about how much easier this would be if she had said it first, or if she were holding me as tightly as I wanted to hold her. But things were never easy around Tisala.

"I love you," I said, careful to keep my eyes on her face. She deserved to see the truth in my face. When she would have spoken, I held up my hand. "I am not saying that because I expect something from you. Unless you are a lot stupider than I think, you already knew how I felt—but I needed to give you the words. I intend to ask you to marry me, and if we survive until next week, I'll do that. Again, I don't need an answer. But I did need to tell you that."

Silence hung over my final words. I couldn't tell anything from her face, and when she finally spoke, it wasn't, directly, about what I'd told her.

"What's happening?" she asked.

I told her about Jakoven, the Bane, and what I intended to do. She heard me out and then said, "Who else will you take?"

"You know the country better than I," I said. "How many do you think I could take and not risk alerting the king's party?"

"Just how many people do you think Jakoven has?" she asked.

I shrugged. "Not many, I'd guess. At least ten, but not more than twenty, probably fewer than that. His wizards and a few guardsmen he'd trust to keep his secrets. Maybe a few more guards that he could eliminate before they have a chance to tell anyone what they've seen."

She swore softly to herself. "Gods, Ward. With such a small party, he'll be able to hear approaching groups easily. We'll have to be mounted, or we'll never catch up to him, and that will make us noisy. Not more than ten, I'd say."

"So I thought," I agreed. "We'll need Axiel. He has some knowledge of magic—it might make the difference between survival and not."

"I've seen him fight," she said, nodding in approval. "I can find him for you—and Tosten, too. He knows which end of his blade is which."

"I know where Garranon is," I said. "I don't know if he'll leave his wife now, but I thought he deserved a chance to avenge Buril if he wants it."

"Lys is tough," said Tisala. "She'll pull herself together if he needs to go."

"If he doesn't come, I'll talk to Duraugh," I said. "I don't want to. If I don't make it, Kellen and Beckram both will need his experience, but it will take more than four people.

Rosem would be nice, but I don't want to try and take him without Kellen."

"What about Oreg?" Tisala asked.

"No," I said. "You know what he is. For longer than I care to think about, he was a slave of the Hurogmeten. When I first met him . . ." I tried to think of a way to describe the terrified, defiant soul who'd offered himself to me with the platinum ring I still wore, though its spell was broken.

I decided finally that his condition after a thousand years of slavery was something I didn't need to share, not even with Tisala. "When I met him, he asked me a riddle as we stood over the bones of a dragon one of my ancestors had killed. He asked me if I would have let the dragon go free, knowing that by chaining it I could have saved Hurog."

I looked away briefly, remembering the sight of the chains that held the dragon long after its death. "I told him no. But he, wise man that he was, didn't believe me. In the end I proved that to save the world I would not only sacrifice Hurog, which I was sworn to protect, but also Oreg himself." I met her eyes. "I won't do it again. This is not Oreg's fight. I won't use him as my ancestor used that poor dragon who died in her chains."

"Out to save the world by yourself again, Ward?" she said.

I flinched at the truth of that, but I answered as honestly as I could. "I am the Hurogmeten. It is my job to protect the dragons that are left, not place them in jeopardy. Even if Jakoven uses the Bane to level the world, Oreg will survive."

"Will he?" she asked softly. "I don't think that he'd survive your death. Everyone needs a reason to live, Ward, even dragons. You didn't see him when you were in the Asylum and he couldn't get to you. I think that if you leave Oreg behind, even if you survive and win, Oreg won't. Letting the dragon go free is more than keeping it safe, you know."

"I won't use him," I said, but the battle was already lost, and even I knew it.

The door at my back opened and I turned on my heel to see Oreg slip in looking apologetic. "I spent a long time," he said to Tisala without looking at me "spying on people and hearing things that I had no business hearing. For the last few years, I've been trying to drop old habits. So when I was walking to my room, and I grew tired and rested my head against the door to Ward's room, it wasn't to eavesdrop. But you can imagine my surprise when instead of Ward declaring his undying love, I heard my own name. *Naturally,* I had to listen to what he had to say."

"Naturally," agreed Tisala, smiling.

He held out a hand and she gave him hers, which he brought to his lips. "How good it is to hear someone else scold him on his tendency to usurp the rights of others under the pretext of protecting them."

Finally he looked at me and I saw a touch of anger in his eyes. "Ward, if I had been more observant in those years when you were growing to manhood in Hurog, I would not have had to ask that riddle. You have never sacrificed anything except yourself. I have apologized for forcing you to do what you had to do to keep the dragon bones from the hands of evil. You suffered from that and I was freed."

He took a deep breath and swallowed his anger. "There's a difference between *using* someone and *asking* them for help—which you know very well. You can't keep everyone safe, Ward." His voice gentled further. "I'm not a child—for all that I look younger than you. I'm not Ciarra or Tosten, who needed you to protect them."

He put his hand behind my neck and pulled me down until my forehead rested against his as he said softly, "*I* am the dragon that would have eaten you, if you'd managed to go defeat Jakoven without asking me to play, too."

I pulled away and laughed ruefully. "Fine. If you come, too, we just might manage to survive."

"Now," he said, "why didn't I hear you proposing to Tisala when I all but told you to? I think you might have scared her off if you'd asked her when you wanted to"—he turned to Tisala—"which would have been within ten minutes of the first time he saw you handle your sword"—back to me—"but if you keep trying to seduce her without telling her how you feel, she's going to think that your purpose is other than honorable. It's not like you to miss your aim, but if you hesitate too long, the rabbit'll escape the snare."

Tisala laughed and made little rabbit ears on the top of her head with her hands.

"Enough, Oreg," I said. But the blush staining my cheeks robbed some of the force from my voice.

"It's all right," said Tisala, still chuckling. "That's the first time anyone ever called me a rabbit. Actually, Oreg, if you'd started listening about five minutes earlier, you would have heard Ward's half of that very conversation. I haven't gotten around to my half yet. Why don't you go see if you can get Axiel and Tosten to meet us in the stables. Tell anyone who asks you that I suggested you three come out hunting with Ward and me." To me she explained, "My father just got word that the southern lords won't be here until late tomorrow. He'll think, at least for a while, that I took you out to entertain you."

"As my lady commands," said Oreg, grinning. He turned on his heel with military precision and shut the door as he left.

"He could still be listening," I said after the door closed behind Oreg.

"I'm older than you," she said baldly.

I waited.

"I'll never be beautiful."

"My dear lady," I said, exasperated. "I don't know if I ought to be angry that you think I am so shallow that I need an ornament at my side to be happy, or if I ought to tell you that when I first saw you wear court dress in your father's hall all those years ago, you made the other ladies fade into obscurity. Or if I should tell you of the heat in my blood every time I see you use your sword."

"At least I don't take my shirt off during sword practice," she accused. "Did you honestly think that I believed you were hot? There was snow on the ground."

I grinned at her, the butterflies in my stomach settling back to where they ought to be. Oreg, bless him, had been right about the effect of my embarrassing outburst on the raft.

"You didn't have to look," I suggested.

To my delight she snorted, sounding very much like Feather. "You're interrupting me," she said unfairly.

I obediently closed my mouth. The humor drained out of her face to be replaced by something that made my heart pound. She stepped forward and touched the side of face. I closed my eyes briefly and turned my head into her touch until she withdrew it.

"I tried so hard not to love you," she whispered. "I didn't want to love a Shavig barbarian. Shavig's winters are too cold."

"At least it doesn't rain all the time," I said, my voice hoarse.

"Ward, I love you. If we both make it out of this alive, I will marry you—gods help you—if you still want to marry me."

Yes! I caught my cry of triumph before it passed my lips, but I grabbed her around the waist and swung her high. She laughed, gripping my shoulders. The joy in my heart was matched by her eyes.

I let her slide down my body, savoring the muscled curves of thighs and belly, the softer touch of her breasts. I stopped her when her mouth was level with mine and tasted her lips with more relief than passion—though that quickly changed.

She hadn't been kissed often. I could tell from the occasional surprised sounds she made. I was out of practice and bit her bottom lip a little too sharply once. When I would have pulled back, though, she returned the favor.

At last, nibbling on the corner of my mouth, Tisala said, "I'm too heavy for this."

I laughed. Aroused as I was, I could have held her forever, but I used the excuse to set her down before I did something we'd both regret.

"If we don't hurry, Oreg will be back up here," I said.

She touched my chest lightly and the sensation burned into my skin. "I'll go tell my father that we're going out hunting."

I KNOCKED LIGHTLY.

Garranon opened the door. "Ward?"

"If you'll give me a minute," I said, "I have a proposition that might interest you."

"Let him in," said his wife from somewhere behind him.

Garranon stepped back and allowed me into his room, shutting the three of us in the small room—four if I counted the exhausted child sleeping in the bed.

"My husband tells me that you believe that Jakoven holds Farsonsbane and that he used it to kill our people." Allysaian sat upright on the edge of the bed and Garranon took up a stance in front of the window. The separation between them was as vast and solid as ice.

"Yes," I said.

"Do you or your wizard have an idea of how to stop him?" she asked.

"Yes, actually, that's what I came to talk to Garranon about, Lady," I said, and, as succinctly as possible, I told them what I intended to do.

When I was through, Garranon shook his head, the expression on his face showing nothing but mild regret. "I have told my lady that I will not leave again."

"He regrets that he had left me all these years and forced me to play the lord rather than the lady," said Allysaian expressionlessly.

A muscle in Garranon's face tightened.

I turned to Garranon. "Do you think that you could have prevented the deaths of your people where your wife did not?"

His eyebrows climbed up his beautiful face. "Of course not." He made a sharp dismissive gesture with his hand. "The only way to have prevented this is if I'd had the courage to kill Jakoven while he slept."

"If you had done that," his wife said hotly, "you would be dead. And Buril would have been razed to the ground as the holding of a regicide, and our people left to the bandits. This is not your fault."

"Isn't it?" he asked.

"No," she said. "No more than it is mine."

"If I had not been his lover . . ." he began.

"There's no profit in that," I said. "My father complained bitterly about you. He used to say that if it hadn't been for you, the king would have divided up Oranstone among his loyal followers, including him. I doubt that was completely true—but I don't know how much of his restraint was for your sake and neither do you."

"My father," said Allysaian as she stood up and touched Garranon's rigid shoulder, "told me that the king gathered the children of the rebels together to kill them and break Oranstone's heart, but he changed his mind abruptly after walking through the cells where the children were held—after seeing you."

Garranon took his wife's hand tightly and looked at me. "Jakoven won't be alone—why do you think you can take him?"

"Oreg can handle anything the wizards throw at him," I said. "With you, Tisala, and Axiel to cover the sword work, I'll take on the Bane. It was my blood that woke it, and I think I know something about how it was made. Enough, maybe, to unmake it."

Allysaian rose onto her toes and kissed Garranon on the cheek. "Go, my lord," she said. "Do what must be done and come back to me."

He bent and kissed her, not a gentle kiss good-bye, but one full of promise.

AXIEL, OREG, AND TOSTEN WERE ALREADY MOUNTED with a second horse tied to their saddles when we got to the stables. Tisala was arguing with one of the stablemen. When she saw us, she pointed at me, and the stableman followed her finger and frowned before turning abruptly and disappearing into the stable.

Tisala handed off the two horses she'd been holding to Garranon and followed the stableman. She returned with another pair of horses.

"Having trouble finding a horse up to my weight?" I asked, eyeing the small, narrow-chested, fine-boned horses she held.

Tisala grinned at me. "These are mine. They could carry you all the way back to Hurog without showing the effects," she said, patting one arched neck fondly. "But you'd die of embarrassment before you'd ridden a mile with your feet dragging in the mud. We have a couple that will do you better, I think."

The stableman came out with a young gray mare much taller and stouter than any of the other horses he'd brought out. There was something about her hindquarters that looked familiar, but her raw-boned head matched the other Oranstone horses. I took the reins and mounted.

"She's not a trained warhorse," warned Tisala. "She's just coming four and is still pretty green."

I nodded my head and sat still, letting the mare adjust to my weight. The stableman came out with my second mount and I took a good look at her before I turned a chiding expression at Tisala. The mare the stableman held was a dead ringer for my Pansy, except that she lacked his thick stallion's neck.

Tisala laughed at my face. "We had your stallion for almost a month," she said. "Do you really think I wouldn't take advantage of it? My father was appalled that I did it without asking."

"Be careful with the dark mare, my lord," advised the stableman as he reluctantly handed over her reins. "She loses her temper if she doesn't understand what you want of her."

"Her sire's the same way," I told him, knowing from the way his hands lingered on her neck that she was a favorite. "I'll take good care of her."

We left Callis without incident, moving at a steady trot. The mare I rode was sensible, for all that she was young, and it didn't take her long before she steadied under me and ignored the antics of her dark sister.

"I thought you said Pansy was a cow," I said.

Tisala snickered. "That was before I saw him in battle. It hurt, though, to write that name on her pedigree."

Tosten, riding beside us, grinned. "The name our father gave him is Stygian, if you'd prefer. That's the one we use on the breeding papers."

She shook her head. "My father's stable master doesn't speak Shavig, and I didn't tell him a pansy was a flower."

It was raining, which surprised no one. Winter in Oranstone was one long rainstorm. But as evening approached, the water poured out of the skies as if some giant were dumping out her mop bucket on our heads—or so Oreg claimed.

"At least we won't freeze to death," replied Garranon in exasperation at Oreg's complaints.

Behind Garranon, Oreg grinned, having worked at getting a rise out of Garranon for the last ten miles. "But the snow you can dress for," whined the dragon in human seeming. "The wet seeps into everything and you can't get warm. And everything is covered in mud."

"He's trying to cheer Garranon up," I told Tisala as the discussion descended into a series of childish comparisons of Oranstone to Shavig.

She laughed and pushed her gelding ahead until she rode shoulder to shoulder with Oreg. "How many Shavigmen does it take to saddle a horse?" she asked.

"At least in Shavig we ride horses instead of ponies," claimed Tosten, riding up to join them.

"I hope you know what you're doing," said Axiel to me under the cover of the resulting hilarity.

I shook my head. "But if I don't do something, Hurog will be next to fall to the Bane." I explained my reasoning and Axiel nodded agreement.

"The Bane is powered by Hurog blood, Axiel," I told him. "I don't know that anyone other than Oreg and I have a chance at it. I thought about asking Haverness's wizard for help—but he's the most powerful wizard who's not bound to the king. If we fail here, he'll be the best chance they have."

"If we fail," said Axiel soberly, "my father will join the fight. If we had the strength we had half a millennia ago that might be enough to turn the tides. But I'm afraid dwarvenkind will fall as easily as the Empire did."

"I hadn't thought of that," I said. "I only thought about having someone I trusted at my back." I thought a moment. "I wish I knew how many people he has with him. But I don't know Jakoven's private guard well enough to *seek* them, and I can't try to *find* his wizards without the risk of alerting them. If you think this is putting your people in danger, Axiel, you need to go back to Callis."

He shook his head. "No. If the Bane survives us, everyone must join in the fight. At least this way my father will be spared endless debate. If I die, he is within his rights to declare war without consulting anyone else."

I gave him a strained smile. "Let us hope it doesn't come to that, eh?"

He nodded his head.

We rode several hours in the dark, several hours past the time when Jakoven's party had stopped ahead of us. We only halted when Tisala determined that the swamp in front of us couldn't be crossed in the dark.

Axiel, Tosten, and Oreg set up camp—such as it was— while Garranon, Tisala, and I consulted her father's maps by my magelight. Tisala showed me where we were and lined the map up with the trail. Then she and Garranon made educated guesses as to where Jakoven was from the information I could give them.

There were only two passes through the mountains into Tallven that Jakoven could be headed for. The first was the pass I had taken into Oranstone four years ago, and the second was more difficult and less used.

If we followed Jakoven at our present pace, we'd catch up to him well into Tallven, but still a day's travel from Estian. If we chose correctly, we had a chance of catching up much sooner, because the direct route to either pass was chock-full of swamp and mire. Jakoven'd have to ride around, and Tisala knew a better route to either pass. If we chose the wrong one, there was a chance that Jakoven would get to Estian before we caught him.

I left Garranon and Tisala discussing the relative merits of both passes and approached Oreg, who was struggling with one of the oilskin tent coverings. My extra hand made short work of the problem.

"I need to talk to you," I said to him.

Oreg found a seat on the raised root of a walnut tree. I crouched in front of him.

"Jakoven probably has his wizards with him," I said. "He has Farsonsbane and he is something of a wizard himself. I don't know how good he is, but Jade Eyes and Arten are both very strong—if ignorant by your standards."

"You want me to take on the wizards while you attack the Bane," he said neutrally.

"There is some connection between the Bane and me," I said. And I worried that if it was I who confronted Jade Eyes, my fear of him would defeat my desire for his death.

He nodded his head. "Have you considered that the connection goes both ways? It might make you an easier victim."

"Yes," I said. "What do you think?"

"You said that you felt it recognized you?"

I nodded my head. "It felt a little like the magic of Hurog but more intelligent. I think it's like the memories of Menogue—still tied to the remembrance of being dragons. I made it curious."

Oreg rubbed his hands together as if they were cold. "Did it feel like one creature or three?"

I closed my eyes, trying to remember. "There was a . . . texture to it, yes. Not really separate, more like a rug where several strands of yarn are bound together."

"So after your blood touched it, it recognized you," he murmured.

"No," I shook my head. "Before. It's hard to explain. I don't think the Bane was ever completely dormant—just powerless. As soon as Jakoven took it out of the bag he'd enspelled to hide the Bane, I could *see* blackness flowing from it, though neither Jakoven nor Jade Eyes seemed to see it. When the black power touched me, it knew me—or maybe it knew Hurog's magic."

"Did it feel evil?"

I shook my head. "No more than Menogue or Hurog."

"And after he used your blood?"

I tried to remember how it had felt. "The stone turned blue, and I felt a wild surge of magic." I remembered something else. "I think it was connected somehow to Jakoven—the stone's blue magic. But the blackness was a separate thing."

"We'll play it the way you want to, if we can," said Oreg finally. "I'll try to stop Jakoven's wizards and leave the Bane to you."

I gave up crouching and sat on another root. It was wet,

but not very muddy. "I wondered if the spell binding the dragon's magic to the stone might not be similar to the one your father used to bind you to the keep."

Oreg nodded. "Probably."

"When I broke the spell that held you to Hurog," I said, with a flash of visceral memory of my knife sinking into Oreg's side, "I felt the weave of the magic binding. I might be able to unbind it."

"That might not be what you ought to do," said Oreg after a moment. "It's not just magic that is bound to the stone, but the spirits of three dragons who are not very happy with the human race right now. Farson tried to use the Bane the way other wizards used a rowan staff—but the only magic he could work with the Bane was destructive, and that was when the spell was new."

"What do you suggest?" I asked.

He shook his head. "I've never gotten as close to the Bane as you have. You'll have to play it as it comes. Just be careful."

We ate the stew Axiel had created with dried meat and bits of this and that. Flavored by hunger and cold, it tasted better than it was. Tisala and Garranon between them had decided that Jakoven was headed for the less well-known pass.

"I wouldn't have thought that a Tallven would even have heard of the pass, but Garranon tells me that Jakoven knows geography," said Tisala before she blew on the stew steaming on the small chunk of dry bread.

Garranon nodded. "He's smarter than he lets on. There'll still be merchants traveling the greater pass to Estian. He won't want to meet anyone. The only people who use the other pass are hunters and bandits. With the Bane and his wizards he has little to fear from bandits, and the hunters on this pass are a wary bunch. They'd never approach a party of strangers."

"I know a path that bypasses most of the swamp that Jakoven seems to be traveling through," said Tisala. "If he's where Ward says he is now, we'll beat him to the pass and wait there."

Tosten had brought his harp, and he played it by the dying fire. We joined in the songs we knew, and he surprised Axiel with a mournful tune sung in the dwarven tongue. Axiel sang the chorus with him and added a verse or two.

"I didn't know you understood Dwarven, Tosten," Axiel said when they'd finished.

Tosten shook his head. "I don't. But your cousin several times removed taught me that one when your folks came to help rebuild the keep. Here's something a little less sad." His fingers plucked a rapid, catchy rift and he sang another of his "Shavig Giant" songs—a little more polished than the last time I'd heard it.

When he was finished, I banked the fire while Oreg checked on the horses. Tisala ducked into the smaller tent while Axiel and Garranon disappeared into the larger one.

Tosten laced his harp case and looked thoughtfully at my face. "Oreg told me Tisala accepted your proposal."

I nodded.

"Ward, our chances of getting out of this aren't good, are they?"

I stopped what I was doing. "No," I said.

He finished lacing his harp. "We decided—Oreg, Garranon, Axiel, and I—that there was only room for four in the big tent." He stood up and glanced at the smaller tent, set apart from the others. "And even that will be crowded. Since you're the biggest of us, we decided you'll have to share with Tisala."

I gave him a slow smile, which he returned briefly. Then his face became serious and he put his hand on my shoulder, "Ward—" he began, before coming to an uncertain halt, unable to say the words. So he said something else. "Ward, I'm glad you are my brother."

"Me, too," I said. Then after he ducked into the larger tent, I said the words I was too much my father's son to say to his face. "I love you, too, Tosten."

"He knows," said Oreg, coming out of the darkness where the horses were making quiet horse-noises. He tossed me my bedroll, which I'd left with my saddle, and took the camp shovel from me and finished banking the fire.

Wordlessly, awkwardly, I rested my hand on his shoulder. Oreg set the shovel aside and patted my hand. "I know, too."

He left me alone by the banked fire. I *looked* for Jakoven and found him in the same place he'd been for the last few hours, camped far enough from us that there was no chance he'd smell our campfire.

I stuck my head into Tisala's tent, my bedroll under my arm.

"They told me there was no room for me in the other tent," I said diffidently.

"Come in, Ward," she said.

In the golden glow of my magelight, I pulled my boots off and set them just inside the tent next to hers. She waited until I had finished and was setting my bedroll beside her blankets before she pulled off her wool tunic to reveal only a thin silk undershirt. I saw a glint of pink shiny skin along her triceps where a sword had nicked her. She didn't look at me when she untied her trousers and folded them for tomorrow. Like a boy, she wore silk shorts under the trousers, but like her top, it was thin and revealed the flesh beneath.

"I can keep my clothes on," I said in a hoarse whisper. "We can sleep together for warmth."

She turned to me then, blushing hard enough that even in the dim glow I could see it. "Is that what you want?"

No! Absolutely not, I thought.

"I will not use this to push you into something you don't want," I said, instead.

"That's not what I asked," she observed. She gripped the bottom of her shirt, and pulled it over her head. I still might have resisted, but the hands that still held her shirt while she sat half naked before me were white-knuckled and shaking.

I closed the distance between us and pulled her head against my shoulder. "Before we begin," I said into the pale softness of her ear, "I need to know if you've done this before." I remembered the bruises the king's torturer had left on her thighs and hoped she'd had a dozen lovers before him.

She nodded against me and whispered, "Once, and I swore

I'd not do it again. I never thought it worth repeating until now."

She obviously didn't know I was aware of that rape. Her wry tone was meant to kept me from feeling sorry for her, and gloss over the incident. I understood the impulse. I ran a hand over her bare back and up under her hair, feeling her tremble as my fingers closed on the back of her neck.

"Ah," I said. "The main thing to remember is that making love is at once the silliest and the most sacred act humans can perform. There is no wrong between us, Tisala, only things that feel good and things that don't. If you like something or if you don't, you have to tell me. Please, it's very important for you to tell me, especially if something hurts."

"All right," she said tightly.

I left her and arranged our blankets as best I could. Nerves had robbed me of much of my passion. I wished I had something better than a bed of coarse blankets over marshy soil.

The first time was full of shy caresses and urgent needs. It was somewhat painful for her still, I thought, though she didn't tell me except with a few involuntary twitches of muscle in her face. The second time was better.

I held Tisala while she slept, and listened to Oreg take watch from Garranon. I'd called for three watches with two sentries a watch, but no one tried to wake either of us. I closed my eyes and savored her warmth against me.

TISALA LISTENED TO HIS QUIET BREATHING AND HELD very still so she wouldn't wake him.

He thought her a warrior, brave and . . . She wondered if he knew just how frightened she had been. He hadn't said anything, but his hands had been very careful as he replaced the nightmarish memories with his caress.

It amazed her how different the sensations of the same touches performed by different men were, what a delicate touch his big hands had, causing pleasure rather than violation.

One of those hands tightened about her and shifted her closer. It might have been a more comfortable position for her sleeping lover, but now her neck bent at an awkward angle.

She smiled as she wiggled until she was in her former position. Let him sleep this night, but if this would be the only night she had with him, she intended to stay awake for the whole of it.

A large arm slid from its resting place under her waist until it was under her hip and heaved, leaving her, somewhat surprised, on top of him. He examined her with sleepy eyes.

"Still awake, eh?" he asked, his voice low with sleep and other, more private things. "Can't have that."

When he was finished with her, she fell asleep before she could remind herself to stay awake.

16
WARD

It is one of those lessons that every child should learn: Don't play with fire, sharp objects, or ancient artifacts.

WE ROSE BEFORE THE WINTER SUN, EATING AND PACKing until it grew light enough to see our way. It had stopped raining, but everything around us was still wet. The trail Tisala led us on was little more than a deer trail, and I on my tall horses suffered the most from the undergrowth and low, wet branches. Consulting maps and the results of my frequent *seeking* for the Bane proved we'd chosen our way correctly: Jakoven was definitely headed toward the secondary pass.

We arrived at the base of the climb shortly before the evening sun went down. We back-trailed a few hundred yards and found a flat area to camp. Jakoven had stopped moving about six miles away, and we assumed that he was camping there.

"Oreg," I said as I helped him set up the tents. "When you followed me to Estian, Jade Eyes felt you—he thought it was me. Is there something you can do so he won't know you're here?"

"How's this?" he asked, and the comforting feeling of his magic disappeared.

I took a deep breath. I hadn't realized how much I counted on the feeling of Oreg's magic to bandage the hole that leaving Hurog tore in my spirit. When I put some power behind my search, though, I could feel him faintly.

"That's better," I said. "Do I need to do something of the same thing?"

Oreg shook his head. "You're always shielded. Your problem has always been that nothing much gets through your shields. That's why you couldn't work magic for such a long time."

"If you really want to take them by surprise," said Axiel, "we ought to confront them now. We can tether the horses here and walk upon Jakoven's camp while they're sleeping."

"Let's go," I agreed. A part of me hoped for one more night, but Axiel was right. If we could take them by surprise, we had a chance. If they knew we were coming, we were dead.

We tethered the horses in the trail where someone would find them if we didn't make it back. We took off our mail and anything else that would clatter, and darkened our faces with the readily available mud before starting out in the darkness.

Travel by stealth at night is slow. By the time we smelled their campfire, it was already second watch. I sent Axiel, with his dwarven eyesight, out to scout the camp and hunkered down with the others under the shelter of a small fir tree.

Something cold and wet touched my forearm. I glanced down and saw it was Tisala's hand. I tucked it against my side, warming it.

Axiel came back too soon with a report. "I make out twelve of them," he said. "At least there's a dozen horses with riding saddles. There are four tents that could hold as many as five men each. He's got three people on watch, two armsmen dressed in the colors of Jakoven's own guard and someone in dark clothing who stinks of foul magic."

"Can you tell which tent Jakoven's in?" I asked. We had to get to Jakoven first, so he couldn't use the Bane.

Axiel shook his head. "They're all alike."

"He'll be in a tent alone," said Garranon with certainty.

"He doesn't trust Jade Eyes enough to sleep with him. All the wizards will be by themselves in another tent. The guardsmen will share the other two. If there's a way to do it, his tent will be surrounded by the others."

Axiel grabbed a handful of stones and wordlessly laid out the camp as he'd seen it. Garranon hesitated over the two central tents.

"One of these will be the wizards' and the other Jakoven's," he said.

"Right," I said. "We all will go in at the same time as quietly as possible. Oreg will take this tent." I pointed at one of the tents Garranon held suspect. "I'll take the tent here. Hopefully, that'll give the two of us the mages. Axiel, Garranon, Tisala, and Tosten stay together and stop here." I set my hand between the tents that held the guards, so that any of the guards had to fight their way through my fighters to get to the wizards. "Wait to strike until the attacks on the mages start or until the sentries call alert. If we can kill the mages before they think to do anything nasty, it'll be the better for us."

"Kill them all," said Garranon. "It'll look bad for Kellen's cause—an assassination rather than justice. But we don't want word of the Bane to make anyone else greedy for it."

"Fine," I said, having come to the same conclusion myself. "Any better suggestions? Any questions or objections? Once we leave this tree, we need to be silent until we reach the camp."

"What about the sentries, Ward?" asked Tosten. "I'm not worried about the guardsmen, but I don't like having a wizard scurrying about."

"I don't like it, either," I agreed. "But what are our chances of taking him out first without alerting the camp?"

"Not good," answered Axiel. "He's too close to the camp. Even the sound of his body dropping is likely to wake someone."

"Our first goal is to get the Bane," I said. "That almost certainly means confronting Jakoven. Remember he's a wizard, and the only safe wizard is a dead one. Oreg or I, whichever one of us gets through with his target first, will have to go after the mage on sentry duty. The rest of you remember that sentry mage and keep to the shadows until the guards come out. Hopefully they'll serve to keep the mage from attacking you for fear of hitting them."

"I can take the mage, before we move on the camp," said Oreg thoughtfully. "I've been used as an assassin before."

I shook my head. "No."

He snorted and appealed to Tisala. "It's really the 'used' he objects to. If I'd just told him I knew how to kill quietly, he'd have let me do it."

"No," I said again, though, indeed, he was right. But there was a better reason. "If Axiel says it can't be done, I'll not risk it. We need surprise on our side."

"So we leave the wizard and hope he doesn't kill one of us before you and Oreg get to him," said my brother.

I nodded. "I don't see any way around it."

So we crept through the mire and underbrush. I silently blessed the dampness that quieted the leaves that littered the ground at the same time as I cursed it for soaking up through leather and cloth. I lost sight of everyone except Tosten as we burrowed separately around the foliage that surrounded Jakoven's camp.

One of the sentries walked out of the shadows not a hand's span from Tosten's outstretched hand. My brother and I froze, breathless, waiting for the man to look down and see Tosten lying on his belly in the mud. Eventually, the sentry continued on his way.

My aunt usually posted sentinels rather than roving guards. She said it was too easy to be seen when you walk, and harder to see an enemy's movement. The only reason to have roving sentries, she claimed, is when the troops are all tired and walking is necessary to stay awake.

Tosten and I continued on our way after exchanging quick, relieved grins. I lost sight of Tosten shortly before I emerged, mud and leaf covered, into the clearing where Jakoven's camp was set.

I sent my magic out searching for the Bane and *found* it in the tent I'd chosen for my own. Oreg would face Jade Eyes, then. Relief and regret swept over me in equal parts.

I crept forward slowly, from one shadow to another. The cloud-covered sky clothed the camp in darkness except for the area right around the banked campfire, so finding a shadowed path to my chosen tent was easy.

I pulled out my knife and slit the side of the tent rather than bother trying to find the flap. The blade was sharp and slid through the wet fabric without making a sound.

Inside the tent it was darker than the starlit night. I crouched just inside the slit I'd made and listened for Jakoven's breathing. But I heard nothing because there was no one there.

Only the Bane lurked in the darkness, invisible. But that didn't matter—I knew just where it was, even without using my ability to *find* things. The power of it filled the tent, calling out to me.

Late in the first summer of rebuilding Hurog, shortly after Oreg had returned, we'd come upon a hidden cache buried under a mound of crumbled stone. I'd reached out to touch a wand of wood covered with faded paint that intrigued me. Oreg's hand had clamped down on my wrist.

"Never a good idea," he'd murmured, "to touch a wizard's toy. Especially when it calls to you. I'll teach you a few of the nastier things you can ward your own treasures with."

And that had been the beginning of his lessons to me.

Would Jakoven have left the Bane here unguarded from the rest of his mages? I thought not, and pulled my hand away. I didn't think Jakoven could activate the thing from a distance. It would be safer here until Oreg or I got a chance to look at it—after I found Jakoven.

So I sheathed my knife, drew my sword, and *looked* for Jakoven. If he felt me, it wouldn't matter; he would know we were there in a matter of moments anyway—as soon as Jakoven's wizards discovered the dragon in their midst. Oreg could kill one wizard silently, but I doubted that he could keep all of them quiet.

I *found* the high king near the edge of the woods. I cursed to myself as I slid out of the tent and sprinted off through the trees as quickly as I could. Haste was more important than stealth now.

Jakoven was the sentry mage. Axiel must not have recognized him. It wasn't his fault. The night was dark, and who would have thought that the high king would stand watch with his men? Certainly not me.

I hadn't made but five strides before the camp erupted in noise and smoke. Oreg's tent burst into explosive flame, and I got a quick glimpse of dark bodies and sparks as steel met steel before the underbrush obscured the camp.

I kept my link to Jakoven, as much to assure myself he wasn't anywhere near the Bane as because I needed it to find him. One of the mages had lit the campsite, and I could see the glow through the branches I clawed my way past.

I burst through one section of clinging branches and all but ran into one of the sentries who had just released a crossbow bolt into the camp. My sword took his head without my slowing a step, as I tried not to think about where the bolt he'd loosed had hit.

There was nothing I could do about my friends until I dealt with Jakoven. I was behind him now. There was a chance he would think any noise I made was his own sentry—the man I'd killed.

Jakoven, for his part, was moving slowly toward the camp—trying, I supposed, to get close enough to tell his men from mine. I was almost upon him when I heard a roar I almost didn't recognize as the king's voice.

"Garranon!" he howled.

Tosten had a song he liked, which I thought silly, about a soldier who finds his wife was a traitor. One of the phrases I'd objected to said something about the man's voice trembling with betrayal and disbelief.

"How," I'd asked, "do betrayal and disbelief sound?"

I heard it now in Jakoven's voice. Felt it in the thunder of power and magic that formed around his person.

I was close enough to have used my sword, but the branches of the trees were too close, hampering my swing, and my sword was not made for thrusting. So I bellowed like a bull moose and charged through the hampering foliage and set my shoulder into Jakoven's stomach before I even saw him with my eyes.

My charge sent us both tumbling down a sharp incline and into the camp's clearing. It also interrupted whatever spell he'd intended for Garranon.

I rolled to my feet and struck in the same motion, but Jakoven's blade met mine and turned it. He let my weapon slide along his blade and replied to my thrust with a series of quick short moves designed to cut rather than maim or kill.

It was an unexpected and effective style. He left several shallow cuts on my arms and a more serious one across my belly. His sword was shorter than mine, which should have been a disadvantage, except that he kept close to me, where my own weapon's length got in my way.

Even so, I was stronger than he. I got one good solid block in and forced him away from me with a rush he couldn't turn. From there I kept him at a distance with the superior reach of sword and arm, making him play my game.

The cuts on my arm bled freely, and I could feel dampness from the slice in my middle all the way to the knees of my trousers. I knew I would have little time to win this before weakness from the loss of blood would seriously hamper me.

Even as the thought registered, Garranon came up behind me calling, "Step back, Ward, I've got him. Bind your wounds before we have to carry you out of here."

We switched places as if we'd practiced the move a thousand times. I looked around, but I couldn't see the rest of the fighting because the tents were in the way. I stripped off my shirt quickly and wrapped it bandage-tight around my waist, just above my navel, tying the arms together to hold it. Hopefully that would stop the worst of the bleeding.

While I tied the makeshift bandaging, I watched Garranon fight Jakoven. The hiss that left my lips had more to do with the beauty of the swordwork I was watching than the burning pain in my abdomen. They were so well matched, I was awed by the speed and savagery of the fight.

"Traitor," breathed Jakoven. "I *saved* you. Saved your brother and allowed you to *keep* your lands when the estates of other men who had smaller roles in the Rebellion than your father were given to those loyal to me."

"You used me," corrected Garranon, all coolness to Jakoven's heat. "And I let you. I knew I could not save my family with my sword, but I could with my body."

"You loved me," said Jakoven.

"Never," replied Garranon. "If I could have taken the breath from your body and not lost all, I would have done so. I paid for spies, and spied myself, feeding the information to Alizon when he broke from your court."

"You lie." Jakoven's voice was confident. "I have never had a more passionate bedmate. Why do you think I kept you all these years?"

"Love is not necessary for sex," replied Garranon composedly. "And that's all it ever was—no matter how good it felt. But weighed against what you have done to my home and to the Five Kingdoms, it is less than nothing."

"You lie," repeated Jakoven, and he missed a block. Garranon's blade slid easily through the simple silk shirt Jakoven wore. The blow was too low to be immediately fatal.

"I loved you," said Jakoven, dropping to his knees, blood dyeing his hands a glistening black. Garranon pulled his weapon free and swung again. The blood-dark blade slid through the high king's throat and the resulting spray of blood covered Garranon, dripping down his face like tears.

I ducked my head, both to examine the worst of the wounds on my forearm and to give Garranon a moment of privacy. There was such grief on his face, I didn't think that he would want anyone else to see it.

"Here," said Garranon. He ripped a strip of cloth from the bottom of his shirt and wound it around my right bicep. I hadn't noticed that one.

"We'd best go see how the rest are faring," he said.

I nodded, but couldn't help but take a last look at Jakoven's still body. I'd been in battle before, and I knew how quickly a man could go from life into death. It only took a single mistake. But it seemed almost anticlimactic to stare at the dead body of the man who'd inflicted so much damage in his life. As if his death wasn't payment enough.

I followed Garranon and caught up to him. We pushed past the tents, and I had just time enough to glimpse Tisala still on her feet when the magelight above us went out.

The hair on the back of my neck rose with the magic that swept over us like a giant wave hitting the surf. I think I even stepped back, because I bumped into Garranon.

"What's that?" he asked.

"Farsonsbane," I said. "Oreg!" I bellowed, turning about as my night vision began to come back to me and shadows turned gradually into more familiar shapes of tents and men.

No one answered me.

Garranon's night sight must have improved faster than mine, because he left my side abruptly to engage one of the shadowy figures before it could complete a strike at someone who was down.

I sprinted toward the tent where the Bane was calling to me, hungry for what I could feed it.

"Oreg?" I called as I ran.

Surely only Oreg could have gotten past Jakoven's safe-guards, but he still didn't answer me. I looked for him with my magic and found him so near the Bane, I thought for a moment that the artifact's magic had misled me.

I stumbled over a body, burnt and torn, and I took a few precious seconds to examine the forehead and eye that were left. Fear that it was Oreg almost kept me from seeing Arten, Jakoven's archmage, in the shape of the brow.

A few feet farther on I found another body, unrecognizable, but the fire that still fed on his flesh was full of Oreg's familiar magic—he was one of the high king's wizards.

Jakoven's tent was dark and still, but the entrance flap was open. I tried to feel Oreg's magic, but if he were using any, it was swallowed up by the magic of the Bane.

Gods, I thought, my mind playing out various scenarios as I slowed to sneak up on the tent. Oreg got through the traps set by Jakoven and tried to break the spell that held the Bane and failed. Or he was tired and was caught by a trap Jakoven set.

I ducked beneath the flap and magelight flared in the tent. There had been so many bodies on the ground, it had never occurred to me that anyone but Oreg would be in the tent with the Bane. But Jade Eyes smiled his beautiful smile at me.

For a moment all I could see was him. My body, remembering what he'd done to it while wearing that smile, broke into a cold sweat. Then I saw Oreg's limp body on the tent floor.

Ignoring Jade Eyes, I took two steps forward and felt Oreg's neck for a pulse—sighing in relief when I felt it. I didn't like the knot that was rising on the back of his head, though. Stala always said that if you hit a man in the head hard enough to knock him out, you had a good chance of killing him.

"Welcome, Ward," whispered Jade Eyes. "I've been waiting for my opportunity to claim the Bane since I first saw it. It is appropriate that you should be here, just as you were when it first called to me."

Crouched beside Oreg, I looked up at Jade Eyes and recognized the madness in his eyes. I wondered if, like my mother, he tasted his own potions or if he was simply crazy. Either way, the slender staff topped with a dragon holding a glowing ruby in its mouth scared me sick.

The Bane's angry red magic blew my hair away from my face and came back to hit me in the shoulder. The blow was as hard as any I've taken, and it was completely unexpected, because there was no change in Jade Eyes's face or body that told me what he intended. It knocked me forward onto my arms, and one of the cuts that had closed reopened. I felt that breeze come back to taste my blood.

"Oh," he breathed. "They like you. Can you hear them? They called me and called me. I visited them every night, but I couldn't break Jakoven's protections. I came in tonight and found your wizard had done all the work for me."

"Who?" asked a voice in my head, breathy and soft. I almost couldn't hear it over Jade Eye's words. *"Who are you?"*

Hurog, I thought.

"We know you." This time the voice was several and much stronger. I saw three dragons, though my eyes were closed. *"Know us, too."*

". . . been working on a spell to release them," continued Jade Eyes, apparently unaware of the other conversation I found myself a part of. "Dragons are immortal. If I can release them from some of the restrictions that Farson placed upon them, they can be dragons again in truth. They will serve me as dragons served the Emperor. Alizon is right," he said intensely. "Jakoven should not be high king."

The blackness began to flow under the violent red of the gem, just as it had the first time I saw it. I realized that this part of the Bane's magic seemed black to me, not because it was evil, but because it was so dense. It slid down the staff in a slow, heavy flow and began pooling on the floor of the tent, covering my hands and lapping over Oreg's body.

This was different, separate from the red magic, and it became more different all the time. It tasted like dragon, though I hadn't realized that dragon magic had a feel to it—a commonality between the magic of Oreg, Hurog, and the Bane.

"It's almost drained now," said Jade Eyes, incorrectly, I thought.

Farsonsbane was hiding its power from him. I shivered when I realized that I understood the Bane because of the connection Jakoven had forged between us with my blood and tears. The magic I saw as red was the power controlled by the mage wielding the Bane. I knew because the Bane told me so. The dark magic was power hoarded by the Bane itself, held in check by the binding Farson had imposed upon it so long ago.

"Jakoven used most of the magic on Buril—after making certain that Garranon wasn't there," continued Jade Eyes, unaware of the secondary communication between the Bane and me. "Peculiar of him, don't you think? I thought he was finished with Garranon. He hasn't taken Garranon since he found me last year. But I know something that Jakoven didn't."

"What's that?" I asked, watching the blackness touch Jade Eyes's feet and wash back like the sea hitting the sand.

"That it is your tears the dragons need—they told me so. *Hurog* means dragon, he said. But he didn't go far enough.

I looked it up. Did you know that *Hurogmeten* means Guardian of Dragons?" He crouched, unaware of the blackness that flowed around the tent. "Your tears will give my immortal dragons back their lives and they will serve me."

He was wrong. The Bane contained the revenants of dragons, and dead things could not be given anything but the semblance of life.

"Dragons aren't immortal," I said, touching my dragon's neck again, because I couldn't see him breathe underneath the layer of blackness that Jade Eyes couldn't perceive: He was not a Hurog. Against my fingers, Oreg's pulse beat steadily. "Dragons live a long time, longer than the dwarves. But they aren't immortal."

His smile broadened. "You don't know much," he said, and tilted the staff just a little.

Pain coursed through me and I lost control of my muscles, falling limply to the floor, unable even to turn my face aside and avoid the painful contact of noise and hard-packed earth.

"Always so quiet, my Ward," whispered Jade Eyes, and he turned my head away from the ground, tisking when he saw the blood flowing from my nose. "I liked that about you. Some people like the screaming, but I enjoy your pain, not noise." He touched his fingers to my upper lip and held his hand up for me to see the dampness of my tears coating his fingertips. "I'm sorry you have to die. But I think that you might be able to take them from me, if I don't kill you before I release them."

"A dragon is no man's slave," I managed to say around the pain. "Nor should he ever be. I think that you'll be like my father and find that it is more than you can safely hold."

"Your father had a *dragon*?" he asked, and the pain ebbed into memory. "They say that there is a dragon at Hurog now. Jakoven said it was illusion."

I took a deep breath. "Listen to me, Jade Eyes. The dragons died to make that gem. You can't bring them back to life. The first rule of magic is not to tamper with the natural order of things. If you break Farson's bindings, you'll only unleash death."

"Yes," said the red tide of magic, *"let me destroy."*

But it didn't have the same living feeling as the black magic that coated me and drank my tears from my cheeks. It was just destructive magic, cold and powerful.

Jade Eyes drew back.

"Did you hear that?" I asked. "There will be no new Empire to rule if you free them."

His face changed abruptly to a hate-filled snarl and he jumped to his feet. "You think you know everything."

He slammed the end of the staff into my diaphragm and I curled up, gasping for breath that wouldn't come. Darkness hovered in front of my eyes, but I remembered my aunt's voice in my ear: "Straighten out, boy. Give your lungs room to work." And I forced my legs straight and drew in a small breath of air. The next breath was larger.

I opened my eyes in time to see him touch the gem with his tear-covered fingers. The black mist of magic grew very still, as if it were waiting.

Jade Eyes snapped his fingers impatiently. "It must need blood, too," he said.

He rolled me flat on my back and drew his knife. He bent and cut the stained bandage from my waist, ripping the fabric off and setting the wound bleeding again. He took the staff and shoved the Bane into my wound.

I felt the icy touch of the gem, felt it feed on me. It sent slivers of agony arcing through my bones, and warm writhing pleasure through my muscles until I couldn't tell which was which.

"Up, Ward, damn it. If you lay like a lump because you've taken a bruise, you'll end up with a slit throat." The memory of my aunt's voice seemed tied into the mist feathering my cheeks with an icy touch that brought some clearness to my head.

With the force of will that had been toughened by my father and my aunt for different purposes, I reached up and gripped the staff with both hands and ripped it out of Jade Eyes's hands.

He must have been using magic on the Bane as well as my blood, because his body convulsed when he lost contact with the staff. He fell, momentarily unconscious, half on top of Oreg.

I pulled the Bane from my flesh, and it was harder than it should have been to do that. Using the staff to aid me, I struggled to my feet, my head hitting the pole that held that section of the tent roof rigid. Then I realized that Jade Eyes must have set a command upon the staff before releasing it.

He'd wanted me dead so no other would have a claim upon the Bane, and the red tide of magic, bloated from my blood, flooded my body in an attempt to carry out Jade Eyes's directive.

I knew the form of several binding spells. Oreg had taught most of them to me.

"If you don't know them," he'd said, *"you can't break them."*

I could see the bindings on the gem when I focused on it. The ties that held the Bane to follow Jade Eyes's command faded under my thrust of magic but not quickly enough. A red tide of pain sliced through me and breathing became difficult.

Hurog blood had given the Bane to Jade Eyes's control. I'd rested the fingers of my right hand on the bloody lump rising on the back of Oreg's head. True dragon's blood, or nearer to it than mine.

Red heat seared my flesh, empty blackness struck me deaf and dumb, and cool blue power touched my skin with ice. Blue for tears, I thought. I couldn't breathe, couldn't see, couldn't hear but for the sound of dragon breath in my ears. Blindly I raised my right hand and felt for the gem. I couldn't feel the staff or the Bane against my fingers, but the cold gem glowed with a wealth of power and I covered it with my hand.

One moment I struggled against the Bane and the next the rush of power was gone. I gulped in air, and my sight returned as if it had never left me.

The gemstone in the mouth of the bronze dragon glowed with cool purple-blue light. I neither felt nor saw either the heavy blackness of the trapped revenants or the red magic that answered to the master of the Bane.

I leaned against the staff, which was the only thing holding me up.

I couldn't sense any magic except for the slight pulse that made the gem glow, illuminating the tent with blueish light. I was too tired to probe the nature of the magic that caused the luminescence, but light could easily have been the result of leftover magic when Farson's spells were released. Blood and tears, I thought, remembering Oreg's belief that the magic could break free.

Oreg had made me kill him to break the spell that bound him to Hurog. It did not seem at all strange to me that those dragon spirits bound to the Bane would be willing to make an equal sacrifice.

There would be time to analyze later. Now there was a battle going on outside the tent—and as soon as I could stand on my own, I needed to get out and help. But even as the thought came to me, I realized that although there was quite a bit of noise, the familiar sound of battle had disappeared sometime while I'd been struggling with Jade Eyes and the Bane.

Jade Eyes.

I started to kneel down and check the mage, but just then he rolled off Oreg. I worried for a moment, because in my current condition a kitten could have knocked me over, but he lay limply on the floor, and Oreg sat up.

Oreg looked around, a hand to his head. He glanced at the Bane, let his gaze linger on Jade Eyes, and said, "Missed all the fun, did I? I can't believe I let him take me from behind."

"No more can I," I agreed, still propped up by the staff. "We need to see what's going on out there." I gestured vaguely toward the entrance flap. "But first, I think we ought to make certain Jade Eyes doesn't do anything we'll regret when he wakes up. There has to be a rope of some kind around here. Since I'm a little under the weather—not having slept through the excitement like some here—that leaves you."

"Jade Eyes?" said Oreg thoughtfully. His right hand moved, drawing the knife in his belt and bringing it across Jade Eyes's throat before I choked out a belated "Stop."

Oreg came to his feet, narrowing his eyes at me—or maybe against the pain of his head injury. "I've heard your nightmares," he said. "I'll not suffer him to live—I gave him a more merciful end than he deserved." To change the subject, he pointed at the Bane. "What are you going to do with that?"

"*I* want nothing to do with it," I said, rather firmly for someone who would have fallen but for my grip on the Farsonsbane staff.

"Wait until they come out," said Haverness's voice clearly from outside the tent. "You don't want to interrupt wizards."

Oreg and I exchanged glances. However our party had fared, it seemed that we had unexpected reinforcements.

Letting the staff take some of my weight, I ducked back out of the tent. A faint trace of light in the east told me that time had passed while I fought the Bane. In the darkness of the early morning, the gem glowed like a fistful of dwarven stones, and in that light I saw that Haverness had brought a small army with him.

I looked around for Tisala, but I saw Kellen first. Facing Oreg and me, at a sword's-length distance, Kellen stood with his blade drawn, Rosem at his right. Haverness waited behind him, and I finally found Tisala at his side, battered but intact. The rest of the people were hidden by the darkness, but there were a lot of them. In fact, as I looked around, I could see that they surrounded the tent.

They must have been waiting half the night for the outcome of the battle in Jakoven's tent. The sight of Oreg and me didn't seem to reassure Kellen. I wondered what results he'd hoped for.

"Sire," I said, not bowing because I was afraid I wouldn't be able to stand up again. "I didn't expect you here."

"Yes," he said. "I rather thought we'd surprise you. It was Garranon who tipped the scales—did you really expect me to believe that he'd go hunting after the attack on Buril?"

"No." I shook my head. "But we needed enough of a head start to catch Jakoven before he became aware of you. We had to take him by surprise before he could use the Bane."

I tipped my head to the staff and swayed a little with the motion.

"Did you?" asked Kellen softly. "Or did you see the chance for power and take it?"

"Kellen's worried that Jakoven's downfall might be a good time for old traditions to reassert themselves," said Haverness, his voice carefully neutral. "The Hurogs are the last of the royal line of Shavig."

I was too exhausted to deal with stupid suspicions, especially, as usual when I was tired, when talking was difficult. I tried to gather my thoughts and had to grip the staff harder to stay on my feet.

"Ward?" Tisala's voice drew my gaze, and I saw her more clearly. Part of me noted uneasily that the light of the gem had followed my gaze without my bidding, but the rest of me was focused on Tisala. I straightened abruptly, anger stiffening my spine. The battering, I realized, had probably come from Jakoven's men, but her hands were bound and she was obviously a prisoner.

I looked back at Kellen, who said quietly, "Is that the Bane, Ward?" His eyes were trying to convey a message to me, but I was too tired and angry to work it out.

"It's not Kellen who doubts you," said my uncle, and I saw that he was here, too. "But when we realized where you were going, a number of the Oranstonian lords who knew your father expressed their doubts. In your place, he would have taken the Bane and used it to gain the throne—and they don't know you."

His words bounced off the rising tide of my wrath, which grew apace when I noticed that he was bound as well.

I waved my hand, drawing on the power of the staff (*"What power?"* asked a small, rational part of me, buried beneath the roil of anger) and the ropes fell from Tisala's wrists. "Tosten, Axiel, Garranon," I said in a voice I hardly recognized.

"Here, Ward," said Garranon behind me. "I'm fine."

"And I," said Axiel.

Tosten said, "Nothing wrong with me that won't mend. Have a care, Ward. Keep your head."

I didn't even have to look at them to release their bonds as well as Duraugh's. The magic of the staff filled me up and powered my *finding* sense until I could have identified every man in the camp, though I'd never seen most of them before.

"Why are my people bound?" I asked gently. "They've done nothing wrong. With this"—I shook the staff—"Jakoven could have leveled a battlefield. Stealth was the only way. So these people risked their lives for you and you make prisoners of them?"

When Tisala came to me, no one tried to stop her. "My love," she said, as if she'd always called me that. "Ward, listen to me. No one was hurt. Farrawell and a few of his ilk believe that claiming the Bane was your purpose from the beginning. There are enough of them here who agree that Kellen had no choice but to confront you."

I listened to her, but I kept my eyes on Kellen. She might say he had no choice, but I knew better. The power that filled me quivered in rage at the thought. And it told me exactly what I could do about Kellen and the Oranstonians who put my people in bonds.

"Ward," said Oreg clearly. "Your eyes are glowing Hurogblue—like the staff."

I turned to the dragon-mage and the awareness that was a part of the Bane's magic knew him as *dragon*. It calmed at his presence, giving me space to understand what he'd said. And as it faded, the urge to destroy Farrawell and Kellen ebbed. But it wasn't gone, just concealed as it had concealed itself from me before.

I took a deep, if shaky breath. "Siphern save me," I whispered. "I thought it was gone." But the Bane had only hidden, waiting to infect me with its ravaging madness.

I knew then that Jade Eyes had been both correct and wrong. Blood and tears had indeed freed the Bane, freed it of any control. Knew moreover what it intended to do, because destruction was all it understood: The Bane was a far more capable Death-Bringer than my little brother's fat gelding.

"Oreg, aid me," I said, but the Bane read my intentions

before I could say anything and launched an attack—not at me, but at Tisala, who held my arm and had no protection against magic.

I threw up a warding around the bronze dragon head even as I pushed Tisala away from me. But the Bane had been storing power for a long time and was sated on dragon's blood. My safeguard wavered, and Tisala collapsed to the ground.

Oreg's hands closed on my shoulders and the barrier stabilized, holding the Bane momentarily.

It gave me time to say, "Away from us. Get back, it's loosed."

Kellen gestured sharply and the people who'd been crowded around us stepped back to the trees. Haverness, though, came forward and picked up Tisala. She moaned as he carried her away and I knew a moment's relief that the Bane hadn't killed her.

Then the Bane began struggling again and I had to turn my concentration elsewhere.

"What do we do?" I asked as I strengthened the warding. "We can't just continue to contain it."

"You were right," Oreg said, "it is connected to you. You understand it best—I'll loan you my strength to do what you can."

"I think I could bind it again," I said.

As if the Bane understood, it redoubled its attack on our barrier. Slowly I gave control of the warding to Oreg, to free my weaving for a more permanent solution.

"If you can," replied Oreg.

I knew one binding spell that would hold the Bane as it had tied Oreg to Hurog—a slave to the whims of the Hurogmeten. I drew my knife with my free hand and awkwardly cut myself without losing my hold on the staff, because that spell began with a sacrifice of blood.

Dragons' voices wailed in pleading terror as I began the spell and they made me hesitate. How could I do this?

The question stalled me further. It had been Oreg's father binding his son to Hurog that had tainted the world with his evil act and my destruction of that binding had begun healing the earth. If I bound these creatures, revenant though they were, would it compound the evil that Farson had started?

As I struggled inwardly, the Bane struck the warding with sudden immense power—as like its previous struggles as an acorn is to a hundred-year oak. Its energies burned through Oreg's weaving as if he were not an ancient dragon, but his strength slowed it enough that I could catch the fraying edges of the warding and hold it together.

But I could feel the Bane regathering its magic for another attempt. It had burnt out Oreg's magic; he wouldn't be able to work magic for hours. That left only me.

The Bane hit my barrier again. I howled in agony and writhed as I sent magic into the warding until I had none left. I searched frantically for more, because if I did not stop it, the Bane would destroy everything and everyone that I loved.

If I hadn't come, Jade Eyes would never have gotten his hands on the Bane. I could feel the patterns of possibilities woven into the gem, where spells once had bound, and knew that Jade Eyes had been right. Without my tears, the bindings would have held for centuries longer. But magic is made more effective through the use of sympathetic intention and symbolism; doors are easier to break open with magic than walls because doors are meant to open and walls to stand firm. The tears and blood of the guardian of dragons made a sharp knife to cut through spells imprisoning dragons.

Haverness had brought his mage and I sucked him dry of power. He didn't fight me, but his magic was a drop compared to Oreg's ocean and neither was adequate, so I cast my net further afield.

Nothing.

I screamed a second time, not just from pain, but from effort and frustration. My hold slipped and I felt the Bane's triumph.

"At last to be free, to burn and consume until there is nothing left."

Then I felt it. Hurog. Over five hundred miles away, the magic of Hurog heard my call and came to me when I couldn't reach it. A thin, cool stream of power spilled over

the warding, taking the governance of the spell gently from
my hands. Hurog touched me and read my desire to neu-
tralize the Bane.

The ward dissolved, replaced by Hurog magic that engulfed the Bane and cleaned it of taint and anger. Dragon
magic absorbed the Bane and left me except for a silk-fine
thread, connecting me to my home.

A pea-sized stone the color of obsidian glass fell out of
the staff to land on a flattish rock. Almost absently I crushed
it with the butt-end of the staff and the little stone dissolved
into powder, drifting away when a stray breeze swept
through the clearing.

I cleared my throat and looked up to meet Kellen's grim
face.

"I'm sorry, sire," I said to him. "It seems the Bane was
more dangerous than I thought." Letting the staff slip through
my grip, I knelt before him and bowed my head. "Let all
here bear witness that the dragons of Hurog do follow Kellen
Tallven, High King of the Five Kingdoms."

The world tilted oddly and someone cried out; I think it
was my brother.

"Idiot," muttered Oreg to me as he and Kellen hauled me
to my feet. "Have you forgotten what I've told you about
destroying magical items? You're lucky you didn't kill
everyone here when you broke the gem."

Garranon was somehow there, stitching up my belly with
thread and needle. "I thought you had this stopped," he said.

I was puzzled for a minute at the abrupt shift of scene,
then realized somewhat muzzily that I must have passed out,
because I was sitting, braced against a tree, and the camp
was lit with morning sun instead of blue gemstone.

"Still prisoners?" I asked.

"No," said Tisala acidly. "You proved to everyone's satisfaction that you had no intention of keeping the Bane's
power for yourself. Kellen declared you a hero, and, after
the impressive fire and spark show you put on, no one decided to argue with him. Next time, I'd appreciate it if you'd
only face one deadly foe at a time. A paranoid king or two,

evil sorcerers, an ancient evil artifact—fine. But not all at
once. It makes it hard to defend you."

I realized that the slender tree that kept me upright was
Tisala, herself. It was her knee that pressed so uncomfortably
against a bruise on my back, but I was too tired to shift away.
It was worth the small hurt to know that she was safe. Garranon distracted me from the bruise when he took another
stitch.

"And you didn't even kill anyone," said Oreg, then added,
"at least none of our allies." I saw that he was lying next to
me with his eyes shut tight against the light.

"Are you all right, Oreg?"

"Damn it, quit wiggling," snapped Garranon. "Unless you
want a few more pinholes to add to your wounds."

"Just a headache," said Oreg when Garranon had finished
speaking. "Axiel tells me I'll feel like living again in a week
or so—about the same time I'll have enough magic to light
a candle. Tosten's in one of the tents with Axiel, who has a
nasty cut on his thigh that someone stitched up."

"My father," supplied Tisala from behind me. "He also
sewed up Tosten's back. He—my father, not Tosten—says
both Axiel and Tosten will mend. He says you are suffering
from blood loss, as well as whatever damage your battle with
the Bane did, but if you haven't died yet, you are unlikely
to at this point. Unless, of course, one of your wounds gets
infected." It didn't sound as if it would bother her.

"Speaking of death," said Oreg, "have I mentioned that
I'm unhappy with you? Destroying something as powerful
as the Bane's gemstone could have left a new valley where
these mountains stand."

Garranon's steady progress across my sore abdomen
paused and then resumed.

"I thought of that," I said, relaxing against Tisala. "But
the magic was gone, eaten by the dragons of Hurog."

"What do you mean?" Kellen rounded Oreg's splayed
body and crouched behind Garranon.

"You're in my light," growled Garranon, and Kellen
moved obligingly to my left.

"What do you mean eaten by Hurog?" asked Kellen again.

"Magic," I said, "is a strange thing."

Tisala laughed against the back of my neck. "Most people think so," she said.

"Most wizards think it's like the wind or the rain," I said. "An uncaring force of nature. And for the most part they're right. But I've been places where that wasn't true. Where the magic is as alive as the trees here, or more so. Menogue is one of them," I told Kellen. "It is as alive as you or I." I hissed as Garranon stuck his needle into a particularly tender spot.

"I could sear it, instead," he offered.

"No," I replied hastily. "Go ahead. Just caught me by surprise."

"The Bane was somewhat more perplexing," I said. "I think the spirits of the dragons were tied into the original spell. Jade Eyes . . ." I paused.

"Yes," said Kellen. "We found his body in Jakoven's tent. Oreg told us he managed to get the Bane before you did."

"Jade Eyes was insane," I said. "He'd been talking to the spirits and they told him how to free them. He thought they'd turn back into dragons. But they were just ravening spirits, not dragons any longer, and only the binding spells kept them from destroying everything. I thought I stopped it, but I was too late. If it hadn't been for Hurog, they'd have killed us all."

The wound across my stomach was deeper than I'd realized, forcing Garranon to stitch up muscle first, then skin. I looked away and continued talking to distract myself. "Hurog is alive, too. When I sought for more magic to hold the Bane, it came and . . . ate the Bane. That's what dragons do with their dead, you know."

"No, I didn't know that. Ward . . ." Kellen began.

I could hear the apology in his voice and waved my hand in dismissal. "If you trusted every barbarian Shavigman who happened upon your way, you wouldn't be much of a king," I said. "However, I hope you don't expect me to destroy ancient artifacts to prove my loyalty on a regular basis."

"Done," he agreed with a grin. Someone called out his name and he excused himself.

Garranon finished stitching and wrapped my middle with cloth that looked as if it had been part of someone's bedroll. When he was finished, Tisala slid backward until my head rested on her knee.

I looked at her face from my new vantage point. Her left eye was swollen shut and she had a bandage wrapped around her upper arm that was stained with blood. She was beautiful and I told her so.

She laughed and kissed my forehead. "Don't be an idiot," she said. She loved me, too.

I closed my eyes, content to rest where I was. Doubtless the politics would continue for a long time yet, but my part was done. Hurog was safe and its dragon was stretched out beside me, safe and whole. The sun was shining through the rain clouds and Tisala's leg was warm under my head. I slept.

About the Author

Patricia Briggs lived a fairly normal life until she learned to read. After that she spent lazy afternoons flying dragonback and looking for magic swords when she wasn't horseback riding in the Rocky Mountains.

Once she graduated from Montana State University with degrees in history and German, she spent her time substitute teaching and writing. She and her family live in the Pacific Northwest, where she is hard at work on her newest project.

Visit her on the web at: www.hurog.com.

From national bestselling author

Patricia Briggs

DRAGON BONES

0-441-00916-6

Ward of Hurog has tried all his life to convince people
he is just a simple, harmless fool...And it's worked. But
now, to regain his kingdom, he must ride into
war—and convince them otherwise.

"Patricia Brigg's novels...are clever, engaging
[and] fast-moving."
—*Romantic Science Fiction & Fantasy*

Available wherever books are sold or
to order call 1-800-788-6262

B054

From "a natural born storyteller" *

PATRICIA BRIGGS

The Hob's Bargain

0-441-00813-5

Hated and feared, magic was banished from the land.
But now, freed from spells of the wicked bloodmages,
magic—both good and evil—returns.
And Aren of Fallbrook feels her own power of sight
strengthen and grow.

Overcome by visions of mayhem and murder, Aren vows to save
her village from the ruthless raiders who have descended upon
it—and killed her family. She strikes a bargain with the Hob, a
magical, humanlike creature who will exact a heavy price to
defend the village—a price Aren herself must pay.

Available wherever books are sold or
to order call 1-800-788-6262

* *Midwest Book Review*

Book One of the Seven Circles trilogy

CIRCLE AT CENTER
by
Douglas Niles

In the realm of the Seven Circles,
a peaceful era is about to end as members of the
various races ban together to incite war.
To protect the land, the Druids decide to recruit
warriors from a world where war is a way of
life—a world called Earth.

❏ 0-441-00960-3

*"Absolutely nobody builds a more convincing fantasy
realm than Doug Niles."*
—R.A. Salvatore

Available wherever books are sold or
to order call 1-800-788-6262

B036

PENGUIN PUTNAM INC.
Online

Your Internet gateway to a virtual environment with
hundreds of entertaining and enlightening books
from Penguin Putnam Inc.

*While you're there, get the latest buzz on
the best authors and books around—*

Tom Clancy, Patricia Cornwell, W.E.B. Griffin,
Nora Roberts, William Gibson, Robin Cook,
Brian Jacques, Catherine Coulter, Stephen King,
Ken Follett, Terry McMillan, and many more!

**Penguin Putnam Online is located at
http://www.penguinputnam.com**

PENGUIN PUTNAM NEWS

Every month you'll get an inside look at our upcoming books and new features on our site. This is an
ongoing effort to provide you with the most
up-to-date information about
our books and authors.

**Subscribe to Penguin Putnam News at
http://www.penguinputnam.com/newsletters**